To St[illegible]

with bes[illegible]

Adolfo

17 June 96

MW01292758

THE STRAW OBELISK

A World War II novel

by

ADOLPH CASO

Copyright 1995
by Branden Publishing Company

Library of Congress Cataloging-in-Publication Data

Caso, Adolph.
The straw obelisk / by Adolph Caso
p. cm.
ISBN 0-8283-2005-5
1. World War, 1939-1945--Italy--Fiction.
I. Title.
PS3553.A794S77 1995
813'.54--dc20 95-1607
CIP

BRANDEN PUBLISHING COMPANY
17 Station Street
Box 843 Brookline Village
Boston, MA 02147

In memory of
Franca and Samuele

CHAPTER 1

Letters bearing the mark of the Red Cross usually meant one of three things: a soldier's death, his transfer, or his return home. Unfortunately, few such letters brought the latter two bits of information.

The clerk who had the responsibility for delivering such letters was a fat woman in her fifties, husbandless and with several children to feed in those post-war days. No one wanted the job of handling that type of mail. She took it on to keep herself and the children from starving.

"Here's one for Maria," said the man behind the little window.

"Maria! Oh! no," she said with deep-felt sorrow.

"Here, take it and be on your way. I don't have time to listen to you. Deliver it and come right back."

"Yes," she answered. In silence, she looked at the letter for a few moments and then went out to her flimsy old bicycle.

It was an early spring morning, cool and vibrant. Birds flew noisily about.

"And me with this letter!" she said to herself. "God! I hope it's good news."

The last twenty she had delivered were death notices. She couldn't bear to witness another mother in anguish.

Stiff on the bike, she pedaled her way to the other side of the village. Almost always, many people laughed at her while the children made fun of her. This morning, there were no children to ridicule her.

"Thank God for that," she said to herself, in no mood to be insulted by anyone, especially this morning with that letter she was bringing to her old and good friend, Maria.

Passing by the church, she held the handlebar by one hand while she crossed herself with the other. As she brought her hand back to the handlebar, she caught sight of Mr. Banno, who was fumbling in front of his house.

"Oh! no, that blabber-mouth again! He'd better not say anything this morning or I'll clobber him, big and fat as he is."

"Ah, here comes my feathered friend. What's the good news this beautiful morning," yelled Mr. Banno, looking at her from beneath his well-worn hat. "You got another of those letters, ha?"

"None of your business."

"Come on now. You can tell me. You know I won't tell."

"Ya, I know. You're as tight-lipped as a hungry cow," she answered without stopping.

Seeing she didn't stop, he yelled to her in a coarse and derisive voice. "Letter for Maria, ha, ha? Samuele? eh! I hope he comes back. Somebody's got to take care of his sister. We have plenty of bitches from Naples. We don't need her. Or is it Marcello? Eh! Stop! Tell me!"

She stopped about thirty feet ahead and turned back to answer. "You've got a young girl. It might just be your turn next."

"Never happen, not in Banno's house," he replied proudly. "You can't say that of yourself--I mean no offense," he added.

"You're nothing but a nosy old bastard..."

"Come now," he interrupted, "that's for Maria, isn't it?"

"Yah, and I hope Samuele comes back to do what he didn't have time to finish with your daughter. I hope to God he does."

"Never fear about that. American officers have stayed at my house. They didn't lay a finger on her. I can't say the same about the Moroccans and you's people."

She stared at him intensely but said nothing. Her eyes said plenty, but Banno wasn't worried. After a few long moments, she turned forward and stepped on the pedal.

Banno yelled from behind. "Aha, what's the matter; you can't take it, eh? Dirty conscience, eh? I hope he comes back; I hope he comes back, just for that. Ha, ha..."

As she pedaled by the curve protected on the upper side by gigantic poplars whose leaves rustled in the breeze, she saw Maria's house about one hundred yards up ahead on the right. Maria was sweeping in front of the doorway; Lucia was preparing vegetables for the noon meal. On the ground sat her year-old baby. The two women looked up.

"I got a letter for you, Maria."

"A letter for me! Samuele! My son, my son," she repeated with tears in her eyes. She took the letter and handed it over to her daughter Lucia to read.

With surging anxiety, Lucia opened the letter and read aloud: "Your son, Samuele, returning home."

Maria was overwhelmed with joy, thanking God for his infinite goodness and calling out her son's name repeatedly. "He is well; he's well!. Thank God..." She had tears in her eyes, and looked up toward heaven, while the other two looked at each other in silence. Lucia was happy, and yet extremely sad because she was worried and afraid. The baby on the ground had been born out of wedlock, with a man already married. She had reason to be afraid, for she knew her brother's character. The whole village knew him, his every fight with friends and strangers, the brutality with which he handled his opponents, his irascible temperament. At one time, Samuele got involved with a neighbor's daughter who had said yes and then no; he gave her such a beating that her father went after him with a gun. To the pre-war village, Samuele was the good-looking, indomitable young man gone to a war whose atrocities could turn him into a decent man or make him worse. This was the question uppermost in Lucia's mind.

"I know how you feel," said the woman to Lucia. You'd better make plans to leave."

"I know; I know," she answered. Her eyes dropped toward her child. Then, looking up at her mother, she said how happy she was that Samuele was returning home. But Maria knew her daughter was not happy. How could she be? Maria also knew her son. But she loved him just the same, the same as she loved Lucia, even though Lucia had been no less exemplary.

"What are you going to do now, Lucia?" Maria asked as she turned her eyes to her only grandchild.

"I'm going to his father," Lucia answered, resolved to meet whatever fate came--to die at the hands of her brother, or to live in the humiliating attic with her child, apart from the rest of Silvestro's family, having to bear the presence of the other woman and of the legal children.

"I've got to go," said the letter carrier. "I'm happy for you, Maria. I was so worried. But I wished he could have come home ... you know what I mean. Lucia, anything I can do, let me know. I can still get around with my old bike."

"You know where I will be. I'd appreciate it if you would let me know when he comes..."

"Sure," she answered. Turning her bike around, she mounted and pedaled away.

A few minutes later, Mr. Banno came by.

"Hello, Maria, I was going to the farm and thought of asking you if everything is all right. I saw fatso taking the letter. Samuele--is well?" he asked as his eyes wondered, looking at the child and at Lucia.

"He is well, thank you. He will be home soon."

"Good, good, Maria. Remember my proposition. Goodby."

"Goodby," she answered, remembering very well his proposition. But she didn't want anything to do with it. She was not going to get involved with her son's affairs. Samuele could marry anyone he wished, land or no land. Her own marriage had been one that united two lots of land into one. The result was that she worked the land to support her children, while her husband took off somewhere out of the country where he died in questionable circumstances. No, she was not going to tell her son anything.

She had other more serious things to think about, mainly the safety of her daughter and grandchild.

"Mother, I'm so afraid,"

"You should be; you should also be ashamed of yourself. I didn't bring you up that way. Why did you do it, why?" Maria asked in a low voice, her heart heavy with sorrow. Her presumed dead son was alive and coming home to threaten her daughter's life, knowing all too well she may lose both. She had reason to think along this line; several such women had been killed by brothers, boy-friends, or husbands coming back from the war. She couldn't expect anything less.

"Pick up your things and go, and pray to God."

Lucia went inside, gathered her few things, and quickly went back outside, where she picked up her child, placed him on her bosom with his face overlooking her shoulder, and left. Maria stood silent, watching her daughter disappear beyond the curve. But from the other direction, her neighbors were already approaching to advise her, to offer help and consolation, some in earnest, others in the manner of Mr. Banno, who had already spread the word. Everyone felt a premonition of death.

"The war has just begun for them," commented one old woman to another as they approached Maria's house.

"As Mr. Banno said," added the other, "these poor boys go off to fight in the war, to suffer so much, then come home to find the family dishonored by the wife or sister. Poor Maria, she's been so good; and her children as rotten as their father. Poor Maria... Oh! Maria, we've heard the good news. If you want, we can intercept Samuele and talk to him before he comes home?"

"Thank you, thank you. Let him come home. He never took advice from anyone before; I doubt he'd take it now. No, thank you. I'm sure it'd be worse. Thank you, thank you," she repeated and walked into the house, shutting the door on the group that had grown larger by the minute. Maria sat down on the chair next to the fireplace, but quickly got up and went toward her back yard where she could not hear the crowd. She thought of God, asking Him for help. She implored Him, knowing the futility at the same time. Her light brown kerchief fell from her head. She pulled it back up, refolding it without thinking what she was doing. The picture of her son appeared to her in a hazy form. About three years had gone by since she had seen him last. While she remembered him as basically good-hearted, even she--his mother--couldn't be so blind as not to admit to his irascible impulses and blind anger. She had experienced many severe beatings at the hands of her husband, often for the most trivial of reasons, and Samuele was worse than his father. In spite of this realization, Maria did not worry for herself, knowing her own responsibility as a mother; she worried over Lucia, whose actions Maria had never condoned. She had talked to her a thousand times, but to no avail.

"What could I do... kill her!" she said to herself. "God, what can I do?" she asked as she walked across the vegetable garden, to gather whatever she could for her son's meal.

"Maria," called a voice from the outside, "open up; it is I, Don Alfonso. I want to talk to you."

She went to the door and let the priest in. About twenty more people had gathered outside.

"Don't they have anything to do?" she asked Don Alfonso.

"People always gather where there's a possibility of violence."

"They won't be disappointed."

"Maria, Maria, how can I help, what can I do? I could intercept him. He might listen."

"You've been preaching against the very thing Lucia did. She didn't listen to your advice. Samuele used to laugh at you. No, thank you, Don Alfonso, thank you."

CHAPTER 2

By evening, the whole village had heard of Samuele's impending return, but no one knew exactly when he was coming. In the past, soldiers had arrived immediately after the Red Cross letter; others had come as many as ten days later. Many villagers, though, felt that Samuele would arrive that very evening, unexpected and unnoticed.

As there had been no correspondence whatever with those who had gone to war, especially during the last two years, most of those who returned learned about their families from the people they met on the street. Everyone, therefore, including the little children, was on the lookout for Samuele, to be the first to tell him what had happened and to counsel him on the actions to take.

The youngsters were particularly anxious to see him, to ask questions about the war, of which they had seen more than children should have seen. The village had been bombed and machine-gunned many times. Innocent people had been killed or wounded. As for the German soldiers under attack, except for one who had been shot in a skirmish with the approaching Americans, no one got as much as a scratch. The children had heard descriptions of battles and about the many enemy soldiers that the local hero soldiers had killed. They had seen with their own eyes the endless moving heavy armor, the trucks, the airplanes, and the soldiers that had passed through the village. To them, these things meant action, adventure, and joy--things only a soldier in war could experience. They waited, therefore, with the expectation that no grown-up could feel.

Finally, at the crossroads at the other end of the village, a truck stopped, and a man got off. It was already dusk, making it difficult for the children to recognize Samuele. They did not know him well, since he had left the village when they were practically babies. A couple of nine-year--old boys made their way to the man who had just gotten off the truck. Indeed, it was Samuele.

The truck took off, leaving Samuele behind. He stood motionless for a while, looking around. He remembered: it was the exact spot where he had been picked up about three years earlier. Nothing had changed. Except for some obvious war scars on walls, the place was still the same. He looked around for a few more moments, then began to walk, carrying nothing but the clothes he was wearing.

In the semi-darkness, Samuele walked slowly toward home, limping heavily--another reason why he was hard to recognize. Nevertheless, he looked suspicious to the two youngsters. They approached him, looked him over, but said nothing. Samuele looked back at them for an instant, paying no attention. He continued to walk; the boys kept behind him. He stopped.

"What do you want, fellows," Samuele asked in a soft but deep voice.

"Are you Samuele?"

"Yes, I am Samuele."

Very excited, they began to barrage him with questions about the war, the guns he had fired, the tanks he had driven, the battles he had been in. "You got shot in your foot, is that why you're limping?"

Samuele looked down at his foot, then slowly turned to the young boy, looked at him for a brief moment, and extended his hand to pat the boy's head. Thinking Samuele was going to hit him, the boy ducked.

"You want to be a soldier?"

"Yes," the boy answered proudly.

"Soldiers are not afraid of other soldiers. You're afraid of me."

"No, I'm not," he answered. Then, with some hesitation, he pulled up to Samuele as the other boy looked on wide-eyed. Samuele placed his hand on the boy's head, ruffling his long hair. Seeing this, the other went closer, and Samuele did likewise to him.

"How many soldiers did you kill?"

"Tell us, Samuele, tell us," entreated the other.

Samuele looked at them in silence, his eyes deep set and bright, marked by soft creases all around. Sadness was permanently imprinted around those eyes which formerly had shone with truculence.

"Aren't you Franca's cousin?"

"You mean my mother's friend, Toni's sister?"

"Yes, yes. How is she, can you tell me?" Samuele asked with trepidation. "How is she, do you know?"

"She's fine. She works the farm."

Samuele patted the two boys once again. He bent down, looked at them, and pulled out of his pocket a piece of candy for each. "And my mother, how is she?"

"She's fine."

"And my sister?"

"She has a little baby."

"Baby!" exclaimed Samuele pulling back from the two boys. "Baby!... When did she get married?"

"She didn't."

Samuele stared at the ground. Then he looked at the boys once again, patted their heads, and walked away, his limping much more marked. He walked slowly, looking at the houses and at the people, not bothering to recognize any of them. As the villagers expected the Samuele they had known, they paid little attention to the solitary man slowly limping his way down the dimly lit street.

The moon was out, pale and full; a halo surrounded it. Samuele looked up and stared at it as it hung above the tall poplars in the direction of his house. He walked with his eyes fixed on that lustrous heavenly body, thinking as he did so many nights--of all the moon had seen throughout its travels: the sufferings, all the joys, the history of mankind. This evening, up there above his village, the moon did not look any different. There were stars in the sky, but the moon floated along its solitary path as though nothing else existed.

"Samuele, Samuele," suddenly and unexpectedly a subdued but insistent voice called from inside an open door. It was Mr. Banno. For a moment, Samuele was startled. Then he looked toward Mr. Banno and greeted him.

"Come in, come in... Rosa!" he yelled to his daughter, "Rosa, Samuele is here, bring out the wine. This calls for celebration."

Mr. Banno spoke so loudly that the neighbors overheard. In no time, several ran out to take a look at Samuele. Before Samuele had a chance to reply, Mr. Banno was already out shaking hands, trying to lead him to the front of his house where Rosa was waiting with a bottle of white wine and glasses. Samuele did not react with enthusiasm, but with a certain timidity which was quickly noticed by everyone even though it was quite dark.

"Come on, Samuele, come in... The rest of you, take off," Mr. Banno declared sternly, as he looked into his neighbors' faces. "I have a lot to tell him, and most of it is confidential. Go on, get away... Samuele, let's go in. You've come back to bad times. But I'll help you; I'll help you get back on your feet. I will, by God...

"*God*!" Samuele repeated in a soft voice, as though he were absent-minded.

"Yah," interrupted one from the crowd, "we know all about your confidential business--*the Bhannò*!"

"Shut up, you blabber-mouth," Mr. Banno shouted with anger, his small blue eyes focused on the man. When the group burst into laughter, Mr. Banno became furious. He accused them of being nosy busybodies. The group only laughed louder, while Samuele looked on emotionless. Seeing Mr. Banno maligned by the derisive neighbors, Samuele raised his hand to calm them down. They reduced their cackle and quickly quieted down to listen to what Samuele had to say.

"Thank you for your hospitality," he said in a low voice. "I'll come back another time, soon. I'm going to be here for a while. So, there's plenty of time."

"Not for the old rubberneck, there ain't," interrupted another voice, amid a burst of laughter.

Mr. Banno let the comment go unanswered. Instead, he looked at Samuele. "I wanted to tell you about your sister; it's very..."

"Thank you for your kind consideration, Mr. Banno. Whatever I have to know about my sister, I will learn at home. Besides, I already know about my sister. Good-night." Samuele turned and walked away, leaving both Mr. Banno and the group dumfounded and perplexed. Was this the ferocious Samuele they knew, or was he somebody else? While no one asked this question aloud, some were already trying to figure out the new Samuele. And the limping!

"...Why, he looks over thirty," commented one in a subdued voice after Samuele had disappeared from view.

In front of his house, Maria was already waiting, standing in the doorway against a dim light coming from inside. On the other side of the street, a group of friends had also gathered and refused to go away in spite of her begging them to leave. They exchanged words with Maria, who politely, continued to ask them to leave. Suddenly, on seeing a man appearing by the poplars, the crowd quieted down to a whisper.

"Maria! Maria!" called out a voice in a hush. "Samuele is coming."

Maria did not move, but suddenly she felt the thundering beat of her heart, her whole inside throbbing with confused excitement. Nevertheless, she remained composed. When the shadow of her son came into view, tears began to flow down her face. A few of the people ran toward Samuele.

"Samuele, be kind to your mother. She has suffered a lot since you went away."

"Be kind," urged an older woman in black; it was the voice of the neighbors across the street.

He looked at them for a few seconds without answering. The he turned toward his house and saw the profile of his mother. He hesitated for a moment; then went forward, his eyes filled with tears, his partially numb foot dragging noticeably. On getting close to his mother, he reached out. Maria, arms outstretched, received her embracing son.

"Mother, I've come back," he whispered, sobbing. "I've come back."

Maria's eyes opened wide; she had never heard her son utter that precious word which now seeming so full of meaning. She felt overwhelmed with an up-surging joy. "Son, my son, Samuele... I thought I'd never see you again. I'm so happy you're back... Let's go inside."

Once in the house, Samuele shut the door behind him, leaving the neighbors dumfounded, befuddled, and anxious.

Inside, Maria and Samuele were too moved, the sobs taking precedence over the words they wanted to say to one another. Finally, in subdued words, she told him she was going to prepare supper. Then she asked him if he wanted anything special. Unable to answer right away, Samuele asked permission to go to his room for a minute. His eyes still watery, he looked around his humble but clean room, glancing at the picture of his father to one side; then at the picture of himself and of Lucia posing with their mother.

He picked it up, brought it near the small light, and paused, first on the smiling image of Lucia, then on the serene face of his mother, then on his own--handsome but arrogant, his youthful eyes hiding a savage expression he just came to understand. He looked up at the mirror, then again at the picture. More than three years had passed since he had posed for that picture. Meanwhile, so much had changed, he thought, all except for his mother, who seemed to have remained herself, exactly as he had left her. He put the picture down, staring at it once more. Then, looking at his reflection in the mirror, he slowly took off his well-worn jacket and placed it on the iron bar at the foot of the bed. With a deliberate move of his hands, he pulled his regular leather wallet from one pocket. Then, he pulled another, much smaller wallet, made of different material, from his breast pocket. He opened the drawer and placed them toward the rear, not without passing his index finger over the little one and looking at it with a steadily, solemn expression of sadness on his face. He then went to the bed and sat on it. Holding his head in his hands, he remained there motionless.

Maria, meanwhile, knowing her son's tastes all too well, prepared the supper: home-fried potatoes that Samuele used to like so much, garden salad, veal cutlet she had bought in anticipation of Samuele's return, and the bread she had baked a few hours before. She also had gotten a bottle of white wine from the cellar and placed it on the small table. She hadn't put a white tablecloth on that table for such a long time. Looking at the table, she felt the room had suddenly made a change, and all boding well.

Much had changed, and above all her son. Maria couldn't figure him out; she couldn't understand his behavior, or, maybe she did. Where had he been? Africa, Germany, perhaps Siberia? No, not Siberia; no one had come back from Siberia. And his foot? Maria hadn't asked. But she intended to do so at the supper table. She was also going to tell him about Lucia, at an opportune time, but especially if she found him in a good mood. How could she break the news? How could she explain Lucia to her son, back with the obvious evidence of mental anguish and physical pain. She didn't know what he had been through, but she could well imagine.

In a soft voice, Maria called out to Samuele, who was still sitting with his head in his hands. He stood up and quickly answered. He walked to the mirror. The marks of his hands were on his face and his eyes bloodshot. He rubbed them a little, then he smoothed his hair with his hands and went downstairs.

The table caught his glance for a moment. Then he looked at his mother before sitting down. Maria poured the wine, filled his plate, and then sat down on the opposite side. As they ate, Maria kept looking at her son's face. Inevitably, her eyes paused on his. Of all, his eyes had gone through the greatest transformation. That savage look had given way to a most expressive sadness which made Maria happy and confident.

"What happened to your foot?" she asked.

"Frost-bite."

"Frost-bite?"

"I'm one of the very few lucky ones, Mother. Too many froze to death. There were hardly any clothes. I had a pair of boots... It wasn't enough."

"My son... you must have suffered a great deal. Thank God, it's all over now."

"Yes, that's over."

Maria noticed the double intent of Samuele's answer and his rather brief comments to the point. She remained silent for a moment, then she made an attempt to bring up the subject of Lucia. "Is there something else?" she asked tenuously.

"Lucia, where is she?"

"You know about her?"

"Yes."

"It happened during the bombardments. We ran away from the village into the hills. You don't know Silvestro. Well, he was the only one who offered us a place to stay. We spent several weeks there. Many nights, when the airplanes were flying above, we ran into the fields where we stayed until morning. Silvestro's wife hadn't been feeling well. As a matter of fact, she's been ill since she had her fourth child. I should have known that something was going on between Lucia and Silvestro, but I didn't think Lucia would ever do a thing like that. What could I do? What can I do? I think I have been a good mother; I've worked. We weren't rich, but neither of you went without bread, even if during the summers you went without shoes. You yourself remember there were people that went barefoot with snow on the ground, and you'll still see them this coming winter. I've tried. A woman can only do so much. You're here now, and you're a man. Things don't have to be the way they were."

"They won't. Things will be better; I'll see to that. Don't worry about Lucia. She'll stay here with us. Has the baby his father's name?"

"No name."

"No name?"

Maria was puzzled, but didn't dare say anything more on the subject. Things seemed too good to be true. But she remained silent, Samuele spoke.

"Where is Lucia now?"

"At Silvestro's house, I hope. She and the baby went there this morning after we received the letter from the Red Cross. I think she's there."

"Very well, I'll go get her in the morning. You'll tell me the way tomorrow."

Samuele was sipping and savoring his wine when someone knocked on the door. Maria raised her head, squinting her eyes and raising her shoulders. Samuele looked at his mother without changing his expression. When the knock became more insistent, Maria asked who it was.

"It is I, Don Alfonso, Maria. Are you all right? Won't you open the door?"

Maria, receiving a nod from Samuele, opened the door. Don Alfonso walked in, expecting to find the house upside down and Maria harmed; instead, he stood there with his mouth wide open in disbelief but with apparent relief, wanting to smile but not daring. Realizing he had given himself away, he quickly broke down. Smiling, he greeted Samuele, who quickly got up to shake hands. The priest was even more surprised when Samuele poured some wine into a glass and offered it to him.

"To our health," said Samuele raising his glass. Then without waiting for an answer, he added: "And I am thankful for being back and to find my family intact."

"And we are happy, very happy indeed; I mean 'happy' to see things I hadn't expected to see... To your health and happiness." Gulping down the wine, a smiling Don Alfonso put the glass on the table. Knowing to leave things well enough alone, he quickly wished them goodnight and good rest, turned as though he was responding to an internal military command, and walked out, where the neighbors were still gathered. On seeing Don Alfonso smiling, they raised their eyebrows in disbelief. They were further startled when they approached him to learn about what he had seen inside, and even more surprised when he told them to leave for their homes, urging the young men first thing in the morning to go join the army, and went on his way. The group then turned their gaze toward Maria, who was standing in the doorway. Saying goodnight, she pulled back and shut the door.

Neither Maria nor Samuele would sleep very much that night. She prayed to God but especially to Mary to whom she repeated countless *Ave Marias* on her old dark beads, while Samuele thought of his past, especially his few secret dates with Franca, whose image had given him consolation during those horrible nights. In the morning, after getting Lucia, he decided he would also walk toward Franca's house with the hope of finding her alone, to talk to her and see what effect his limping might have on her. Above all, he wondered whether she might still love him, now that so much time had gone by and so many things had happened.

In his bedroom, he sat on his bed. After having taken off his shoes, he rubbed the bluish stump of his foot, then reclined on the bed. After a bit of tossing and turning, and with one foot snugly under the other, Samuele finally closed his eyes, his head on his arm, his hand clutching the edge of the mattress. For the first time in so long, he fell asleep completely relaxed, not having to worry that he might be killed by enemy fire or die from the pervasive hunger and persistent cold as had happened to so many of his comrades. With his head sunk deep into the pillow, he finally relaxed his shoulders under the sheet snugly taut around his neck.

CHAPTER 3

As usual, Maria got up early the next morning. While her son slept, she went on quietly with her routine. But this morning she was happy, happier than she had ever been before. She went to the chicken coop to pick up fresh eggs; then to the cellar to get the earthen pot full of homemade sausages preserved in melted lard. Once again, she placed a bottle of white wine on the table still covered with the white cloth from the evening meal. Occasionally she sneaked upstairs to see if Samuele might be up. But not until a little after nine did he give signs of movement. Maria immediately called up to him, and he answered that he would be down shortly.

Maria was ready when he came down. She scraped a spoonful of the refined lard, pulled out four sausages, and put them in the pan, which was already on the fire. She then broke four eggs. While she did this, with Samuele watching attentively, Maria explained the way to Lucia's hiding place.

The breakfast was exactly what Samuele had been waiting for. He ate heartily and drank almost half-a-bottle of the white wine. At the end he cleaned the dish off with bread crust, drank another half glass of wine, and went on his way to get his sister.

The sun was shining brightly. An early spring breeze blew across the plateau; Samuele felt the air and was filled with excitement. He glanced up at the top of the poplars and walked toward them as he had done so many times. This time, though, as he passed them, as though in review, he noticed the many scars on their trunks, scars that had not been there before. One in particular, the one in the center, had a good hunk gouged out. A heavy truck or tank must have run into it. By some miracle, however, the tree remained tall and very much alive.

Samuele hadn't been alone but a few moments when his old neighbors began to gather around. He shook hands with all and moved on, avoiding answering questions concerning his military experiences. But the children were the most vociferous.

"Is it true you killed a hundred soldiers?" asked one.

"No," interrupted another, "he killed two hundred... Isn't it true, Samuele?"

Samuele smiled affectionately but continued to talk to the grown-ups. Finally, Mr. Banno walked over.

"Let's go, spread out," he ordered as he pushed his way toward Samuele. One of the children pulled back, sticking his tongue out and twirling his hands on his ears. "You fresh brat... Go home... Hello, Samuele, how are you this morning? You know, I wanted to talk with you about that piece of land. I remember how you and my Rosa used to get along so well together. Well, you know the high cost of good land. I just want you to know that my land can be yours."

"I'm interested in buying farmland. When you're ready to sell, please do me the favor of letting me know."

Mr. Banno raised his head and pulled back slightly, not expecting this answer at all; it had several implications to be thought out. Mr. Banno stared at Samuele. Lifting his eyebrows, he jerked his head up and down, suspecting something was afoot, but not sure what to make of it. Momentarily perplexed, he hesitated, thinking that he should perhaps defer the conversation to a more opportune time, that it might be wiser to stop talking altogether. The temptation was too great, however.

"Did you come back with a lot of money?" he asked, then immediately placed his hand over his mouth.

"That's a little personal, don't you think, Mr. Banno?"

"Sure, sure, Samuele. Good, good... We'll talk about it another time. That's right, we have plenty of time. By the way, are you good for that glass of white wine? I always keep a few bottles for important people, and this year's vintage is exceptional. You know how good a wine-maker I am, Samuele?"

"Yes I know. There'll be another time. Right now, I'm on my way to get my sister Lucia. But, don't worry; I'll be dropping in on you before you know it. Goodby, Mr. Banno."

"By, Sam..."

Samuele walked away smartly so as not to give Mr. Banno a chance to detain him any longer. As he walked way, his limping was very noticeable. It almost disappeared, however, when walking in full stride. Passing by the church, he glanced at it hastily without slowing down. Don Alfonso, who stood in front of his house, had watched everything. When Samuele approached, Don Alfonso greeted him.

"Good morning, Samuele. How are you this fine morning?" Don Alfonso asked, slightly embarrassed.

"Oh! good morning, Don Alfonso. I am fine, thank you."

"I just watched you pass by the church."

"Yes."

"You haven't given up your faith in God, I hope. When you passed by, you made no attempt to cross yourself. Our religion..."

"God!" Samuele repeated in a soft voice. "If it hadn't been for God, I wouldn't be here today. In spite of Him, many did die, however. Maybe they had lost their faith," Samuele stated in a tone which left Don Alfonso puzzled. Like Mr. Banno, Don Alfonso, too, raised his eyebrows.

"I'm on the way to get my sister Lucia. I'm running a little late. Goodby, Don Alfonso," Samuele said, thus avoiding further questions of elucidation from the priest.

Speechless, Don Alfonso consented by bowing his head and watched Samuele sprint forward, this time stopping for no other neighbor.

After about an hour of fast pacing through back streets and pathways, Samuele reached what should have been Silvestro's house. At the ranch, Samuele was stopped by a huge, barking dog, threatening with its teeth ready to attack. Samuele froze. The dog stopped barking but growled, pulling his nose back and grinding its long pointed teeth. Samuele's heart jumped, but he did not move. After having gained a little confidence, Samuele tried to talk to the animal:

"Easy, boy, whoa, fellow..." Samuele said in vain, knowing he was neither striking the right chord to calm it down, nor himself able to back out, for surely, the dog would have jumped him. Fortunately, a woman's voice from within called out and the dog reduced its growl. Soon after, the woman appeared on the pathway and with an obvious caution to keep herself in equilibrium, she approached Samuele.

She was thin from undernourishment. Her eyes were sunk in their sockets, her complexion pale.

"Who are you?" she asked, her words the lamentation of a person near death, with just enough energy to seek some distraction from boredom. After feebly sending the dog away--an astonishment for Samuele that she was obeyed--she turned to Samuele.

"I am Samuele, Lucia's brother. I am told she's here."

"Lucia! Yes, she is here. She ran away when she heard the dog bark. But she won't go far. If I had had the strength, I would have let her have it. And then I'd let him have it. They deserve nothing less. But, here I am, about to die...any moment. And my children, my poor children !"

"I've come to take her back home with me. I am very sorry for the troubles she has caused you. I know you took her in; it wasn't fair, I know. May I come forward?"

The fragile woman made a motion with her hands, and Samuele began to walk toward the house. She followed behind slowly, her foot not sure. Samuele turned his head to look at her, only to be motioned to continue walking.

"Silvestro--that is my husband--is out in the field," she informed Samuele in a continuous trembling voice.

Samuele stopped and turned around. "Yes," he said. "Where is Lucia hiding?"

"Down there, see, below that hill," she said, lifting her weak arm and pointing in that direction. "She took the baby with her."

"Thank you."

"You're limping quite a bit. Your sister had signed you off for dead, same as with me. But I'm not dead yet, and I'm not planning to die any time soon. And you! How come you didn't make it convenient for your sister?"

"We all make mistakes," he answered, walking away perturbed, his head bent as if he were again walking away from death--so customary an experience of his last three years! Having moved away a little, he turned, his eyes focusing on the woman, who stood there motionless at the edge of the walkway, her body a starkly sad remnant of a body in decay. But, he was not looking at her for the reason she might have thought, for, once again, she raised her arm motioning to Samuele to continue in the direction she had specified. Samuele, however, kept his eyes poised on her face. After a few moments, he turned around and continued on his way. His limping more evident, he did not look back any more.

At the bottom of the hill, Lucia waited, hidden in an abandoned straw hut, looking outside through the openings of thatched straws. She held the baby in her arms, distraught over the possibility he may cry. She caressed him over and over again, putting her finger over her puckered lips, keeping her eyes glued to the openings at the same time. But instead of keeping silent, the baby smiled. Lucia then ignored him altogether. The baby looked up at his mother's desolate face, his eyes full of mirth and his mouth wide with gurgling smiles. Then, "Ma, ma, mm, mm..." At that instant, the figure of Samuele appeared on the pathway and was fast approaching.

Lucia's face filled with terror as her heart leapt. With the baby clutched close to her breast, she prayed to God, while the child mumbled and sputtered. "Please, please," she said, closing her eyes full of anguish. The baby, on the other hand, began to smile and babble once more. Lucia placed her hand over his mouth. He pulled back and smiled. Of all the times to be happy, she thought, her eyes closed out of desperation. She looked out to see whether her brother was carrying his shotgun. On not seeing one, she became a little relieved. But, then, he might have a pistol in his pocket. On seeing Samuele closer to the hut, Lucia crouched to one corner, clutching her baby tightly against her breast. When he tried to break away, he began to whimper from the pain. Lucia reacted by drawing him closer, almost suffocating him. With one jerk of his arm, he pulled back long enough to catch his breath, and emitting a shriek that while piercing the heart of his mother, also reached the ears of Samuele, who was but a few yards away.

"Lucia!" he exclaimed. "Lucia, come out. I'm not going to hurt you," he said in a controlled soft voice.

She did not answer, but cringed to a point of hysteria.

"Come out, Lucia," Samuele repeated. She wanted to answer, but couldn't. When he appeared at the door, she felt a paralysis like she had never felt before. Samuele poked his head and looked down to a baby whining in the clutch of his mother's arms. Samuele moved closer. Without saying a word, Samuele extended his hands toward the baby. With her back pushing against the straining straw wall, Lucia released the baby, who, by now, was crying aloud with tears streaming down his eyes.

"I'm not going to hurt him," Samuele repeated in a soft voice, "and I'm not going to hurt you. Now, come on out."

Lucia didn't not move, her body still in shock.

"That's alright," he said, trying to reassure her. "I know how you feel," he continued, remembering the many soldiers in similar shock. "Up, get up. I said I'm not going to hurt you. Let's go; I'm taking you home. That's where you're going to stay from now on. And we're giving our name to the baby. Come on, don't be afraid. Get up," he beseeched in a softer low voice. "Come on up. Here, let me have the baby."

Fearfully, she began to move. Samuele bent down to get the crying child, tears streaming down his face as he looked at his new uncle. Lucia got up but remained in the corner.

"Come here. I am your brother."

Lucia said nothing. Her eyes began to get watery, however. In a few seconds, she began to sob. Samuele grasped her by the arm and pulled her up to him, holding her close. Lucia burst into tears, uncontrollably. On seeing his mother cry, the baby joined in, emitting shrills as if someone were killing him.

"No, no, don't cry. Don't cry, Lucia. We're going home," Samuele said, caressing her and holding the child in the other arm. "We're going home. Stop crying. Come on, stop."

For Lucia, it was easier said than done. She couldn't stop if she wanted to, at least, not for the time being. The baby, however, responding to his uncle's soothing voice, quickly shifted from shrills, to sobs, to moist eyes, to serious expression, and to a faint smile when tickled under the chin. After about a couple of minutes, Lucia tried to speak.

"Forgive me... I didn't mean to do all this to you and to our Mother... Forgive..." she said amid sobs, "forgive me," she repeated with insistence. "What have I done, what have I done to you?"

"What you have you done? What have you done compared to what has been done? Lucia, you've done nothing, nothing. I assure you," he said, rubbing his chin on her face, while the baby looked on. Tears were beginning to appear again on his small face.

Lucia finally began to gain control over her emotions. "I am sorry, Samuele. I'm sorry. Please forgive me," she asked again.

He did not answer. If he had not already forgiven, he would not have been there. The problem was with the rest of the people, he thought--relatives and friends alike. Were they also going to forgive--to forgive according to their religion--forgiveness which extends and makes life possible from the first sinful act, to the numberless ones that follow, to the very last?

Samuele, with the child in his arms, and clutching Lucia's hand firmly, backed his way out of the hut into the pathway. With Lucia slightly behind, brother and sister walked up to the house. There, within the doorway, caught between the outdoor light pressing on her and the darkness of the room pulling her inside, the fragile woman stood upright, one elbow anchored on the square stone of the doorway. She just stood there, motionless, her eyes fixed on and moving with Lucia. At that moment, Samuele realized the squalor of the place: no flowers anywhere, the walls full of holes, no bench of any kind, rocks scattered about, and even the open barn was filled with odd branches mixed with hay. Sparrows chirped above a couple of chickens pecking aimlessly around the branches and hay. And the dog, which had acted so ferociously before, sat on a dry patch of ground, his head pointing toward Lucia, but not moving.

"It's only a mutt!" Samuele exclaimed to himself. Then, shifting his eyes, he captured the transparent eyes of the woman, who kept staring at Lucia, but unable to bring her into focus.

Her hand still being held by that of Samuele, Lucia, who continued to stand slightly behind Samuele, spoke first.

"We're going home, but I do want to thank you for your patience."

The woman paid no heed. Then, in an ephemeral burst of energy, she countered the horrible words of embarrassment:

"You're nothing but a whore." Turning to Samuele, and in the same whining voice, she said, "You must be much worse."

Pulling Lucia forward, Samuele looked into his sister's eyes. "Don't pay any attention to that." With his eyes on the woman, he said, "We understand how you feel. We all have problems of our own. We wish no harm to you or to your husband, and especially to your children. If I can be of service to all of you, let me know. Goodbye and best wishes."

Without waiting for an answer, Samuele turned around and, with nephew in arms, he once again pulled Lucia forward on their way home, under the condemning but powerless glare of the woman.

They walked for over a mile when Lucia finally spoke.

"It is my fault. I have humiliated you too."

"We could have done without it. Now, what's done is done. I don't want to hear about it any more," he said firmly. "We're here now, not on the moon."

Lucia looked at her brother with a puzzled expression, but did not challenge him. Instead, she asked about his foot, only to get the stereotypical answer he had given others: he had fallen asleep without covering his foot against an unexpected cold night.

When they approached the village, Lucia began to walk with her head down

"No!" he ordered. "Up with it, or you will never be able to live here, or elsewhere. Up, and face the people: let them know you have made a mistake but that you also have the courage to face up to your mistake. Besides, it's your mistake and not theirs."

Forcing a gentle smile, Lucia looked up and walked as Samuele had ordered.

When she was greeted by her neighbors, she answered with words and smiles, causing a variety of unusual expressions.

When Don Alfonso saw the trio, he did not act as joyful as he the evening before, making no bones about either, alarmed over the precedent that Samuele was setting. Don Alfonso understood well the mistake Lucia had committed, but Samuele should not be condoning it so openly.

"You should have been more discreet," Don Alfonso said as he approached them, his voice vacillating.

"Discreet!" repeated Samuele without making any effort to hide his annoyance. "What do you mean?" he asked, his words very defined and clear, his voice without sign of weakness.

"The precedent you're setting, that's what I mean," retorted the priest.

"If I set precedents, I do it for myself and for my family. I don't set them for others, and I don't give a damn for the precedents others set."

"I didn't mean to upset you, Samuele," Don Alfonso said defensively. Then, in a soft voice, he turned his glance toward Lucia, who dared not intervene, though she wished she could disappear from sight, sink into the ground. "You probably could have avoided the main street," continued the priest, "what, with your child and all."

"No!" answered Samuele abruptly, his arm automatically squeezing his nephew to his chest, "absolutely not." Then, turning to Lucia, he took her hand once more. "Come on, we had better go."

Lucia did not speak; she nodded her approval with her head bent toward the ground. Samuele let go of her hand, placed his arm around her waist and led her on, leaving Don Alfonso behind, awkward and embarrassed. No one, not even the old woman had the effrontery of Don Alfonso. On their way home, as a matter of fact, the people waved their hands in salutation and those closer bid them good day, and for some reason, the children were not around.

"I hope Mr. Banno is not around," Lucia thought to herself as they approached his house. Luckily, on passing by, they saw no sign of that meddler. "Thank God," she whispered to herself. Samuele picked it up.

"You were expecting Mr. Banno?"

Lucia nodded, prematurely, however, for Mr. Banno was there, in his garden with his daughter, Rosa, who called to her father. On noticing Lucia, he looked up, commenting sarcastically to his bosomy daughter: "There she goes, a woman that should have been lynched by her brother; instead, she is being protected by him. What's the world come to these days?" he asked himself rhetorically, almost absentmindedly, his complexion bit more red than usual. Turning his heavy head to Rosa, he added, "I thing he could be a good provider. I'm sure he could take good care of you the rest of your life. We have to play our cards right, and we will!"

Rosa did not answer. Instead, she stared at Samuele, her large lips slightly open, her eyelids semi closed, but not saying a word and still watching as Samuele, Lucia and the child disappeared into the curve.

Having reached the poplars, Lucia gave a sigh of relief. With her brother to her side, however, she felt reassured.

When they got home, Samuele and Lucia found the door closed. Lucia suggested they go to the rear of the house where their mother might be at the stall caring for the livestock. They walked back and found Maria fetching hay from the stack. On seeing Lucia and Samuele still holding the child, Maria felt extremely happy.

Samuele had not yet seen the stall. Maria quickly went toward them to ask Samuele if he wanted to see the animals. Though Franca was on his mind, he obliged his mother. "Come here," she said proudly, "I've got something special to show you." She took him by the hand as though he were still a child, and led him inside the stall. To one side there stood a young and sturdy bullock, unusual for its size and apparent strength. The animal was already as big as a fully grown one and much handsomer than he had ever seen. Looking at his new owner approaching, the bullock turned around, raising its muzzle and sniffing through its nose. Samuele went close, marveling at its size. He caressed it on its huge neck, while Maria proudly stood behind.

"We'll sell it at the fair of the Straw Obelisk. He'll fetch a good sum," Maria said. But Samuele did not hear her. He kept on stroking the animal's neck and head, and the bullock seemed pleased. It extended its neck, getting closer to Samuele. A few rabbits below chewed on the hay, moving their noses from side to side. At the other end of the stable, the bullock's mother mooed loudly; she hadn't yet received her portion of feed.

"Oh! I forgot," exclaimed Maria. "I haven't fed her yet."

"Wait, I'll go," he said, as he handed the child over to Lucia.

Outside, he picked up the wooden fork, stuck it several times into the odorous stack, and came up with a heavy forkful which he deposited in the manger. Several rabbits quickly scurried over to eat the remnants dropping from the stuffed manger. Samuele patted the cow on its side, went back to Maria and told her he was going to visit Franca.

"Oh," Maria said, surprised; her reservation obvious. Then she added: "I wish you luck, son. But Franca has a brother of questionable character, and a mother... well, enough of that... Her father Ernesto, on the other hand, has always been level-headed and commands respect throughout the village. But, please, beware of Toni. I have yet to hear one good thing about him."

"Wasn't he drafted?"

"No," Maria answered disgustedly. "He has something wrong with his leg, but I don't believe it. Same thing with your friend Enrico; he skipped the draft too."

"Maybe they were smart. Well, I'd better be going. I'll see you in a while," Samuele said, passing by the child and patting him on the head. The two smiled at each other as though they had known each other for a long time.

CHAPTER 4

About one mile from Samuele's house lived Franca, a sensitive young woman in her very early twenties. As there was a lot of work around the farm and house, she helped out in the field and in the house.

Franca had known Samuele very well since she was about sixteen, when she fell secretly in love with him and had kept on thinking about him through the war. And, like Lucia, she too had even given him up for dead. But now there he was, back at home. Outside of his foot, she was told, he was quite well, but that he was acting strange. She knew he would be trying to see her, but did not know how or when. Within her, she felt an excitement that gave her little peace.

She wandered about the house, now feeding the chickens, then the rabbits. She went to the well, filled the tank with water, then washed her hands.

"Again!" Franca's mother yelled from inside the door. She had noticed Franca's rather erratic behavior. "What's the matter with you this morning! This is not time to feed the animals. And what's this with your hands? How many times have you washed them this morning? Get the sack and go fill it. Your father and brother will be getting home soon with the animals."

Without a word, Franca went inside the house, picked up the burlap bag, and walked down the pathway toward the place where she and Samuele used to meet.

"Where are you going?" asked the mother in a harsh tone.

"To get the leaves, where else?" Franca retorted, the strong statement betrayed by her weak voice. She turned and walked away, her mother threateningly waving her hands to insure that Franca came back with a sack full of leaves.

Walking down the hill, Franca passed her hands through her hair, pulling the fine strands away from her face and tying them on each side of her head. She checked her white blouse, straightened her skirt and looked at her worn-out sandals. Then she looked at her legs, bending down to pass her hand over the rough skin.

Above her, birds chirped on the trees replete with fresh leaves, and on one branch, two sparrows were wooing each other. It was spring, and suddenly she felt it in her heart. She stared at them as they flew from branch to branch, the male ruffling its feathers. Below, amid the wild grass, white lilies were making their way up. She touched one with her finger, then bent down to bring her face close to them, to smell their perfume, to feel their freshness. In the past, she would have picked them, made them into a nosegay, and worn it on her blouse. This day, she was satisfied to admire them, realizing that if she touched them she would damage their delicate buds. And the thought of Samuele did not leave her.

Samuele, in fact, had left for the war just about three years ago. Before leaving, he had given her a bunch of those lilies. But except for a couple of letters she had received during the first month or two, she got no more letters after that. Nevertheless, she remembered his handsome face, the high forehead, the light brown hair, his wide chest, and strong arms. She also remembered the wild expression in Samuele's eyes, and cherished the kisses she tried to avoid--the kisses she enjoyed to the point that she could have become completely his if he had wanted to. Luckily for her, Samuele never went beyond the kisses, no matter how passionate, and this made Franca feel there was something special in their relationship. Yet, she also knew that he did abstain from having sex with other women. Nevertheless, Franca remained a virgin for two other good reasons: her mother and her brother. Heaven help her if she had been like Lucia, or Rachele, or like so many other women who, either out of need, or passion, or fate, had fallen by the wayside. In her heart, she felt they had done the wrong thing. But, to each his own. As for Franca, she knew that she wouldn't be alive let alone think those thoughts if she had been like the other women.

Since Samuele had left, however, other men had approached Franca's father and Franca herself, but she never felt anything for them, even those from well-to-do families. Secretly, Franca kept on dreaming and hoping that Samuele would return and take her away. Above everything else, she longed to be a woman--a full woman, knowing that only Samuele could make that possible. But now that the moment was approaching, she felt awkward, anxious, and less than a woman.

Throwing the sack over her shoulders, she got up and walked down to the corner of the farm, below which ran the main road of the village. There, surrounded by low-lying trees with branches laden with leaves, Franca pursued her chore. Holding the sack with one hand, she trimmed the branches with the other, making a noise audible to anyone below.

Samuele, who had just reached the corner below, on hearing the rustling, looked up from behind the bushes and saw Franca. Slightly overcome with emotion, he stood there, looking at her, contemplating her every movement. Franca was more beautiful than before, wholesome looking, strong, vigorous, decisive: a complete woman, he concluded, one with the earth at peace with itself. There she was, in front of him--not on the moon--but on this beautiful earth.

The more he looked at her, the more his heart throbbed. He wanted to go right to her, to hold her and kiss her as he used to do. This time, however, he did not dare, not because he lacked courage or dare, but because he did not feel secure, his foot and all. Would she still want him, he asked himself, now that he was no longer the Samuele of three years ago--physically and mentally?

He looked while Franca continued to strip the branches of their leaves and thrusting them into the sack without as much as one dropping to ground. Finally, having made her fill, she paused for a moment. Then, as she was about to lift the sack onto her back, Samuele appeared from below, startling Franca.

"May I?" he asked, repeating himself as he walked toward her with an obvious limp. Staring into his eyes at first, she unwittingly looked at his foot, dashing Samuele's spirit.

"Samuele!" she exclaimed, her hands crossed over her breast, bosom. Oh, Samuele, I'm so happy to see you. You're finally back!"

"Yes..." he mumbled, "thanks to you," he added, his heart uplifted. Not knowing what to make of those words, she waited for Samuele with outstretched arms. Once in front of her, he placed his arms around her while she slipped her hands around his back. His head deep into her shoulder, Samuele hid his tears, not knowing that she too was crying. After a few seconds, they broke their embrace. Looking into her eyes, Samuele spoke.

"Did you give me up for dead too?"

Shaking her head, Franca stared back, a ponderous expression on her face.

"Samuele..." she answered in a chastising tone.

"Are you as happy in seeing me as I am of seeing you?"

With Franca nodding her approval, Samuele extended his arms once again, and Franca fell into them as they kissed.

Theirs was not the passionate kiss of their youth; their lips now lingered softly together--a sweetness having replaced the torrid kisses of yesteryear. With their eyes closed, they relaxed in a prolonged kiss, as Samuele brought his hand over Franca's breast.

"I've loved you... I love you," Samuele said in a whisper. "I thought I'd never be back to tell you that. About two years ago, I began to realize how much you meant to me," he continued in a low voice, his lips touching the side of her soft face. "And I always feared you wouldn't have waited, that you wouldn't have loved me."

"I always loved you... And I still do," she answered, stretching her arms around his neck. "I do, and I've been waiting for you to come back and take me away from here. I've been so unhappy."

At those words, Samuele pulled back a little, wanting to take her hand to kiss it. As he tried to do so, Franca protested.

"No, no! Please, Samuele."

He insisted, however. He took her hand and placed it on his face. Franca withdrew it from under his hand. They were too rough; they were the hands of men that did manual labor, and she was ashamed.

"When I heard you were back, I tried to make myself pretty. I tried to look like the woman I feel I'd want to be, but I couldn't. I was worried you wouldn't like me this way."

Samuele smiled. "And I was afraid you wouldn't have liked me this way." Then he kissed her again. With her arms locked around Samuele's neck, she reassured him of her love.

"And my foot?" he asked her. "I'm not what I was physically. I am in worse shape than I look."

"If you're ill, I'll cure you. You could have the whole leg missing and I'd still be loving you. Thank God you're back."

"God!" he whispered to himself as though Franca was not present. Then, as if he were completely unaware of his remark, he proposed to walk Franca home, to meet her parents to let them know their intentions...

"No!" she replied. "This is not the time. Let me talk to my father first. Maybe I will talk to my mother first." Franca turned aside to pick up the sack. "I must go now," she said. "My father and Toni should be returning any moment," she said, as she moved to pick up the sack to put it on her back, not noticing Samuele, who had already moved to get it.

"I'll get it. Let me take it up."

"No, I'll do it. You go on home now. I'll let you know what they say the next time we meet."

"Here, let me help you with it."

"No, I'm not picking it up until you leave and are out of sight. Please, go now," she beseeched.

Embracing her once again, Samuele kissed her tenderly, and walked toward the road below. With her hands on the sack, Franca looked at him limping away until he was out of sight. Then, with a heave, she placed the sack over her shoulder and walked home.

CHAPTER 5

Ernesto, Franca's father, was already home sitting at the table waiting for his lunch when Franca arrived.

"Hurry up," ordered her mother from the kitchen. "The animals are hungry and your father is waiting here. "What's kept you so long?"

Without answering, Franca immediately spread the leaves in front of the animals tethered to the fig trees. Then she went inside where her mother immediately began to complain.

"I don't know what's the matter with her today. Just a while ago she fed the chickens, then she washed her hands. I don't know what the matter with your daughter," she said to her husband.

"Yah, I know... Just put something on the table," he ordered effortlessly, pouring from a bottle of red wine into a not too large glass. But, instead of filling the glass, he stopped halfway, pushed the glass to one side and began to drink from the bottle.

"Where do you get these thimbles, anyway!" he half exclaimed half asked, after a long draw. Neither of the two women answered. As Franca put the bread on the table, she looked at her father's large reddish face and full set of graying hair. She wanted to speak to him, but didn't dare. Then she walked toward the door to get away from the heavy air inside. As she stood by the door, she looked down the road. On seeing her brother coming up from below on his motorcycle, she felt her heart jump, fearing he might have seen Samuele.

The sound of the motorcycle soon reached the ears of Franca's mother, who, with deliberate solicitude, quickly went to the door. Pushing Franca aside, she looked at her son Toni, her face full smiles, as she waited for Toni to dismount.

"Let's get the food on the table," shouted Ernesto. Franca immediately went over to the fireplace, got the hot pan containing the fried potatoes and peppers, and placed it on the table. Then she got a plate and a fork. As she was filling the dish, Toni entered. Distracted by Toni's unusual entrance, Franca spilled some peppers on the table.

"What's the matter with you today?" said Ernesto, fed-up first with his wife, and now even with Franca.

"I know what's the matter with her," interrupted Toni sarcastically.

"Oh... you do?" asked Ernesto, his voice contemptuously prolonging his words, unconvinced that his son might really know.

"Yah, I know," Toni repeated with emphasis. Then, turning to Franca, and with his finger pointed at her at her, he accused her of having seen Samuele. "I just saw him below. He was coming from this direction."

"Is that right?" interjected the father in a ridiculing tone. "Did you see them together?"

"No, but I'm sure..."

"You should be sure of one thing and one thing only, that you've been a knucklehead and you will always be one. Just shut up and let that mother of yours set the rest of this damned table before I bounce it over her head. I've been working like a slave all morning, and I don't want to hear any crap."

The wife quickly went to get the food, having noticed her husband a bit more irascible than usual. In no time the four were seated at the table eating their lunch in complete silence. Not even the dog dared to move. Though the others drank from their glasses, Ernesto continued to drink from the bottle. Every time he raised it to his lips, the dog looked up at his master. With the bottle still up to his mouth, Ernesto dunked a piece of bread in the juice of his dish and threw it up in the air. On seeing the mutt jump and catching the bread, Ernesto smiled with satisfaction.

"He's smarter than you," he said to his son, noting his futile attempts in teaching him anything.

"You're always picking on him," interrupted the mother. Ernesto let the observation go as though she had made no sound at all.

"Where were you all morning long?" Ernesto asked, his eyes fixed on Toni's. "There's the field to be planted, and you're gallivanting on your motorbike. Hell of a thing I did when I bought it for you. And I bet I know who you were with--the other good-for-nothing Enrico. Of the two, I don't know who is the worse, except that you're both alike."

"I went to the market to see what price we can get for the calf."

"Did I tell you to go, or, did your mother tell you to go?"

Mother and son exchanged glances. Then Tony answered in a defensive tone. "No one told me. You're always accusing me of not taking the initiative or of showing any interest of the farm, but when I try..."

"You try staying around here and go when I tell you..."

"And Samuele?" asked Toni. Franca's eyes opened wide. Hiding the obvious terror on her face, she quickly turned aside.

"Samuele!" exclaimed Ernesto. "He's come back from the war!" Pulling the sleeve up on his arm, he continued. "You've forgotten I was in the first world war," he said pointing to the scar on his arm. "My biggest mistake was keeping you from the draft. What a disgrace! I listened to her... Look at her, she cried night and day when you were called."

Having heard the same story repeated over and over again, the woman just ignored her husband. Instead, and through rote, she refilled her son's dish without realizing there was still plenty of food on the plate. Ernesto looked on, shaking his head. Toni remained neutral.

"Fill mine, too," erupted Ernesto, startling his wife.

Then, getting her wits back, she retorted: "Do it yourself; I'm not your servant."

"Not my servant, eh!" Ernesto repeated in a soft voice, barely audible to the rest, ironically philosophizing to himself. Then, with a tremendous shout, he yelled: "You should be so lucky." Pausing a few brief moments, he continued in a more calm but resolute manner. "Any more lip from you," pointing at his wife, "and any more nonsense from you," pointing at his son, "I'll give you both such a whipping as you never had before. Just mark my word. Now, get the goddamned dish filled as I ordered you."

That word *ordered* made her inner core cringe; yet, unbeknown to her, she was a greater slave to her son, the difference being that she loathed her husband and blessed every inch her son walked on. As for her daughter, she didn't think much one way or another, but certainly she considered Franca a nuisance more often than not, and regardless of the argument, she always took the side of Toni.

The woman filled the dish as her son and daughter looked on in silence, hoping the quarrel would terminate soon, for, they had seen their mother well beaten up, and even Franca did not want to see that happen again. While their mother served their father, they sat at the table waiting for him to eat. On seeing him eat, they also ate, and no one said a word. Even the dog stayed to one side, his tail between his legs, somehow remembering his master's irascibility. In that manner, they spent the rest of lunch.

When Ernesto finally took his siesta, Toni, who was shining his motorcycle with his mother standing by, called out to Franca. Knowing that sooner or later she would have to face them, Franca went over, ready to do battle, especially with Toni. Her mother began in a soft and understanding tone:

"What do you want with a man like Samuele? I don't think he's good enough for you, and for us. Now, I am told he limps. Besides, he has very little land besides and the house--well, his mother, and now his sister and baby--the house wouldn't be big enough for you as well. Franca, as everyone knows, is just the kind of woman she is, and Maria, regardless of what other do-gooders say about her, can't be much better. I know these kinds of people well. You'd go there and you'd be their servant..." she said, looking directly into the face of Franca, bored by her mother's sermon. "...Toni knows so many people. Many of them have titles, and we'll find a nice man..."

"I know his friends," Franca interrupted, the sarcasm directed at them. At that moment, she realized where she stood: her father, no matter how crude, would be her salvation.

"I'm warning you," threatened Toni. "You keep away from him, or, what should have happened to his sister will happen to you."

Franca did not answer. Instead she stared at him in defiance, cutting him down with her looks alone, almost in the manner of her father. Then with words full of sarcasm and disdain, she answered: "You're talking from that dirty, stinking conscience of yours." Franca turned around and left her brother and mother speechless and motionless--both looking at her as she disappeared through the door. When the dog approached them, wagging his tail and pointing his nose up Toni's leg, he brutally kicked the dog in the stomach. Wailing loudly, the dog ran outside, through a group of chickens peacefully pecking away at the ground.

They jumped and tossed wildly through the air in frightened excitement.

CHAPTER 6

Those tall poplars, retaining the curve on the upper side of the road, had always attracted Samuele since he was a boy, having admired them throughout his life, their image always in his mind, especially during the atrocious days of his many encampments; their tremendous height and sturdiness still amazed him. In the summer, they provided him cool shade; in winter, they shielded him from the cold. When the wind blew, they turned it to music, and the various melodies remained in his heart throughout his army career. But the thing he liked the most about them was the rustling of the leaves in spring. Theirs was a symphonic tapping he could hear directly from his home. On the branches filled with gilded leaves, the goldfinches made their nests, more often than not, joining their singing to the poplar's tapping.

Beneath them, sitting on a large rock Samuele listened to those sounds for the first time in so long, and felt the light breeze crossing the plateau, just enough to make the air balmy and to set the leaves rustling. Samuele looked up to their summits, and down to the ground. But his eyes almost always came to rest on the trunk of the largest poplar with its big gash. Though the bark was creating a ring around the gash, the surface of the wound was already drying.

He had seen nothing but death in the past few years, and although he had overcome its trauma--at least temporarily--signs of death still depressed him deeply. Having made a vow to assist any struggling living thing, even it if meant placing his own life at risk, that thought alleviated the trauma. And although he was not thinking exactly about his vow, he was responding to the conditioned reflex to act on behalf of others, as he had done so many times, even though his actions too often had proven futile in the face of man-made death. There, in front of him, the tree trunk showed its huge scar, and he felt helpless in assuaging the pain of the tree or of his own pain inside. Samuele stuck his foot out and touched the tree with his shoe, a sign of mutual respect, admiration and solidarity, even though he could not do anything to bring his foot back to normal or of healing the scar on the tree, except to learn how to live with it, doing the best he could. Life, after all, was, and is still, precious.

His daydreaming--torrid and lyrical--came to an abrupt end with the appearance of Enrico, the friend of those wanton and irresponsible days. Enrico approached Samuele with his usual jovial flair filled with apparent exuberant affection.

"Samuele! How the hell are you? Say, you look much older. How are you?" he asked, extending his hand to shake Samuele's. Enrico put his arms around Samuele and hugged him with affection and laughter. "I'd never thought you'd be back, you old devil. But, I'm glad. Boy, we did so many things together... Remember! There's more to be done now, I can assure you. But now, tell me, how are you, you old devil? What the hell did you do in the war? I was told you got shot in the foot--that's why you're limping now--isn't that right? But you look good, though, let me hand it to you. Jesus, you look good. Are we going to have a time," Enrico went on. Samuele simply kept on smiling, amused. "Yah, you ought to see what I'm latching onto.

Legs like this," he said bringing his hands together. "What flesh, Samuele. But remember, hands off! Listen, I'm dying to make her, but so far, no luck. I want you to help me. You were always pretty good with the women--not that I was too shabby myself--but now that you've been in the war and all that, you got your foot shot off, you know, some women go for that. Hey, come on, what do you say? And how the hell are you? By God, you look good. That little hair you lost sure made a difference. What do you say... Come on, let's go over my house. You're not doing anything right now, are you..."

"No."

"Well, that's fine. Well, then, come on, let's go. Hey," he said as he put his arm around Samuele's waist, and beginning to walk, "have you seen Rosa yet? Well, I tell you, she's something else, I tell you. You know, Mr. Banno talks a lot...not like us, you know what I mean...we're after, you and me, that is--we're after facts. You know, we got a deal going--can't tell you all the details now, but I tell you, Sam, there's plenty, and it's all good. Come on, let's go over the house. My mother is waiting for me. She's always preparing something good to eat. But let's stop by Rosa first. I'm sure she's taking some spring-summer sun in her back yard...ha, ha, ha...remember that barn? It's still there. Rosa, I'm telling you, wouldn't be what she is today if it hadn't been for us. She's more beautiful now, but promise, we can't touch her, but we can still have some fun though. We can tease her... She's good at that. Come on," he urged as he hugged Samuele with over-abundant affection. "Come on, tell me something. You haven't said a word."

"I couldn't get one in edgewise if I wanted to."

"Oh, come one, Samuele, I'm so glad to see you. You can't imagine. Anyway, what do you say, are you game?"

"I'm game, and you needn't worry."

"About what?" Enrico asked, a puzzled expression on his face.

"Didn't you just talk about Rosa?"

"Oh, Rosa, of course. You were always sharp. Hey, you really got your ass shot off, didn't you? Just look at the way you limp. Well, that's all done with. I tell you, you should have done what I did. I told you. But you wanted to be a hero. Now, look at you. You're back with your ass shot off... Hey, look, there she is!" he exclaimed. "Rosa doesn't have the legs of my sweet *jeova*, no sir, I tell you... You know, remember now, Rosa's already taken."

Enrico was about to continue talking, when Samuele interrupted him as they had gotten within hearing-distance of Rosa.

"*Already taken*, what does that mean?" Samuele asked, his forehead full of furrows.

"Never mind. We're picking up where we left off, as though nothing ever happened--no war, no nothing..."

"You've changed a lot in these years. I can see. You do a lot more thinking and a lot less talking."

"Action, Samuele, action. That's me. Well, you know, time goes by. Me, I've had a ball. You should have stayed here..."

"There's Rosa," interrupted Samuele.

"Hi, Rosa, look who I've got. You haven't seen him yet, have you? Well, here he is, the old bruiser. He's got his foot shot off--you can see him limp--he almost got something else shot off--you know what I mean. But aren't we glad he didn't. Remember..."

"I do," she answered with a tolerating smile. "Hi, Samuele. I was hoping you'd be coming by." While Rosa spoke, Enrico jabbed Samuele in his side, smiling happily.

"Hi, Rosa," greeted Samuele. How are you? You look great."

"Yah, I told you she did. She's as good as they come. The best in our village, the best all around, the best in the world. Tell us you never saw anyone like Rosa, not even at the front. Tell us... Look," Enrico said, pointing at her, "you haven't seen anyone like her in the war, did you?" he asked with a smile, his hand extended at the same level as Rosa's full breast, her nipples pushing out.

Rosa picked it right up. Smiling, she brought her arm out to strike down Enrico's extended hand.

"You're still the old teaser. You haven't changed a bit," Rosa said, her eyes on Samuele.

"I've changed; Samuele just said so," Enrico added.

"Maybe in some things; but for the better, I'm sure," she retorted with a big smile that turned into laughter. Enrico, too, laughed. Soon Samuele did likewise.

"Remember, Samuele, remember the fun we used to have. Remember Rosa. Those were the good old days. But I just told Samuele, I'm glad he's back. So what if he limps, we can still have a good time, don't you think? Besides, with his hair line up a little he looks much older, don't you think? You women like that, right, Rosa?" he babbled on, as if he were monopolizing the conversation.

"I suppose so," she answered. Then turning again to Samuele, she became a bit serious. "I remember when I used to have such a crush on you. We had a lot of fun together."

"I guess we did," interrupted Enrico, his voice scraping a little. "Yah, we all had a ball, didn't we. Rosa, you've heard about Samuele, haven't you. I am told he killed I don't know how many soldiers. Have you heard?" he asked, no allowing Samuele to comment on Rosa's admission.

Samuele stopped smiling. Noticing the change, Rosa quickly intervened.

"I don't think Samuele likes to talk about those things," she commented. "Tell me, Samuele, what are you going to do now that you are back?"

"Work the farm and raise cattle."

"What! Are you crazy? *Work the farm and raise cattle*? Are you well? Come on, Samuele. Life is short, isn't that right, Rosa? Tell him, life is short. Life is short, I'm telling you. It isn't much longer for women; especially the ones as beautiful as Rosa. Tell him, Rosa, I tell you."

"*Life is short*, Samuele," Rosa said in a straight face, then bursting into laughter and throwing her arms up against Enrico's chest. He laughed too, but quickly put his arms around her and drew her against him. Squeezing her tightly, Enrico turned and winked at Samuele, raising his eyebrows at the same time. When Enrico drew so close as to feel her breast, Rosa pushed him back.

"Come to think of it," interjected Enrico, "Samuele has been away for a long time. I bet you haven't even kissed him or shook his hand to welcome him back, have you, Rosa?"

"I don't think he wants to," she answered.

"I mean, after all, unless...you know what I mean," Enrico said.

Rosa knew too well what he meant. But keeping in the spirit of the conversation, she extended her hand to Samuele. "Welcome back Mr. Samuele. We all missed you."

Samuele extended his hand. She took his hand and held on tightly. When he tried to break the handshake, he couldn't. Rosa held on, smiling effervescently. Samuele tried again to pull back, but to no avail. Rosa held on, drawing him toward her just as Enrico had done with her. Instead of backing up, Samuele drew her toward him, both to Rosa's delight and to Enrico's surprise. When she was directly in front of him, their chests almost touching, Samuele looked at her, smiled, winked at Enrico, who was looking on nervously, and kissed her smack on her forehead, making a concomitant noise.

Rosa did not lose her composure. With both arms around Samuele's neck and playfully, Rosa suddenly brought her mouth onto Samuele's and kissed him hard. Off-guard, Samuele did not move, all the more because he felt the passion of her kiss and at the same time not wanting to lead her on or reveal to Enrico what was taking place.

When Rosa continued with what seemed more than a game kiss, Enrico took on a serious expression. His forehead wrinkled, he place both his hands between Samuele and Rosa, physically separating Rosa from Samuele. "Hey, you guys!" he complained.

Her eyes fixed on Samuele, Rosa turned her face slightly toward Enrico. "Isn't that what you wanted me to do?" she asked.

Enrico was embarrassed because he had expected Rosa to do that to him, if anything, and not to Samuele. On seeing his troubled dejection, Rosa turned to Enrico, and with obvious fanfare, kissed him on the mouth, thus restoring his equanimity. The kiss, however, had neither the passion nor the depth of Rosa's previous kiss. Nevertheless, Enrico was happy.

Unexpectedly from below, Mr. Banno began to call out to his daughter. Rosa pulled back from the two men. "Oh, Jesus, my father's coming. Go on, take off before he sees you..."

"Rosa, where are you, Rosa!" Mr. Banno repeated as he appeared from below. "There you are. What are you doing here? Why didn't you answer?"

"Daddy, you just called. You didn't give me a chance. I was about to answer you when you appeared... Enrico and Samuele were passing by. They stopped to say hello. They've only been here a couple seconds. You know, I hadn't really said hello to Samuele."

"Samuele knows he can come to our home any time he wants to."

"And me, Mr. Portabandiera...I mean Mr. Banno?" asked Enrico with artificial obsequiousness.

"Not you," Mr. Banno said, his eyes semi-closed from the frown above. To make no bones about his dislike for Enrico, Mr. Banno continued. "I told you to stay away from my daughter; I told you not to come to this house."

"But, Mr. Banno," observed Enrico in a serious tone, "Samuele was just telling Rosa and me about the gold he found in Russia. You didn't know that, did you?" Enrico asked with a sub-rosa expression (no pun intended). "It's a secret. I told you this because we trust you to keep secrets. You won't say anything to anyone about Samuele's secret, will you?" Enrico asked, to the surprise of Samuele, who couldn't quite know what to make of Enrico's quick thinking and delivery.

"Who, me! Banno Portabandiera! Even you know I can keep secrets... Well, Rosa let's go. Your mother is not feeling well... Samuele, remember, my wine is the best in the region," he said, placing his hand to one side of his mouth and turning his thumb into his cheek. Then forming an "o" with thumb and index finger, he extended his hand, telling Samuele how exquisite his wine was.

"Aren't you going to offer me any? The world knows how great your wine is, and I haven't had any, not even this much," interjected Enrico, rubbing his own index finger over his thumb, subtly. "My mouth is watering already. I heard it mentioned in Naples, then in Bari. The world knows about it, and here am I, sixty miles from Naples and sixty miles from Bari, and, only a couple hundred feet from you, Sir--Mr. Banno's famous cellar, and I haven't had the honor, the distinguishing honor of having tasted it yet."

Proudly, and with a broad smile, Mr. Banno answered that Enrico would have to go to Naples if he wanted to taste it. Better still, Mr. Banno, no fool when it came to give and take, added, "Try going to the North Pole. I understand there's still a bottle there, waiting just for you. But be sure to bring some grease with you." With this, Mr. Banno left with Rosa by his side, not before Rosa had secretly looked deeply into Samuele's eyes without saying anything, and turning her head toward Samuele from time to time. When they were about to go into the house, Mr. Banno turned around to give one last glance at the two young men. Enrico shrugged his shoulders; then, when Rosa and her father had gone inside, he bend forward, puckered his lips and shook his head at an incredulous Samuele in semi shock.

"What's the matter with her?" Rosa asked her father on entering the kitchen.

"Headache, the usual thing... Is it true, what Enrico said: Samuele has come back with gold? I always knew there was a lot of gold in Russia."

"He's going to raise cattle, he said."

"*Raise cattle*! Is that right? How can you do that without money? Mm..." he moaned, tightening his lips. "Mm... It sounds interesting. I told you, Rosa, Samuele didn't come back empty-handed as people say. No, Rosa, my pretty flower, he didn't."

CHAPTER 7

On the way to Enrico's house, Samuele did not say much, as Enrico did all the talking. Outside of some remarks having a sense of novelty, everything else Enrico said had become repetitious. Samuele listened throughout; his mind, however, was elsewhere: Franca.

"What's the matter?" Enrico asked, realizing he was getting little response from Samuele. "Are you thinking about Rosa's kiss?"

"Oh, ya... yes. I must have been thinking about that and the bottle of wine being reserved for you in the North Pole."

The two men walked along the pathway lined by fruit trees bearing many-colored buds. They were behind the church when Don Alfonso came out of the back door. Enrico stopped, pulling Samuele behind a fully-leaved tree out of sight of the priest. While waiting at Enrico's urgent request, Samuele asked for a reason.

"You know," Enrico answered, "lately, well, really, a few years, I haven't been going to church. He's talked to my mother. Well, I still didn't go. Now, he's worried. We have a missionary--some sort of new religion, I don't know what it is, and I don't care a hoot about it. You know me: I ain't no giant in the field of religion and philosophy. Anyhow, there's a young missionary whom I call *my jeova*. She's come here because we are poor and ignorant. Many people say the church keeps us poor and ignorant. I don't believe it. We're poor and ignorant because we want to be. Besides, the land doesn't offer much around here. Well, that's besides the point. The point being is that people think she's going to bring salvation... I don't know what else she may be bringing to them. I know what she's brought me. What a hunk, Samuele. I tell you, Samuele...a hunk. I thought Rosa had it, you know. But now...well, me, you know what I'm interested in. You ought to see her legs," he said, bringing his hands together to demonstrate the approximate size of the missionary's legs. Enrico was so completely engrossed in his description that for a few moments he was actually serious, especially in his description of her body, and truly consumed by an inner passion coupled by an evident desire to consummate a sexual relation, by whatever means.

"What's the matter with our church?" asked Samuele, matter of fact.

"Tell Don Alfonso to bring in good-looking nuns, and I'll go to church. Did you see what he's got there now? She's something else, I tell you, Sam," Enrico said, shaking his head, a serious expression on his face, not realizing the irreverence in his words. Samuele did not respond. Enrico's disrespect was in words alone. Samuele was amused by Enrico's statement that he wasn't much on religion and philosophy.

"Who is this missionary?"

"Tina. Isn't that a beautiful name? Wait till you see her."

"Does she have an audience? Are the people listening to her?"

"You know, there's oddballs all over. Yah, she's got some followers...like me!" he admitted with a big grin. "But she's latching on to me. You know why," he asked, running his hands through his black wavy hair.

While the two remained hidden behind the tree, Don Alfonso walked around the garden, pausing at times to concentrate on the beauty of the trees in bloom.

While Samuele followed the priest with his eyes, Enrico became impatient.

"Why the hell doesn't he go... Hey, he's coming toward us. Come on, let's go," Enrico urged.

"It seems you're afraid of him," observed Samuele in a calm voice.

"Come on, come on. We can go back this way. He won't see us. Come on, let's go."

Enrico grabbed Samuele by the arm and led him away down a steep path that brought them down to the main road. As they climbed down, Samuele observed how familiar Enrico was with the surroundings.

"You know we killed a viper in here some time ago. She must have come from woods over there... Hey, look who's coming from below," said Enrico as he came to the edge of the road. Samuele stepped forward to glance down.

From below, Toni, whip in hand, walked on one side of the macadam road, leading his two cows. Enrico made his way down the bank, followed by Samuele. Toni came within talking distance but avoided looking their way. He frowned and looked straight at the ground. Then to hide his nervousness, he pulled the reins of the animals with one hand, clicked his tongue for the cows to move faster. When they did not respond to his command, he unleashed his whip on their back.

Surprised by Toni's obvious hostility, Enrico first paused, then spoke up. "Hey, Toni! Didn't you see us? Guess who we just saw."

Toni's face turned livid, a fierce and angry expression quickly apparent on his face.

"Don't bother me," he retorted, continuing on his way and double whipping the poor animals.

"Don't you see who's back? This is Samuele. Don't you recognize him? Look, he got his foot shot off..."

"I don't give a goddamn about his foot. He could have got his heart shot off for all I care."

Enrico was shocked. Without saying a word, he turned to look at Samuele, who seemed only mildly bothered by Toni's harsh words. When Toni had disappeared from view, Enrico was literally confused. "To think that only last night we were together and had such a great time. I wonder what's eating him. And you--the three of us--why, we were called the three musketeers. Now, all of a sudden, damn it: something's happened. I bet it's his father. He's always had it in for Toni's beating the draft and all that... Looking at you, Toni and I surely saved our asses..."

"Aren't we headed toward your house? Your mother must be waiting, don't you think?"

"I don't know what to think... Yah, yah, let's go. But I can't figure out Toni. He'll tell me later, I'm sure. Come on, let's go. We can't keep my mother waiting much longer."

CHAPTER 8

Teresa, Enrico's mother, was waiting for her son at the door. She was of light skin and brownish hair. That morning she had put a bit of lipstick to enlarge her thin lips. Hanging from her ears were two large wheel-like earrings, and her dress was light and colorful. A while before, she had turned on the radio which was playing a series of Neapolitan songs sung by a young tenor and accompanied by an orchestra of mandolins and guitars. Teresa hummed along in complete disharmony with the subtle and sensitive music. When she saw her son, she yelled out to him to hurry because the food was getting cold.

"Coming, coming, mother... Look who I brought with me. Do you have enough for Samuele as well?"

"There's always plenty of food for any friends of yours. Welcome, Samuele. I'm so happy to see you back," she greeted in a thin voice, just short of being squeaky. She looked at the two and quickly observed that Enrico was taller. "I always thought you were about the same height," she added in admiration of her son.

"Can't you see, he's limping."

"Sure I can, Enrico. He should have stayed behind as you did. You know, Samuele, Enrico missed you a lot. He always talked about you, always."

"How are you," greeted Samuele. She shook his hand. Then looking at her son, she commented on Samuele's receding hair.

"I told him the same thing," blurted Enrico. Samuele smiled pleasantly, and they smiled along with him, thinking that Samuele found their remarks amusing.

"By the way," Teresa said to her son after he and Samuele had sat down at the table and were already eating chicken *cacciatore*, "the clerk delivered another Red Cross letter, but she didn't say to whom she delivered it... You know, Samuele, when I learned there was one on you I was terrified; I was so afraid something terrible may have happened to you. But now I understand you went to get your sister and you took her back to the house. That was very nice of you, but how's that going to affect your future?"

"I haven't thought about that yet. I will when the time comes."

"Do you have any plans on what you are going to do? Enrico will be going to the University of Naples to become a doctor."

"No, I don't know yet."

"Didn't you just say that you were going to raise cattle?" Enrico asked.

"I just said it for lack of words."

"Yah, you also said you were going to be a farmer. I didn't quite understand you when you said that, because you always hated anything to do with farms."

"If you'll be working your farm, you won't have to worry about your future," Teresa added. Samuele smiled. "But let me tell you the latest on your friend, Enrico here," she continued. She continued for a long time telling Samuele about Tina and how she had fallen madly in love with her son. While she told the story, she twisted her hands together, her fingers interlocked. She looked up to the ceiling, enraptured.

Samuele looked at her, but his mind was on the music coming from the radio. Noticing that Samuele was not giving her his full attention as she thought he should, and observing he was enjoying the music, she walked over to the radio and shut it off.

"Go on with what you were saying. It is very interesting," Samuele said. Teresa smiled with satisfaction.

"Sure, let me tell you. Well, Tina is the daughter of an army sergeant..."

With the same enthusiasm as before, Teresa went on to tell how much Tina had traveled as a result of being in the army, how one day she came across some modern missionaries preaching a new religion, how Tina became interested in it, the school Tina attended, the help she had given to the poor, and on and on. But in the end, she took pride in the fact that such a cultivated and ambitious young woman should fall in love with her son, Enrico. She admitted, however, that Tina's feelings toward Enrico couldn't have been any more natural than they were, for, Enrico was very handsome, if not the most handsome in the village, and definitely the only one that had kept up intellectually. She pointed to the radio and at some newspapers. "Tell me," she inquired of Samuele, "how the war affected people in so many ways." Poor Tina, going from place to place. If she had come here in the first place. What's important is that she came here. But no, tell me, how did the war affect you?

"You should have been here, Samuele. All the terrible things that happened to us. We went through hell. All those soldiers, and the airplanes. It's a good thing you weren't here. But Enrico did very well, though. You know, he learned so many languages. He can speak German. You should have heard him; he spoke in that language just as you and I are speaking now. Then the Americans came, and in no time he learned English. And you know, he also learned French from the Moroccans."

"Enrico was always smart in school. It doesn't surprise me," Samuele said.

"I know," she answered. "He was always ahead of his class. One time, after you left, he even went ahead of his teacher; that bastard got mad and failed Enrico. You know, there's a lot of jealousy in this world. Anyhow, Enrico is going to the University now," she said with apparent pride.

But if the words *air head* needed definition, Teresa would have been a perfect candidate.

Samuele got up from the table and said that he should be going home because his mother was waiting for him, and neither mother nor son seemed disturbed by the announcement.

"Sure," said Enrico.

"I'll be back another time. Thank you very much for the lunch," Samuele said in a low voice and walked out, with Teresa and Enrico following him to the door. Samuele turned to them, and in the most serious tone, with apparent sympathy for what they had suffered through the war, said, "The war has changed many things, and affected so many people. I am happy it had little consequences to you. You have not changed at all... Your hospitality was and is tops. The chicken was delicious, Teresa."

Enrico walked his friend to the street. Before saying goodby, he talked about his mother.

She'd do anything for me," he said. "Do you know what I call her? Saint Terry. Oh, you should see her laugh when I say that."

"Yes, you have a saint of a mother. Well, goodbye."

"What's with this *goodbye* shit. We live less than half a kilometer away from each other."

Samuele walked away, his head bent. At first, he walked in a hurry; then, when he was a distance from Enrico's house, he slowed down. Finally, he came to a stop. He turned around and slowly glanced over the landscape and looked at the small stone houses, his sad eyes expressing what his heart was feeling, heavy over his inability to decide whether these were the people for whom he had gone to war, or the type of people who had brought about the war.

CHAPTER 9

Lucia's friend, Rachele, with her five-year-old daughter, walked hurriedly along the road. Hardly anyone said hello to her; nor would she have been aware if even any of her few friends had greeted her. She walked so fast that her daughter had difficulty staying up, the poor child seeing the sheer terror on her mother's face but unable to understand the source nor its meaning. But she tried to walk as fast as she could. Dragging her daughter, Rachele walked as though she were a ghost, no one noticing her evident terror or caring to notice. Though there were people on the road, Rachele walked as though she were in a desert. Not even the little girl attracted any attention. Having picked up her pace, and realizing her child's valorous effort in trying to keep up, Rachele bent to pick her up. When their eyes met, Rachele became emotional. With tears streaming down her face, she gently pushed her daughter's face between her shoulder and neck, thus hiding the greater flow of tears. The least she could do now was to give her daughter some safe haven.

Rachele was a slender tallish woman in her twenties, with brownish hair usually falling on her shoulders. For the first time in a long while one could see the complete form of her eyes: large and brown in color. Her eyelashes were long and her eyebrows curved down to below the center line of her eyes. Although Rachele wore makeup, she was unable to hide altogether her naturally manly features. That morning, her make-up accentuated the very features she had been trying to cover. Not beautiful according to the standards of her day, nevertheless, with her distinctive facial and body features, she was certainly attractive and often admired by the perspicacious few.

This morning, she wore a striped cotton skirt and a silk blouse with buttons running down the center--the same blouse she formerly wore with the top buttons unbuttoned. Now, she wore it buttoned all the way up to her long neck. She pulled her hair to the back of her head in a knot, away from her face. In her recent past she wore her hair to the front, moving it from side to side to create moods of sensuality; this morning, she kept her face clear, perhaps because she wanted to be unmistaken about the depth and degree of her anguished terror.

With child in arms, and her face wiped dry with her handkerchief, Rachele stopped in front of Maria's house. Looking at the door, she felt her heart pump. Overcome by the fear of rejection, she felt her knees buckle and almost fell to the ground. Her equilibrium shattered, she attempted to go to the door, but couldn't. Finally, after a few moments of hesitation, with a long step forward, she made her way to the door. Trembling, she knocked on the door hard and fast, and waited.

Inside, Maria and her children were getting ready to go to the stall to care for the stock. Hearing the loud, insistent knock, Maria rushed to open the door.

"Maria, please let me in. I want to talk with Samuele. Please let me in," she urged desperately.

Maria opened the door; then closed it behind Rachel.

"What's the matter?" asked Lucia. "Here, let me have the baby."

"I just got the letter. Marcello is coming back; Marcello is coming back. Oh, my God, what am I going to do; what am I going to do?" she repeated with tremendous anxiety.

"Tell me, Samuele, won't you be so kind as to help me. I'm so afraid; I'm terrified. Please, Samuele, I came over just to see you. For the sake of my baby, please help me. You were Marcello's friend. I understand you were together at the front."

"You knew we were at the front!"

"Yes, yes. Oh, God..." Rachele exclaimed.

At the word *God*, Samuele raised his eyebrows, and his eyes became bright. Rachele did not notice. She went on: "I know what you mean, Samuele, I know, and I am so sorry. I'm so sorry," she repeated as she burst into tears. "I thought he was lost; we thought you both were lost," she said, weeping profusely. "Marcello was so good... He did not deserve this, he didn't, he didn't."

"That is correct," interjected Samuele coldly, "He didn't." Lucia and Maria looked at Samuele, startled by his apparent harshness.

"I don't expect Marcello to be as kind as you were with Lucia. I know my situation is different. Who's going to care for my daughter if something happens to me? Who?"

The little girl in Lucia's arms looked in silence at her tearful mother, and only occasionally glancing at the little boy who was playing in one corner with a small wooden spool.

"You should have thought about your daughter before you began...whatever it is you did."

"I thought we were all going to die and that the end of the world was coming--for everybody. There wasn't much purpose in living any more, there wasn't, Samuele."

"There was, I tell you, and there still is a purpose," Samuele shouted. "But you took the easy way out--the solution of the moment regardless of anything or of anyone, as though there are no consequences to our actions."

"There was no pleasure, Samuele, no pleasure, no, never, in no way, believe me. I feel like a prostitute, and there can't be any pleasure in that, believe me. Turmoil throughout. No pleasure, Samuele, none whatsoever, none. Can you understand that?"

"Where was your mother all this time?'"

"My mother! Poor woman, leave her out of this," replied Rachele as she looked at Maria.

"Don't worry," interrupted Lucia unconvincingly.

"I wish I could say the same thing," replied Samuele.

"My God, oh, my God!" exclaimed Rachele.

"God! God," repeated Samuele automatically. "God!" he shouted. "What did you do to Him? What did you do to the people around you?"

"Samuele," Maria beseeched in a gentle voice. "We all make mistakes. Rachele is no different. In the end, we all have to forgive each other."

"There is no such thing as forgiveness, Mother, and you know it, because facts and deeds cannot be erased. All we do is simply live with it; we can only learn to live with it, that's all. But we don't forgive, and it isn't fair."

"Christ forgave worse crimes," retorted Maria.

"Christ, Christ, that's all we say, and we always use His name when we want something."

Rachele stopped crying, and the tears stopped coming down. Nor did she speak any more. Her previous intuition was now verified: hope had suddenly vanished. She stood there impassively, looking at them and not seeing them. Lucia placed her hand on Rachele's arm.

"Why don't you leave the child with us until Marcello comes. Meanwhile you can go to that uncle of yours up in the hills and hide there until Marcello comes. We'll intercede for you. If all is well, we'll send someone to get you."

Rachele nodded, then after having looked into the eyes of all those present, and especially into her daughter's eyes, she paused for a moment longer, her eyes fixed on those of her daughter. Unable to restrain herself, she sprang toward the little girl to hug her in the most tender of ways, knowing that most likely this would the last embrace the girl was to have had from her mother. Of that, Rachele was absolutely sure. She released her daughter to Lucia, looked once again into the faces of the three, and ran towards the door, opening it with a decisive pull and slamming it shut behind her.

Samuele turned to his mother, who was left speechless and with heavy heart. Maria asked her son if he knew something more about Marcello, and he answered that he did: both had spent the better part of the first two years together, having been in Russia and then through Germany---the concentration camps, the Jews. In Russia, they were briefly separated during one of the more fearful battles wherein the Russians made carnage of the Italians. Many had died and Samuele thought that Marcello had also died. But by whatever miracle, they were re-united in the same camp where the Russians perpetrated the most savage torture on the prisoners.

"Marcello always spoke about Rachele and his daughter. He used to say that whatever he survived, he pulled through because of his strong desire to see them. 'God help me if anything happens to them,' he'd say. But, for some reason, deep in his heart, he would survive to have to face a greater tragedy. We all had the same fear. He's gone through a lot, mother, an awful lot, and I can't predict what he might do to Rachele, and I would not take any chances... Nothing we can do now. We may as well go take care the animals... Come on, kids," Samuele said to the two children, bending down. First he picked up the little boy; then, turning toward Lucia, Samuele took the girl and holding her in his other arm, walked with them to the barn where the cows were already mooing, the pigs scraping against the wooden doors, and the dog running back and forth across the path.

"Coming," shouted Samuele, "coming."

CHAPTER 10

Early next morning, Rachele made her way toward the church. She bypassed Maria's house without pausing. When under the poplar trees, however, she stopped by the one bearing the scar. She first looked at the thick trunk, then at the green wheat field beyond the road.

She had seen the accident: the huge truck with its front literally wrapped around the tree trunk and the three soldiers without injuries. Not having the means to break the vehicle loose from the tree, the soldiers were forced to stand by until the next morning.

They were Americans with plenty of supplies. They offered Rachele cigarettes and soap, telling her that they would have more gifts toward evening. That's how it got started. Now, on looking over the field, she fixed her eyes on the rose bush covering the well stones, where formerly rows of corn stood tall. Recalling that night, she put her hand over her half-opened mouth. How she wished now she had stayed home! Instead, she had rationalized that her husband was most likely dead and that she might as well live a little before she would meet the same fate. When it was too late, she learned that having spent the night with the Americans was neither fun nor rewarding. But, then, it was already too late, and she could not take back the night before.

Rachele kept holding her hand over her mouth, her eyes wide open with fright. Suddenly, she felt nausea. In despair, she rushed away and began to run. On seeing Mr. Banno in front of his house, Rachele stopped running and began to walk, her eyes wild with fear, as Mr. Banno, the self proclaimed champion of morals, had become the bane of women like Lucia and now Rachele. Of all the people to have to deal with, she thought, it would have had to be him. In despising him, she also admitted *mea culpa*.

Banno began to comment, "My, what have we got here so early? What brings you this way? You hardly come by here, Rachele. Maybe you got a little unexpected letter?"

"What I got is none of your business."

"You certainly are brash for a woman in your situation. I bet you're going to church."

"What of it, if I am?"

"No, I just thought the church wasn't made for whores, that's all."

Rachele was not surprised at that statement. She had heard that word many times before, even from her mother. But while she took it from others, in spite of her torment, she was not going to take it from him.

"Worse people than whores became saints, and those like you professing to be good ended up in hell, and I am sure the devils will receive you with open arms. Hell is where you belong," she shrieked and ran away leaving Mr. Banno no chance to reply. Mr. Banno, however, shrugged his shoulder, and went on with his chores.

At the church, old women dressed in black were filing out the door, Mass having finished. They looked at Rachele with scorn and indignation. "You, in this place!" said one.

"I suppose you come here because you have a clean conscience," retorted Rachele, who, in spite of her grief, was never lost for words.

"The impertinence!" exclaimed another white-haired woman. Then, holding her tongue, Rachele continued on her way into the church.

"And don't forget," added Rachele without hesitation, "not all the apostles saw the light at first."

"Yah, we know the kind of *light* you've been seeing," interrupted another toothless crone. "Well, I saw a bit myself in my days, if you don't mind my saying so," she added, a wicked smile in her eyes that at other times would have made Rachele laugh. "That's why I'm coming here. Go on in, Don Alfonso is getting undressed."

"You have seen the *light*, haven't you?" Rachele asked. "Do you think there is salvation for us?"

"Horrible thing to think about. Me," the toothless woman said, shrugging her shoulders and spreading her arms, "I'll think about that after I'm dead."

Dan Alfonso was in the process of taking off his stole when Rachele appeared through the doorway of the sacristy. Instead of going in, she waited at the door, hoping the priest would see her and ask her in though he had his back turned toward he door. Unexpectedly, Rachele heard her name.

"Come in, Rachele. I've been waiting for you," said Don Alfonso without turning and still going through his motions of taking off his vestments and replacing them with his street clothes. "Come in," Don Alfonso repeated.

Frightened, Rachele hesitatingly made her way toward him. She looked at him as he turned to face her. "Please you hear my confession?" she asked in a low and soft voice

"Yes, of course."

"My husband, Marcello, is coming home--maybe tomorrow..."

"...I know."

"My hours are counted. I want to make an attempt at being ready."

"Sure, sure. Wait for me at the confession booth."

Rachele walked back through the door and walked to a seat next to the booth toward the center of the church to one side. She looked at the painted cherubs on the wall, then she paused at an oil Pietà hanging on the upper wall of the altar: the body of Christ, in the style of Michelangelo, resting in the arms of his mother, her fragile legs serving as pillow to his heavy body, and his face bearing an expression of serenity while that of the mother bore the expression of despair. "He didn't do anything, and look what happened to him," Rachele thought. She looked to the other side, at the statue of the bronze Christ with his hands and feet pinned to a large wooden cross. Across his chest there were two blood-spurting wounds. But although thorns bored down on his head, Christ's face was serene, without traces of pain. In a niche not far from the bronze Christ stood St. Michael. In his red skirt, he stood astride a fire-breathing monster with its tail wrapped around the legs of the Saint plunging his lance into the monster's neck. To the left of the niche, a painting of St. Gerard hung on the wall with two signs, one asking for contributions and another asking donors not to throw cigarettes and combs into the receptacle which contained more combs, cigarettes and handkerchiefs than money. "God, how we trespass," Rachele said to herself. Then, turning toward the door of the sacristy, she waited for Don Alfonso to appear.

A few moments later, she saw the door open and the priest coming out. At his signal, Rachele walked to the booth, knelt, and waited until the priest was seated inside before crossing herself. Don Alfonso drew the curtain in front of him and began confession. About twenty-five minutes later, Rachele crossed herself once again, got up and walked to the altar, where she knelt in prayer. Don Alfonso, meanwhile, went into the sacristy, where he rang for the Mother Superior, who quickly appeared to help him with his vestments. "I have to give communion," he said.

"Yes," she answered, and said no more. She helped Don Alfonso, handling the garments gently, being sure of details, and gracious throughout. With her fragile white hands, she picked up the tray and followed Don Alfonso to the altar. Rachele closed her eyes for a moment, then watched as the priest took out the consecrated host. In no time, Don Alfonso was in front of her. After taking up the host from the gilded chalice, he raised it far above Rachele's head, made the sign of the cross with it, and brought it down to the level of her mouth. The bespectacled Mother Superior promptly held the tray below Rachele's chin, and Don Alfonso delivered the host.

With the host in her mouth, Rachele closed her eyes, crossing her hands over her breast. She remained in that position for a long while, opening her eyes well after the priest and the nun had left the altar.

Having said her prayers, Rachele got up, crossed herself, and walked slowly toward the exit, stopping to glance at a copy of Leonardo da Vinci's *Last Supper*. "How fitting," she said, and walked straight toward the door where she dipped her hand into the bowl of holy water. Having crossed herself once again, she turned and, throwing a kiss to the altar, she walked out of the church.

CHAPTER 11

Samuele was in the yard walking his young bullock around the yard when Don Alfonso approached from outside. Before interrupting Samuele, the priest waited to pause in admiration at the combination of this strange, limping man walking with that animal, the largest bull he had ever seen for its young age; he stood there in awe, struck by the friendly relationship between the powerful animal and his master, enjoying what he was seeing.

But, how could he be thinking about such things when earlier he had given what surely was the last communion to poor Rachele; after all, he was there to talk with Samuele about Marcello's imminent return.

Hoping in his heart that Marcello might turn out to be somewhat like Samuele, Don Alfonso reluctantly walked forward.

"Good morning, Samuele, how are you? What a beautiful animal! The first time I've seen it. Are you keeping it a secret?"

"No," Samuele answered. "No, not at all. I was very surprised myself when I first saw him. I had never seen anything like it," he commented, caressing the animal effortlessly. "He's something. I think I will train him: he reacts well, and seems he has taken a liking to me."

"Are you going to keep it?"

"My mother wanted to sell him, but I decided to keep him. I'm planning on raising cattle. What do you think?"

"Not a bad idea. Good livestock is hard to come by these days. What little is available is both bad and expensive."

In the presence of the bull, Don Alfonso listened to Samuele talk about his future short and long-range plans. But perforce, Don Alfonso had to broach the subject of Rachele. Samuele, who knew the reason for the priest's visit, waited for Don Alfonso to speak first.

"Rachele was in to see me this morning. I gave her communion--more like the last rights. She doesn't think she's going to live very long. She's concerned about Marcello, who could be returning any moment, and she's scared stiff. You know," he continued, changing his tone of voice, "I didn't tolerate her behavior then, as I did not tolerate that of your sister. But, as you said, we can't kill them--not that it ever entered my mind, I want you to be sure to understand that--we have to do something to help them make their lives meaningful and worth while. What you have done with Lucia is wonderful. She seems like a different woman; she's come alive. The war left scars on everyone. I just wish many more people would bear the hardships and disappointments as you have. You're truly exemplary, and I appreciate it," Don Alfonso added in a genuine tone.

"I don't know as I have completely recovered, or, as you imply, adjusted. But I'm grateful for your kind words."

"What can we do for Rachele?" the priest, a distraught expression on his face.

"We have to wait and see," replied Samuele almost automatically.

"Wait and see!"

"What would you suggest?"

"I don't know; that is why I came here. I just don't know and I feel so helpless, and here I am, a priest!"

"It's difficult to predict what a man like Marcello might do. It is true we spent a lot of time together. We've seen," Samuele said in a lower his voice but looking directly into Don Alfonso's yes, "we've seen many people die, and not all of them soldiers. No matter where we went, we saw death. We saw death from the moment we crossed the border into Russia and Germany. Death, Don Alfonso, death all over. And we, do you know how many times we came close to it? Do you know that I--me, I gave him up for dead too. I committed the same sin as most of you did here. I don't know what he might do. I don't know if he's tired of looking at death or whether he is seeking it. Hopefully, he might be sick of it or even fed up with it. If he's fed up, then things won't be good either for himself or the people around him. I hope that is not the case."

"You talk as though there is no hope."

"If I do, I don't mean to. He should be tired of death; he should he tired of hearing humans giving off their last wailing: untold voices calling out to *God*, others to *Die*, to *Dios*, to *Jehovah*, to *Dieu*, to *Deus*, to *Christ*, to *Mary*, to *Allah*, to *Bor*, to *Moses*. Yes, to *Moses*, to *Moses*, Samuele repeated emphatically, his eyes closing tight each time he pronounced the various renditions of the word God. Then, opening his eyes, he continued. "God was on their lips down to their last breath--especially on their last breath. And we, we observed and observed. Everyone observed. I'm sure the whole world observed. We all observed. Some of us swore we'd do anything to try not to hear it any more, or to keep others from saying it. It matters little what we said or promised. We were decimated, slaughtered worse than animals, and always conscious of our doom. Do you see this!" Samuele said in a trembling voice, as he pulled the small wallet from his breast pocket. "Do you see this; do you know what it is?" he asked with insistence.

Don Alfonso took the wallet into his hands, but not without hesitation, not so much from fear of handling the strange-looking object but more because of the passion with which Samuele had spoken. Samuele's obvious conviction had shown more than a trace of vehemence. Don Alfonso turned the wallet over in his hands. Not understanding its significance, he concluded it must have been important by the manner of Samuele's reaction.

"You don't know, do you?" Samuele charged as he pulled the wallet from Don Alfonso's hands and quickly putting it back into his own pocket.

"I don't understand," Don Alfonso admitted candidly but reservedly. "I don't understand the meaning of all this. What are you trying to tell me, Samuele? Tell me; I will listen. Tell me that you suffered a lot. You needn't tell me; I can see you have. You suffered; I can see it in your eyes. You have seen a lot of suffering, haven't you, my son? You have, I can tell," Don Alfonso said putting his hand on Samuele's shoulder. "I know you have, you must have. You must have suffered a lot, otherwise you wouldn't be what you are. You will be rewarded, God ..."

"God! God... God, God, God, God..."

"God will reward you, Samuele," Don Alfonso said reassuringly, breaking Samuele's sudden spell. Feeling that it would perhaps be better to change the subject, Don Alfonso started to talk about the bull, which, throughout the exchange, had stood silently and practically motionless behind his master, closing only his eyelids and swinging his tail to fend off the pesky flies. "That is a beautiful animal, Samuele. No pagan deity ever had such an animal sacrificed in his behalf, I am ..."

"Nor will any god see it sacrificed."

Don Alfonso was speechless. Nevertheless, he stared into the eyes of Samuele, who too remained silent. Suddenly, Samuele turned away from the priest to wrap his arms around the neck of the bull, pressing his face hard against it.

"My child," Don Alfonso began again, in an inaudible voice. "We will do Thy will," he added, raising his eyes towards heaven. Then, placing his hand gently on Samuele's back, Don Alfonso bade him farewell.

CHAPTER 12

Franca kept herself busy that morning, mainly washing all sorts of things, besides having washed the dishes and clothes.

In the afternoon, while her father rested, she continued to wash. And though it was a rather warm day, Franca wore heavy stockings--a thing neither she nor anybody else was apt to do. Having noticed the stockings, her mother frowned but said nothing. While Franca continued to wash next to the well, her mother, unable to resist any longer, finally walked over.

"Why are you washing those rags?"

"Because I want to."

"And why are you wearing those heavy stockings?"

"I just want to," Franca answered. Without looking at her mother, Franca kept on scrubbing the old clothes. Exasperated, her mother left. Soon, she returned with an armful of dirty clothes, mostly heavy linen. Franca looked up to listen to her mother.

"Now that you're in the mood to wash, here is another load."

"Take them back. I'll do them tomorrow."

"Why not now?"

"Because I'm tired, that's why."

"And I suppose you're going to take a rest now."

"Yes."

"Where, down by the curve?"

"If I want to."

"Stay away from that clubfoot, if you know what's good for you. He's no good for you. He's got no pot for himself nor a bed for you."

"You'll have to get the bed regardless, whether I marry Samuele or somebody else," Franca answered without stopping her washing. Then she stood up, and with her mother still holding the clothes in her arms, Franca became more brash. "What do you have against him? It can't be his foot, I'm sure. Can it be his sister? I know all about your dead sister: did she and her baby die of natural cause; and who is your brother-in-law?" she asked with full sarcasm. "Is it money? They don't have as much as we have, that's true. But, is our life the better for it? Is it any better than the animals we're raising? Or, is it something else? Is it your son? He's been a bastard for as long as I can remember, but never as rotten as he is now. He's always trying to make everyone, including one of my old school friends. He's rotten through and through, and you always stick up for him. You're even proud of him."

"A man is a man and he's got to do his things."

"And what's a woman to do, be his victim? Is that what you are saying? Then, how come you treat my father as though he's a fool? Do you think I will become Samuele's victim? But, why is it alright for other women to become his victim and not me to Samuele? I want to know because you make no sense to me. Nothing makes sense in this house."

"You wouldn't dare do such a thing."

"But it's all right for your son to do that."

"A man is different, I told you."

"You can be sure Samuele is different, 'way different from your son. He wants to marry me and doesn't want me to be his victim, though I'm ready to be his. All he has to do is ask. I want to, and I would," she said defiantly and without hesitation, startling her mother, whose eyes opened wide, a flash of anger traveling over her face. Suddenly, she swung her arm out and caught Franca's cheek with a tremendous and loud slap. Franca's face reddened from the sting and from anger. "You will not do any such thing," commanded her mother. "That clubfoot has no honor. He'll never put foot in this house for as long as I am alive. We have our honor," she concluded, haughtily beating her hand on her chest.

"You... you call this honor. It's filth; it's mud! It's nothing but dishonor, and you're calling it honor. You've always been as blind as a bat, and now you're also corrupt. I can't stand you, and I can't stand that animal brother of mine, the filthy bastard," she cried out emotionally as she held her moist hand over her livid face where the print of her mother's hand was already showing its outline.

The quarrel of the two women had awakened Ernesto.

"What the hell is going on down there?" he bellowed.

The women turned in his direction. "Just remember what I told you," warned the mother in a menacing but low voice.

"I'm going to do what's good for me. I know what honor is all about, not you. You never knew; otherwise my father wouldn't be treating you this way. Besides, I'm not here as an accommodation for you or for your son."

"I'm warning you," her mother said with insistence. "I'm warning you," she repeated, pointing her finger at her young laughter.

"And I'm telling you that I'm going to see who I want and not who you or that pig wants."

Not giving in, Franca infuriated her mother even more. But for fear of having her husband intervene in the argument, she left Franca and went back to the house with the dirty clothes in her arms. She passed in front of her grumbling husband, but did not answer. She walked straight for the door where the hen had gathered with several of her chicks. Instead of avoiding the little creatures, she walked through them, scattering them in every direction. The hen quickly rallied the desperate little chicks together and led them away. Ernesto, meanwhile, muttered some very unkind words to his wife, complaining about the fact that people who worked were being denied rightful rest and peace any more. Then raising his voice, he commanded the wife to get the animals ready.

Meanwhile, Samuele slept outside his stall in the open air, surrounded by chickens and roosters, rabbits scurrying about, and his dog sleeping on the ground next to his master. From inside the stall, the cows mooed as they chewed their cud.

It was his first real siesta in years. And to rest in such an arcadic setting as his own place made his sleep more enjoyable as revealed through an expression of contentedness on his face. The sounds of the animals did not disturb him, though each sound caused Samuele's forehead to wrinkle. Finally, the young bull began to bellow causing Samuele an abrupt awakening.

Looking into the clear sky, then getting to his feet, he stretched his arms, while the dog wagged its tail. Samuele returned the glance, and the dog, as if to thank his master for the consideration, rose to his feet. Samuele bent down to caress its head. Another tremendous bellow from inside made Samuele quickly go to the stall. As he entered, he saw the bull turn to look. He walked toward the animal. When Samuele got close, he stroked the bull; then, patting its neck, he stared into its eyes which stared right back while Samuele continued to pat him and to stare.

"I've got to go now," Samuele said, as if were engaging the bull in a conversation. "You know where I have to go. I think I'd better wait a while, though, don't you think? Her people are not taking too kindly to me. But we're not that bad, are we? Surely we're not bad. I can't figure out what goes through people's minds, what makes them feel they're better than others. You don't have that worry, do you? Here you are, big, sturdy, and beautiful, more beautiful than any other animal I have ever seen, and yet you don't act any different from the mangy ones. You ought to have seen what some of our mangy human beings do to each other; you ought to have seen what they did to each other and to us the last three years. Unbelievable!. You should have seen what they almost did to me. Thank God that's over. We have different battles to fight now, and most them are battles we wage with ourselves. Believe me, they can be just as harsh and more fierce because there is bitterness, unlike the exterminations in Germany. The Germans did not do it out of bitterness... Well, come on, let's go outside. I want to do a little training with you before I go see Franca."

Samuele untied the bull and walked to the open air, the dog following behind, its tail wagging happily. Samuele led the bull around the farm, letting the animal sneak some wheat stocks and leaves along the way. Returning to the front of the stall, Samuele attempted to teach the young bull how to walk backward, the first try proving unsuccessful, but there was plenty of time to train the animal and to tame it to the point that it could work with efficiency and speed.

"Is it necessary to do all that?" asked Maria, seeing her son so taken up with the animal. "Why, why are you doing all this?"

"I don't really know. I just think he understands me. I think I can teach him to do things."

A few minutes after Maria had arrived, Lucia also came out with the two children. Seeing Samuele with the bull, the little ones ran to him. Afraid they might get hurt, Lucia seized them by their hands and pulled them back, letting them go only when her Samuele told her to release them.

With great and noisy excitement, they ran, the little girl getting there first. After having patted her head, Samuele took his nephew by one arm and lifted him up onto the bull's neck. The animal squirmed a little but soon quieted down on hearing his master's reassuring voice. Meanwhile, the boy shouted with joy while the little girl jumped up and down on her feet.

Toward late afternoon, Samuele finally decided to walk in the general direction of Franca's house hoping to meet her somehow. While under the noisy poplars, as there was a light breeze, he remembered the old well, just below a small ridge not far from the curve, and wondered if the bush of red roses was still standing. Slowly, he made his way toward the well, along the old pathway, filled with overgrown grass and stones loosely scattered on the surface.

In a short time, he reached the small circular rock wall rising above the abandoned well. Just behind it, was the rose bush full of red roses. Samuele looked at them. On noticing the prettiest, he plucked about six, smelled them, and began to make his way back to the poplars. As he walked, he noticed rows of corn already breaking through the surface of the land, remembering that this particular lot of land belonged to Mr. Banno, who was very good at growing corn. Now that he had planned on raising cattle, he said to himself, he would be needing plenty of corn. But this was not the time to be thinking about such things. He had to think about Franca.

With anxiety in his heart, he found himself once again on the dirt road leading to Franca's house. As he walked, he hoped to find Franca alone, but that if she were not alone he would attempt to talk to her nevertheless. Above all, however, he did not want to meet Toni. For reasons he could not fathom, Samuele felt that meeting with that man at this time would have disastrous results.

Arriving at the corner where he had met Franca the last time, and not finding her there, he decided to walk around through the farm. After about five minutes of careful wandering among the grape vines and fig trees, he looked at a lot of land below to the west and saw Ernesto next to

Toni, who was driving the team of oxen yoked to the plow. To the extreme end of the field, Franca's mother planted corn where the surface had already been tilled and ready for planting.

On seeing them engaged with assuredly plenty of work ahead of them, Samuele quickly dashed up to the house. Franca was in the courtyard feeding the little chicks, holding two of them in her hands and caressing them, when her dog barked. Samuele quickly called to Franca, who, recognizing her sweetheart, immediately ordered the dog to stop barking.

"Samuele!" Franca exclaimed in a whisper.

"I brought you some roses," Samuele announced with a smile. "May I come over?"

"You needn't ask," she answered, kissing the chicks before letting them on the ground. She ran to him and fell into his open arms. "I am so happy you came; I'm so happy," she repeated like a child receiving an unexpected gift. She drew him to her and kissed him. Samuele, holding the roses with one hand over her shoulder, returned the kiss.

"May I give you the roses?" he asked in a soft voice. I picked them just for you. For a moment, I thought I was not going to be able to give them to you. Do you like them?"

Franca was overcome with emotion. Roses! Whoever had ever thought of giving her roses? she thought; yet, they grew everywhere. They wouldn't have cost anyone anything. Worse, no one gave that beautiful and fragrant flower to anyone--not even lovers.

"They're beautiful,!" she exclaimed, holding them close to her nose. "They're the most beautiful roses I have ever seen. They are beautiful, Samuele, very beautiful." Then, with an unexpected leap, she threw her arms around Samuele. He pulled her up and kissed her with greater passion. Franca drew closer, her lips pressed hard on his mouth, her breast throbbing against his chest. She moved her head from side to side drawing in the sweet breath of excitement. "Samuele, Samuele," she whispered between kisses. "I want to be yours, completely yours, just yours. Take me away; please take me away from this place," she pleaded. "I can't stay here any more; take me away, please!" she kept pleading, tears beginning to flow from her eyes. "Take me away," she repeated once again as she looked up at Samuele, who remained confused, because he sensed that something had happened and did not know what. Whatever it was, however, it must have involved him.

"Come, let's go for a walk. Come..." He took her hand, and this time, she gave it to him willingly, Samuele noticing and commenting on the softness of her skin. As he caressed it with his thumb, he looked at her. Franca understood and began to smile through the few remaining tears.

"We can go by the corner in the wheat field. Do you think anybody will see us?" Then added impatiently: "I don't care who sees us. What we do is our business."

"What's the matter, Franca? How come you're so tense? Why do you talk that way? We care about others, at least I do. I care about you. I love you."

"I do, too; I love you so very much," she spoke reassuringly.

In no time, they were in the green wheat field, walking through rows of growing stalks until they came to a place far enough away from the road as not to be heard or seen.

"Why the stockings?" Samuele asked in a light tone.

Franca smiled as she cuddled to him, kissing him on the lips. "I've been washing all day. I washed all day yesterday. I want to be what women ought to be. I don't like myself the way I am now."

"You're a woman," he answered with a smile. "It doesn't matter if your hands are soft or hard, or your legs, for that matter. What counts is you, the person. It is you I love."

"Yes, I know. But I want to be appealing to you."

Samuele smiled once again and Franca laughed with him whole-heatedly. She raised the roses to smell them. Noting the stems had no thorns, she asked, a great wide smile crossing her face.

"What did you do to them?"

"I snapped them off for fear you might scratch yourself."

Franca laughed aloud. "What, these hands!" she exclaimed, unable to contain her happiness. She laughed as though nothing had happened before, as though nothing existed other than her immediate world, there in the wheat field together with her sweetheart who admired and loved her. She did not know that her mother, having heard the dog bark, had gone to the house, and not finding her daughter, was already going back to tell her husband and son. At that moment, Franca thought about nothing other than Samuele, the knight who had finally arrived to deliver her. She laughed with joy.

"Hold it," Samuele said, his finger over his lips. "There, see: the goldfinch must be nesting nearby. Maybe in this vine. Let's look."

The little yellow bird flew from branch to branch with food in its mouth, not daring to bring it to the young ones, for, the nest was right above the intruders. Finally, in one leap, she landed on a small branch right above Franca's and Samuele's heads. Seeing their mother, the little ones quickly began to chirp, and from below, the two lovers could see them extend their necks with their receptive beaks wide open.

Franca was overwhelmed, not because she had not seen that scene before, but because she was witnessing it now with the man she hoped would give her the chance of playing that very role as the mother goldfinch. As she watched, she imagined feeding her own milk to their own children.

"That's what I want to be!" she exclaimed with emotion, "and my family doesn't want to understand that." Turning to

Samuele with a serious face, she gazed into his eyes. Her lips half closed, her heart beating heavily, she let Samuele kiss her again. Then while Samuele put his hand to her lips to caress them, she kissed his fingers gently. Bringing his hand through her hair to the back of her head, and holding her firm, he pulled Franca toward him down to the ground, then turning her over, he kissed her passionately. With the other hand, he unbuttoned her blouse. Holding her breath, she allowed Samuele to move his hand to her youthful breast. Samuele moaned with joy, and Franca did likewise. He kissed her harder and longer. Their passion at its peak, Franca spread her legs, inviting Samuele to consummate their love. But though Samuele kept kissing her on the mouth and on cupping then kissing her breast, he went no further, and Franca understandingly accepted the limits.

"How I longed for this moment," Samuele confessed, still holding her breast. "I thought I would never be enjoying these moments."

"But you're here; we're here, and you're making me happy. I wish I didn't have to go back up there."

"You must. I think we ought to go now. I want to come to speak with your father about us. If someone should see us, it might jeopardize our relationship."

"Nothing can," Franca answered, convinced that absolutely nothing could stand in their way.

Samuele found her strong attitude perturbing, for he hadn't expected Franca to be so sure about what she wanted. Nevertheless, he understood why, and made no attempt to answer her.

Suddenly and unexpectedly, they heard Franca's mother call from above, shattering their idyllic moment. Worse, they saw Toni and his mother returning and searching around obviously looking to catch Franca in a compromising situation.

"My God!" Franca exclaimed, bringing her blouse over her breast. "They're looking for me!"

"God! God!"

"Samuele! What's the matter with you. Can't you see, they're coming down this way?"

"Yes, oh, yes, I understand. When they call your name, answer them."

"What!" Franca's eyes opened wide for fear.

"Don't be afraid. Just answer that you are here."

"I'll do one better," she said, emboldened by Samuele's stand. She buttoned her blouse and then pulled her hair with one hand. "When they come closer, I will ask them if they are looking for me."

"No, you mustn't."

"Are you afraid?" Franca asked.

"No."

When Franca's mother and brother had come within hearing distance, Franca rose to her feet.

"Are you looking for me?" she asked. Looking straight at their startled faces, Franca threw down the gauntlet. "I'm here with my lover, Samuele... Samuele, stand up so they can see you."

Samuele stood up. "I don't want you to think that we did anything wrong. We had to talk to each other about our future." Samuele said, as he and Franca came out of the wheat field, Samuele leading the way. No one said a word. Finally, when Franca came out in the open, with marked deliberation, her mother moved closer toward Franca.

"Take this," she said, swinging her arm wildly, catching the other side of Franca's face. So hard was the slap that Franca found herself stumbling in front of Toni. He grabbed the sister by the arms and shook her violently, calling her a prostitute.

"Wait a second," Samuele yelled, moving toward Toni. He seized Franca by one arm and pulled her away from Toni. To the surprise of his mother, who had forbidden him from doing anything rash, Toni immediately put his hand into his pocket.

"Toni, no!" his mother yelled, knowing that that kind of violence always proved mutually disastrous.

"This is only the beginning," Toni retorted. "I'm going to do you in for sure. Not now, but another time. You can count on it."

"I'm not here to fight you. I am here because I love your sister and I want to marry her."

Those words made Franca's mother laugh derisively.

"Is that so!" she answered in clear ridicule. "You want to marry my daughter? Have you forgotten you're a clubfoot, and did you already forget about your sister? So, you want to marry my daughter and give her your reputation?"

"You're cruel, but I didn't think you could sink so low," interrupted Franca angrily.

"Shut up, you bitch," commanded Toni. "Go on home; I'll see you later... Go on, take her home," Toni ordered.

Sensing the threat, Franca suddenly sprinted off in search of her father, who had just tied the oxen in the stall.

With screams of despair, she asked her father to run down and stop what might turn out to be a tragic fight.

Both ran frantically down the dirt road. While Franca told her father what had happened, they saw Toni and Samuele scuffing on the ground with Toni's mother intervening on her son's side, kicking Samuele whenever she could. By the time Ernesto and Franca arrived, Toni and his mother had Samuele pinned to the ground, but were unable to hold him down. With one hand, Ernesto rudely pushed his wife to one side. At the sight of his father, Toni almost froze on top of Samuele, who, seeing his opponent neutralized, quickly pushed him off. Toni fell toward his father. Ernest grabbed Toni by one arm, twisted him around mercilessly, shoving him forward with a great kick to the back thigh. Then moving to the front of Toni, Ernesto he raised his foot and kicked his son brutally in the shins causing the young man to shout with pain.

"I'll take care of you later," he said to his petrified wife, "you filthy bitch."

The woman instantly turned and ran with her son toward the house. When they were at a safe distance, Toni turned around. With a wild expression on his face, he threatened Samuele. Ernesto picked up a rock and threw it full force at Toni, missing him and his wife by a few inches.

"I'll be home soon. Wait for me there," Ernesto ordered the retreating two, who kept on walking daring not to look back.

Throughout the family quarrel, Samuele looked on without saying a word, but remained beside Franca. Ernesto turned and stared at Samuele.

"So, you're back from the war, and now you think you have the license to do as you please."

"No, not at all. I'm back from the war, but I left the fighting behind. I came to talk to Franca because we love each other, and I wanted your permission."

"Is that so?"

"Yes, that's exactly so," replied Samuele, unshaken.

"And why didn't you come to see me?"

"I am here for that reason. But I wanted to speak with Franca first. That seems normal, don't you?"

"I guess you're right."

"Toni thinks he can do better for Franca."

"I don't doubt that," Ernesto retorted, his eyes looking down to Samuele's foot.

"I'm not the same, that is true. But neither of you went through what I did, and the experience must be worth something. It is to me, and it should have some meaning for others, otherwise, what is the use of anything. We may as well all die."

"I understand, and I can see you've got a bum foot."

"He didn't get it by staying home either," interrupted Franca. "He got it at the front where your son should have been. Samuele came back with a bad foot, but he's back as a man. And your son, who avoided the draft, stayed behind and is more savage than wild beasts. You said it yourself yesterday when you showed your scar from the first war. Does it make you any less because you can hide it?"

Ernesto remained silent for a moment, thinking about Franca's words, which were too true to contradict.

"What is it you want, Samuel?" he asked in a calmer tone.

"I want nothing except your daughter in marriage before the year is up, if nothing happens to the contrary."

Ernesto had not expected such a forward and honest--sounding statement. He was pleased, yet he did not let on about it one way or another. He stared at Samuele and Samuele stared right back. Then he looked at Franca.

"And what do you say to all this?"

"I don't want to live in your house any longer with those two," she answered right back, delightfully stunned over her father's allowance.

"That's not what I mean. How about him?"

"We want your blessing."

"Those are not things that concern me. You do what you want, but don't come crying to me if things don't work out. Anyhow, I'm not deciding now. You, go on home," Ernesto ordered Samuele, "and don't come back until you hear from me, one way or another. As for you, let's go home. I have bigger matters to attend to... Samuele, don't pin your hopes too high. I don't particularly like your family and I don't think a great deal of you. Besides, I don't really think you can take care of my daughter, never mind raise a family."

"I've come back from hell without the help of anyone; but raising a family is a different story. Yes, I would need the help of Franca, and our children would want to know their grandparents; we would all need your help. As for my family, we're pretty lucky, thanks to my mother. But I want to ask you for a personal favor, if I may," Samuele said, in a controlled monotone that lent a lot more to the literal meaning of his words.

"Is that so," Ernesto remarked... "This guy's got balls," he said to himself secretly.

"I'm raising cattle. I understand you have one or two good examples for sale. I'll buy them from you, though I'd prefer you'd give them to Franca and me."

"Come on, let's go home," Ernesto said, looking at his daughter. "We got that little matter to take care of." Then, noticing the roses Franca still held in her hand, he asked where she got them. Instead of answering, she smiled and looked at Samuele. Shrugging his shoulders, Samuele put his hand on her shoulder and nudged her toward home. On arriving near the house, Ernesto put his arm around Franca's waist.

Samuele stood watching the two until they walked out of sight. Then he turned around and walked home. As he came to the dirt road that crossed the one that led to Franca's house, he looked at the high mountains, plainly visible in the distance, the sky being so clear. "They're south of Naples," he said to himself. "They're so far, yet I can see them so clearly." Then, continuing to talk to himself in disbelief of what he was seeing, he wondered why he had not noticed them before.

He walked leisurely along almost without a trace of limping, his eyes wandering in the distance, at the vast Irpinia Valley surrounded by high mountains. Occasional hills interrupted the smooth surface, mostly covered with green fields of wheat moving in the wind as waves at sea. He could also see the tall poplars, and two miles beyond them, the craggy hills with their torrents and steep ravines.

He breathed deeply, very deep, as he resumed walking. His eyes filled with the astonishing panorama, he walked forward, not without thinking of Franca and of those secret moments he had just enjoyed with her.

CHAPTER 13

On Sunday morning, farmers from the surrounding areas gathered in the ample but hilly town square full of merchants selling their wares. Dressed for the occasion, almost every farmer joined the townspeople at the various masses being said throughout the morning. Their main interest, however, revolved around the open market divided into specific sections: dry goods in one, food specialties in another, livestock at the perimeter, and so on, creating a veritable network of comings and goings much as ants around their nest. In this busy and colorful atmosphere, clients looked for specific deals, while vendors sought to make as much profit as possible. Each side engaged the other in earnest, and almost every deal closed to the benefit of both. The naïve looking and listening would conclude that the client got the deal of a lifetime and the merchant a royal screwing: "You've taken food from my children's mouths," the merchants would say, raising their hands to their heads and squeezing their temples. Everyone--spectator, merchant, and client alike--was totally engrossed in the business at hand.

Their faces did not show traces of the ravages of the recent war which had taken lives from almost every town and village. Yet, during that spring morning, everyone acted with confidence of a better future. At the same time, however, they did not lose sight of their present moment which they pursued as if it were the very essence of their being. But even in such serious pursuits, they found room for laughter and jokes, with the men often congregating in small groups in their tall-tale telling.

Further up the street, Enrico and his mother were buying a rabbit for dinner. The elementary school teacher was at the corner store buying week-old newspapers because he could not afford the latest ones. The Cavaliere, as he was known in the town, dressed in a white suit and wearing a large straw hat on his head, wandered through the market and single mindedly ending up where large animals were being bartered. Once there, he only stopped to look at the best oxen and bulls. At the other end of the section, Samuele, having sold his two calves, was buying a team of four Calabrian oxen when the Cavaliere walked by.

Attracted by the distinguished man, Samuele was impressed by his bearing. Maria explained that the Cavaliere was the man in charge and the restorer of the Straw Obelisk. Samuele nodded to his mother, and quickly returned to the cattle dealer, who was holding fast on his original price.

"Listen to me now," Samuele urged. "I'm trying to raise cattle. You know what that means, don't you?" The rotund but severe looking man stared into Samuele's eyes. Samuele continued unperturbed. "If you give me a break, I'll get started and I'll be buying many more of these, and I will be buying them from you. It's not easy to start, as you very well know, especially for someone who's just come back from the war. You know how much soldiers make in our army. You were in it! Cut your price by one-third because that's all I have. Here it is. Take it, and let's be done with it."

The man was almost convinced and was about to say yes when instead he uttered a "no". Disappointed, Samuele shrugged his shoulders and asked his mother to go look elsewhere.

As mother and son walked away, Ernesto and Franca appeared from down the street. On seeing Samuele, Franca quickly asked her father to go speak with them. At first Ernesto said no; then he accommodated his daughter.

"What's the problem?" Ernesto asked Samuele.

"Nothing," answered Samuele, surprised to see them. "I tried to buy those four animals but the owner wouldn't budge on the price."

"That fat guy down there?"

"Yes, that's the one."

"Come on, let's go. If you want them, he'll sell them to you, provided you really want to buy them. We were in the first war together."

The four walked through the crowd, Maria and Franca walking behind Ernesto and Samuele, who discussed the bid. On arriving, the rotund red-cheeked man let out a gleeful shout at Ernesto.

"What's this I hear, refusing Samuele's bid?"

"Look, if he wants them, he can have them, but only because you're with him; otherwise, I wouldn't. Look, they're four beautiful animals."

"You've never sold anything other than the best. How are you?" Ernesto asked, bringing his hand forward to shake. The man extended his, and the two shook hands firmly. Franca and Samuele looked at each other while the two men chatted privately. After a few moments, Samuele stepped forward and gave the money to Ernesto's friend, who, upon accepting, reminded Samuele on whom to see for additional purchases.

With the help of Maria and Franca, Samuele walked the animals away while Ernesto stayed behind with his friend.

"He's a fine young man," Ernesto admitted to his old friend. " I treated him harshly, but he turned out to be a nice young man. He was a son of a bitch; then he went into the army, and, look at him now. He has certainly changed for the better and he wants to marry my daughter. You know, I'm giving him a hard time about it, but I approve. My son, on the other hand, has turned out to be a louse. I am worried about him. Anyhow, I think Samuele's going to do something for this town. He's got good ideas and is serious. Give him a hand when you can. He's been through a lot, as you've seen, much more than you and I ever saw. He wants to marry my daughter, but I can't just open my home to him. Besides, that wife of mine and that son of hers are dead against Samuele. Well, thanks a lot, and don't forget to drop by for a drink. I've got some great wine."

"Goodby, Ernesto. I'll be by soon."

Joining the three, Ernesto said he had another appointment and that he and Franca had to go. Samuele thanked Ernesto, who in turn offered to help any time Samuele needed it. Samuele then said goodby to Franca, who answered with a smile.

At the market, Lucia and the two children waited for Samuele and Maria, Lucia having bought the meat for the Sunday dinner, as was the general custom. When Lucia saw her brother leading the four calves, she smiled with joy, and walked toward him to congratulate him. Samuele handed her the ropes, then picked up his little nephew first then Rachele's daughter and sat them both on the back of one of the animals, holding them as Lucia walked them home. Maria, meanwhile, walked behind, secretly enjoying the scene unfolding ahead of her.

As they walked, they greeted the people coming from the opposite direction, stopping when Enrico, bundle in hand, walked up to them. He asked Samuele to accompany him, because he wanted to introduce him to Tina, waiting in front of her house. Samuele handed the calves over to his mother and sister and went off with Enrico.

In the short walk to the market, Samuele said hello to practically everyone who walked by, whereas Enrico avoided looking straight into the people's faces. Whenever they passed a young woman, however, Enrico went out of his way to smile, making sure to control the degree of his salutation, always making more fuss over the more attractive young ones.

"Stop wasting your breath on the old ones," Enrico told a chuckling Samuele. "Just concentrate on the young ones."

"All right, all right," answered Samuele, who had reasons to be happy: so much had gone right for him that morning.

"When you see the old ones coming, turn your face to me as though you're involved in a deep discussion with me. That's all you have to do," Enrico continued in a spirited manner that made Samuele burst out laughing.

Enrico kept-up his spirited monologue until they came within sight of Tina's house. On seeing her seated in front of the house, Enrico pointed her out to Samuele, who, looking at her steadily, tried not to be too obvious.

"Look at her," Enrico pointed out, "look at her breasts, those legs; they drive me crazy mad, I tell you. I spend hours, whole sleepless hours, thinking about her. You can't imagine, Samuele, how she drives me. I've got to have her, Sam...," he emphasized, closing his lips tightly. "When I'm close to her, I go nuts, nuts, I tell you. That's why I haven't dared say or do anything yet."

"For fear of failing or of being rejected?"

"I want her to feel I'm serious about her stupid religion until you know what."

"You haven't changed a bit. A woman means only one thing to you."

"Oh, yes, Samuele, I think about that all the time, and my *jeova* is next--come hell or high water, or, *fire and brimstone* as she says," Enrico said, laughing heartily, thinking he had made some terrific pun.

"Isn't your mother also a woman?"

"Come on, Samuele, you're breaking my balls."

Tina was sitting on a sturdy straw chair, holding a book in one hand but not reading it. She wore a light but tight red sweater--her breast accentuated especially because she was a bit on the heavy side, and a plaid skirt falling over her knees. She wore her reddish and slightly long hair down to her shoulders. Her complexion was milky white, her eyes blue and deep-set, and her protruding lips were rounded and meaty.

She liked seating there on Sunday morning because everyone going to the market had to pass in front of her house, giving her a chance to wave her hand at them and greeting them with a hearty *good morning.* The older women, of course, resenting the amount of lipstick on her mouth and the rouge on her cheeks, hardly responded to Tina's salutation; the men, on the other hand, either tipped their hats or gave quick nods with their heads, to the reprimanding frowns of their accompanying women with their terse accusatory words of *Puttana!*

Tina was a rarity among the indigenous catholics in that as a representative of a foreign religion, she was making good use of her sexuality in order to attract the attention of an otherwise condemnatory populace. She sat with her head erect, her breast fully out, her legs slightly open, but never to the extent of being offensive, closing them cautiously when the older ladies passed by.

On approaching Tina, Enrico put his left arm out, and with his other hand on his mouth, he forced Samuele to stop in silence. He gazed at her indulgently, his tongue moving between his wet lips.

"Samuele," Enrico said, his hand still across Samuele's chest, "well, isn't she a sight to behold? Hold back, I don't want her to see us yet..."

"Don't you think you've looked enough. She's bound to turn around, and if she sees us, she may think you're a darn fool."

"You're right, Samuele... Ciao Tina!"

"Oh! hi, Enrico. I didn't notice you were there."

"I thought introducing you to my old my friend Samuele. Remember, I already spoke to you about him. He's just back from the war..."

"Oh, yes," she said, getting up. With hand extended, she fixed her eyes into those of Samuele as though she were in a momentary hypnosis. "I have heard about you. I like the way you handled yourself with your family too. It is indeed a pleasure to meet a man like you."

"My pleasure, I assure you," answered Samuele with a smile. Enrico, meanwhile, looked at the ground.

"Oh, I hope this will not be the last we see of each other. I am here on missionary work. Everyone is of a personal interest to me."

"Some more than others," interjected Samuele.

"Oh, yes, naturally. We're all human beings, after all."

"Any luck with your proselytizing?" Samuele asked straight faced.

"Ah, yes, well... I think very well," she answered, not sure what to make of Samuele's word. "Yes, things are going fine considering. Enrico has been coming for lessons on a regular basis, and he is doing very well, too," she said, looking at Enrico, who quickly came to life.

"That's because she's a good teacher."

"Oh, no, no. Don't believe him, Samuele. Sometimes he is too easy with his compliments. Oh, I just wish some of his friends would also come, like you, Samuele."

"I brought you Toni," Enrico added, not sure on where the conversation was going.

"Yes, oh yes, Toni is too set in his ways, and I don't think he's serious enough."

"Look, Samuele, look who's coming, if it's not Mr. Banno himself wearing sunglasses!" Enrico commented. Waiting in silence for Mr. Banno to come closer, Enrico could not resist. "Good morning Mr. Banno, sir, how are you today, this beautiful sunny morning."

"I'm fine," he answered dryly. Then turning to Samuele, Mr. Banno asked how he was, all the time avoiding looking at Tina.

"Did you see the four cows Samuele bought this morning?"

"No, I didn't... Did you, Samuele?"

"Of course he did. Next year, they're each going to have twins, and the year after, triplets. Samuele is going to be a very rich man around here."

"I notice you bought sun glasses, Mr. Banno," said Samuele.

But before Mr. Banno could answer, Enrico beat him to the punch.

"You bought them from the Neapolitan salesman, just below the church, didn't you?. My aunt bought three for the price of one. She tried to give me a pair but I didn't want them. I wouldn't be caught dead with those cheap glasses. What did you pay for them, one pair for the price of two?"

Mr. Banno felt embarrassed but only temporarily. "For your information, young imbecile, I got five for the price of one... Well, goodby, Samuele. Remember, I still got that wine."

"Don't worry, we'll be over shortly."

"Not you! But, Enrico, have you noticed? Too much blood flows to your head. Try putting a dozen leeches on your face as well."

"Give my best regards to Rosa."

"Goodby, Mr. Banno," Tina interjected. But Mr. Banno, shrugging his shoulders, continued on his way.

"That man is amazing," commented Enrico ironically, making Samuele and Tina smile, and he quickly joined in a hearty laughter.

"Tell me, have you contacted many people?"

"Ah, yes, Samuele, several people are coming for lessons, and even Rachele, for instance, has come by."

"Rachele! And I suppose my sister?"

"Yes, but she didn't want to come."

"You know Rachele's husband is returning."

"Oh, yes, I know. And I think it's just dreadful for her to hide in that God-forsaken place. She should stay right here and face him. Up there, she has no protection at all."

"Why didn't you tell her that?"

"Oh, because she went to the priest instead of coming to me."

"What is your magic formula?"

"Ha, we don't have magic formulas. We simply work. We just work with and for the people."

"Very commendable indeed."

"Hey, won't you give me the chance to tell you all about my religion?"

"An hour, that's all..."

On hearing the last sentence, Enrico raised his eyebrows and looked away from Tina, acting as though he could not stand being there in her presence, so great was his passion. He knew he had to bear with her until an opportune moment. As he listened to the conversation between Samuele and Tina, he understood that his friend was not going to come through. Samuele seemed too interested, and Enrico could not decide whether his friend was more interested in Tina or in her religion. However, when Samuele's sarcasm coupled with his obvious disbelief in anything she professed became more than clear, Tina opted to close on the *one hour* offer, to the dismay of Enrico.

"...One hour. that's all, Samuele."

"I have many things to do; I'm very busy. Besides, I have had plenty of religion, of all kinds."

"Hey, we don't have to talk about religion."

"You're a missionary."

"Well, would it be more amenable if a woman by the name of Tina were to ask you over?"

"Now you're talking."

"You will accept then?"

Tina found Samuele appealing and Enrico finally understood. Having no time to lose, Enrico had to get Samuele away before she got to him. As Enrico was thinking of a way to get Samuele away, Don Alfonso appeared from below, walking toward them.

"Well, will you accept?" asked Tina of Samuele.

"I can't give you an answer right now. But there's plenty of time."

"Look! interrupted Enrico, "the priest's coming."

Tina quickly looked. As she saw the robed man approaching, she pulled her skirt down in a manner that did not attract the attention of her two admirers.

"Hello, Don Alfonso!" greeted Enrico.

"Good morning, Enrico, good morning, Samuele. And how are you, young lady?"

"Oh, fine, thank you," Tina answered bowing her head.

"Are you enjoying yourself? You are in the presence of two very handsome young men of our town."

"Oh, Don, Alfonso," interrupted Enrico, "Samuele and I were about to leave. Do you mind if we walked with you? I want to ask you about the up-coming feast."

"By all means. But I'm sure you can ask me some other time if you wish. Besides, the feast is not until late in September, as you well know."

"But if you're in a hurry and don't want our company, that's all right, Don Alfonso."

"No, I'm not in a hurry. Well, come on then. But are you sure Tina will not object to your coming along with me?"

"Oh, they will be in good hands," Tina assured naively.

"You also keep them well, Tina, don't you?"

"She does," interrupted Samuele. "She does, I can vouch for that. Yes, Don Alfonso, we were about to leave and may as well walk home with you. I would also like to hear questions he has of you."

Samuele and Enrico began to walk with the priest, not before Tina reminded Samuele that it was Tina that had asked for the appointment and not the missionary lady. Samuele did not answer, having gone off as though he hadn't heard her last remarks. Enrico, on the other hand, surely heard.

CHAPTER 14

The three men walked along the road toward the church. Enrico's house was midway between Tina's and the church. Don Alfonso accepted Enrico's request with suspicion. He had known Enrico since he was born, and in view of Enrico's activities throughout the war, Don Alfonso did not particularly like him or his mother. In Don Alfonso's eyes, Enrico was egocentric, superficially playful, jovial and calm, but clever in hiding strong carnal tendencies.

Don Alfonso's suspicion proved to be true. Enrico, as a matter of fact, did not have any question about the feast. Samuele, on the other hand, showed a lot of genuine interest, wanting to know all about it, and Don Alfonso obliged:

For the first time since before the war began, fireworks were going to be included in the celebration. Two orchestras, one of them a band, were going to play throughout the greater part of the day and in the evening. The streets were going to be decorated with electrically lit displays, and merchants from all over the region had already written requesting space. In the morning a huge animal fair was going to be held; in the afternoon, fruit growers and candy manufacturers were going to compete for decoration prizes. But the biggest attraction was definitely going to be the pulling of the Straw Obelisk.

"The Cavaliere has been steadily working for the past years, revising and re-doing the defective parts and has added new ones. Actually, the reason why we are going to celebrate late this year is because of him. I have seen some of the new panels, and all I can say is that it is going to be the most beautiful obelisk that will have been drawn. This year, the Cavaliere has already started to canvass the region's cattle owner for the best specimen, and has even planned a trip to Calabria to search for the best. Remember, the Obelisk will stand about eight stories tall and be heavier than ever before. He's going to be very choosy, both with the animals and with the trainers," Don Alfonso declared enthusiastically.

While Samuele listened with deep interest, Enrico remained completely absent from the conversation, the thought of Tina making him morose. He just could not get her out of his mind. At least one time, Enrico moaned aloud, causing the priest to look at him with a frown.

"What's the matter?" asked Don Alfonso.

"Nothing. I was just thinking about something, that's all."

"Tina!" interjected Samuele with a kidding smile. His face reddening, Enrico admitted he had been thinking about Tina, a forced smile on his face to hide his embarrassment.

Don Alfonso continued with his description of the coming event. This time, Don Alfonso's accumulative details became of little interest to Samuele as well. While the priest talked, Samuele went into his own revelry wherein he went back to his younger days of the pull: the excitement that marked the major event: the straining bulls with ferocious looks in their eyes, the Cavaliere directing from the platform on the first stage, the sturdy and strong rope men, the steep hills, the roar of the accompanying crowd, his holding on to the last stick of the rope--things going through Samuele's mind, in full color, contrasts, action, danger, and a suspense he would never forget, the routine, though slightly out of focus, rousing his mind to tremendous excitement.

"I'm going to be there," Samuele said, interrupting Don Alfonso in the middle of a sentence.

"I hope so," responded the priest, raising his eyebrows. "Now, what is the matter with you?" he asked.

"I was just remembering the...the whole thing. I had practically forgotten a good amount actually," Samuele admitted with a smile.

Enrico, on the other hand, struggling with an unsuppressible eroticism, was trying to think of a way to seduce Tina. He had to, otherwise he would go out of his mind. "I will not have any peace," he said to himself, his eyes askance. The picture of Tina flashed through his mind in many forms, and in all of them he found himself kissing her passionately. In his vicarious ecstacy, Enrico unconsciously kept biting his lips as though he was tasting something and not having anything in his mouth.

"Your lips hurting you?" asked Don Alfonso in a low voice, with a curiosity that startled Enrico.

"No," he answered. "I was thinking about the bulls pulling the Obelisk... like Samuele."

"I didn't think the coming feast meant so much the two of you."

"It's just the excitement," explained Samuele.

"Don't forget: we're celebrating the glory of our Madonna. If we celebrate the feast with that thought in mind, we will have great success, honor, and unlimited rewards."

"Yes, Don Alfonso," agreed Samuele.

At that point, from the opposite direction came Toni. Seeing him, Enrico suddenly lit up with enthusiasm, unlike Samuele and Don Alfonso, who kept explaining to Samuele about the connection between honoring the Madonna and celebrating the feast.

"Good morning, Don Alfonso," greeted Toni, first looking at Enrico and then at the priest.

"Good morning, Toni," Don Alfonso answered. Then, turning toward Samuele once again, he continued with his explanation.

Toni had bypassed them by about forty feet when Enrico suddenly spoke up.

"I forgot to get the matches for my mother. Here, Samuele, hold the meat for a second. I'll ask Toni to pick them up for me." He handed the bundle to Samuele and ran down to Toni, calling out for him to wait.

While Enrico exchanged words with Toni, Don Alfonso unconvinced about Enrico, began to question Samuele.

"What is your connection with Enrico and Tina?" asked Don Alfonso.

"We grew up together and spent every day of our lives together up to the war. So many things have changed and don't know what to make of him. As for Tina, I don't know her. She told me she's doing missionary work. Obviously, you haven't done that good a job with your people," Samuele said half serious.

"The war brought many changes and not many good ones. Tina is very young and attractive woman. But as with my youth, and yours, I am sure, knowledge and understanding become facile acquisitions. When young, we have idealism, so many utopias. Reality, however, becomes real through learning, reflection, and age. I haven't heard anything bad about her, but sometimes I do wonder about her motives. I am more doubtful about Enrico...here he is. He's coming back."

"I'm glad I caught him, otherwise I would have had to make another trip. Here, give me the meat, Samuele."

Don Alfonso looked closely at Enrico, who, all of a sudden acted with haste.

"If you don't mind," Enrico said, "I'll take the short-cut home. I didn't realize how late it is. Mother asked me to hurry, as she was preparing dinner for relatives visiting us today. Samuele, I'll see you later. Goodby Don Alfonso.

I'll tell my mother I had the pleasure of walking home with you."

"Yes, do that, Enrico. God be with you."

Enrico climbed down the side of the road. Once out of their sight, he threw down the bundle and began to run back in the direction from which he had been coming, keeping himself below the edge of the road to avoid running into the people still going to or coming from the market. In a few minutes, he reached Tina's house. As he paused to regain his breath, he stared at Tina sitting, as before, on the bench. In joyous composure, he approached Tina.

"Hi, Tina, it's me. I've come back."

"Oh, Enrico, it's you! What's brings you back?"

"I have an hour or so before dinner. I thought we could go over some points I missed the last time," he answered as he looked up her legs still slightly apart. Noticing his stare and smiling coyly, Tina brought her legs together.

"Sure, Enrico, let's go inside."

"If you don't mind, Tina, I prefer outside. The weather is too good to be inside. Look at hills, the countryside is so beautiful, isn't it?"

Both looked out at the enchanting panorama: fields of wheat, fruit trees, vines...

"We think of religion here, but wouldn't it be better out there in the middle of so much beauty. I bet you I can find a thousand violets by the brook, and all for you."

"I love violets."

"I know."

"How do you know?"

"I know you better than you know me, and I think about you more than you think of you," Enrico admitted, looking at her in an outward serious expression. Inside, however, he trembled with passion. Not completely revealing his feeling to her, he would occasionally look away from her as though he was waiting for someone to come. Finally, someone appeared from the field across from Tina's house.

It was Toni. Climbing up to the road, he greeted Tina and then Enrico, who, surprised to see him, asked what he was carrying in his hands.

"Violets."

"For Tina?" asked Enrico.

"No, not for Tina. I'm sorry. But there are so many more by the brook. Got get them yourself. You have two legs, don't you?" Toni asked, challengingly. "Now, if you don't mind, I'm on the way to church. These violets are for the Madonna, and they won't stay fresh for long," Toni added matter of fact, turning around abruptly, in time to hide his smirk.

Enrico quickly turned to Tina and asked to go together. She hesitated. Then Toni added that they could easily find the flowers--a whole bunch right by the tall oak at the brook's edge alongside the wheat field.

"Come on Tina, get your orange book and let's be gone. Come, get your book. I'll take my lesson by the brook."

"Oh, oh, yes. That's a good idea." Tina went inside to freshen up.

"Were you able to do it, Toni?" Enrico asked, winking his eye.

"All set," Toni winked back. "I planted all I could get. They're just over the edge behind the hedge under the oak. The wheat is very tall there. No one will see you. Good luck."

"Thanks, Toni, I owe you one. I'll see you later."

When Tina finally came with her book, she asked the whereabouts of Toni, and was satisfied with Enrico's explanations that Toni also had other things to do and had no time, but that Toni had entrusted him to give her his best wishes.

"My, you smell good," he said, his nose moving up her neck.

The two walked to the other side of the road. First to climb down and facing Tina, Enrico extended his arms out to her. After having passed her book to him, she then clutched his hand firmly, and deliberately slow, she allowed Enrico to help her down, making sure to stumble. Not missing a beat, Enrico held her close to his chest while he turned his head on both sides, looking for a safe place to land. Then making believe he himself had lost his equilibrium, he stumbled. Giggling, Tina quickly called out to Enrico, who, wrapping his arms around her, fell to the ground with her on top of him. When Enrico came to a complete stop and did not release her, Tina objected mildly.

"Oh, come on. Remember," she said while in a prone position, her breast and face directly above Enrico, "we're going to get violets, aren't we?"

"Yes," answered Enrico with a confident smile. "I didn't realize you were so beautiful, though," he said as he squeezed her body against his and then separating. Tina brushed her clothes with her hands and pulled her sweater down over her breast. Taking the book in one hand, he held her hand with the other, saying that the surface of the pathway was uneven, and that she might fall.

They walked slowly down the solitary path, surrounded by tall bushes in which crows and blackbirds noisily winged away from the intruders.

"I wish you had never come to the village," Enrico confessed as he squeezed her hand and rubbed his thumb over her soft skin.

"Oh, why?"

"Because you've stolen my heart. I haven't been sleeping for weeks, and I'm always thinking of you. You are the most beautiful woman I've ever seen," he said in a sincere tone. And Tina, not minding the compliment, knew she was not beautiful. "I've been asking myself if I am in love with you, even tried to convince myself I was not. Instead, here I am telling that I am in love you."

"Oh, well, Enrico, you know why I am here. We must not let our emotions interfere with our mission. Oh, yes, we have to control our feelings."

"Of course, but I can't help the way I've been feeling the last several months. But I really want to know all about you, about the things you do, who you are, because I even thought of proposing to you."

"Oh, no, Enrico," she said with a smile. Enrico put his hand around her waist and drew her close.

"Only if you want to. Besides, there's plenty of time... Look, there's the oak!"

Walking a bit faster, they reached the shallow brook. Enrico crossed on the large stepping stones. Once over he extended his hand, and Tina crossed, doing a quick pirouette on the rock.

"Oh, it's so beautiful out here," she said ecstatically. Enrico agreed and led her toward the base of the huge oak. He climbed over the edge, walked around the bushes until he saw the flowers, looked around for the patch of tall wheat that Toni had described, and, satisfied, extended his hand to Tina.

"I've already spotted some violets," Enrico said, staring at the undulating wheat.

"Help me up," she answered.

With one sure pull, Enrico brought her up, pulling her squarely against his chest. He quickly tried to kiss her, but Tina pulled back.

"Oh, we mustn't," she said. "Where are the violets?"

"There, see."

"Oh, they're beautiful, but they're so few!"

"There are hundreds along the edge. As a matter of fact, they're even in the wheat field right about there."

When Tina bent down to pick them, Enrico knelt in front of her. He plucked a few and handed them to her. As he looked up, he closed his eyes. Then he immediately looked down. After having picked enough for a little bouquet of the truly odorous flowers, he rose to his feet. As he handed them to her, he took her into his arms and kissed her passionately. Tina resisted feebly at first. When Enrico continued holding her close and kissing her wildly, she soon dropped the flowers and began to indulge herself. After flinging her arms around Enrico, and with her mouth tight against his, she allowed Enrico to have his way. The more she heard him say she was the most beautiful woman on earth, the more passionate she became, enjoying both the adulation and the kisses alike. In between breaths, Enrico led her to the patch of tall wheat. After bending the stocks to form a bedding, he pulled Tina down. Kissing her naked breast, he drew his body over hers. In one instant, he found himself ecstatically inside a receptive Tina, who moaned with joy. In no time, and with one large heave that brought pain to Tina, Enrico, reached his climax. Suddenly, he lay listless on her body. Tina continued to kiss him until he slid off of her. Still excited, Tina brought her hands down to his crotch, but to no avail. On realizing what had happened, Tina remained next to him for a few but long moments of deep and silent soul-searching. Looking into eyes that had neither seen her body nor that of any other woman, Tina got up. Her voluptuous body in full view, she gathered her clothes and got dressed. Squashing the violets with one foot, she walked to the edge of the brook, and rushed home for her prophylaxis.

Enrico, meanwhile, remained on the ground, seemingly bewildered over the whole affair. "To think," he said to himself, "she wanted to get laid more than I, and I was not up to it. Worse, there was no need for this whole charade. If only she had been sincere," he thought. "But, there'll be other times..."

Enrico's mother, after having waited for about two hours, decided to go look for her son, fearing something had happened to him.

After knocking on Samuele's door, and expecting him to answer, Teresa felt a bit uncomfortable to see Maria, who, noticing Teresa's slight apprehension, quickly escorted her into the kitchen. Teresa was surprised to see them all sitting at the table made bright by a bouquet of flowers at its center, and the children well behaved and enjoying their Sunday dinner.

Dressed in her usual colorful fashion, Teresa asked Samuele the whereabouts of her son Enrico. After Samuele explained that Enrico was walking home with Don Alfonso and himself, and exactly where Enrico had left to do some errand, Teresa excused herself and went back outside. Troubled by what she had heard, begrudgingly, she decided to stop by Don Alfonso.

With a weak pull, Teresa brought the hammer to the rim of the small bell. In a moment, Don Alfonso's maid opened the door.

"Come in, Teresa, come in. You haven't been around in a while. Come in; tell me, what can I help you with?" called Don Alfonso, who was eating alone.

"Nothing, it's just that Enrico is not home yet, and being that he walked home with you, I thought he might be here with you or with his friend Samuele. He is not there and obviously he's not here. Did you say something to upset him?"

"No, Teresa. But what makes you think I would say anything to upset him? I don't think I did. Do I say things to upset people?"

"I know you don't, but sometimes one never knows. You know, he's the only one I have. Sometimes I worry about him."

"That you should."

"Then you did say something to him."

Wiping his mouth with his napkin, he told her that she should worry about him, that it didn't seem to him that her son was purely interested in Tina's religion as much as he was in Tina. "You had better worry about him, lest something happens. The story he had something to do all of a sudden, and his wanting to walk with me to ask about the feast--it doesn't take a genius to see through it all. Teresa, it doesn't take a psychiatrist to see through your son. I just hope all is well with him, and that if I can be of help--genuine help--I am at your disposal, because, Teresa, I'm somewhat worried about his soul and less about him coming home late for your Sunday dinner. And by the way," Don Alfonso continued, pointing his finger at her, "you should be thinking about your own soul a bit more. I hardly see you at Mass."

"I come whenever I can, Don Alfonso," she answered in low voice, avoiding the priest's glance. "We're all so busy," she stated without conviction, and blushing enough to accentuate her rouge.

"You're not working the fields; you're living comfortably on your husband's income. I notice the many dresses you wear, and, now, even the rouge, like Tina. She also wears rouge. Did you notice?"

"No, I didn't. But I'd better be going. Enrico may have returned, and he will not find me there. Goodbye, Don Alfonso," Teresa said in a low, squeaky voice.

"Don't worry, Teresa, he'll be home. God be with you and with your son. And don't forget, I want to see you more often in church."

"Yes, Don Alfonso. Goodbye," she answered subserviently, and hurried out the room.

Trying to appear svelte in dress and in stride, an unnerved Teresa rushed home to find Enrico at the front of the door sitting on the wide ledge between the bundle and the orange book.

"Thank God, you're here. Where have you been? I was so worried."

On seeing his mother so distraught, Enrico walked toward her, apologizing for having been late. When Teresa did not answer him, with a big smile, he put his arms around her, and telling her how beautiful she was, he asked for her forgiveness.

"All right," she answered.

"I am so happy; I think Tina likes me. I didn't think she liked me, but this morning she proved it. I thought she was interested in me because of the religious lessons, you know. But now I think she likes me."

"Were you with her all this time? Were you close to her? I can smell perfume on you."

"No, Mother, it isn't what you think. We sat rather close at the table. My clothes must have rubbed against her."

"And the book?"

"She gave it to me because she said I was a good student, and because she wants me to bring my friends to her. To make her happy, I promised her that one day I would also bring you to her for at least one class. Mother, I am sure you will like her."

"No, Enrico. I was up to see if Don Alfonso knew of your whereabouts, and he wasn't very nice to me. All I need is go to Tina for religious lessons."

"What do you care, Mother? Anyhow, no one need know about it. You go once. Then, if you don't like it, you won't have to go again. Besides, with these religions, they're all alike."

"I don't understand you."

"What's there to understand? Tina has come to us with a new religion. I think we all should at least know what it is. How can we know if Don Alfonso is on the right track. Don't you agree?"

"I agree; I haven't won an argument with you yet. Well, bring the meat inside. You must be hungry."

"Yes, mother, very."

"I'll cook a couple extra pieces for you."

CHAPTER 15

After Teresa left, Maria asked Samuele about Enrico, and he answered that Enrico should be of no concern. Enrico simply had a mad crush on Tina that time would cure, he explained. Knowing better, Maria decided to bring her son up-to-date. In her eyes and in those of others, Enrico was notorious during the war for his many shady deals both with enemy and allied soldiers, that he had been with every prostitute from Naples or tried to seduce every woman in town, and that for some reason, women with any amount of *salt* had very negative feelings about him. Furthermore, Maria explained, Enrico had a way of getting what he wanted and then break his word.

Having made no bones about how she felt about Enrico, Maria also gave her opinion of Teresa, though admitting, before Samuele could retort, that she, herself, in view of Lucia's behavior, should not be the one to render criticisms. Lucia, sitting next to her, looked at the ground on hearing her mother's comments.

"Don't think Teresa has been virtuous either," Maria continued. "Because her husband had gone to Argentina, Teresa entertained just about every officer that came down the pike, under the guise of friendship visits between the new alliance. Naturally, she entertained only in the daytime, as she stated publicly so many times."

"Why are you telling me all this?"

"Because Enrico was your friend. I objected to him then; I object to him now."

"That's true, I remember. But did I listen to you then?"

"No!"

"What makes you think I would now?"

"I always wanted you to be your own person."

"You need not worry, Mother. True friends are scarce these days. Just because one speaks to an individual does mean they're friends," Samuele observed in a low voice, somewhat provoked at his mother for having brought up the subject. He understood her feelings, however, and let it go at that.

Instead of going on with the conversation, Samuele went over to the two children who were playing in a corner, picked them up, and placed them one on each knee. After tickling them to smiles and laughter, Samuele turned to his sister to ask how the two were getting along, concerned about the little girl but being sure not to show concern obvious to the little girl.

"They're getting along fine," Lucia answered, a serious expression on her face.

"She's eating, and all that?"

"Yes."

"Does she miss her mother?"

"I think she does, but she hasn't said anything about her. Last night, in bed, she came close to me. I held her close until she fell asleep. While sleeping, she continued to cling to me."

Samuele looked at the little girl with sad eyes, thinking of how unfortunate she was. Her father was about to return to an empty home to find his daughter in the care of friends, and his wife in hiding.

Samuele asked Lucia if the girl talked about her father. Lucia answered that she only knew that Rachele was so ashamed about what had happened that she never mentioned the word "father" in front of her child. In any event, according to Rachele, the little girl was too young to understand the idea of fatherhood.

"Too young? I doubt it. She may not know the words, and she may not know what to say. You can be sure she's missed somebody. And that someone is coming back. Marcello could be coming back to fulfill the ideals of fatherhood for which he is eminently qualified, and this child, instead, is going to miss out on both fatherhood and motherhood. Some mother she was born to!"

The last words cut deep into his sister's and mother's hearts although Samuele had not meant to direct his remarks at them. It was only the consequence of their actions that made mother and daughter also feel a sense of guilt. Maria had already accepted blame, and Samuele knew it, though he could not separate his mother--or, rather, she would not separate herself from the sense of guilt. And Lucia, while she may have been forgiven, at least superficially, could not under any circumstances forget the humiliation she had caused her family as a whole and to her mother and brother in particular. On a day when so much had gone so well, a simple visit from Teresa had caused so much sadness and gloom.

"And the children--what could they be blamed for?" Samuele asked rhetorically. "Come on, kids, we're going to the yard. You're going to be riding the bull. Come, come on," Samuele exclaimed with laughter as he lifted the boy in the air. After placing him on one shoulder, he picked up the little girl. With both of them on his shoulders, he walked out of the kitchen with the children holding on, grabbing his hair with one hand, and his hands with the other. As Samuele jumped up and down, the children laughed and giggled.

"Out to the yard!" Samuele repeated, to the great satisfaction of the two riders.

Maria and Lucia, looking on as the trio disappeared out the door, continued to discuss the situation. More than Lucia, Maria kept saying how thankful they should be, for Samuele had turned out to be the opposite of what she had expected. She told her daughter to feel grateful in that she was spared the sure fate of Rachele.

"I feel as helpless about Rachele as I felt about you. I prayed a lot, and my prayers came through. I'm praying for Rachele, but she needs more than just mine."

"How about the police, can't they do anything?"

"The police! What can they do short of putting people in jail after the crimes are committed. You know what's happened to all the others? They went around with gun permits in their pockets and could have killed their victims in front of the police and the police could only act after the killing."

"It's all so cruel."

"It is, isn't it? The worst is that it doesn't stop. It goes on, and only rarely do things turn out for the better. You're one of the few exceptions. We have a lot to be thankful for, an awful lot. The last two days, I've been praying almost exclusively for Rachele, up in those hills, all by herself. We don't even know if she found anyone there. We know how she felt when she got the letter, and I can just imagine how Marcello is going to feel when he knocks on the door looking for his wife and child, and no one answers. Some neighbor will finally tell him that his wife turned out to be a whore and that friends like Lucia are holding his daughter: a friend helping a similar friend. There was time when friendship meant something, and I am thankful that people talk to us as much as they do, no thanks to you."

Lucia listened without saying a word. When Maria finally finished talking, she still said nothing. There wasn't much she could say or do to right the wrong. Living with that sense of guilt was punishment enough, made more unpleasant by Samuele surprise change of heart. In view of what her mother had just said, Lucia felt that death might have been a better way out. Instead, she had added to her brother's burden. She saw it and sensed--as her mother did-

-her brother's internal strife and conflicts. In silence and to herself, she deduced that her brother had turned away from the very punishment she should have been receiving. But there she was, part of his household, and he was playing with her illegitimate son as though he were his own son. If only Samuele had taken his belt out on her. Instead, he took her into his arms and brought her home.

The mental torment went on in each of the two women, and the atmosphere in the kitchen was heavy. Neither spoke nor looked at each other. When finally the kitchen chores were completed, Lucia went to see if she could help with the livestock.

Samuele and the children were near the bull tethered by the fig tree. Samuele caressed the huge animal while the children watched eagerly, hoping Samuele would lift them up onto the animal's powerful back and ride around the yard.

Samuele talked to the bull, and the animal seemed to understand. Often he moved his neck as if agreeing to what his master was saying. The children's eyes were glued on the face of the animal, awed by the bull's response.

"Watch," warned Samuele, "the bull is going to say something." As he caressed its huge neck, talking at the same time, the bull suddenly let out a tremendous bellow. The children drew back in alarm. They had expected the animal to talk, as Samuele had said, and not to bellow so loudly. Seeing they were frightened, Samuele laughed, and they quickly began to laugh as well. Then, Samuele, telling them to approach, offered to give them their long-awaited ride. Samuele did not have to ask them a second time. One at a time, he lifted them up. After cautioning them not to sway, he ordered the bull to start walking.

"There's precious cargo on your back," he told him. The bull turned its head and looked into Samuele's eyes.

Lucia couldn't believe her eyes.

CHAPTER 16

It was evening. On the moonlit street, villagers walked along the edge of the road. Occasional couples walked by, then random groups of adults and young children running in every direction playing hide-go-seek.

There was no traffic to disturb the children or their elders, and the only noise heard was that of the happy scurrying children, who did not even see the lights of the dilapidated bus approaching from the opposite direction. They often made fun of the vehicle, a post World War I specimen still in service because the newer ones had been used on behalf of the War, and the few worthwhile things left behind were confiscated by the retreating Germans.

The rickety vehicle made a stop--a very unusual one, for, it never stopped there. Nevertheless, hardly anyone cared, though most of the inhabitants noticed the bus stopping. Nor did anyone care about the passenger getting off near Rachele's house, which was set to one side and somewhat hidden from view.

It was Marcello--tall, rather lanky, with at least a three-day beard on his face, long hair, some falling over his forehead almost to his eyes. After he got off, he stepped aside to allow the bus to drive on, and then he began walking toward his home, a little bundle over his back. It contained, among other things, some clothes he had bought in Naples for his two women, having personally chosen them, feeling sure they would be pleased with his choice.

As he walked toward his home, he wondered, as he had done so many times, what his little girl would say on seeing him, and whether she would recognize him. In a few moments, when he was close to his house, he paused for a few seconds. There was enough moonlight for him to distinguish its corners, its solid stone walls, its doors, its elm tree in the front, the little fenced-in garden to the right, the flat stones that led from the street to the front door, and the empty barn to one side.

There was no sign of a light from within, however. Yet, it wasn't that late, he wondered without concern, his eyes full of anxiety despite the presence of a glow due to his expectation of his impending meeting with his wife and child: how was he going to act? Did his daughter look like him or his wife?

He walked slowly, his steps short. He bent slightly forward, but not from the weight of his bundle. On reaching the front of the house, he still saw no light. Nevertheless he walked onto the flat stones to the front door. He raised his hand to knock. Instead, as he was about to bring his bony fist onto the wood, he stopped. He listened for a few moments. When he heard no sign of life inside, his heart suddenly began to beat fast. He brought his heavy fist down on the wood and waited for an answer. When he heard no response, he knocked again, harder this time. He knocked again and again. He began to call out his wife's name. Moving to one of the windows, he beat on the glass, calling out Rachele's name. He ran to the front of the house and beat on the door. Realizing no one was home, he decided to seat down on the stone and to wait: she must have gone to visit her mother or friends. After all, she did not know he was coming. However, he thought, she was bound to return sooner or later.

He had waited so many months, he could wait a few more moments, even longer. Dejectedly, he waited, looking in every direction of the street. When shadows of people appeared, he stared in their direction hoping they'd be his wife and daughter. When he saw they were neighbors, he remained seated, unobserved by those who walked by. An hour passed, and still there was no sign of them. He stood up and walked to the water fountain on the side of the road about fifty feet away, where he pushed the button and, with his face toward the deep dark sky, he let the cool water drop into his mouth. Passing his hand over his mouth, he walked back to the house and sat down again. Another twenty or more minutes passed, and no one came. But a woman, carrying a water bucket on her head, stopped by the fountain. While she was filling the shiny copper bucket, Marcello felt the urge of going over to ask her about Rachele, but decided not to. The woman finally filled the bucket, lifted it to her head, and, with one hand holding it steady, she walked away like a ghost. Marcello waited. The minutes, meanwhile, grew longer. Another thirty went by. Hoping Rachele might still be inside, probably sleeping heavily, he got up and knocked on the door again. At first, he knocked quietly; then he began to knock hard and to yell his wife's name. He knocked so hard that the skin of his knuckles began to peel and break. Another woman appeared by the fountain with a bucket on her head. Hearing Marcello knock and call out Rachele's name, the woman, her hands over her breast, in a whisper called out the name of God. It was Marcello, and Rachele had run away.

"Marcello, is it you?" the elderly woman asked after having put down the bucket.

Marcello, who had his face pressed onto the top of the door, immediately stopped. Then, with a sudden turn of the head, he looked in the direction of the fountain.

"Yes, it is I. Marcello! Who are you?" he asked, his voice trembling.

"You don't know me. I moved here during the bombardments. Rachele has talked to me about you."

"Rachele! Rachele! Where is she? Where has she gone with my daughter?"

The woman began to walk over with Marcello staring at her as she approached. By her manner, he sensed something was wrong.

"She's not here," she said. "Rachele will not come back this evening. She's away; she's run away. She thought you had died." "Died!" he exclaimed, knowing full well what had happened.

"Yes, she thought you were dead..." Marcello's eyes opened wide, a fierce expression flashing across his face, but saying nothing, however. He let the woman talk. "Your daughter is with Samuele. Do you know him?"

"Samuele! He's alive? He's come back? He's here with his mother and sister? He's alive?"

"Yes, he is alive. He is well except for his foot. I understand part of it froze off in Siberia. Outside of that, he is well."

"My child is there?"

"Yes."

"Where is Rachele?"

"I don't know."

"Did she go to Naples, or to the hills?"

"I don't know. The Red Cross letter arrived just a while ago. She couldn't be too far."

"She's in the hills, over at her relative's house?" he asked in an excited voice.

"I don't know!" the woman answered, frightened by Marcello's tone. "I don't know," she repeated. "But, please," she began to implore, "don't harm her. Rachele is not a bad woman. What happened to her happened to so many others. The war! Marcello, the war. Oh, God, believe me, the little I know her, she's a good woman who just made a mistake. Spare her. There've been worse ones."

"I'll decide that. Thank you for the information," he answered in a cold, impassive voice. Leaving the bundle on the ground, he walked away from the woman in the direction of Samuele's house. The woman held her arms across her breast as she looked at Marcello disappear in the silence of darkness just as he had appeared.

As fast as Marcello tried to walk, he could not quite move fast enough. He did not walk very long either before he was recognized. Old friends approached him with their greetings which he ignored. Above all, he refused advice or further information about his wife. While the grown-ups understood Marcello's state of mind and let him go on his way, the children that gathered around him persisted in asking him embarrassing questions about the war, the soldiers he had killed... much as they had done with Samuele. Though Marcello told them to go home, and though he would not answer their questions, they walked along with him, to his great annoyance. Marcello avoided them for a while. Finally, when they did not leave him, he became furious with rage. With awful, unkind words, he ordered them to go to their mothers. Though his voice roared, the children retreated only a few meters. When he began to walk again, the children at first hesitated; then picked up walking behind him. The nine-year-old child who had spoken with Samuele joined the group. Unaware of Marcello's disposition, he began to ask the same questions. Turned on him like a ferocious beast, Marcello picked up the dumfounded boy by the arms and pushed him against the wall of a neighbor's house, threatening at the top of his lungs that if he and the rest didn't go home he would strangle each and every one of them. Seeing their friend pinned to the wall, the other boys quickly took to their heels and disappeared.

"Do you understand?" Marcello yelled at the frightened boy, his eyes full of tears, his face grimacing with fear. He looked into Marcello's ferocious eyes and understood that he had but one choice. Sobbing, and with extreme fright, the boy answered with an almost inaudible yes. Marcello put him down. As the boy ran away, Marcello reached him with a kick, lifting him off the ground. From then on, until Marcello reached Samuele's house, no one disturbed him anymore, though the whole town now knew about Marcello, who was already being described as the *man of action*, the one who was going to accomplish *needed* justice. In truth, some privately rejoiced over the possibility that a killing was going to take place. Some even protested that Rachele, by taking to the hills, was going to deny them the spectacle. Some made Marcello understand their wish, a thing that infuriated him all the more.

Don Alfonso got word of Marcello's arrival and quickly rushed to Samuele's house, where Marcello stood outside the door waiting to knock. On seeing him, Don Alfonso shouted to Marcello, who, seeing Don Alfonso, waited for the priest to approach.

"Marcello?" Don Alfonso said in a soft voice.

"What do you want?" Marcello answered in a rough and unkind tone.

"Nothing, really. I haven't seen you in about three years. Remember, we were good friends. I just wanted to see if there was something I could do to help."

"You had your chance and didn't. I don't need you now. I don't want you. I don't want to have anything to do with any of the things you stand for."

"You haven't given up the word of God, Marcello, have you?"

"What God?" Marcello answered with cruel derision. "If he is there, he's nothing but a filthy beast," he spurted out. Then, closing his mouth, Marcello felt a tremor on his lips. His eyes became more fierce--the white shining with greater truculence in the bright moonlight. Don Alfonso dropped back, so great was his surprise at meeting with so resolute a man, a quality he did not remember Marcello to have had. Marcello would have put his hands on the priest just as quickly as on anyone else, and it mattered not whether he was Don Alfonso, the family friend and priest, or the devil himself.

Marcello's loud voice brought Samuele from inside. When the door opened, Marcello turned to see who it was, while Don Alfonso looked with the hope of seeing Samuele. Slowly, Samuele opened the door. He first saw the priest, who was directly in front. Then he turned to the side of the door and saw his old friend Marcello. After shouting Marcello's name, Samuele, a grave expression on his face, eagerly moved to shake the hand of his comrade-in-arms. Marcello shook hands, but not with the same enthusiasm, while Samuele put his arm over Marcello's shoulder. The two had fought together, survived several Russian prisoner of war camps and a concentration camp in Germany, only to separate thereafter, each thinking the other had died. Incredibly, they had returned by way of hell, still alive, back in their own town.

"Thank God, you're both alive," Don Alfonso interjected while Samuele held Marcello with his arm.

"It was luck," retorted Marcello. "... pure luck," he repeated in a softer tone, his head touching that of Samuele.

"Whatever it was, we're back and alive. And we can be thankful," Samuele added emphatically.

"Maybe you can," Marcello commented with an obvious bitterness.

"Your daughter is inside."

"Is she up?"

"No."

"Good. Let her sleep."

"Well, come in. I'm sure you want to see her anyway. Afterward, we'll have a bite to eat."

"I don't want to see her."

Samuele felt a cold chill run down his spine. Don Alfonso started to say something to appease Marcello. Instead, on catching Marcello's truculent eyes, Don Alfonso found himself making an awkward gesture with his hand; his lips moved, but no voice came out of his mouth.

"What the hell are you doing there? Go the hell back to your church and leave us alone."

"Marcello!" interrupted Samuele with concern. "He hasn't done anything to you. Be mad at Rachele..."

"That bitch has seen her last days."

"Marcello!" repeated Samuele.

"I best be going, Samuele. I hope you will calm him down," Don Alfonso said. Then turning to Marcello, the priest continued in a soft voice full of anguish. "I am sure that after tonight's rest you will feel better tomorrow morning. Goodnight, my young friends, and God be with you." The priest turned and walked away, saddened over his impotency in the face of a tragedy about to happen. The wrinkles on his face more marked, he looked to the ground. On passing by the tall poplars, he turned his eyes toward heaven, imploring the Virgin Mary to intercede on behalf of Rachele. He was so concentrated on his prayer that he didn't even notice the presence of the skyward poplars. His mind was fixed on the image of a frustrated and mindless Marcello bent on executing Rachele and thereby fulfilling justice, that senseless justice consummated everywhere by a most ferocious of blood instinct. "Marcello... oh, God, get some sense into him. There are other ways. Please help us find a better way..."

"Don Alfonso, Don Alfonso!" called Mr. Banno, coming toward the priest. "Marcello is here," he announced with a satisfied smile on his face.

"I'm returning from Samuele's house. Marcello is there in...with Samuele," Don Alfonso said, about to fall into heresy. "He's there with Samuele and in the hands of God. You should be returning to your home; it's much shorter to go back to your home. You belong in your home, especially this evening."

"I know where I belong," answered Mr. Banno impertinently, and took off for Samuele's house. When he got there, he found the two men about to enter the house.

"Samuele, Samuele, wait. It's me, Banno."

Samuele turned around, and Marcello likewise, both waiting for the gasping Mr. Banno to address them.

"Hi, Marcello, I'm glad to see you back. There's a lot of justice, a lot of cleaning up. I want to help you in whatever way I can."

"You're the same old nosy bastard we left behind. Someone should have shaven off that long nose of yours. But, there's still time for that, being it's still on your face. Someone will do it before you kick the bucket." Turning his back to Mr. Banno, Marcello walked inside with Samuele behind, his hand on Marcello's shoulder, the other shutting the door behind them.

Inside, Maria and Lucia were standing, one by the fireplace, where a little fire was burning, and the other by the table, both very tense. Maria, who was bent over the fire, greeted Marcello, and Lucia did likewise. Marcello first walked over to Maria, then to Lucia to shake hands. The women had serious expressions on their faces. After Marcello was invited to sit down, Lucia brought a bottle of white wine to the table. Samuele poured it into the glasses and welcomed his old comrade back to civilian life. During the toast, Marcello did not utter a sound; he simply looked into Samuele's eyes and drank his wine in a gulp. Maria offered to cook something, but Marcello refused to accept. Nevertheless, she put on the table a loaf of bread, sausages under olive oil, fresh cheese, and peppers under vinegar.

Samuele cut the bread, then sliced the sausages and passed them to Marcello, who took a slice of bread and some of the sausage. As soon as Samuele saw Marcello begin to eat, he poured more wine into the glasses. Maria and Lucia locked on, hoping to hear something about Marcello's plans, especially because Marcello's child was upstairs sleeping, and Rachele probably worrying herself to death. Maria thought of mentioning the child, but decided not to, deferring to her son.

Marcello did not say how much he appreciated the delicious bread and sausages, because he thought for sure those very things would have tasted better if he had had them at his house with Rachele overlooking his shoulder and with the baby on his lap, holding her with one hand and eating and drinking with the other. Instead, there he was at the home of his friend eating someone else's bread and wine, and to receive shelter for himself and his child, having little choice by to accept the invitation to spend the night with Samuele.

While Maria and Lucia were upstairs fixing the bed for Marcello, Samuele took the opportunity to ask him about his plans. He asked Marcello first to go see his child and then talk about resolving the problem with his wife.

"Do you want them to bring the baby down here, or do you want to go up to see her. She's very pretty."

"Samuele, I do wish to see her at this time. And I don't want her to see me. Nor do I want her to know I ever existed."

"But you do exist. You're her father."

"I know that."

"Then, you're not making sense."

"Nothing makes sense."

"Why don't you want to see your daughter?"

"Samuele, please! I just went through it with the priest out there. I don't intend to have to go through the same thing again with you."

"Don't worry, Marcello--no pressure of any kind, except, you're not getting any sympathy from me. We had to put up with so much, we needn't add to it, except that we have to be true to ourselves. You and I have to be true to ourselves, otherwise, the value of what we did will have no meaning--not the meaning you and I gave it.

"You haven't forgotten, I am sure. Besides, what you do here is your business; we no longer need each other's help. Here, we don't have to worry about survival. No guns are aimed at us, no communist soldier commanding us. Togliatti is not here to identify Italian black and German brown shirts to make execution more promptly terminal--remember how we were saved? You said we were proletarians. Otherwise, we'd be in those graves and in those rivers whose waters still run with our soldiers' blood. And we carried bodies to those waters and to those graves. Never a mark of any kind. You and I agreed to carry their grave marks in our hearts and in our minds," Samuele continued in a monotone, with Marcello remaining silent, his eyes moving from those of Samuele to an empty space in the dark corner of the room.

"We don't have to worry about the cold, and there is always something to eat. No one to tell us where to sleep with or with whom to sleep. No one will tell us to go here or there, when, how, and why. Here, you may choose me as your friend, or you may reject me. You can tell the priest where to go. But you cannot deny the fact that upstairs your child is sleeping. She's yours. She is your responsibility, not mine or anyone else's. My sister's child is also here. She's not married, as you know. Her baby also has a right to a father, and doesn't have one. Your daughter has a real father, and you're trying to deny her what is legally and naturally hers. After all we went through, after the thousands of people we've seen go *peacefully* to their death, after the many times you swore you'd love your own baby to death if you pulled through--don't you remember how many times you said it when we saw other children heartlessly executed. How many times, how many children! You're not forgetting all of a sudden, are you?. Have you forgotten the miseries, the inhumanity, the nothingness we were reduced to. Yet, we clung to each other and made it. The thought of that little girl upstairs pulled you through while so many of our friends fell to those savage brutes. Remember the indignity in seeing so many civilized people fall prey to those brutes. Remember how many times we used the word *indignity*? The thing is, most succumbed, and you and I--because we stuck together, because we had memories and dreams, we defeated our enemies by staying alive. Because, while we are eating this bread and sausages, and drinking this great wine, I guarantee you that those Russian brutes do not have a pot to piss in, let alone enough food or decent living quarters. Remember they gave us crap only when they had it; remember they ate the same crap we often threw away. Then we went through Germany and saw what those people did to other people. Between the Communists in Russia and the Nazis in Germany, they probably tie for having had the worst mass murderers the world has known.

"Remember, we survived in spite of them, because even though a few of us survived, for as insignificant as it may seem, ours was the real victory. We're here, Marcello! We made it! Ours was never the end but always the beginning no matter where we were or how badly we fared. I've begun again, right here, and I'm afraid that you haven't come back to start again; you've come to end, to put an end to our victory. Marcello, you can't let them be the winners, not after all we've been through, not after we've returned. The things the Russians and Germans did cannot compare to the things Lucia and Rachele did. No one here has killed anyone, no one except fools, and we have our share.

"When Lucia heard I was coming back, she ran away. She was scared and had every right to be. The few of us fortunate to be back, we cannot become the criminals we've condemned. We detested them then, even in our sleep. You may have already forgotten all that. Perhaps this will help you remember," Samuele said, in a trembling voice.

He put his hand into his pocket, and pulled out the peculiar wallet which he gently placed on the table. Samuele stared at it and Marcello did likewise, both maintaining a deep and, what seemed, a long silence, while their eyes remained fixed on the object.

They had taken it from an abandoned shop in Germany, alongside a few bars of soap, to discover, afterward, that both the soap and wallet had the same origin: bones and skin of a human being.

After realizing what it was made of, Samuele and Marcello decided to keep the wallet. As there was only one, Samuele opted to hold it, as a reminder and proof of the degree of men's inhumanity against other human beings, both agreeing to refer to it whenever either might contemplate or be involved in acts of violence against others.

"You've forgotten, haven't you!" Samuele charged with anger. "You've forgotten the agreement we made, that you yourself suggested. I didn't suggest it! Now, you're bent on doing what those brutes did. You want to become like those ferocious brutes we left behind. Go upstairs and take that child into your arms. Kiss her, and be thankful. We're here. We're alive. You're alive with your wife and daughter. Rachele was not as mean and cruel as you and I were prior to being drafted. She didn't do the things we did during the first months of our military service. Remember those young women--those poor bastards! What we did to them. Animals! Marcello, that's what we were, except that animals do not behave beyond their instincts. What these people have done is nothing compared to what we did, you and I. What we did--and, now, you have the gall to refuse to see your child. If only I had one, any child, from any woman. I don't have one, and I doubt I ever will. You know what I mean.

"You have a child, and you're trying to cut her off. You're trying to cut yourself off. Go upstairs to see her. Tomorrow morning, we'll go get your wife. You can start over again. Make it the beginning, not the end. Rachele is not a bad woman. She still loves you. You can learn to love her again. You may even love her as before. Nothing is ever the same when something like this happens. But so many things happen, so many things. Forgive. You've got to learn to forgive, Marcello. Forgive. If it weren't for this none of us would be around now. We would be destroyed by our own acts, our own crimes. Forgive Marcello. Learn how to forgive yourself. Do you hear what I am saying, or am I talking to a stone wall? Answer me," Samuele demanded, his eyes flashing with anger.

Marcello looked impassively, detached, but not unconcerned. He had heard Samuele; he heard his friend and had understood his comrade-in-arms, except that he didn't believe in those words any more. Everything was empty. His soul had left his body.

"I am an animal, and what I feel is instinct. I have urges. I am an animal. I always thought I was one, but never really believed in it. I am one now, Samuele. I am an animal, a pig, a snake; in addition, I am a worthless bastard with no right to live. I never really had the right. Why! Why did I pull out of that line? Why? Why was I spared? Why were we spared? I thought there was a God who had helped me. What a hoax! I wasn't killed. I wish I had been. I wish the hell I had. I resigned myself to it, just like the rest of those poor bastards. And what would have been the sense? Death was such a sure thing. How did we escape it, how did we? I thought there was a God. We used to say there was. There isn't, Samuele. We are worse than the animals. They're hungry, they kill, and they eat, and never know that they themselves might be the next meal for others. We know, and that's about all: in one form or other, maybe not now, not tomorrow, but for sure the following day. Our days are numbered. And if we live longer, we only do that to serve the scheme of others. We die knowing we're dying. Look at that," Marcello looked at the wallet on the table. Samuele stared at it. "Look at it," he repeated with tremendous emotion. "Look at it, look!" Marcello exclaimed, raising his voice.

Maria and Lucia, who were upstairs and had heard most of the conversation, decided to return to the kitchen. When they appeared, Marcello and Samuele stopped talking. Samuele quickly reached for the wallet, and, before either of the women could see it, he put it back into his pocket.

Snatching some bread, Samuele brought it to his mouth, but did not eat it. Instead, he held it in his hands. Marcello, meanwhile, looked silently into Maria's face, then stared at Lucia, who lowered her face in shame. Realizing he was embarrassing her, Marcello immediately stopped staring. Maria asked Marcello to go up to see his child so that afterward they could all go to bed.

"I'm not going to see her tonight, Maria, but I would like to get some sleep, if you don't mind."

"If you tell me the time you'll be getting up, I'll have a good breakfast ready for you and Samuele."

"It'll be a little late, if you don't mind. But don't worry about me. I'll just grab something when I get up... Are you going to bed?" Marcello asked of Samuele.

"Yes... Go see her first."

"Look, Samuele, I know what I am doing. Please let me alone. If you don't want me here, I can leave. I think I can always break down the door of my house."

"I don't want you to leave. You're wrong, dead wrong. You haven't seen your daughter in years, and you don't know what she looks like. You yearned to see her. Now you're here, and you don't want to see her. She's sleeping next to our room."

"No, Samuele. Absolutely not."

Without saying another word, the four went upstairs. Maria and Lucia joined the two children; Samuele and Marcello went to the other room. On his way up, Marcello looked closely at the stairway and the flimsy black door off the small bedroom where a makeshift bed had been added. Before getting into bed, Samuele placed the wallet on the old bureau and then turned to Marcello. Both looked at each other for a few seconds. Finally, after saying good-night, they got into their beds. Samuele turned off the pale light hanging from the faded ceiling.

In the other room, Lucia was already in bed with the two children. Maria, on the other hand, was kneeling before a picture of the Immaculate Conception, praying earnestly. After about an hour, she went to bed, her head bent low, exceedingly sad and worried over what she felt might occur the following day.

Samuele was also worried. Unable to sleep, he kept his eyes closed. Unbeknown to Samuele, Marcello did the same. Occasionally they opened their eyes to see if the other was asleep. Marcello was in a better position to see Samuele, as some light came through the partially opened window. Outside, the moon shone brighter than ever.

In his makeshift bed, Marcello thought about the things he had done and what he had seen during the war. He wondered about the many enemy soldiers he might have killed--he had killed many, all innocent *bastards*, as innocent as he was in doing the killing. What a feeling it was to kill and to know that his turn may be next! He remembered his friends laying dead next to him, their mutilated and bloody bodies always making him sick to his stomach. What had they done to deserve that king of man-made death? What had he done to deserve that atrocious punishment? As if that weren't enough, now he had to endure the kind of humiliation he had not thought about. Marcello turned to one side, his face toward the wall. He opened his eyes.

"What a life!" he said to himself. What kind of humanity was this and of which he was part--evil everywhere! The programmed mass killings he had seen, that last-minute human wailing, those voices crying out, the experiments, the special details--why did they endure those things knowing that death was imminent--and the manner of death! And he was the witness to only a small part. What happened elsewhere? No, life was not worth living, and those who made life unlivable must die.

He remembered the day when Togliatti--Palmiro himself--the Italian communist leader working on behalf of the Soviet Union, the one who identified the Italian soldiers: if they were recognizable Fascists or had Fascist leanings, he assigned to one side to be summarily executed; those still standing attended indoctrination classes, quickly becoming proletarians. Of these, few survived, however, Marcello and Samuele being among them.

Togliatti had brought other news from home: Mussolini, together with his mistress Clara Petacci had been captured outside the city of Milan and hung upside down, their bodies abused by the angry mob. They got their right justice, Marcello thought to himself, and some people dared call it uncivilized justice. What contrast! Those who spat at the dead bodies were called crude and uncivilized; those who planned for the mass-extermination of whole populations were respected everywhere. As he reasoned within himself, he stared at the wall impassively. Those thoughts made him want to choke. Nevertheless, he kept on thinking, reasoning, asking why, asking himself why. Why did Rachele abandon herself to the detriment of her baby and husband? Soon, she'd be abandoning her own life. So many people abandon their lives to satisfy the whims of who-knows-what hunger. Rachele could easily have given up her life. Having played her part with the monster, she must not be allowed to go on. Yes, Marcello had his own account to settle, and he was going to settle it once and for all, except that his settlement would be with the monster within, and not even with those distant brutes.

How about his little girl? She'd be better off with both parents gone forever. She'd stand a better chance on living a proper life. It was better, too, if she never saw her father.

Marcello's mental rambling was not limited to him. Samuele often did the same thing, and it was hardly daydreaming.

From the other bed, Samuele looked at his tormented friend. He knew Marcello was not asleep. If only he could do something, anything, to assuage his friend's feelings. He would even pray to God. Yes, he would pray to God. With this thought, Samuele finally closed his eyes to the desolate room. But sleep is not always a cure. Samuele had hoped that the night's sleep might have helped in uplifting Marcello's state, with the hope to find Marcello in a better frame of mind and willing to discuss the future in the morning.

Eventually, Marcello, too, fell asleep, but projected no hope of any kind. All he thought about before closing his eyes was that sleep should not betray him. Neither his sleep nor that of others should betray him, especially at that moment.

The two slept in the noiseless room, its walls marked by the moon's rays coming from openings by the windows.

Toward early morning, its beams fell on the surface of the chest of drawers with some of the light reflecting off of the wallet. Outside, birds were already beginning to chirp, while roosters everywhere began announcing daybreak.

Maria awoke as usual. Silently, she dressed and went downstairs to begin to prepare for her daily chores. It was still dark when she got downstairs. She went to one side of the kitchen where she picked up branches for the fire. As she lit the fire, she heard the birds chirping outside. Strange, she thought to herself, that she should be hearing them now as she always heard them on opening the door. Short of shrugging her shoulders at something she felt more than she was able to rationalize, she went on with her chores. As the small flame began to envelope the larger branches, she looked toward the door. Sensing something was wrong, she walked toward it to find it was open. Yet, she remembered having closed it. She looked to see if anyone might have tampered with the lock from the outside. On finding it in tact, and noticing the door opened from the inside, she immediately thought of Marcello. She ran upstairs and opened the door to find Marcello's bed empty. She looked around the room, and all she could see was her son still sleeping. Regretfully, she went to her son and awoke him.

"Marcello is gone! The door was open! He must have gone after Rachele."

Samuele's heart began to palpitate with a sudden rhythm. He jumped out of bed, got his clothes, and quickly put them on, telling his mother that he was going after Marcello.

"I hope he won't find her," Samuele said, fear in his eyes. Maria watched while her son rushed about getting his things. Then, without saying a word, he ran outside.

The moon was still shining, though light from the east was already filtering through the cool countryside. A small breeze permeated the air, making the leaves quiver noisily. The tall poplars stood dark on one side, their leaves at the top already reflecting transparent silvery rays.

Samuele hurried through the countryside, unaware of the bountiful nature he had been marveling about since his return. He ran as hard as he could, stopping to walk occasionally to catch his breath, his foot functioning as though it were normal.

At his approach, the birds feeding in the fields and bushes flew away in fright. Samuele ran desperately downhill and panted heavily uphill. In no time, he was at the foot of the big hills where the pathway became much more rugged, with rocks scattered every where and huge boulders on either side of the torrent-tormented pathway. Samuele jumped from side to side, realizing that if he wanted to keep Marcello from committing his crime, he would have to get there before Marcello did. Not knowing when Marcello had left, Samuele could not take chances of slowing down, though occasionally he had to slow down to avoid collapsing altogether. After about thirty minutes of running and walking up the crooked and steep path, he came to the side of the mountain. Up from there, at about half a kilometer, he could see the house where Rachele was staying. As he came from below, the whole sky suddenly opened. To the east the sun's rays were already filtering down from the distant peaks. Samuele could clearly see the sun but did not pause to look at it; he ran along the path that clung to one side of the steep, precipitous hill. Below it, the drop was so long that at its bottom it was still dark. Samuele, however, did not bother to look below, his eyes fixed forward, hoping to see Marcello or any one else. Above all, he wanted to see Rachele. Having walked around the last blind curve, he finally could see the house. As he went around the final bend, he saw Marcello straight ahead, looking like a giant, and standing below the branches of a great oak above the steep cliff. He had a rope in his hand and seemed to be looking up at the branches. Come to a sudden stop, Samuele hid behind a hedge and waited to see what his friend was doing. When Marcello began to throw one end of the rope over the branch that hung above the cliff, Samuele quickly understood and immediately rushed forward, startling the un-expecting Marcello, who stood almost motionless, with one end of the rope in his hand.

"What are you doing?" Samuele shouted, breathing heavily.

"Go back home and take care of my daughter."

"She's cared for. Where's Rachele?"

"You needn't worry about her any longer. She's resting in peace. Soon you won't be worrying about me. Go back home, Samuele!"

"Have you seen her?"

"Yes."

"Where is she?"

"In bed."

"You haven't harmed her!"

"She got her due."

"Let's go up together; I want to see her."

"Go ahead; I'll wait here."

"All right," Samuele answered walking forward. As he was about to bypass Marcello, Samuele suddenly jumped on his friend. Marcello tried to dodge him but couldn't. Both fell to the ground, Marcello screaming to Samuele to leave him alone. Struggling to get a hold of Marcello, Samuele fell to the ground with Marcello on top of him. Finally, Samuele got the rope away from Marcello. As he did, Samuele lost his grip on his friend, who, coming suddenly to his feet, moved toward the back side of the pathway while Samuele was still on the ground. Without losing a moment, Marcello sprinted toward the edge of the cliff. Samuele quickly moved in his way, raising his head. Marcello, who had already started to run, could not change his direction and ran into Samuele's head. The impact brought them both sprawling onto the ground, with Marcello landing on the edge of the cliff. Samuele quickly got up and pounced on Marcello, taking hold of his opponent's arms, only to find that Marcello did not react. Samuele quickly raised his head and turned Marcello's face. Seeing his eyes closed, he got up on his knees and looked for the rope. Without wasting one moment, he tied the hands of his helpless friend, then, wrapping the rope around his whole body, he dragged Marcello up to an old stump and tied the rope snugly around it.

After making sure that his knots were secure, he began to run uphill toward the solitary little house, whose rough white stone walls could be seen from afar. As he approached the house, he looked around for signs of life. Other than the few chickens pecking around the house, he saw no sign of either Rachele or of her relatives. He ran to the front door, pushed it open, and called out to Rachele. When no one answered, he ran up the stairs to the bedroom. On reaching the top of the stairs, he saw Rachele in the bed, the side of her face reposed on the pillow, the rest of her body neatly covered with the white sheet up to her neck. Samuele softly called her name. On getting no response, Samuele pulled back the sheet. Looking at her nude body, he whispered Rachele's name once more.

"Rachele," he gently called out again, not wanting to startle her. As she did not answer, he called her name another time, and still she did not answer. He moved to one side and looked into her face. Noticing that she was not breathing, he moved her head up, placing his hand on her warm forehead. Then he pulled off the sheet altogether and turned her over to see if there were any wounds. Not seeing traces of blood or bruises, he put his hand below her left breast, holding his hand over her heart for a few tense moments. When he did not feel the heartbeat, he leaned over and placed his ear on it. Not hearing anything, he quickly put his hand over her mouth and nose. He pulled her lips apart to discover they were badly battered on the inside. He could see that Marcello had suffocated her with the pillow. Samuele opened her mouth, checked her tongue, and as he had done many times before, pinched her nose with his finger and began to breathe down her mouth, keeping a steady cadence. Anxiously, he kept pushing his breath down through her mouth, and still Rachele did not respond. He continued giving her artificial respiration for twenty minutes. He moved her arms to one side, then from side to side. He pressed on her stomach, then on her heart.

Once again he began frantically to breathe into her mouth and kept on for another fifteen minutes. Almost completely exhausted and realizing there was nothing more he could do, he slumped on her breast, his eyes filled with tears. Though he tried to keep himself from crying, he began to sob. After a while, he raised his head, picked up the end of the sheet and covered her entire body. Walking backward toward the stairway, he turned and ran downstairs.

From the front of the door, Samuele looked down to the tree where a diminutive Marcello was still laying on the ground, his hands tied to the tree.

"She's dead," Samuele said, his face full of anguish.

"I know she's dead. I killed her," answered Marcello, who, having gained his consciousness, squirmed trying to look up at Samuele.

"We made a promise to each other that, once out of the war, we would not kill anyone or anything, that we would try to save lives, not to destroy them. Couldn't you just have given her a beating she deserved and let it go at that?"

"No, Samuele, no. No reason to burden people further; there is no reason to. Let me loose and go on your way."

"I'm not letting you loose."

"Yes, you are. You have no right to keep me bound."

"I'm taking you to the police."

"No!" Marcello yelled, his voice making an echo below.

"I'm taking you in, whether you like it or not," Samuele answered in a quiet but resolute tone.

"No, no! I've got to die. Let me loose. Throw me over the cliff. Let me go, let me go!" Marcello yelled desperately.

Samuele unwound the rope from around Marcello's legs, making sure that the hands were bound tightly behind his back. Marcello kept on squirming, trying to get away. As he tried to leap up, he felt the slack of the rope tightening, causing him to fall heavily on the ground.

"I can tie your legs again and keep you tied to this stump if you wish. I can then go to the police who will then come to get you. What do you prefer?"

"Let me go. Untie me. I want to die and nothing else. It's my life; I don't want it. Get these goddam ropes off of me. Get them off. I want to die now. I don't want to wait. I don't want her to see me. Don't tell her I ever existed. Get the ropes off. Just don't say you saw me. Let me go free," Marcello yelled, tears flowing from his eyes on recalling his little girl.

"I can take you there myself or I can go get them. What do you want?"

"Let me go free."

"All right, let's go. I'm taking you in."

"No! No! Get the ropes off of me."

Samuele slowly undid the knot around the stump. Holding the rope tightly in his hands with its end twice around his right hand, Samuele ordered Marcello to get up.

"No!" he yelled desperately at the top of his lungs. "I beg you, Samuele, I beg you, let me go. I want to die. Let me die. I want to die," he repeated in earnest.

"I know you do, Marcello. But I can't break our promise. Remember, we made a solemn oath not to kill and to save lives as much as possible. This suicide of yours would mean murder to me. And I'm not about to break that promise, especially now, and especially with you."

"Samuele, I now understand that things are easier said than done. I understand it now. I also understand that I cannot go on living with the thought of my little girl out there. Please, Samuele, the pain and the punishment will be far greater if I stay alive than if I'm dead. You cannot punish me that way. We never agreed to that."

"Get up! Here, I'll help you. Come on, no tricks, and no more nonsense." Samuele bent down to pull Marcello up. As he did so, Marcello turned suddenly and kicked Samuele in the stomach. Samuele bent, almost doubling with pain.

Marcello leaped to his feet and rushed toward the edge of the ravine. Samuele tightened on the rope. Just as Marcello was about to reach the edge, Samuele pulled the rope with all his strength, causing Marcello to fall dead weight face down on the rough ground.

"I'm taking you in, even if I have to batter you on the way. Now, get up." Keeping a little slack in the rope, Samuele moved to help Marcello up. Seeing the side of his friend's face badly scratched, Samuele drew Marcello to the side of the pathway, making him sit down. Then pulling his handkerchief from his pocket, he cleaned the dirt and blood from Marcello's face. The cuts were rather deep and the blood kept on flowing.

"I'm going to have to tie the handkerchief around your face. You're bleeding a lot. See what you made me do? Here, let me tie it. Turn your face, and no more tricks." Samuele tied the handkerchief snugly over the side, being sure to keep it from obstructing Marcello's sight. Then, grasping one strand of rope that was wound around Marcello's chest, Samuele pulled his friend up and began to walk, keeping Marcello on his right side, away from the edge of the cliff. Slowly, they made their way down the precipitous path, Marcello walking with his head bent toward the ground. Samuele tried to converse, but Marcello did not utter one single word all the way. The only time that Samuele got any reaction at all, and it was only a short glare, was when Samuele reminded Marcello of his strong belief in God.

The two walked on slowly, Samuele limping heavily. His foot began to hurt him, but he said nothing. Marcello noticed it. As they walked, Marcello, with his head bent low, looked at his friend's tired feet. However, Marcello realizing that the closer they came to the town, the fewer chances of a get-a-way, thought about ways of taking advantage of Samuele's weakness. Samuele, who had gone through many similar situations, knew all too well Marcello's thoughts.

"Remember, no tricks," Samuele said, getting a better grip on the rope, with the hope of dissuading Marcello from trying anything. Samuele knew the effect of show of force.

"You're no better than our captors," Marcello responded, having realized it was too late for him to attempt a get-away. They were on flat land, and the ropes so tightly wound around him kept him in pain. Marcello resigned, therefore, to be taken in peaceably.

When Samuele and Marcello arrived at the edge of the town, the sun was shining bright. The villagers were moving about with their daily chores. On seeing Samuele leading Marcello in that fashion, they all got very excited. Immediately the news spread. Before the two could arrive at the station, manned by two policemen, a group of people had already gathered there to witness the unusual incident, puzzled by the event wherein Samuele was bringing in his own friend, and not sure whether to admire him or hate him the more.

Amid comments and questions from the noisy and inquisitive crowd, Samuele and Marcello made their way to the front door where one of the uniformed policemen was on duty. Marcello never raised his head, though many people tried to cheer him up by telling him he had done the right thing. Many of them went so far as to assure him that they would start a collection for his defense. Marcello, however, kept his head bent and avoided any eye contact with them.

Mr. Banno, who was in front of the door next to the policeman, waited for Marcello to get close, then jumped in front of them to praise Marcello for his courage. He put his hand on Marcello's shoulder promising him that he, Mr. Banno, would see to it that justice would be on his side. Mr. Banno tried to get some sort of response, but Marcello, after a brief defiant glance, continued on his way, allowing

Samuele to escort him inside. When both were inside the office, the policeman ordered the crowd to disperse, and closed the door.

Inside, Samuele unbound Marcello. On feeling the last strand of rope off him, Marcello spread his arms out. The policeman ran his hands through Marcello's clothes. Not finding anything, and having been told by Samuele that Marcello had tried to commit suicide, the policeman took away Marcello's belt. Then he stripped Marcello down to the waist. As the policeman did that, the marks of the rope became evident. Samuele felt sorry and apologized to Marcello, who did not answer.

"And the face," the policeman asked.

"He tried to get away, and fell on his face when I pulled the rope," Samuele answered to the policeman's satisfaction. Then he turned to Marcello. "You should have told me the rope was tight. I would have loosened it if you had said something."

Marcello did not answer. The policeman then spoke. "Before admitting you, you have to make a statement. Sit down here," the policeman ordered. After putting Marcello's shirt on his back, the policeman asked Marcello to make a statement. Marcello nodded and sat down.

"I killed my wife Rachele early this morning by putting a pillow on her mouth and nose and holding it there until she no longer moved. After having waited a few minutes to insure she was dead, I covered her with the sheet and left. No one was around at the time that I killed her. I also planned to kill myself by hanging. I was just throwing the rope over the branch of a tree when Samuele arrived. He jumped me and took away the rope. He bound me and left me tied to a stump and went up to the house to see Rachele. After a long while he came back. I tried to get away but failed, and he's taken me here. That's all."

"Did your wife resist?"

"Hardly. She expected to die. It was clearly visible on her face when she saw me."

"What happened to your face?"

"In the fight with Samuele, I fell to the ground."

"I see. Anything else you want to say?"

"No."

"Very well. Take him to the cell, and check out his bruises," the policeman instructed his assistant. Marcello got up and walked peacefully to the cell followed by the policeman, while Samuele remained behind.

"What he said, is it true?" asked the policeman of Samuele.

"It is."

"Did you check on Rachele. Was she dead."

"She's dead."

"Marcello said you stayed away a long time."

"Yes. When I got there she had been dead for only a few minutes. Her body was warm. I tried to give her artificial respiration. She didn't respond. I'm sure she is dead."

While the two talked, the crowd outside grew larger and noisier. From inside, they could hear Mr. Banno, who spoke loudest and more than anyone else. Unexpectedly, the door opened and in marched Mr. Banno, desirous to know for himself and the crowd the disposition of Marcello.

"He is in jail," the policeman stated. Then, calling his aide, the policeman instructed him to prepare another cell for Mr. Banno, unless, of course, Mr. Banno were to go outside and mind his own business. Mr. Banno quickly turned around and ran for the door. On stepping out, he was jeered by the crowd hailing him with derision.

"They put him in jail," he reported.

"No kidding," answered one. "He's just killed his wife."

"Very funny," retorted Mr. Banno. "She deserved it. If anyone did, it was her."

Inside, Samuele and the policemen discussed other details; outside, the crowd grew larger. Mr. Banno defended himself valorously from the group that continued to deride him with comments that went from the vulgar to the comical.

"You're all fools, I tell you," he yelled to the laughing crowd. "We have a hero who is in jail and you're laughing..."

"...at you, Banno," cried out a voice from the side. The crowd burst into laughter and immediately stopped laughing when the door opened unexpectedly and Samuele stepped out. The crowd turned to him. Some cheered, others clapped their hands. They knew Samuele had saved Marcello's life. That took courage, some thought. They demonstrated their appreciation and respect by their exuberant cheers. But they weren't just happy because Samuele had saved Marcello. Though they did not say so openly, they were even happier over the fact that Rachele had been killed. Sensing that the people were overjoyed at the recent death, he became angry, and began to yell at the top of his lungs. Quickly, the crowd stopped, dumfounded to listen to what their unpredictable man had to say.

"What are you cheering about? We've had one tragedy; we almost had another, and you're all laughing and joking. You ought to be ashamed of yourselves. You're acting as though you've done nothing wrong in your lives. No scars on your conscience, is that right?. Go on home and take care of your own affairs. There's plenty of work to be done; go do it. Clean up your yards; clean up your lives. I'm trying to do that very thing for myself. What kind of people are you? Aren't we men and women? We weren't born hyenas; does the spilling of human blood make you happy?" Samuele shouted with vehemence. At those words, the crowd became silent. On seeing many with their heads bowed in shame, Samuele continued in a softer voice. "Let us all go home. Go home; that's where you belong. You and I don't belong here."

"We only wanted to help," intervened Mr. Banno, causing the people to raise their heads, waiting to hear Samuele's answer.

"You can help by going home. Marcello had been under tremendous pressure. He almost committed suicide. Do you think he is in the mood to listen to you out here?"

"We think what he did is right and we want him to know it," Mr. Banno reiterated.

"What you think is right may not be what I may think is right. Now, go on home. You all have work to do."

"Who are you to tell us what to do. Just because you were in the war doesn't give you the right to tell us what to do. Who do you think you are?" Mr. Banno contended in a voice that was far less strong than his statement which was further weakened by the recurrent hissing and giggling on the part of the crowd. Several children had also gathered; they laughed the loudest when Mr. Banno spoke. Feeling ridiculed and humiliated, he reacted in a manner he had not intended. "Women who bring shame to their families have to be punished. Marcello did right, and both you and these darn fools around me don't think he needs help..."

"...pass the hat to him," yelled a voice from behind. "That'll shut his trap."

"No one has the right to do what Marcello did," Samuele reiterated, feeling frustrated.

"Action is always better than no action. At least Marcello's cleansed his name." Mr. Banno's counter point exasperated the crowed. Whether or not they agreed with Mr. Banno's stand, his insinuation was made mute by the crowed's persistently derisive and insolent boos.

Samuele, who had had enough by now, fixed his eyes on Mr. Banno.

"I am not living in shame, I assure you. My sister's sins are hers and her alone, just as your sins are yours and some of your sins are far greater than those of my sister. As for you, Mr. Portabandiera, you're quick to judge others and to draw conclusions which have little if any bearing on you. We're all tempted one time or another. Wait till all is over in your household."

"No one can say anything about my family. My Rosa is a perfect example of what all young ladies ought to be."

"You can say that again," interrupted a voice from the crowd. The crowd looked and laughed. They knew Mr. Banno's Rosa all too well. Laughing at each other, some brought their hands up with fingers representing horns and moving them up and down.

As they frolicked, Samuele looked on amazed, unable to believe his very eyes. A while before, a man had been taken in for having killed another human being, and the crowd had already forgotten about the very thing they had gathered for.

There in front of him stood Mr. Banno. Were it not for his obvious stupidity and the fact that the people knew him well, Mr. Banno could have been a candidate to higher office much as Mussolini, Hitler and Stalin. Not having much other recourse with which to counteract the obviously disrespectful display of the people, Mr. Banno, who felt like a misunderstood champion, began to speak again. "Laugh, you fools. Laugh all you want. The only honorable man is inside behind bars..."

"...and he has killed," Samuele answered with deep-rooted conviction.

"...and you, Samuele," Mr. Banno retorted with sarcasm, "how many did you kill?"

At those words, the crowd became tense. Samuele, realizing he should not have engaged in any conversation of any kind, moved away through the crowd. "I've had better conversations with asses," he said as he passed by Mr. Banno.

Separating into two parts, the crowd allowed Samuele to pass through. As he left, they cheered, and soon dispersed, leaving Mr. Banno mumbling to himself. He had been left almost alone when Don Alfonso appeared from below.

"Christ," Mr. Banno said to himself, "all I need is him now. I'd better be going." Turning in the opposite direction, he left with his head bowed.

CHAPTER 17

The time to harvest the wheat had come, and farmers all around were busy cutting the golden stems whose kernels were to guarantee the villagers precious bread for the coming year. Old men and women, young folks and children, all joined in on the harvest. The men handled the sickles while the women and children gathered the stalks to form them into sheafs. As they worked they would occasionally break into song. When one group working in one field stopped singing, a group from another field would pick up, reminiscent of the chorus in *Cavalleria Rusticana*. At times all would sing together, making the valley and hills come alive. The children formed their own choir, and their voices could be distinguished from those of the women and men. They did not sing the ballads of the elderly; they sang simple jingles and *ritornelli*. They were not old enough to appreciate and sing about the subject-matter of the ballads of their elders. The harder they worked, the harder they sang. On the roads of the countryside, tractor--led threshers moved about, stopping at every place where the sheafs had been accumulated into tall well-designed wheat stacks. While men and machines worked in these areas, men and animals did likewise in the more remote farms.

Samuele had gotten a position as the operator of one of the tractors, his responsibility being to set up the tractor to the huge threshing machine and to help the farmers process the sheafs. He was happy going from one trashing place to another, though he worked very hard. At lunch time, he enjoyed walking to nearby farmers singing in the fields. Whenever he stayed a bit too long, the farmers would call him back to start the engine, and he would rush back. He also looked forward to the early evening when he would stop to maintain the machinery and shut everything down, thus giving him a chance to hear the other farmers sing in the fields. There was no time to lose, they would say. And Samuele would answer that they were right. He understood that the wheat had to be threshed in an allotted amount of time, especially when the weather was good and the corn fields were already sprouting their beards.

"Aren't you tired?" asked Maria of Samuele on his return late in the evening. "You've never done this before. Don't you think you're overdoing it? You ought to take it easy."

"It's not going to last forever. I can take it."

"Where will you be tomorrow?"

"At Franca's. Mr. Banno has his wheat there too."

"Why don't you give up the job? We have plenty to do around here."

"You talk as though something were going to happen. What's bothering you? Is it Franca? Are you against my seeing her?"

"No, Samuele. I think she is a fine woman. I think you would be happy with her."

"Then what?"

"I just think you are working too hard, that's all."

Early next morning, Samuele made his way to Franca's farm, where he had already set up the tractor and the huge belt-driven threshing machine. When he got there everyone was ready for the day's work. He greeted them and without saying much more, started the tractor. After a brief period of warming up, he signaled to Ernesto that all was ready.

Toni climbed to the top of the thresher, while two others climbed to the top of the wheat stack. Ernesto signaled back to Samuele, who engaged the gears. The tremendous clattering scared the animals at first, but after a while, the chickens were all back around the machine, pecking at the grain.

The two men on the stack each in turn handed one sheaf of wheat to Toni, who in turn broke the binding and shoved the wheat stalks head first into the thresher's opening. Occasionally he looked down at Samuele, who, together with Ernesto, held the burlap sacks at the bottom of the thresher. The women lined up to one side to carry the sacks away, while Ernesto helped lift the heavy sacks on top of the women's heads, his daughter Franca being one of them. With straw dust in her hair and clothes, she came up on her turn. Samuele looked at her, but Franca turned her glance toward her father, who noticed his daughter's strange behavior but did not try to understand why. Ernest motioned her to stoop a little as he placed the sack of wheat on her head. Staggering slightly, Franca quickly regained her balance. In humiliation, she walked away silently, with Samuele looking at her as she walked around to the back where she disappeared amidst the dust gushing out of the machine's jet.

By noon, as predicted, they had finished with Ernesto's wheat. Samuele stopped the machines, and the farmers stopped working. All walked to the well to wash up before lunch, which was being served by Ernesto's family. While they waited to wash, Franca and her mother set the table outside under the sprawling elm tree. As they sat, they heard from afar the other machines come to a halt. But some singing was still going on. In a few moments, though, that too stopped. With the exception of a few localized discussions, the whole valley became silent under the burning sun, intermittently broken by the noisy cicadas scattered among the trees. Even the birds seemed to take refuge among the cool leaves in the trees or among the tall rows of corn stalks.

At the table, Ernesto sat next to Samuele. Toni sat with the two men at the other end of the table with the women sitting at one side. Franca and her mother did not sit down, as they were serving.

When Franca came out with the food, Samuele looked up at her, but Franca avoided his glance. Toni, though he made believe he was interested in his discussion with two farmer friends, looked out the corner of his eye at Samuele and at his sister. When Franca brought the food to Toni, their eyes met. Neither spoke, but it was obvious there were threats on both sides.

"Tell your mother to get the wine out here right away," Ernesto told Franca. Franca turned back to look at her father but instead she caught Samuele's glance. Embarrassed, she immediately walked away awkwardly.

"This is the year for our *aglianico*," commented Ernesto to Samuele, obviously proud of his wine, which, in truth, could rank with the best in the world. "We have not had a harvest like this in years. Too bad the region produces so little of this venerable wine."

"Everyone seems satisfied. Even my mother made more than she expected."

"Now that you are raising cattle, make good use of your thatch. It'll come in handy in the winter. You'll need all you can get."

"Some farmers have offered it to me; I've been adding to my haystack and will be building another with this year's harvest."

"Good. Are you buying more cows?"

"I'm not in any hurry, but I won't let a good deal go by. I just got a couple more the other day. They're Swiss."

"Good. Maybe you can get the people to start using more milk. As for you, you can always make cheese. You know, people still don't appreciate our local cheese. The cheese we make from November to April is the best in the world... Where's that wife of mine? I always have to yell to get her attention. Here," he said, turning to one of the women, "go inside and get wine and water. And tell that wife of mine to hurry up with the food."

As the woman was about to walk to the door, Franca appeared with the bottles. Behind her came her mother. The woman took one of the bottles from Franca and walked back to the table.

"What's taking you so long!" Ernesto complained to his wife.

"You're always complaining," she said, a slightly forced smile on her face. "We'll see tonight if you'll be complaining when the Bannos serve."

"I don't give a goddam about tonight. Get the stuff now and don't bother me about tonight, " Ernesto said loudly. Then, in a complete low tone, he turned to Samuele matter-of-factly. "Don't make the mistake I made when I got married. I should have clamped down on her right from the first day. Now it's too late."

"Sing, go ahead, sing all you want," taunted his wife. "You weren't a choice then, and you're not now."

"I have no intention of bickering with you now. Just shut your trap and get things done on time. We have no time to waste."

The woman did not answer. In her anger, she slammed the plate on the table, spilling some of the food.

"Look at the cow," commented Ernesto.

Everyone looked up. The woman, furious, looked at her husband with a fierce expression on her face, but let the insult go unanswered.

"Go on and eat," Ernesto urged his guests, on seeing they had stopped. "Go on. This is routine for us; I thought you knew."

Though Ernesto had complained about his wife's service, the guests were satisfied with the meal she and Franca had prepared. At the end of the meal, several complimented the two women. Ernesto could not resist adding more comments, however.

"If the meal was good, you can be sure it was Franca's doing," Ernesto said, unable to give his wife any credit.

Franca almost smiled at the compliment. Samuele looked at Franca, who almost looked back, but didn't. Toni, on the other hand, was angry with rage. What his father was doing was inexcusable. It was true there was never much affection between them, but to go so far as to show his feelings in front of all those people was a tremendous rebuff for Toni, who, after all, was working just as hard as anybody else. He was so irritated that he got up from the table and walked away. But Ernesto was not about to let him off without adding something to make his son angrier than he was already.

"And there's her son; they make a fine couple."

Toni turned. Biting his lips, he glared at his father. Feeling uncomfortable, one of the men intervened on behalf of Toni.

"Ernesto, you're being cruel to your wife and son. You shouldn't act like that. Toni worked very hard. I don't understand why you are abusing him this way."

"He knows why. And so does she. Listen--listen--I' going to ask him where he is going... Where are you going?"

"None of your goddam business," Toni answered with vehemence.

"You're going inside to your mother, aren't you. You're still attached to her apron. You're not man enough to take anything that comes hard. You can't take that, can you?"

"If I can't, it's only because I take after you."

"No, sir. You take after her. Go ahead; go. She's waiting inside to wipe your mouth."

"Ernesto! What are you trying to do?" the man intervened. But Ernesto did not answer. Toni meanwhile had turned his back and gone inside. He was so enraged that he could have strangled his father with his bare hands. And Toni was big, and strong enough to be able to do it, too, though Ernesto was bigger and heavier.

Throughout the family quarrel, Samuele remained silent. He was, however, not missing the opportunity of studying Toni's expressions. To a certain extent, Samuele knew why Ernesto was driving his son, but to go so far was wrong. Ernesto was alienating his son to the point of no return. Perhaps Ernesto had understood the danger point and stopped in time. As for Samuele, he had also understood that should anyone step in Toni's way for whatever reason, during any one of his mad moods, he might just become a savage animal. It was because of the same thought that the man had intervened on behalf of Toni.

"Watch! His mother will come out to threaten me," Ernesto told his guests.

"Ernesto, you're carrying it too far," protested a second man. But no sooner had he finished saying this than Toni's mother appeared through the door.

"You'll end up on the pitchfork one of these days," she said.

Ernesto paid no attention to her; instead, he turned to his guests to affirm his prediction. He then waved his arm at her as if to tell her to get lost, and told Samuele that it was siesta time. Before getting up, he left word that he wanted to be awakened in half an hour. He also expressed hope that Banno and his people would be coming soon so that after they finished with the present wheat, they could immediately start with Mr. Banno's. Ernesto got up and moved to his favorite afternoon spot under the mulberry tree. The rest of the farmers also scattered about, each finding a place to rest.

Samuele, on the other hand, did not rest. He walked around the place hoping Franca would come to talk to him. But she didn't. He could not see that she was looking at him from behind the window upstairs. She had just been warned by both her brother and mother to stay away from Samuele if she wanted to avoid tragedy. Besides, she felt so unwomanly that she was ashamed to meet her lover. Samuele went from place to place, looking at the vines full of red grapes--the *aglianico*, the elm trees, the pears, apples, almonds, walnuts, and especially the fig trees so full of the maturing figs. Each time he stopped to observe, he nonchalantly looked at the house. When he saw no sign of Franca, he would go on to the next tree. But each time Samuele stopped to look back, Franca rejoiced. Not for too much longer, however, for Samuele, tired of lingering, went out into the field. Stopping by a lone poplar, he decided to sit under it and rest.

From there he overlooked the entire valley. He could also look across to the distant mountain range of the Appennines. As he glanced over the beautiful but arid land, a cicada began to sing from above the tree. He turned his head up to admire the solo performance. Amid so many tribulations and in a land whose fertility had been lost to centuries of wind and rain, and to the yearly harvests that had gotten meager with each passing season, still there was so much beauty.

Samuele broke a couple of straws and unconsciously bent them into many different forms while his eyes encompassed the vast panorama. Above, the cicada kept up its singing. From below, about fifteen feet to his right, a long gray-black snake slowly made its way through the straws. Not expecting such a visitor, when the snake came close, Samuele was startled and immediately jumped to his feet in fright. The reptile, not expecting to find anyone either, quickly changed direction. Samuele began to smile at having been so frightened by a little snake he had not seen since he had left the village for the army. Whereas before he would have killed the harmless reptile--he couldn't even remember how many he had killed--now, he watched it slide away, observing its mouth with its tongue darting out.

While Samuele was engrossed with the path of the reptile, Franca sneaked up from behind. Hoping to scare him, she softly emitted a *boo*. Samuele turned quickly, and without hesitating, he ran into her extended arms and into a close embrace, kissing passionately. To avoid the possibility of being seen from above, they walked below to a fence of wild bush that shielded them from the house.

"I thought you wouldn't come," he said.

"I can't stay long. My brother is as mad as a dog. He said that if he sees me with you, he'll do something to the both of us.

"Let's not talk about him," Samuele said as he held her against his chest. He kissed her and she kissed back. "Open your mouth," he asked softly. She obeyed, and closed her eyes. Samuele pressed his mouth on hers as he drew her tight against him. Franca felt her body vibrate. She tightened her hold around his neck and enjoyed the passionate kisses of her lover.

"I love you--I love you," she whispered, touching the side of his face with her mouth. Samuele kissed her on the neck. "Kiss me again, before I go."

Samuele drew her up against him, her mouth half-open, Her lips quivering. Samuele kissed her once again. Then, drawing her body away, but keeping her lips against his, Franca pulled completely away and ran toward the house. Samuele stared at her slim and agile form as she disappeared from view. On his lips he could still feel the sweetness of her kiss. He put his hand up and touched his lips with his finger.

"I'm glad I didn't die," he said to himself. "I am glad I did not die. Life can be so wonderful." He raised his head toward the sky when another cicada on a nearby tree began to sing, after the one above him on the poplar had stopped. And from the distant farms he could hear the noise of the threshing machines, telling him it was time to get back to his work.

His head still skyward, he began to walk toward the house, not noticing that Mr. Banno, his wife, and Rosa were approaching from below. Seeing Samuele alone, Mr. Banno shouted to him to wait.

"Hurry up, Mr. Banno," answered Samuele in a happy voice. When the three arrived, Samuele greeted them in a friendly manner. Noticing Samuele's good humor, and never wanting from seizing the moment, Mr. Banno asked if later, during one of the breaks, they could talk about a few things. Samuele agreed. Then, the two men began to walk forward while the two women followed behind, Rosa somewhat upset because Samuele had hardly looked at her.

Rosa stared at Samuele's back, not minding his limping. But, as she looked at Samuele, she realized that he was out of her reach. She would have to settle for Toni, hoping to get some sign from him before the day ended.

Up above, from the threshing area, Ernesto's dog barked to announce the new arrivals. Ernesto got up from his place and walked over to meet them.

"Why, if it's not the flag-bearer himself in flesh and bone! How are you, Mr. Banno? I haven't seen you in ages."

"Not bad for an old goat. At least, not too badly for as long as my wife here helps me out with a few things. Otherwise, life could be a bit more unpleasant."

"I know what you mean. Thank God, I don't need mine yet."

"Excuse me," interrupted Samuele, "I'd better go start the machines. I'll wait for your signal when to engage the gears."

The two women also left to join Franca and her mother in the kitchen. They had brought with them the food for the evening meal and wanted to get started with the preparation.

"Fine man, that Samuele," Ernesto confessed to Mr. Banno after the women had gone. "He likes Franca. He told me he wants to marry her, but I'm not sure yet."

"Oh! is that right? When did this all happen? I didn't know anything about it."

"I thought for sure you'd know if anyone did. You of all people!"

"Well!" Mr. Banno answered, scratching his head, making it obvious to Ernesto that he was thinking about something and not saying anything about it. "Well," he repeated. Before he could add to that *well!*, Samuele started the machines whose noise drowned out their conversation. Mr. Banno motioned to Ernesto to move to the side and to get started without delay.

In no time all hands were in their assigned places and the threshing began immediately. After about one hour's steady work, they finished with Ernesto's lot. As they changed over the crew, the men and women took a five--minute break. Franca carried the wine bottles and Rosa brought cool water to the workers, who were already wiping the sweat from their brows as they waited for their drinks. The men, for the most part, all drank the wine, while the women drank the water. Franca passed by her brother.

"I'd rather have water," he said sarcastically. Without a return glance or an answer, Franca continued on to where Samuele, Mr. Banno, and her father were working. While they took turns at the wine, Rosa was offering water to Toni. Seeing that Mr. Banno was looking his way, Toni held the bottle to his mouth making believe he was drinking.

"I bought you a gold ring. When can I come over? I want to try it on you," he said, winking at her to be careful not to let on they were talking. Rosa put up her hand to shake the dust from her hair.

"Any evening at sunset, near the well behind my house. Pass by the street in front of the house. I'll signal you from the window." She put her hand down to dust her skirt; then she dusted her blouse on her breast. Toni stared as he drank the cool water, which had never tasted as good. He drank as though he had had nothing to drink in days. He had also forgotten about the recent quarrel with his father.

The plan he and Enrico had thought out was beginning to work. Now, all he had to do was to get the gilded ring Enrico himself had used for several previous conquests. Rosa, not even thinking about such tricks, dreaming already about the ring, even if it might mean making love with Tony, took the bottle of water from him. Without letting on about her unexpected happiness, she carried the bottle from one worker to another. The farmers, especially the men, smiled at her; some even stared at her voluptuous body, which Rosa did not mind.

Toward late afternoon, while all were working at full capacity, Mr. Banno approached Samuele, who had been left alone by Ernesto.

"Samuele," said Mr. Banno with a furtive motion of the hand. "I have something important to talk to you about. Continue with your work. Here, I'll help you. I want this to be a secret between you and me."

Samuele looked up at the rotund, reddish-complexioned man, who, not long ago, had recently opposed him so vehemently in public.

"You needn't apologize for your behavior in front of the police station. What's done is done. I don't believe in apologies."

Mr. Banno, who had already forgotten all about the incident--Marcello being a faint recollection, was somewhat taken aback. He remained speechless for a few seconds, but not long enough to let on about his awkward feeling. He had not anticipated Samuele's reaction.

"Oh, yes, yes. I had been meaning to come see you about that. But you know, with the harvest and all, I really forgot. Actually, I didn't have the time. You know how it is these days."

"I know how it is these days. Here, hold the bag," Samuele instructed as the grain fell down the chute off the noisy machine. "Sure, sure. But I wanted to make you a proposition."

Samuele looked up, wanting to be sure to look into Mr. Banno's eyes when speaking.

"You know the land near yours? I mentioned it briefly to you about it before. It's up for sale!"

"What!"

"You heard me. Promise, if you are not interested, you will not say anything to anyone. Promise!"

"I'm interested if the price is right."

"The price is right. Oh, watch out: Ernesto is coming. Not a word." Mr. Banno acted busier than he actually was, holding the burlap sack. At the same time that Ernesto appeared, one of the women also came up. She stooped to pick up the sack and Mr. Banno helped her lift it. Then, as she balanced the weight on her head and was about to walk away, Mr. Banno pushed her off, with his hand on her buttock. The woman protested to the laughter of Mr. Banno and Ernesto.

"The old goat is still at it," Ernesto commented to Samuele.

Samuele did not respond one way or another; he simply went on with his work, which pleased Ernesto. Samuele was thinking about the proposition, the manner in which it was presented, the exclusion of the daughter, and above all, the secrecy of the whole thing. Mr. Banno must have had something up his sleeve. But Samuele was willing to gamble, needing the land to expand his business. Yet, he could not be overly anxious. He was going to let Mr. Banno make the next move before he would say or do anything.

Before making his next move, Mr. Banno kept his eyes and ears open to see if he could get more information on the rumors that Toni might be interested in Rosa. As a matter of fact, he had instructed his wife to be on the alert too. And she, having found no great objections on the part of Toni's mother, went directly to her husband to inform him. Mr. Banno was very pleased to hear the news. Earlier he had seen Toni exchange glances with Rosa. They made it quite obvious something was up between them. Mr. Banno made no attempt to find out, either. His hunch was right, and now he was going to play his card.

Toward evening, after Samuele had shut off the engines of the tractor and the noise had completely subsided, Mr. Banno approached Samuele once again.

"You're staying for supper, aren't you? You know, Rosa prepared supper."

"Sure, Mr. Banno, I'm planning on staying."

"Not because Rosa cooked the meal?"

"I wasn't thinking about that." Samuele acted neither surprised nor overjoyed.

Mr. Banno watched Samuele's reaction closely. When Samuele went on with his work, Mr. Banno began to speak once again.

"Do you know what Rosa prepared?"

"It doesn't matter. If it's edible, I'll eat it."

"She made something special. She knew you were going to be here."

"I don't think so, Mr. Banno."

Mr. Banno hesitated before answering. Samuele just seemed a little too disinterested in what Mr. Banno was saying about his daughter.

"Of course, you know Franca is also helping with the table."

"Franca!" Samuele answered, looking up. Noticing that Mr. Banno was watching him closely, Samuele felt awkward. He also felt as if he had given himself away to Mr. Banno, who became full of smiles. "What difference does that make?" continued Samuele, ineffectually.

"Well," Mr. Banno answered, a satisfied expression on his face. "It may not make that much difference, and you may be right. How about the land I offered for sale. Are you interested?"

"Depends on the price. Or, should I say, condition."

"What condition! Once you pay for it, the land is yours. You're able to pay for it, aren't you?"

"You're only interested in the money, is that right?"

"Oh, yes, cold cash. But remember, if you are interested, not a word to anybody."

"Why the secrecy?"

"Remember, I asked you, and you promised!"

"I remember."

"Are you buying or not?"

"I said I was interested."

"Then, everything else is none of your business. All you should care about is one fact: the land becomes legally yours."

"All right."

"Good. Watch it now. Some of the women are coming this way... You'd better hurry up. Supper is about ready, isn't that right?" he asked one of the women coming out of the kitchen. She was the same woman Mr. Banno had helped push forward with his hand. Remembering his action, she ignored him altogether, calling him a pig, however. Her friend understood what she had said and burst out in laughter.

"Can't trust these women, can you?" Mr. Banno commented.

"Strange you should say that. Rosa is of marrying age," Samuele replied.

"Let's get down to business. How much are you willing to offer for the land."

"Nothing."

"What do you mean!"

"You're selling; I'm not."

"I'm going to make you a special offer simply because you were in the war. Otherwise, I wouldn't. A million lire!"

Samuele looked surprised, though he knew the land was worth much more than that. Nevertheless, he was going to try to get the price down.

"No deal," Samuele answered without raising his voice.

"What do you mean?"

"I don't have that kind of money."

"But I..."

"...You'll have to do a lot better than that."

"Eight hundred thousand?"

"It's getting more reasonable."

"What do you mean?" Mr. Banno asked, signs of frustration filling his face. Samuele remained expressionless.

"Take off a couple more and I might think about it."

"I'm not going to take off any more than one. Take it or leave it. The price is seven hundred thousand."

"Can I give you an answer tomorrow?"

"No!" Mr. Banno answered angrily.

"It's a deal. On your way home this evening, stop by the house. Two hundred thousand down payment, right?"

Mr. Banno smiled. He had been willing to sell the land for much less. As a matter of fact, anything he got for it would have been something extra in his pocket. With Samuele and Franca getting married eventually, and the likelihood of Toni and Rosa following suit, Mr. Banno would retain the land in the family. Plus, he would have seven hundred thousand in his pocket. With that money, he could provide a great dowry as well as a great banquet for his daughter.

Mr. Banno was gambling, and he knew it. But the odds were good. Besides, he had gambled before, and he always won.

With tremendous satisfaction, he went into the dimly lit kitchen where the table was nearly set. The women were busy running around, getting the last few things ready. In the presence of the two mothers and Franca, Mr. Banno went to his daughter. Putting one arm around her, he hugged her while she held a couple of plates in her hand.

"You're getting along very well here. I've never seen four women get along so well. It's great; it's great."

Rosa felt very awkward being hugged by her father in that manner. Franca, too, looked up. She found Mr. Banno's action, especially his words, very strange. Something must have happened to have made him suddenly so happy. Franca looked at her mother to see if her expression might reveal the secret. Nothing unusual appeared on her face. As a matter of fact, all four of them looked at each other in search of an answer. Mr. Banno finally broke the silence.

"Well, women, go on. Don't let me stop you. I'll get the rest ready. Beautiful table! Rosa, go on, go on with your work." He released her, and she went on clumsily trying to smile.

Rosa's mother, meanwhile, remained silent and expressionless, staying almost always in one of the corners of the kitchen. Though she knew what had taken place, hardly any of the rest of the women paid much attention to the short, stubby woman. No matter what she did, she never changed her passive expression, even when suffering pain.

At the supper table, Mr. Banno made himself the center of attention, for no reason other than that he spoke the most and the loudest. A braggart from the word go, he continued talking *ad nauseam*.

"Here," interrupted Ernesto, "have a drink, will you!"

"Oh, yes, my friend, thank you. Come on, everybody, let's all fill up--remember, it is my wine; you may drink all you want--and let's toast the harvest. We haven't seen a better one in years. Come on, everybody, fill up. The war is over!"

Amid chatter and the noise from moving plates and glasses, the farmers filled up. Why not! Mr. Banno had never given anything to anyone before. While they all wondered what might have happened, they weren't so much concerned about that as they were at joining in what appeared to be a quasi-banquet.

"To the harvest!" Mr. Banno exclaimed, raising his glass.

"To the harvest and whatever else may follow," answered the farmers. Toni, Samuele, and Franca joined in the drinking, but remained silent. Ernesto acted exuberant.

"Let's have another round; it's Mr. Banno's wine."

"Yah, yah," the farmers answered.

"How many bottles do you think they brought?" interrupted Ernesto's wife. "You've just about finished the wine, and we haven't started supper yet."

"Why doesn't someone do something to her?" Ernesto answered with apparent disgust. "Look at her," he continued, inviting the group to fix their eyes on her. "Look at her: killjoy in the flesh. If you want to have another round and afterward get the beating of your life, just say another word, or if you want the beating I have been saving for you, let the wine run out."

When Ernesto spoke, no one said a word or dared move, though they were all hoping the woman would spare them another embarrassment. But Mr. Banno did not remain silent for long.

"There's plenty of wine. Come on, let's drink up."

The men refilled their glasses and drank, while most of the women looked on. Samuele also drank. He looked around, however, and noticed Toni to be abnormally reticent. He also noticed that Toni was avoiding looking at Rosa, and Rosa did likewise, though she did not succeed. Samuele felt something was up, but couldn't figure out what was behind the strange behavior. Surely Mr. Banno must have had an inkling, otherwise he would not have been so easy to bargain with or been so free with his wine. Samuele remained silent but observant.

The food was placed on the table, and the farmers began to eat heartily. Almost everyone in turn mumbled his or her approval over the antipasto of home-made *prosciutto*, *salumetti*, and *formaggio*, which they consumed almost instantly. The *tagliatelle* covered with a light tomato sauce was served, and once again the farmers, who had put in a hard day, joyfully accepted second servings of the delightful pasta. But the *coniglio* (rabbit) cooked in white wine and herbs made them really react. As they ate, they drank, and as they drank, they heard Mr. Banno brag about the delicious food Rosa had cooked, all on her own, which, of course, was not true. Even as Mr. Banno told the lie, his wife stood to one side with the same neutral expression as before. Were not for the fact that once in a while she spoke, thereby moving her lips, one would think she wore a permanent mask. As her husband spoke, Mr. Banno turned his head toward Ernesto to get his approval. Ernesto, not knowing what was behind Mr. Banno's words, agreed wholeheartedly.

"Delicious," he commented, licking some of the gravy dripping down one side of his mouth, "just superb. You have a fine cook in that daughter of yours. Yes, a fine cook," he added, his eyes staring at his empty plate.

"Rosa!" Mr. Banno responded, and Rosa quickly went to re-fill Ernesto's plate, to the envy of Ernesto's resentful wife. As Rosa passed by Toni, Mr. Banno caught their glance, and was now convinced, more than ever, he had made a deal. Once again, he offered another toast, and the farmers naturally accepted with enthusiasm.

Franca brought out more wine, and even poured some into Samuele's glass, smiling as she did so. Toni turned the other way.

"Don't forget your father," said Ernesto benevolently, causing Mr. Banno to raise his eyebrows.

"Me too," interrupted Mr. Banno. Franca moved over to fill his glass. After she had filled it to the very top, Mr. Banno went on speaking. "I'm so glad you all like my wine. I made it from the grapes of our old vines, and last year's *aglianico* is the best ever--the kind to drink at special occasions." A smile of contentment filling his eyes, he turned to Franca. "Fill Toni's glass, Franca; it's empty..."

"...Certainly," she answered with a slight hesitation.

"...Or would you rather Rosa fill it?" Mr. Banno added, turning to Toni, and leaving Franca cold. Toni agreed. "You didn't say much this afternoon and hardly a word this evening, *my son*. Is something bothering you?"

"He quarrelled with his father," answered one farmer.

"Don't be angry. Your father, here, is an old crock. Don't let it bother you. This is time to celebrate... Hurry up, Rosa; pour the wine. Toni's thirsty."

When Rosa poured the wine, Toni finally smiled. He looked for an instant into Rosa's abundant breast then quickly looked into the direction of Mr. Banno, while the two men sitting next to Toni raised their eyebrows on seeing Rosa bending to pour the wine for Toni. The women smiled un-enviously, except for Franca's mother gesturing with her hand, and Rosa's mother looking on impassively.

"To Toni," said Mr. Banno, raising his glass.

"To Toni," answered the rest, including Samuele.

CHAPTER 18

Nicola, the town veterinarian, had the responsibility of going around the farms to collect donations for the coming feast.

In the past, the traditional donations consisted of either flower, wheat, or sheafs of wheat. Presently, however, the donations were necessarily in the form of money, except that many farmers still contributed either wheat or other farm products which were collected and then sold to raise money for fireworks, music, and other incidentals to the feast. The only item specifically set aside for money raising, with a minimum fixed amount, was the single strand of rope to the Madonna. This passive strand was auctioned and reserved for the highest bidder.

Because Nicola knew a lot about animals--and because he was genuinely humble as a person and as a professional that often he joked with his friends saying that all he knew about cows was that one was bigger than another--he was also entrusted by the Cavaliere with the responsibility of finding unusually strong and well-behaved oxen or bulls to pull the obelisk on the day of the feast.

The large-nosed, rosy cheeked veterinarian, his forehead very large due to his receding hair, was a jovial but serious man, one who had been chosen for the position both for his personal integrity and for his knowledge of the countryside and of the people.

He visited Samuele's house to ask for a donation, but he also went there with the hope that Samuele would invite him to look over the stable, having heard about the young bull Samuele was raising. Not being credulous, he wanted to check it out for himself.

When he went to knock on the door and found it closed, Nicola made his way around the house to the stable. There, outside in the courtyard, Samuele was exercising the bull, the size of which amazed Nicola. Instead of going toward Samuele, he stepped aside and hid behind a tree to observe what was going on before announcing himself. From behind the tree, he also saw Lucia carrying large bundles of green corn stalks into the stable, while Maria was carrying two buckets of milk. Under the large tree in front of the stable door, sitting on the stone slab, the two children playfully looked at Samuele and at the bull; they were patiently waiting for Samuele to finish with the training to get their promised ride. When Samuele finally finished, he signaled to them, and the children scurried to his side. Samuele first picked up the boy, then the girl, and placed them on the animal's back. Then, with a smack of his tongue, Samuele commanded the docile animal forward, going around the yard a few times. When Samuele told them the ride was over, the children asked for a last ride, and Samuele agreed.

"Hang on, though, we're going to try to make him walk backward part of the way, all right?"

It was more than all right for the children, who were thrilled at the suggestion, showing their approval by shouting with enthusiasm. Toward the middle of the ride, Samuele stopped the animal. Warning the children to hold fast, Samuele smacked his tongue, put one hand on the animal's hind leg, and gently pushed the bull backward, speaking to it at the same time. During the first attempt, the children remained completely silent, especially when the animal failed to walk backward. Seeing the bull was not responding to the new order, Samuele ordered it to stop. After patting it affectionately, he tried again. Giving his initial order, Samuele placed his hand once again on the hind leg, and gently forced the animal backward. The bull hesitated, but not for very long. Soon it began to move its feet backward. Samuele insisted with his order, though he never raised his voice or showed disappointment. The animal took a few awkward steps to the praises of Samuele, who kept his hand on the hind leg and pushing gently. Slowly, the bull began to take regular steps, and soon was walking backward without difficulty. When the children saw Samuele congratulate the bull at the end of the brief walk, they burst into cheers while Samuele laughed with pride.

"You have reason to be proud," said Nicola, as he walked out. "Excuse me, Samuele, I was standing behind the tree. I think you have a beautiful and intelligent animal. I've never seen such a big bull nor any man do what you were doing."

Nicola's eyes moved from the bull to Samuele, then to the bull again, and then to Samuele. It seemed as though he wanted to concentrate on everything at same time but did not have enough vision to take it all in simultaneously.

"You remember me, don't you, Samuele. I am Nicola, the veterinarian. I am going around to collect for the feast. I was supposed to do something else, but I'm not allowed to say anything about it. Others will. Well, how much will you contribute this year? You know it is the first pull since the beginning of the war. We want this feast to be bigger and better than all others. The war is over, and we have, in spite of everything, to be grateful for what we have. I know all about you."

"Sure, I remember you," Samuele answered, putting out his hand to shake Nicola's hand. "Wait, let me get these two off before they talk me into another ride... Come on, off with you!"

"No, no, no! Please, one more time," asked the girl. Smiling, Samuele picked up the boy. Nicola, without being asked, took the girl dawn.

"Thank you," Samuele said. "How are the contributions coming this year?"

"The people are giving. They're happy over the wheat harvest, and the corn and grapes look good too. We all have reasons to be happy. There's an a unusual optimism in the air, and this may explain why they are so giving this year. As for you, I'm told you're not doing too badly yourself. You bought that beautiful piece of land. Mr. Banno must have been crazy selling, or else he's got something up his sleeve. We all know him well, the old gizzard. Anyway, you got a deal and I am glad it was you to get it. You deserve it."

"Thank you."

"You deserve it. Our surviving soldiers deserve breaks of this type and not of the other, you know what I mean... Say, would you mind showing me your stable?"

Samuele did not hesitate to bring Nicola into the stable. As the two walked between the rows of small and large animals, Nicola was impressed by the number of heads Samuele had accumulated. As they inspected them, Lucia went on with her work, and Maria also returned to continue with her milking. Nicola congratulated Maria, who, thanking him, smiled.

"Everyone has been talking about you, you know, the way you've handled your affairs. I think you did the right thing. Well, I'm sure you're busy. I have many more farms and houses to visit."

"I understand," Samuele answered. Then turning to Lucia, he asked her to go inside and get thirty thousand lire. On hearing the generous sum, Nicola objected ineffectively, but was really only too happy to receive it.

While Lucia left the stable, the two walked to where Samuele had tied the bull. Nicola kept on staring at the impressive animal.

"I can't get over it. I just can't. Here it is, under my very nose," Nicola commented, placing his hand on the bull's large nose and rubbing it, "and I didn't know how big and beautiful it truly is. I've got to hand it to you, Samuele. You've done well. By the way, you'll be coming to the feast, right?"

"Certainly."

"You won't forget this year's pull for as long as you live, I promise you. The Obelisk has several new panels, and it stands some nine stories high. It's structure is truly grandiose and fantastic, I tell you. We can all be proud of it. Our Cavaliere has been working day and night. I'm telling you, he's created a masterpiece."

"A masterpiece?"

"A true masterpiece. People from all the entire valley will be coming to the feast, to see the obelisk, and to take part in the pull. I guarantee it."

After a few minutes, Lucia returned and gave the money to Samuele. Then, Lucia took her son into her arms, and placed her other hand on little girl's shoulder. Nicola thanked Lucia for the money. As she nodded with a smile and walked away with the children, Nicola moved over to the bull. Running his hand the length of the bull's neck, causing it to turn its head toward him, Nicola patted its thick skin and left the yard.

Exhilarated, Samuele walked over to the stall where his mother was milking and Lucia filling the manger with green corn stalks she herself had cut from the field. The children, meanwhile, were running among the animals chasing the rabbits. When the little girl finally caught a little white one, she ran over to the boy to let him hold it. Samuele felt thrilled. Things were better than he ever imagined and life was well worth living. He walked over to his mother and placed his hand on her shoulder.

CHAPTER 19

The following day, toward late afternoon, Samuele received an unexpected visit from the Cavaliere.

Dressed in a white light suit, wearing a large brimmed hat, the tall slim man knocked on the door of Samuele's house. Maria opened the door. On seeing the Cavaliere, Maria bowed, as most people did to the distinguished man. As an artist, he brought fame to the townspeople, who, in appreciation of his work as the custodian and renovator of the artistic straw embroidery on the Straw Obelisk, at times acted a bit too obsequious for his taste.

"Good evening, Maria," he said, as Maria looked up at him. "I've come to speak with your son, Samuele. Is he available?"

"Yes, Cavaliere, he's at the stable. Has he done something wrong?"

"Absolutely not. In fact, all I hear about him are good things. Yes, Maria, I understand he is a very changed young man. Anyhow, I'm here because I was told he can do me and the town a great favor."

"By all means, if he can he will. Let's go to the back."

Maria walked in front of the gentleman, who looked around observing the surroundings. Coming into the yard, she pointed to Samuele resting next to the his bull tied to the fig tree. Neither was moving; it seemed as if they were taking a rest after a hard workout.

The Cavaliere was impressed by the bull's size and its apparent docility. He walked toward them with his eyes fixed on the animal. Samuele turned on hearing them coming. Seeing his mother with the gentleman dressed in white, Samuele quickly walked toward them with a certain anxiety.

"The Cavaliere has come to ask you something," Maria said, a slight smile on her face.

"Good evening, Samuele. I've heard a lot about you."

"How do you do, sir. I am very happy to meet... Mother, won't you get some wine?"

Maria, quickly left. The Cavaliere turned to the bull.

"I've never seen one this big before. I was told he was big, but I didn't expect him to be this big. If he handles well, I would like you to train him to be on the team to pull the Obelisk. There will be six teams in all, for a total of twelve. The sturdiest and best trained animal gets the front right position. Do you think you may be interested?"

"Yes, sir, I would be interested. Anything I can do, I will be happy to do my part."

While the two men talked, the bull occasionally turned its huge neck toward them. The Cavaliere was impressed with the sensibility of the animal. It had remained in its place without the least complaint. Normally, such animals acted-up in front of strangers. At times, they even became ferocious. As a matter of need, however, the Cavaliere was looking for docility and strength above everything else. He had chosen less powerful oxen in the past if they were more manageable. Passing his hand over the animal's neck, the Cavaliere asked Samuele to walk it. Samuele asked if he would rather see it with two children on its back. At this, the Cavaliere became even more surprised.

"Come with me; we'll go to the back where they're playing. He seems to like children."

Samuele led the way to the back. When the children saw the bull, they quickly ran towards it, knowing they were in for a ride. When they saw the gentleman dressed in white, however, they hesitated.

"Do you want a ride?" asked Samuele. The boy quickly got into position for the lift onto the bull's back. The girl did the same, and soon the two were riding under the watchful eyes of the Cavaliere, who could not believe what he was seeing. Samuele commanded the animal, which executed all the orders. At one point, Samuele ordered the bull to stop. Afterward, he ordered it to walk backward. The children turned their heads to see where they were going, and the Cavaliere was simply amazed.

"That's fine," he told Samuele. "But why are you doing all this? Why are you training this animal?"

"Just because he understands. There is no other reason. He responds very well, better than some human beings, if you know what I mean. As a result, I just want to see how far I can go with him. I think it is quite a challenge."

"And you have no other reason?"

"What other reason is there? People don't always have to have reasons to do things."

"You're right. Are you planning on harnessing the bull?"

"I've thought of it."

"If it responds well, will you do us the favor of being on the team to pull the Obelisk?"

"Yes, if you wish."

"You realize how dangerous it is; we haven't had a feast during the war years and just about everyone lacks experience. If you accept, you will have to have further training. Most of all, the animal would have to get used to the noisy and shifting crowds. Do you think you can help us in this?"

"I'll do my best, as I have said before. I am honored that you should ask me to be part of the feast. I'll train him further, and he'll get used to noise. I'll do my best."

While they talked, the children listened silently, keeping their eyes on the two men. They did not understand what was being planned, but sensed that something big was about to take place.

"How about you, Samuele, will you be able to make it?" the Cavaliere asked point blank, his eyes pointing to Samuele's foot. Feeling a little embarrassed, Samuele did not answer. "You understand," continued the Cavaliere, "it's nothing personal. I ask similar questions of everyone on the team. The man leading the animals is under a terrific strain. Mentally and physically, he's got to be able to handle many things at once. Again, as I said, there is nothing personal; I just have to be sure, you understand and that you would be able to undertake the physical and psychological stress, that's all."

"I understand, and I'm glad you asked. If you hadn't, you would not be at ease. I can assure you I'm all right. I limp, but I limped my way back home from Russia and Germany. I am fully recovered. I can sustain long distances and demanding work. I learned how to put up with a lot. I can assure you that both physically and mentally, I am well--at least, I feel I am. However, should you believe I'm not worthy or capable in any way, you just tell me. There'd be no problems or acrimony from me. You know your requirements. Judge accordingly. If I can be of assistance any way you desire, by all means...and to the degree you need. I will be available."

"Thank you. I am glad you did not take it personal."

"I'm used to it... We'd better go back now. My mother must be ready with the wine. As soon as I can, I'll harness him. By the time the feast comes, I should have him completely trained... Yes, I remember how important that is. There, there's my mother," he said, pointing to her. With the Cavaliere walking at his side, Samuele led the bull to the open yard with the two children sitting stiffly on its back, a smile on their lips.

Maria had brought out a bottle of white wine and the glasses. The Cavaliere walked toward her while Samuele walked the bull to the fig tree, where he tied the huge animal. After letting the children down, he joined the guest. After striking the rims of their glasses for best wishes, the two men sipped the wine, while Maria looked on with satisfaction and pride. To think that a man as important as the Cavaliere was actually there, drinking wine with her son and asking him to help with the Obelisk! No one had ever paid attention to her family before. But now, her son Samuele was changing everything. She was happy to note that the change was what she, in all her ignorance, had hoped but never dreamed of fulfilling.

Samuele, Maria thought, had been so much like his father, at least prior to the war, and now, just the opposite. Silently she thanked God. An unusual expression of serenity and satisfaction filled her being, and her face filled with light even if there were no smiles on her lips.

The Cavaliere looked at Maria for one moment; then he began to stare. Thinking he wanted more wine, Maria picked up the bottle and began to refill the glass.

"No, thank you," he said. "I was just noticing the expression of happiness on your face. I haven't seen this kind in many years."

"I am very proud of Samuele."

"You should be. I have heard all kinds of things about him and some were not complimentary."

"At time, Samuele left something to be desired, as all boys do, I guess."

While the two talked, Samuele listened without saying a word. Soon the Cavaliere finished his wine and left, assuring Samuele he would be in touch with him.

CHAPTER 20

While Samuele was having supper at the kitchen table with a child on each side of him, his sister Lucia came in from outside to tell him that Toni had just passed by. Samuele merely shrugged his shoulders and continued to eat, while Lucia went on with her chores. Maria, who was by the fireplace, stirred the potatoes frying in the pan. She asked her son if he was happy about the Cavaliere's proposition and Samuele answered that he was excited and honored, the feeling of happiness clearly visible on his face, as if in a reverie. His need to pursue his plan for the evening, however, brought him back to his present reality.

"Are the potatoes ready?" he asked.

Maria turned to look at him. It seemed strange that he should ask her about the potatoes, something he had never done before.

"Are you going someplace?" she asked. "Here, the potatoes are ready."

"Oh, good. I just wanted to go to Franca's to tell her all about it. I thought she might like to know."

When Samuele stepped outside, the sun was disappearing beyond the Appennines. A cool wind blew across the valley and the poplars already seemed like giants standing on guard duty. Though things were distinguishable at close range, a light bluish mist permeated the air. Samuele walked under the huge trees. Beyond them, to one side, he went onto a small pathway that led to the unused well, approximately five-hundred feet from the main road. On each side of the road there were tall rows of corn stalks, the ears of maize already showing their multi-colored silk. Samuele noted and appreciated the beautiful colors. Slowly, he made his way toward the well, making sure not to trip over the rocks scattered on the pathway. Some were rather large, and he thought that they should be removed to make the passageway easier. But then, he thought, hardly anyone went there anyway.

Soon the walls of the well appeared before his eyes. Behind it, rising far above the circular stone rim, were several rose bushes with the beautiful flowers going unobserved, except for the moon. High up in the sky, above the cylindrical wall of the abandoned well, that large round face was also standing watch. Samuele made his way around the wall, plucking the best-formed, most odorous roses, carefully and noiselessly breaking about ten stems from the main branches. Then, holding them together in a bunch, he put them close to his nose to smell them. Happy that the roses were as beautiful as they were odorous, he went on plucking some more.

Suddenly, from within the corn field, he heard what seemed like human groaning. Come to a standstill, he turned his head in that direction, waiting to hear and locate the sound. After a few moments, he heard the groaning again, this time accompanied by some rustling. Having located the noise, he slid noiselessly between the rows of green leaves of corn to the spot. There, between two rows of corn, he saw Rosa's face with Toni's deep between her shoulder and neck. Her mouth was open, her eyes closed while Toni above was moving rhythmically to an impending orgasm. Sensing the presence of someone, Rosa suddenly opened her eyes. On seeing Samuele, the sensual expression of her face quickly changed to one of horror. With a heave, she pushed Toni to one side, warning him of Samuele's presence. As Toni turned, Rosa jumped to her feet. Grabbing her dress, she covered her bare breasts. Then, without saying a word, she turned and ran, disappearing in an instant. Toni, on the other hand, his semen lost on corn leaves, calmly and silently began to get dressed.

"Rosa, wait," called Samuele. But Rosa had already gone. Instead, Toni answered, telling Samuele to wait.

Moving back to the well, Samuele stood against the side of the wall holding the bunch of roses in one hand, his foot resting on one of the stones on the ground. "You're always sticking your nose into my business," Toni said with an accusing tone.

"I didn't know you and Rosa were there. I came here to get some roses..."

"...For my sister!" Toni stated in a low but harsh and ominous voice.

"Yes, for Franca."

"I told you to stay away from her."

"Why, because you think I might do with your sister what you're doing with Rosa? Is that what you think? Is that what you're afraid of? You think I am a threat to your home and to your family, is that it? Is that why you don't want me to see your sister?

"But you don't know me. I don't want to see Franca for the same reason you're seeing Rosa..."

"...You're not going to be seeing Franca, ever again."

"Is that a threat?"

"It's a statement."

"How do you plan on doing it?"

"...With this," he said as he pulled a knife from his pocket. "I'm going to slash your throat and cut you into a thousand pieces."

"Animals kill for food. You'd do what animals have better sense not to do?"

"...And then I'm going to throw you in this hole."

"I have no intention of fighting with you, Toni. We were never boyhood friends; I'm older than you. I don't know you, and you do not know me. There's no reason why we can't be friends. I proposed to Franca, and unless something drastic were to happen, we'll be marrying soon. Even if that weren't so, I still have no intention of fighting with you. There's no need. I want to be your friend..."

"...You have no choice. I'm not going to fight with you; I'm going to slaughter you."

"I didn't come here to fight," Samuele said in a beseeching tone.

"Fate brought you here," Toni said resolutely. He pulled out his stiletto. As he held it up, he pressed the button, releasing the shining blade. Samuele pushed tight against the stone wall, letting the roses fall on the rim, half falling within the well, the others to the ground.

"Put that away."

"Only after I do you in and have you cut into pieces."

"Put it away. You're forgetting I was trained to fight tougher men than you."

"With those odds, all the more reason to take you on," Toni answered, drawing near.

With his eyes fixed on Samuele, he moved in, thrusting his arm forward toward Samuele's chest. Samuele turned and avoided the thrust. Toni quickly turned again and went toward Samuele, who, with his arms out, his back bent, pulled slowly away as Toni pressed on with the shiny blade in hand. Samuele kept his eyes on Toni, looking for a move by which he might grab Toni to disarm him. Toni, however, pressed on, his eyes fully concentrated on those of Samuele. Suddenly, he thrust the blade into Samuele, who moved aside, but not enough to avoid the blade which cut into the muscle of Samuele's upper left arm. With blood suddenly beginning to gush out, Samuele took a big breath. Realizing his partial success, Toni eagerly moved on. With a quick glance from the wound on his arm to Toni's face,

Samuele moved from side to side, knowing that unless he got the knife away, he would be too weak to continue. As he moved toward the wall, Samuele tripped on one of the rocks, landing on the ground. Toni jumped, his knife pointed at Samuele's chest. As the blade came down, Samuele moved to one side and Toni sank the blade into the ground. Samuele moved over and grabbed Toni's arm. As they clutched they tossed on the ground, making their way toward the rosebush. In an instant, Samuele twisted Toni's arm with all his strength. But Toni held on. Slipping one arm around Samuele's neck, Toni attempted to apply a strangle-hold. Samuele, with all his strength, put his hands up, and brought Toni's hand down into the rosebush. As the thorns stuck deep into his hand, Toni released the blade with a tremendous shout. Once again, Toni got a grip around Samuele's neck. Samuele swung his arm, landing a solid blow to Toni's face. Toni swung back, but his hand once again caught the rose bush full of hardy thorns. Desperately, Tony pulled his hand which was bleeding profusely, but still kept his hold on Samuele. With a quick and decisive move, Samuele pushed to one side, breaking Toni's hold. He quickly jumped on Toni, who fell to the ground. Gaining a position on top, Samuele began to hit him savagely. With blood coming from his nose, Toni tried to throw Samuele off to no avail. In control, Samuele kept on hitting Toni. Squirming and moving violently to one side, Toni tossed Samuele off. Samuele, however, quickly regained his balance and jumped on Toni, pinning his arms to the ground and holding them down with his knees. Toni, almost completely exhausted and breathing deeply, tried in vain to get away. Suddenly, Samuele bent forward. Picking up a large rock next to the wall, he raised it high above Toni's face. With a wild and ferocious look on his face, he paused for an instant. Then as he was about to crush Toni's face, Toni desperately invoked the word *God*.

"God, help me," he shouted, his mouth open wide.

Samuele froze. Having brought the heavy rock down to the level of Toni's eyes, Samuele stopped, his eyes staring at it, forgetful of Toni pinned under his knees. Noticing that Samuele had become momentarily fixed, Toni raised his legs and shot them forward, cause Samuele to lose his balance. The rock fell from his hand just as Toni pulled his head from below Samuele's legs. Samuele did not move. With his hands out as though he was still clutching the rock, he began to repeat Toni's word.

"God!" he said. After a brief moment, and without changing his position, he repeated God's name again, while blood dripped from his hand and arm.

Having freed himself from Samuele, and noticing Samuele motionless and still on his knees, Toni staggered on the ground for a few seconds. Then, getting up on his feet, Toni, who could finally have easily killed Samuele, ran down the path, leaving Samuele on his knees, talking to himself in an obvious trance.

"God! God! God!" Samuele repeated, not knowing that God may have just spared his life. Raising his voice, he continued. "God! God! God..." repeating it at least another ten times and pausing only when out of breath. With his arms still out as though he were clutching the rock that was to kill Toni, Samuele kept on repeating God's name.

Shouting at the top of his lungs, he called out to God "God! God! God! God!" for about a half-hour. Meanwhile, the material of his torn shirt was clinging to the wound and beginning to coagulate, as he unconsciously went on repeating God's name. His voice coarse by now, he nevertheless continued to a whisper.

"God! God!" he repeated.

Up above, the moon had regained its full orange color, reflecting its light all over the valley. After about an hour, Samuele got up. Voiceless, but with his lips moving, he kept on repeating God's name. Suddenly, he began to walk, first into the cornfield, then into another. Aimlessly, he walked by a bare field, across another that had been recently plowed, finally reaching a ravine full of abandoned ancient grottos and tunnels. Without falling, he made his way down to the mid level, his lips moving, his eyes staring but not seeing. As he limped across another field, and with his eyes fixed on the moon, he kept on descending without knowing where, why, or whom he might meet, unlike Dante in his *Inferno*. Samuele's lips continued moving, not from the kind of cold he had suffered in the real hell of the Russian camps, but from an unexplainable compulsion hidden deep within his subconscious and refusing to surface into consciousness.

"God! God!" he kept repeating to himself voicelessly like an automaton being pulled, by who knows what gravity, further down the ravine, his limping more noticeable except to himself. He crossed yet another field until he came to a blind bend in the ravine. Stepping off, he landed face down on the ground. On coming to rest about halfway down, he got up and began to walk again, his teeth now chattering feverishly. He stepped off only to fall again, this time finding himself--if that can be said of a man on automatic pilot--at the bottom of the precipice very nearly exhausted. However he did it, he managed to get up and walk along the clay ground until he stumbled into a cavity, falling into it head-first. Then, fixing himself with his body on the ground and his head sticking up above the uneven parapet of the cave, he looked from side to side, his lips continuously moving. Having looked up into the sky, he suddenly slumped down, his arms stretched out, his face resting on the cool and humid clay.

Toni, after having attempted to wash himself off, returned home. Though he tried to go to his room undetected, Franca saw him. Noticing his badly bruised face and cut-up hand, she quickly became alarmed and frightened. She went close to her brother.

"What happened?" she asked, her tone revealing more fear about Samuele than concern for her brother's battered face and body.

"None of your goddam business. Leave me alone!"

"No, you got to tell me."

"Get out'f here," he commanded, crunching his teeth.

"I'm not going unless you tell."

"You son-of-a-bitch..."

"...That's what I think of you."

Toni picked up a heavy stick and went toward Franca, who quickly ran to the kitchen where Ernesto was sitting down sipping his wine. Hearing Franca's call for help, he rushed out. Seeing his father, Toni came to an immediate and frantic stop as his sister ran for shelter.

"Look at him: he's been in a fight and doesn't want to say with whom. I think it was Samuele," Franca said aloud.

"He's been in a fight. Just look at his face and hands," Ernesto said without much concern. "I can see you were in a fight. I can also see that whoever fought you could have bashed in your brains. Did he spare you? I wouldn't've." Then, he turned to Franca. "Call your mother; she'll want to lick his wounds. Go ahead; she's upstairs getting the bed ready."

"But I want to know if it was Samuele!"

"Even if it were, and I agree with you, he must be a great man. Your brother, here, is the one that got more than he bargained for. You can see for yourself--what a mess!. Don't worry, if the other party is Samuele, be assured he is well and in good health. Go, go, get your mother. Her little boy needs his mother. Tell her to come down; her small son needs breast feeding."

Franca left, not too convinced of her father's assurances. While she was away, Ernesto looked squarely at his battered son.

"Tell me," he said, "have you learned a lesson from tonight's fight?"

Toni looked at his father but did not answer. Ernesto repeated the question with greater emphasis. This time, though he hesitated, Toni answered in the affirmative.

"Was your life spared?"

Toni did not expect that question. Though his eyes hurt, he opened them wide.

"Well!" insisted Ernesto.

"Yes," Toni answered, humiliated.

"Good. Go ahead to your mother now, and never raise your hand to your sister again, do you hear, if you don't want me to break both your arms."

Toni looked up, understanding that if his father had been in Samuele's position, he would have been dead by now.

"Well!" his father insisted once again.

"Yes," Toni answered, walking away.

From above, Toni's mother was already showing worrying concern about her son, her voice clearly reaching Ernesto and Toni.

"There she goes; she hasn't seen the shape you're in and she already thinks you're dead. Wait till she sees you."

Toni walked past his father. Giving him one last furtive glance, he walked inside to join his mother. On seeing him, his mother uttered a scream.

CHAPTER 21

By midnight, everyone at Franca's house had gone to bed and sleeping. Franca, however, lay awake on her bed.

Outside, all was quiet and peaceful under the bright light of the moon, except for the crickets. Even the dog slept soundly. Since Ernesto had killed the fox that had feasted on his chickens and ducks, the dog slept more heavily. Toward one o'clock in the morning, the dog was awakened from noises from below.

On hearing the dog growl, Franca quickly rushed to the window. Suddenly the dog began to bark, causing Ernesto to awaken. Having gone for his shotgun, he posted himself behind the window. Downstairs, the dog continued to bark and growl. After a few moments, a voice called out to Ernesto. It was Maria. Recognizing the voice, Franca quickly opened the window.

"Maria, Maria! Is that you?"

"Yes," Maria answered over the dog's barking. Meanwhile, Ernesto, having opened the window and quieted his dog, told Maria to approach the house.

"I am looking for Samuele," Maria answered in a loud voice.

Stopping short by the door when the dog began to growl again, Maria waited for the door to open, relieved in seeing Franca rushing toward her.

"What's happened?" Franca asked with concern.

"Samuele didn't return home. He said he was coming to see you. Was he here?"

"No! He didn't come here. He wasn't here all night."

Excited, Franca ran upstairs to her brother. Meanwhile, Ernesto had come down to talk with Maria. After Maria had explained about Samuele, Ernesto ran upstairs to his son's room, where Franca, having already awakened him, was asking Toni the whereabouts of Samuele, but Toni would not answer. Toni also refused to answer his father's questions until Ernesto got mad. Grabbing Toni by his bruised head, Ernest literally sat him up on the bed.

"Where is Samuele?" Ernesto asked in a loud voice.

"I don't know," Toni answered in a weak voice. He was hurting all over and was unable to answer to the satisfaction of his father. At this time, Toni's mother entered the room, demanding to know what was happening, and quickly rushing to Toni's side. Franca tried to explain, but her father interrupted. Ernesto grabbed his wife the shoulders, turned her against the wall, and holding her shoulders, he pushed her out the door, telling her to stay out. Toni looked on helplessly, realizing his father meant business.

Ernesto returned to Toni's bedside under the staring eyes of a terrified Franca, who had never seen her father so angry.

"Let's start from the beginning," Ernesto said in a calmly controlled voice. "Tell me what happened tonight; tell me everything from start to finish and do not leave out any details, and don't tell any lies. Do you understand?"

"Yes."

In a weak, at times inaudible voice, Toni told his father exactly what had happened from the time he was with Rosa, to the moment he saw Samuele, to the time he left Samuele by the well. Toni also told his father about the knife wound, how they had struggled, and how Samuele was about to crush his head with the rock. As Toni talked, Ernesto listened without lifting his eyes from his son. On hearing that Toni had left Samuele alive, Franca felt relieved. Ernesto, on the other hand, was seized by a tremendous burst of anger.

As Toni had slumped into his bed while telling what had happened, when having no more to add, Ernesto pulled his son up with a savage pull. Then, swinging back, he slapped Toni's battered face with uncontrollable fury. Franca ran to her father, clasping her arms around him.

"Please, please, leave him alone. Let's go look for Samuele. Father, father, please!" she screamed in despair.

Responding to his daughter's words, Ernesto stopped, releasing Toni, who, almost unconscious and in terrible pain, slumped once again into his bed. Ernesto and Franca left the room, hurrying downstairs to Maria, who was anxiously waiting.

"Come on, Maria, let's go. Toni and Samuele had a fight. Toni is badly beaten and Samuele must be severely wounded."

"My God! To think that he had planned to come here to tell Franca some wonderful news. The Cavaliere has asked Samuele to help out with the Obelisk. Instead, joy has turned to grief. Oh, God, I hope he is well. I hope we find him."

While Toni was being comforted by his mother, Ernesto, Franca, and Maria left to go to search for Samuele. On the way, they decided to stop by Mr. Banno's to check on Rosa. Ernesto wishfully thought that Samuele may have gone there to see Rosa instead.

In no time, they were in front of Mr. Banno's unlit house. Ernesto knocked on the door. When no one answered, he picked up a rock and began beating on the door, calling to Mr. Banno at the same time. Finally, on seeing a light from above, Ernesto stopped pounding on the door, but continued to entreating Mr. Banno to hurry.

"What's going on out there?" Mr. Banno yelled from his half-opened window. "What's all the noise?"

"Hurry down. It's me, Ernesto. Come down right away. Something has happened to Samuele."

While Mr. Banno made his way down to open the door, the three remained close together, waiting for Banno to appear.

"Did Samuele come here tonight?" Ernesto asked without wasting time.

When Mr. Banno answered that he hadn't seen Samuele at all, Ernesto ordered him to tell Rosa to come down.

"Why?" Mr. Banno asked, resentful of the intrusion.

"Because Toni was with her tonight."

"What do you mean 'was with her tonight?' What are you talking about? My daughter was home all night long. We all went to bed soon after sun down..."

"...Hurry up, you're wasting time. Call her down and let her tell us what happened. Samuele may be dying for all we know."

"My daughter has no story to tell," Mr. Banno answered resolutely.

Ernesto got so furious that he threatened to go up himself if Mr. Banno would not immediately comply. Faced with that possibility, and finally believing that something very serious must have happened for Ernesto to act that way, Mr. Banno went up to get Rosa. In a couple of minutes, Mr. Banno was down with Rosa. Ernesto wasted no time in speaking to her.

"Toni told me he fought with Samuele. Is that true?"

"I didn't see them fight..."

"...See, I told you, Ernesto. Rosa was in all night," Mr. Banno interrupted.

Not paying any attention to him, Ernesto went on questioning Rosa.

"Toni told me he was with you in the cornfield next to the abandoned well."

Rosa did not answer at first. Then she said no.

"Yes, by God, Toni said so. Either you are lying or Toni is. If it is Toni, you can be sure he will be dead by tomorrow. Now, hurry up and tell me if you saw Samuele."

"Now, just wait a minute," interrupted Mr. Banno, who was listening with his mouth wide open.

Ernesto pushed him aside, warning him not to interrupt again. Seeing Ernesto's resolution, Mr. Banno stepped back to join the two women who were looking on mortified.

"Well, woman, hurry up. Samuele may be dying out there. We have to find him and fast."

"I only saw him for a moment very early in the evening."

"By the well?"

"Yes," she answered with hesitation.

Ernesto turned to Maria and Franca and quickly made their way to the well as their best bet in tracing Samuele's whereabouts, leaving behind a distraught Rosa together with her desolate father. They rushed to the path that led to the well and made their way to it.

The moon being bright, the three looked around the well for any traces of Samuele, each following a single direction, their heads bent to the ground. At one side, near the rose bush, Maria stumbled over the knife. She picked it up, looked at its stained blade, and quickly called Ernesto, her heart pumping hard.

"Let's see," Ernesto said pulling the knife away from Maria's hand. After looking at it closely, first upside down, then sideways. After a thorough inspection, during which time the two women waited with their hearts in their hands, Ernesto raised his head.

"It's Toni's and the blood must be Samuele's, because Toni did not have any knife wounds. The problem is, Maria, that unless he went for help, he may be bleeding to death. Of course, I'm only thinking the worst. If Samuele doesn't know what to do in such cases, with all that he's been through, I don't know who else would. I suggest we look more around here. If we find no traces, it means he's gone for help and we'll have to wait till morning."

"What if he doesn't make it?" Maria asked in a low voice.

Franca, meanwhile, listened to both but said nothing. She felt as though the man she loved may have been taken from her permanently. Though she listened, she kept on walking, looking for traces of her lover's whereabouts.

"Let's look by the corn field," Ernesto said.

The three continued their search, all tending to walk away and around the stone cylindrical wall. Finally, not conscious of her direction, Franca found herself in front of the well. Stumbling on a rock, she looked at the wall. There, somewhat scattered, she saw the roses. As she moved closer, she noticed a few others on the ground. Without calling the attention of Maria or of her father, she gathered the flowers together into a bunch and held them close to her breast, the roses being of the type she had secretly received before from Samuele. She knew, therefore, that Samuele had met his fate because of her. As she held the roses close to her, she began to cry, tears rolling down her face.

Seeing her standing still, Ernesto called out to his daughter, asking if she had found something. Without betraying her find, she shook her head and began to walk around again.

The three covered every inch of ground around the well and in the cornfield as well. Finally, Ernesto called Maria and Franca together to tell them their efforts right now were futile.

"We'll start out early in the morning. I'll start right from my house. Come on now, Maria, we'll take you home. There isn't anything we can do now. Nothing. I'm sure Samuel knows what to do. Come, let's go."

Without answering, Maria began to walk toward the main road, Ernesto following close behind, while Franca remained still for a few seconds to allow for a distance to build between herself and her father.

When they reached Maria's house, Franca remained on the street. When she and her father began to walk home, she again walked behind. Holding the roses close to her breast, she began to cry again, with more tears rolling down her already wet face.

CHAPTER 22

The next morning at cock crow, Franca got up quietly. Without bothering to wash or to groom, she sneaked outside into the gray light of early morning, and went unnoticed even to the animals semi asleep. Only the dog lifted its head to Franca.

Without looking back, she started down the path, walking fast, turning back from time to time, then running as fast as she could, cutting across fields until she came to the well. Her unexpected presence startled the many birds in their early feeding. She also encountered a couple of wild rabbits and wondered why they were still alive in fox country.

When she got to the well, she looked around for signs. Though the sun had not appeared on the eastern horizon, there was enough light for her to see. After circling around a couple of times, she found Samuele's trail. She followed it through the multi-colored cornfield to the open field full of clear footprints leading to the ravine, a dangerous place both because of its rugged terrain and the wild animals that lived there. Though no one had ever been molested, the possibility of Samuele being attacked must have been great, due to his condition. Besides, no one had spent the night out there, as best as Franca could recall.

Nevertheless, she thought of the worst possible things happening to Samuele. With her head bent toward the ground, she walked fast over the footprints. Her uncombed hair fell down her back, her light skirt spread out each time she leapt over the drainage ditches separating the fields. When she came to the edge of the ravine, she looked for a pathway, as the footprints were no longer visible. She was about to call out Samuele's name when she discovered more footprints in the field below. Relieved, she ran to one side which was not as steep and where she could hold on to the sparse bushes. In no time she was in the open field below, following the foot prints once again. As the field slanted steeply downward, she began to run, picking up speed. Suddenly, she reached another edge, almost falling over the edge, for she could not stop immediately. She was able to hold on to some of the underbrush and come to a complete stop. However, there were no footprints. This part of the ravine was much steeper and almost completely obstructed by higher and ticker underbrush and large oaks. Unable to see below, she crept from side to side, looking for a pathway or some sign of what was below. When she did not find a way down, she began to call out the name of Samuele! At the sound of her voice, a couple of jack-rabbits sprinted from their burrows, their unexpected noise startling Franca, who was relieved on seeing they were rabbits. "Samuele!" she called out as she ran along the edge looking for a way down. "Samuele!" she called out again, but no answer. Gasping, she finally found a place that was not as steep, and with the same precautions she had taken to descent the first part of the ravine, she made her way down to the bottom where she found a pathway running parallel to the edge of the last and steepest cliff with its brook whose water ran noisily downhill. Standing on the clay pathway, she looked around at the rugged land scape. Suddenly, she felt a humid cold penetrating her body.

"Samuele, Samuele!" she called, as she moved downstream. At about fifty feet from where she had descended, she came upon other footprints and was relieved in noting they were the same she had been following.

"Samuele!" she shouted, then stopped to listen for a response.

Running downhill, she could see snake holes and caves along the clay wall of the ravine. Below, a haze arose above a small but noisy water drop.

"Samuele!" she called and stopped to listen once again. "Samuele! Samuele!" she repeated in desperation. On getting no answer, she was seized by a fit of hysteria. "Samuele, Samuele, Samuele," she called out at the top of her lungs, searching the landscape "Samuele!" she frantically called out again. Not getting an answer, and not seeing any footprints on the hard surface, she sprinted along. After having run for another hundred yards or so, she stopped once again. "Samuele!" she yelled persistently. Then, she waited. "He's not dead, I hope," she said to herself, a shiver running through her body both for the thought and the cold. Up ahead, out of sight, was the cave with Samuele slumped over still sleeping.

"Samuele, Samuele!" Franca cried out.

This time, on hearing the voice, Samuele opened his eyes. Raising his head, he groaned from the pervading pain. Staring out into space, he moved his lips, whispering the name of God. When he heard Franca's distinctive voice calling his name, he shook with tremors, confused by Franca's voice and dazed by the incoming enemy deadly fire power. His hands covering his ears, he did not know whether to raise his head over the parapet or sink lower into his fox hole. And Franca? What was she doing in hell? His lips moving as before, he looked out, his eye barely above the parapet: everything in front of him was unreal and hazy, including Franca's persistent call.

"Samuele!" she kept on crying out, her voice carrying a distinct tone of despair. "Samuele!" she continued.

Each time she uttered his name, Samuele reacted a bit more as things in front of him began to take more and more shape with the voice coming insistently closer. Finally, he stopped repeating the name of God and began to whisper Franca's name as he looked in her direction.

Suddenly, her silhouette appeared before his eyes. He looked at her in disbelief.

"Franca, it's you," he finally whispered, as one coming out of a coma. She did not hear him.

"Samuele!" she cried out.

"Here! here!" he responded excitedly, his physical pain more acute. "Here, here I am," he repeated. But his voice did not carry. Finally, struggling to his feet, he leaned out, the word Franca on his lips.

On seeing him, Franca reacted with a burst of joy, her eyes opening wide.

"Samuele!" she shouted as she rushed to him. On seeing him in full view, she raised her hands to her mouth in disbelief of what she was seeing. "My God!" she exclaimed in a toned-down voice as she looked at the battered face, the dried blood on his arm, and the bruised hand covered with thorns. With tears in her eyes, and the name of Samuele stuck in her throat, she rushed to him, locking her arms around him. With obvious difficulty, Samuele clasped his hands around her waist as best he could.

"My God! Oh, my God!" she continued.

"God! God!" he repeated, causing Franca to look up at him.

"Thank God, you're alive. Thank God. I was sure you'd be dead. I thought I'd never find you alive. I thought I'd never see you again. Thank God."

"God!" he repeated after her.

"Yes," she said as she pressed her face against his chest.

When Samuele repeated God's name, Franca looked up at him again, finding it strange he should say only that word. On looking at the battered face, she could see that

Samuele was still in trauma. Lifting his hand, she looked at the stubs around which blood had dried in ringlets. She turned his hand and brought the palm to her mouth. She held the other hand and kissed it as well. Then she looked at his arm covered by a shirt glued to the wound by dried blood. Then she looked again at his face. She had to look at him again to be assured that what she was seeing was real and not hallucinations.

"Come! Here, hold on to me. Let's get out of this place," she pleaded softly, lifting Samuele's arm over her shoulder, helping him down near the brook. She went to the water and drenched the large white handkerchief she had taken from Samuele's pocket. She then ran back to him and began to gently wash his face. Samuele reacted to the pain with wrinkles to his forehead. Franca noticed the added strain and stopped. She asked him if it hurt, and he nodded in the affirmative. Putting her hand to his mouth, she caressed his lips and kissed him softly.

Franca was cleaning Samuele's bruised hand when from above in the distance, she heard a voice calling. Franca paused to listen while exchanging glances with Samuele. Not hearing another sound, she went on removing the broken thorns and cleaning the plasma around the wounds. While she passed the freshly wet cloth over his hand, Samuele placed his other hand over her shoulder causing Franca to look up to his lucid eyes. Though he was looking at her, she noticed his thoughts seemed elsewhere. Yet, he uttered no sound.

"You've suffered a lot, I can tell," Franca remarked, her tone neither a question nor an exclamation. She fixed her eyes on his and waited for him to speak. He didn't, however, but kept staring at her in silence. Then, turning her eyes to his hand, she continued to pull the rest of the thorns. Meanwhile, Samuele broke his silence by muttering the name of God.

"Yes, yes," she answered, "thank God all is going well. Thank God. Oh! How much you must have suffered. As if what you went through in Russia wasn't enough; you had to come back to this."

"I almost killed your brother," Samuele finally emitted a full sentence, though in a whisper.

"He deserves to die, but not by you, my darling. Some day someone else will."

"No, no, no," Samuele answered turning his head sideways. "There's too much killing, too much. I almost killed your brother."

"He deserved it," insisted Franca.

"No, he didn't."

"Didn't he try to kill you? So he said."

Shaking his head, he paused. Looking away across to the other side of the brook, he began to speak again. "No one has the right to kill, in anger or otherwise."

"You have seen enough of death. Is that right?"

Samuele did not answer. There was no need to tell her or anyone else about the things he had seen and done.

"I'm sorry," she added, on seeing his unwillingness to answer her question. "I'm sorry. I love you."

Samuele looked into her soft and understanding eyes, caressing them gently. Franca placed his hand into hers and kissed it several times. Moved, Samuele drew her close and kissed her as best he could, assuring her that he loved her and thankful to her for saving his life. She moved her face under his and kissed him back.

While she was telling Samuele how much she loved him, they heard a woman's voice from up the ravine. It was Maria.

"It's your mother!"

"Mother!" Samuele attempted to call out. But his voice did not carry.

Placing the wet handkerchief on Samuele's leg, Franca raced upward in the direction of the voice, yelling and running toward Maria, who was still calling.

"Maria, Maria!" yelled Franca. "Down here, down here. Samuele is here, he's here!"

"Franca, Franca, I hear you," Maria answered from above.

While Franca waited below, Maria made her way down. Exhilarated, Franca told Maria that Samuele was well. Then, leading the way, she helped Maria down the last part of the steep hill, and in no time, they were standing in front of Samuele.

On seeing her son in that condition, Maria covered her face with her hands.

"My son!" Maria cried out. "My son!" she repeated as she stared into his battered face.

"Mother, I'm all right."

"Why, why?" she said, moving up to him. "None of this happened to you in the war. You had to come back here for this." Maria was angry and her voice showed it.

"No, Mother, we're human beings regardless of what's happened."

"What are you doing here? Why didn't you come home?"

"I don't know. I'm not used to returning home after these things, I guess."

With an expression of acute sorrow, Maria closed her eyes for a few seconds. Samuele coughed slightly.

"Are you ready to come home now?"

"Yes, I'm ready. I'm causing you anguish. I'm sorry."

Slowly, the three began to walk uphill. After they had made their way up the first part of the ravine and were crossing the field leading to the second one, about three--quarters of the way up, they heard a noise from somewhere up above. They stopped to look. After pausing a few seconds, Maria saw Ernesto coming down the steep descent, his head lowered so as not to trip.

"Father!" called Franca.

Ernesto was speechless. As they advanced toward him, he started to walk toward them. Finally they joined and began to walk toward home. On making the transition over the edge of the ravine, they came to a stop to look at the sun emitting its strong light from the east. Franca turned to Samuele, held his hand tightly and looking deep into his eyes said, "The sun is up."

Samuele squeezed her hand tight. With tears in his eyes, he led her on, staying slightly ahead of her. Behind them, with their heads bowed, the two parents followed gratefully.

CHAPTER 23

Besides delivering mail, the fat postal clerk often delivered verbal messages for a fee.

Some time after the Toni-Rosa incident, she rode her bicycle toward Samuele's house. By the proud expression on her face one could easily tell that she had something important to deliver, for, she pedaled briskly and eagerly.

On approaching Mr. Banno's house, and seeing him outside the door, she could not resist stopping.

"Don't you want to know where I'm going?" she asked, a smirk on her round face, her voice carrying an obviously insolent irony.

Mr. Banno, rather despondent, was enduring a good share of ridicule by many of his neighbors, the type he himself dished out without compassion. When he did not respond, the postal clerk continued in full glory.

"Well, don't you want to know?" she asked tantalizingly.

"I don't care," he answered, his voice weak, his face pallid, his eyes, which formerly shone brightly, full of gloom. All of a sudden, Mr. Banno had grown old by at least ten years.

The fat woman noticed his apathy, but could neither be charitable nor lose the opportunity to get even. She remembered and resented the manner with which he had dealt with her throughout the years, his braggadocio when it concerned his family, and his vehemence in putting down those of lesser fortune such as she.

"How come you don't care any more, Mr. Banno? You always stuck your long nose into other people's business. Did something happen to you lately? Or, should I ask: did something happen to one of your dearly beloved?"

Mr. Banno looked at the squared chin of the fat lady. In front of her, he felt defeated and humiliated. Without saying it, he was asking for pity. But she was not going to let him off so easy, and he understood it.

"You don't remember, eh! What's the matter, you've lost your voice... Why, the big mouth of the town has lost its voice! Are we finally spared? Oh, by the way, I almost forgot to ask: how is your little... I mean, big virgin? I don't see her around much, so I cannot ask her."

"I never liked you before; I don't like you now," Mr. Banno answered tartly.

"So, you are talking. You do have a voice. I thought you had lost it. Too bad, too bad you didn't lose it. You know, Mr. Banno, people are still wondering if the ring Toni gave your daughter, in exchange for...you know what--well, people are wondering what carat gold. Some are saying it is forty-eight carats. Is it possible? Tell me, what shall I say when they tell them me that the ring is gold inside and copper-coated outside.

"Well, I've got to go now. Oh, I almost forgot another thing," she continued, a perpetual smile of sarcasm filling every crack of her fat and round face which stood out like putty. Mr. Banno noticed it all, but did not have the will to retort. Without the least sympathy she went on.

"I got a message for Lucia this time. You know, Lucia, Samuele's sister, the one that has the baby. It seems she's getting a proposal. Do you think Toni will be proposing to Rosa? Or don't you think him worthwhile? Well, I've got to go now. Goodby, stupid. It couldn't have happened to a better fathead."

With a smile that turned into a coarse laugh, she stepped on the pedal and moved on, sitting straight and upright on the fragile and diminutive two-wheeler. Mr. Banno followed her with an apathetic and indifferent look as she disappeared beyond the tall poplars.

When the fat woman reached her destination she found Samuele answering the door.

Samuele's face was practically free of scars except for his hands still showing signs of bruises. The cut on his arm had healed so well that just three days earlier the doctor took out the stitches.

"I am happy to see you," the postal clerk said with a smile of satisfaction. "You know I'm the one who brought the good news to your mother, the letter from the Red Cross saying you were alive and returning home. Well, I'm back again with some more good news, I think. But I cannot tell you. I have to tell Lucia. Is she in?"

"She's out back. You know the way to the yard, don't you?"

"Sure do, sure do. Well, I got go. You look good, much better than I thought. And by the way, congratulations on the land you bought from Mr. Banno, the ass. I'm very happy for you. You've done the right thing. Don't forget now, when you and Franca get married, be sure to invite me. I have to make another wedding sooner, I hope. Well, I can't say any more. I've got to go see Lucia."

The fat woman disappeared behind the house, leaving Samuele wondering just what her exuberant babbling was all about. But he was not going to question her, preferring I will him to hear it from Lucia herself.

With a serious expression on his face, he went inside, where he was soon joined by Lucia, who entered with a great big smile on her face. Looking at her gleaming face, Samuele asked the reason behind the clerk's visit.

"Silvestro wants to marry me. His wife died, and he wants me back."

"That's good news. But, do you like him?"

"Yes, of course."

"Are you sure?"

"Yes, I am sure. Why are you asking?"

"I don't want you to do things you don't want to. What I mean is, I don't want you to do this because of me. I want you to get married, of course, but to the man you want."

"I want him."

"Have you told Mother?"

"Yes, and she's very happy," she answered. But Lucia did not tell the whole truth.

Her mother advised Lucia to talk with Silvestro first before telling Samuele; however, Lucia could not resist telling her brother, for she was sure of Silvestro. Girlish, Lucia told Samuele he would like Silvestro.

"I will like him if you do," he answered. "When will I meet him?" he asked, having noticed his sister's almost uncontained happiness.

"Soon, very soon. I didn't give him my answer yet. I wanted to talk to you first."

"You didn't have to. You do what is best for you. Remember, you also have a son."

With a smile on her face, and eyes that revealed her inner joy, Lucia nodded. Then, with a gentle sprint, she returned to her mother to tell her about Samuele's positive reaction.

After Lucia left, Samuele sat down to think about the news he had just heard. He saw that Lucia was happy, but he was not sure whether she was happy because she was getting married, or getting married to repay him for his kindness and understanding.

Reflecting on this new situation, he nevertheless felt a certain exhilaration. Lucia acted so naturally happy--something he hadn't seen for such a long time, that he almost forgot how many more things there were to be discovered. Life could not be cruel all the time, and that this latest was proof that life was worthwhile. It had to be, otherwise he would not have survived the battlefield, the marches, the cold, the camps, the hunger, and the recent mental and physical torments.

Down the road, the fat woman stopped once again in front of Mr. Banno's house. Balancing herself with one foot on the ground, with her back perpendicularly plump on the hidden saddle, she once again tormented Mr. Banno doing his chores at the side of the house.

"I have delivered the message. Don't you want to know what it said, Mr. Banno?" she asked. Mr. Banno didn't even turn in her direction. Determined to get his attention and to get even with him one more time, she pressed on.

"Lucia is getting married," she stated matter-of-factly. "When is your little... I mean, big virgin getting married? Will you be inviting me to the wedding? I have left-over baby bottles and nipples: I thought I could give those as gifts. Or might Rosa need them sooner?"

Mr. Banno looked up, raising his head altogether, and staring at the fat woman smiling triumphantly, knowing all too well what she was up to, and knowing, deep down that she was justified. Yes, she was cruel, but no less cruel than he had been. Nevertheless, he felt he had to put an end to her pestering insolence.

"Thank you," he answered in an even voice. "Just drop them off on your next trip."

Hearing him speak so seriously, the fat woman stopped smiling. Without another word, she began to giggle. Laughing out loud, she placed her foot on the worn pedal and pushed off, continuing with her hysterical laugh.

CHAPTER 24

Having heard from the doctor that Samuele had been involved in a serious fight, the Cavaliere decided to visit him to assure himself of Samuele's health as well as the status of bull's training.

Now that Samuele had almost completely recuperated, he had planned on trying to place the bull under yoke, and had already made preparations for this important event.

On arriving at Samuele's house, the Cavaliere once again waited at the entrance, as he did not want to interrupt activities taking place within.

Looking in from the side of the house, the Cavaliere observed the big animal tied under the sprawling fig tree, the children looking on, and Samuele raising a large, heavy timber onto a wooden horse, then roping it around the elm tree and extended outward at a suitable height, Samuele's intention being to simulate the tackle of two draft animals under yoke and thereby begin to train his bull.

Samuele had barely succeeded in roping the end of the heavy timber when the Cavaliere made his presence known.

After greeting him, Samuele invited the Cavaliere to join him in the yard. On seeing the strange contraption at close range, the Cavaliere asked about its purpose.

"I'm planning to train the bull with it," Samuele explained, somewhat surprised at himself in that he was not expecting to explain it to anyone. "Notice," he continued, "once I raise the end, I can tie it up onto the yoke, and the bull can either stand still or walk around. I tied it to rotate around the tree. I can tighten it according to the amount of weight I want the animal to bear and control it with this pole."

The Cavaliere listened and watched, and, concluding that Samuele was truly ingenious, he asked Samuele to yoke the animal for the experiment. Samuele quickly walked and got the bull. With the help of the Cavaliere, Samuele yoked the animal to the timber. Then, holding up the other end of the yoke, Samuele slipped its steel ring over the end of the log. To make the other end lighter, he took off the oxbow. After fastening the ring to the log, Samuele moved to the right side of the bull, and, together with the Cavaliere, watched the animal standing by the log without a sign of protest. The two men were satisfied as were the children, who began to cheer on seeing their pet bull under yoke, the boy obviously knowing he was in for more and better rides.

When Samuele finally decided to make the bull walk, he found the bull running head-on to the end of the log, as there was no counter-weight on the other side for a second animal. Stopping it before causing any harm, Samuele tied the other end of the yoke (in the form of a triangle) to the front and back of the central timber so that when the animal pulled forward the rope would hold the yoke in position. That in place, Samuele tried once again. This time, the animal walked forward, walking around the tree with Samuele keeping his hand on its neck. The Cavaliere, holding the children by the hand, stood watching as Samuele completed several passes.

"The trouble with that," commented the Cavaliere, "is that the animal may learn to walk in a fixed direction. Going around in a circular fashion is contrary to the actual terrain which, because it is rugged, the pull may have to be omni-directional."

"You're right. We'll make him go the other direction as well."

Standing close to the animal, the two men paused. The children, familiar with draft animals, were waiting to the same thing taking place there. When they saw no sign of this, the girl asked Samuele when he was going to get a cow from the stable. The two men looked at each other.

"Why not?" Samuele said. "After all, he'll have to get used to another animal. Wait a second, I'll go get the other animal while you untie the other end of the yoke."

Samuele went into the stall. In a few seconds, he appeared with his cow. As they approached, the bull turned to see what was happening. The cow, strange to all this, moved forward cautiously; then, unexpectedly, it stopped altogether. Pulling on the rope, Samuele encouraged her to continue walking. Instead, the cow planted her front feet solidly on the ground and refused to move. Samuele, seeing she was scared, decided to wait. Moving to her side, he began to caress her neck. Meanwhile, the children urged Samuele to hurry up. Surprised by their eagerness, the Cavaliere bent down. Putting his arms around both of them, he told them to be patient.

After a few minutes, Samuele attempted to make the cow go forward. Moving very slowly, she finally moved into position next to the towering bull. Her eyes were turned toward the bull, which, in turn, stared at her. Samuele slipped the oxbow under her neck and hooked it to the crosspiece. Then, kicking aside the rope he had dropped, he pulled back. With one hand held fast on the cow's neck, he ordered the team to go forward. The bull reacted to Samuele's order, but the cow stood still. Samuele quickly ordered the bull to stop. After having paused for a couple more seconds, Samuele attempted to make both go forward. The bull quickly obeyed, but the cow once again hesitated. Samuele continued prodding until finally she began to move forward in short steps. Slowly, Samuele led them around the tree in a complete circle, with the bull pacing himself to the speed of the cow. The Cavaliere and Samuele noticed that the bull had an uncanny sense of direction and weight distribution. Extremely pleased by the results, the two adults congratulated each other while the children immediately asked to be placed on each of the two animals.

"Not this time," answered Samuele. "Some other time, maybe." But when they grumbled with disappointment, Samuele weakened. "I'll take you around afterward," he added, bringing the children to shouts of joy and the Cavaliere to smiles of great satisfaction.

After about thirty minutes of working out with the animals, Samuele decided to stop and fulfill his promise to the children.

After placing his nephew on the bull and the girl on the cow, he cautiously ordered the team to move forward. Reacting with typical docility, the animals moved ahead to the cheers of the children.

Satisfied that things were even better than expected, the distinguished Cavaliere left Samuele's yard, knowing that his Obelisk would be pulled by one of the best combinations of man and animal.

CHAPTER 25

While Samuele and the children were in the yard---Samuele was working and the children following him around--a man of medium height stopped in front of the house. It was Silvestro come to make plans for the marriage ceremony.

He stood outside in front of the door, afraid to knock for fear of having to face Samuele, whom he didn't even know. There he stood, in his faded corduroy jacket with unmatched trousers. He was also wearing a pair of American military boots and a shirt whose collar was much too big for the size of his neck, about an inch of space between his Adam's apple and the first button of his collar. He also wore a bright tie, of the style often preferred by younger and more exuberant people. On his head he wore a light brown straw hat which covered his well-trimmed and very curly hair. His forehead was reddish with obvious lines crossing it. Beneath his thick eyebrows beamed deep green eyes partly covered by eyelids that never seemed completely opened. His nose was rather large, and so was his mouth. There were deep grooves on each side of his mouth with wrinkles running to smaller ones around his eyes.

Silvestro was a man in his middle thirties, having lived all of his life on the farm and knew nothing else but the hard work of his un-benign land whose harvests had been meager indeed. He was so conditioned by his labor that on his countenance he resembled the rugged land where even flowers had a difficult time pushing through the hard surface. Many things were there, perhaps from generations gone by. Yet, he never asked how or why they were there. He didn't even know how to ask.

He stood there in front of the door, looking around, pausing for long moments looking at the poplars, then across the countryside, comparing it with his property, and concluding that this land was much more manageable and fertile. These thoughts helped assuage his fear, but not for very long.

He turned toward the door, and, with his eyes half-opened, knocked and waited for an answer. Lucia was inside but did not hear the knock.

Somewhat frustrated, and even more fearful than before, he finally knocked with a bit more vigor. This time, Lucia heard and immediately knew it was Silvestro. She had been waiting for him, having made sure that Samuele not be present when Silvestro arrived.

A natural glow appeared on Lucia's face, and more than ever, she seemed unusually beautiful. She ran to the door and opened it with a quick turn. When Silvestro saw it was Lucia, a slight smile of relief appeared on his lips.

"Come in, Silvestro," Lucia said, extending her hand to him.

"How are you?" he asked as he gave her his hand, allowing her to bring him in. He stopped in the center of the room, looking around for signs of Samuele, standing there feeling timidly awkward. Lucia noticed his embarrassment.

"No one is here," she said in a calm voice.

"Did you say something to your brother?"

"Yes. Samuele wants to meet you."

"What!"

"Don't be afraid. You don't know my brother. I

didn't know him either when I told you all those things about him. He's not the man I thought he was. He's wonderful and I am sure you will like him."

Silvestro raised his eyebrows making the lines of his forehead more marked. But the manner in which Lucia described her new brother reassured him, resulting in his eyes opening a bit wider.

"He won't mind us getting married?"

"No. He wants what I want."

"You want me?"

"Yes."

"You know where I live with all the other children..."

"...Yes, I know. I also know what my responsibilities are," she answered in a serious tone, a subdued smile on her face.

"I need you. You don't need me."

"I need you," she answered, more serious than before. "I'm about thirty now. I should know what I want. Dreams come true in many ways. I never thought my dreams would ever be coming true this way."

Silvestro opened his eyes wider than ever before revealing a color more beautiful than Lucia had ever seen before. He even smiled, showing his nicotine-stained teeth.

"I need someone right away. When can you come?"

"As soon as we're married."

"When will that be?"

"When we want. My brother will help us. Come, let's go out to the yard. He's there with our son."

"Our boy!" he exclaimed.

Silvestro had had four girls with his deceased wife but always wanted a boy and felt pride with his natural son.

"He's big now, and he has an older friend. Both spend a lot of time with Samuele, who lets them ride on the bull. Come, you'll see. Come, let's go."

Side by side, Lucia and Silvestro walked to the yard but no one was there because Samuele, the children, and Maria were in the stall attending the animals. While they walked slowly across the yard, Silvestro closed his eyes a bit. Finally, on reaching the door of the stall, Lucia called inside.

The first to come out were the children. Lucia picked up her son. With a smile, she showed the boy to his father.

"He looks like you, doesn't he?"

Silvestro nodded. He extended his hand and caressed the boy's face. Lucia got close to Silvestro so the boy could touch his father. As she did, the boy grabbed his father by his pear-shaped nose and squeezed it hard enough to make Silvestro pull away. Lucia laughed, and soon Silvestro joined her with a small smile. They quickly stopped laughing on seeing Samuele appear from inside. Silvestro drew back while Lucia stepped aside.

"This is my brother," she said.

Samuele stared at Silvestro with a serious expression on his face. Then, looking at Silvestro squarely in his eyes, Samuele extended his hand to his future brother-in-law. With obvious hesitation, Silvestro extended his hand.

"How are you?" Silvestro asked, shaking hands, his eyes practically closed.

"What's this I hear," Samuele asked, retrieving his hand. "You're planning on marrying my sister?"

"If she wants to, yes," he said, obviously intimidated.

"Apparently she does. Why do you want to marry my sister?"

"I need her."

"*I need her*, that's good. You simply need her?"

"What do you want me to say?"

"I just wanted to hear your reasons."

"I have four children at home. They can't help me much. I try as best I can, all alone, but I can't. When Lucia was there, she helped me. Now that my wife is dead--you know she was sick a long time--I thought it better for Lucia and me to get married."

"She's not coming there to be your servant and the servant to your children, is she?"

"She won't be coming to loaf around, that's for sure. She won't want to. There's too much work and I can't do it alone. Besides, the girls need a mother. They're used to Lucia. They like her, and they asked me to come here."

"I see," responded Samuele, knowing all there was to know. Besides, what else could he say, as he had already made up his mind about giving them his blessing. Then, unexpectedly, the boy, who had been listening quietly, extended his hands for his uncle's neck. Lucia quickly released him. While in Samuele's arms, he began to pull on his uncle's ears.

"He just pulled my nose," interjected Silvestro with a smile.

"He's a fresh one, this one. All he wants to do is ride the bull." Samuele stopped for a few seconds, then he continued, "Here," he said, taking the child and holding him out to Silvestro, "here, take him. He's your son." These last words carried a tremendous charge.

Silvestro took the child. As he held his only boy, Silvestro opened his eyes the widest ever. He glanced at Lucia, and, on seeing her smile, he turned to his son and kissed him.

"Call Mother," Samuele told Lucia. "We need to start making plans."

Lucia went inside. Holding the little girl's hand, Samuele walked toward the center of the yard with Silvestro walking to one side.

"All I expect from you is that you treat my sister like a human being, because that's what we all are, regardless of where we come from."

"I understand, and I want to thank you. I'm sorry for the trouble I caused you. I am very sorry. I hope to make up for it, and I guarantee you I will, you'll see."

"Don't worry about us. What happened cannot be changed but we can try to work toward a better future, however. That's what we ought to strive to do."

Silvestro agreed, nodding his head. The two sat under the elm tree to wait for the two women to come out. In a few minutes, Maria and Lucia appeared. Maria nodded to Silvestro, who quickly got up to greet her.

"We can give the baby a name now," Silvestro said to Maria.

Samuele, who found that statement strange, asked him to explain, and Silvestro quickly recounted that when he and Lucia wanted to name the child, Maria had objected because she wanted a full, legal name for the child, and that she would give her consent at the appropriate time.

"Actually," Silvestro went on to explain, making Maria smile, "her word was law. That's why the boy is without an official name."

"What you and Lucia did was very wrong," Maria stated in a serious tone.

"Yes," Silvestro admitted, looking at the ground, Lucia doing likewise.

"I don't know if I agree with my mother, but she must have had her good reasons," Samuele said. "But now, you needn't look down anymore. You're very lucky. Things don't usually happen this way and I'm sure you both realize it."

Lucia and Silvestro looked at each other, their eyes showing concomitant guilt and happiness.

"This is all such good news that we ought to celebrate. Why don't you all stay in the yard while I go down and get a bottle of wine. Maybe Silvestro would like to see the animals. I'm sure he knows a lot about them too. He raises them himself," Maria said, the smile on her face revealing an inner happiness she had not shown for years.

After all the hardships and suffering, she was about to see her family settled once and for all just as she had desired, though not completely so. Nevertheless, things had turned out much better than anticipated, even if she were to consider Samuele's almost fatal incident with Toni.

With the children leading the way, Lucia stayed in the yard while Samuele and Silvestro went into the stall and Maria to the wine cellar. Soon, Samuele appeared, leading the bull by the rope with Silvestro walking behind.

On seeing the bull, the children began to shout. Knowing what they wanted, Samuele mounted them on the animal's back to Silvestro's surprise. Samuele walked them around the outer ring of the yard a couple of times. Then, with the help of Silvestro, Samuele yoked the bull under his contraption happy to show his future brother-in-law what the animal was capable of doing. Silvestro stood incredulous, his eyes wide open, probably the widest he had opened them in years, and never shining with as much color as now. Lucia noticed the new expression on the wrinkled face of her husband-to-be and smiled, holding her hand on her child's head. Unconsciously, she bent down to her son. Hugging him, she told him his name.

"I am so happy for you, my little Samuele, I am so happy," Lucia said, acting from instinct and unaware of the little girl who, with an innocent smile on her face, looked on. On noticing the girl's eyes, Lucia stopped smiling. Extending her arm to her, Lucia held the little girl close to her breast. Then, with an unexpected burst, she got up on her feet and lifted the two children with her, their feet dangling below as they giggled over the unexpected lift.

"Do you know what his name is?" Lucia asked of the little girl.

"No," she answered.

"Samuele, just like uncle Samuele."

"Samuele!" the girl repeated with a giggle.

"Yes," replied Lucia, "that's right," Lucia ascertained as her child looking on not quite understanding what was happening. "That's right," she affirmed as she looked into her son's eyes, "your name is Samuele in honor of your uncle, who is always giving you rides."

Little Samuele didn't pay much attention to his mother; instead, he looked in the direction of his uncle.

"Silvestro, stand next to me," Samuele asked, wanting to show where his actual partner might be during the pull. Silvestro moved into position, maintaining it as they went around in a circle.

"What do you think?" asked Samuele after stopping.

"Never seen anything like it. The animal acts like a human being; I can tell by the way he looks at you. Your whole stable looks good too. Without a doubt you have the best cattle of the region."

"We're going to raise cattle."

"That's good. I have two little calves myself. The mother is practically out of milk. Can I give them to you?"

"Bring them down, but don't think you're giving them to me. In our family, everything belongs to all of us. I hope you feel the same way too."

"Sure, but I don't have much."

"Neither do I," answered Samuele. He was about to add to his statement when Maria came out with the wine.

"It seems all of a sudden we're always drinking for one reason or another," Samuele commented with a smile.

"What's happened in the last few days won't happen again. Here, Silvestro, take your glass."

After Maria had filled all the four glasses, Samuele raised his glass. "To our health," he cheered.

"To my children," Maria said. "Thank God you're safe and sound."

"God!" Samuele repeated in a low voice, his jovial expression changing to a brooding one.

"To our future," interjected Lucia. "Let's all drink up."

The four adults drank their wine. Then, unexpectedly, Lucia threw her arms around her brother's neck and kissed him on his face. Embarrassed, Samuele stepped back, but in vain. Lucia persisted in her embrace until Samuele put his arms around her affectionately.

CHAPTER 26

Having made arrangements with Don Alfonso, in the late afternoon, Samuele went to Franca to ask her to be the witness with him at Lucia's wedding.

He hadn't been at Franca's house since the fight with Toni. But now that the scars had been almost completely healed--and hoping the same would was true for Toni, Samuele ventured to take the chance.

There was no one outside. On approaching the house, Samuele heard the dog bark. Franca quickly appeared in the doorway. When she saw Samuele approaching, she turned to tell who was coming, and immediately began to walk toward her lover, with the dog following behind, wagging its tail.

"Samuele!" she yelled.

"Franca," he answered in a soft voice, "I've come to ask you something," he said as he extended his hand to hers.

"Ask me now before they come out."

"I'd rather ask you in front of your parents. How are you? I haven't seen you in a long time. You look beautiful."

Franca smiled. "I've been taking care of myself, making sure not to do any work that might ruin my complexion. I want you to like me more than anything else in this world, including other women."

"I can't love you more than I do."

"You can love me more," Franca with a lilt as she moved toward him, wanting to be kissed.

Seeing someone appear at the doorway, Samuele took Franca by her hand and drew her to one side, telling her that someone was watching.

"Later on," he said.

"I've been waiting for you to come."

"Your father is there. Come on, let's go."

While the two walked to the front door, Ernesto waited for them with a serious expression on his face. Samuele immediately sensed that something was wrong.

"It's about time you came. We've been waiting for you."

"You could have let me know," answered Samuele.

Franca, who had no idea of her father's intentions, looked puzzled and worried. Anxiously, she waited for him to speak.

"I see," Ernesto commented, "there are no scars on you. I'm glad of that. I wished you had come before. But, it doesn't matter. I am glad you finally did come."

"I wasn't aware that you wanted to see me. Well, here I am."

"Come on inside."

Ernesto went inside. Franca and Samuele followed immediately after.

Inside, at the table, Toni was seated with his mother at the table. When Samuele appeared, neither Toni nor his mother looked up. Noticing their unusual behavior, Ernesto looked at them.

"Aren't you going to welcome Samuele?" he asked in a low tone.

Begrudgingly, Toni looked up. "Hello," he said with a sudden glint. Then, lowering his eyes, he looked at the table.

"And how about you, aren't you going to welcome Samuele into our home?" Ernesto asked his wife.

"Hello," she said, and lowered her eyes to look at the table.

Feeling embarrassed and awkward, Samuele could easily tell that they were not welcoming him of their own free will. Franca, too, felt awkward and wondered about her father's purpose.

"Hello," answered Samuele, looking at the woman first, then at Toni with his left arm in a sling.

"Aren't you going to get up and shake Samuele's hand?" continued Ernesto.

Toni got up. With a sign of submission, he walked toward a speechless Samuele. Slowly, and hardly looking up, Toni put his apathetic hand forward. Extending his hand, Samuele hesitatingly shook Toni's hand. Noticing all eyes on himself, Samuele decided to make the best of the bizarre situation. He was about to ask why Toni was in a cast when the better part of him told him not to, realizing the question might bring added humiliation to Toni.

"That was a hell of a fight we had. I'm glad we're both well."

"You could've killed me if you had wanted to," Toni answered on his own.

"You turned out tougher than expected."

"And I thought you'd be a cinch," Toni answered candidly.

Seeing that things were not really going as he had planned, Ernesto interrupted.

"I understand Samuele spared your life."

Toni's eyes dropped. Samuele looked on with compassion, understanding the point Ernesto was trying to make, but feeling it was overdone.

"What's done is done. I have no rancor against you, Toni. I always wanted to be your friend and I still do. But I don't want you to be my friend because your father is making you. It's not the kind of friendship I want. It is not what I want," Samuele repeated as he turned toward Ernesto.

Paying no attention to Samuele, Ernesto turned to his wife.

"Are you going to shake Samuele's hand?" he asked in a soft voice. The woman got up, walked around the table, and went toward her future son-in-law.

"You need not do this, if you don't want to," said Samuele.

"He's kept us in this house until you came. He almost killed Toni. He promised to kill us both if we refused to apologize."

"I never understood your antagonism toward me. But you don't have to do this. I don't want you to. I cannot accept this submission."

The woman, however, extended her hand to Samuele.

"It's, true, we didn't like you. We weren't friendly to you all."

"As I just said, what's happened, happened," he said as he moved forward toward the woman, who kept her hand extended.

Reluctantly, Samuele shook her hand. With his face turned on Ernesto, he began to speak.

"Oh, what you've done!" Samuele complained to Ernesto. It's not what I want. I never wanted this," he continued in a grieved tone.

"I realize you're hurting more. You can take it and I know you understand whereas they couldn't. They could only understand brute force. That's all--just brute force! I warned them and explained to both that they were up to no good. They didn't understand because they did not want to understand. As a result, you almost lost your life, thanks to my son. See how far the idiots went? No, I know I am hurting you more. But I want to be sure they understand once and for all the harm they did to you, to themselves, to Franca and to me. If I claim him as my son, he has to act like one. He has to change. That's all. Do you understand what I'm saying, Samuele? Do you see what I am trying to do, Toni? Do you understand what you almost did? You have to have reason to kill. You attempted to kill Samuele without good reasons. Do you understand what I am talking about."

"Yes, I understand," answered Toni.

"Up to this moment, you had to do and say only what I allowed you to do and say. From now on, you're free to do as you wish. You can speak your mind."

"I understand," Toni answered, accepting his father preachy speech.

"He spared your life when he had every reason to kill you and didn't."

"That is correct," Toni answered with obvious patience.

"How about you, do you see what you led your son to do. If it had been someone else, you would have lost your precious son. Do you understand that you almost caused his death?"

"I do."

"Are you sure?"

"Then. are you going to apologize then?" he asked in an angry tone.

"Now, just wait a minute," interrupted Samuele.

"He's right," the woman said in complete submission. "He is right. You could have killed my son and you didn't. I am grateful and I owe you at least this much. I never wanted you for my son-in-law. I don't want you now. But the fact still remains you spared Toni's life."

"You're as mean as ever," Franca interjected sarcastically.

"It's all right, Franca," Ernesto said. "It's better to be open than to be sneaky. Now you know where you stand."

While the humiliated but stern woman looked at the ground, Samuele felt extremely sad, not over the woman's rejection as much as for the state of submission she was reduced to by her husband. Yet, Samuele appreciated her fierce temperament.

Without looking up, the woman, followed by her daughter's stare, walked slowly around the table to where she had been sitting. Then, lifting her eyes, she told them that she said what she felt in her heart and that they could do whatever they wanted to her.

"No one is going to do anything to you," Ernesto answered. "No one attempted to do anything to you. You still have it wrong. It was you who did things to others, and for no good reason. Maybe, I should have."

"No, Ernesto, no. It's over now," Samuele said. Then, turning to the woman, he continued. "I admire you for saying what you feel, and I respect you for it. I don't agree with you, however. I love Franca very much and I believe she loves me. There isn't much that you or anyone else can do about it. It's love, and I sincerely love your daughter. Why should I love her and not love someone else? I don't know. I just hope you understand and respect my feelings. Simply because we do not see eye to eye doesn't mean the end of the world has to come, which was your mistake. You thought the end of the world was going to come if Franca married me. I can assure you, the world will not come to an end even if we marry someone else.

"If this thing I feel could be turned off, then I would bow out. It's not the case, however. If Franca should feel differently, I would give her up. But if she loves me, as I think she does, then you will have to tolerate us. You will have to bow out. I do not force my feelings and beliefs on others, and I will not allow others to force their beliefs or feeling on me."

"Well said, Samuele. You can be sure that from now on no one will stand in your way," Ernesto said, catching Franca's glance.

At this, Franca smiled. "I love him," she simply said.

"No one asked you to say anything," Ernesto retorted with his own smile which lifted the heavy atmosphere. "You're as stubborn as your mother. When you get something in that thick skull of yours, there's nothing anyone can do to make you change your mind. I've learned this much, you see. Your mother is still learning. She's so much like you that she can't even recognize it."

"I am very happy about all this," interrupted Samuele. "I didn't come here to receive or make speeches. I would like to tell you why I am here. May I?"

"By all means," answered Ernesto with a feeling of self-confidence. "By all means," he repeated without giving Samuele the opportunity to continue with his request. "Yes, you may now state the reason why you came... Just wait a second, though. Let's get some wine on the table, first... Go on," he told his wife. "Be quick with a bottle of the special white wine. This calls for a celebration, regardless of what Samuele has to say. I really thought we already discussed the reason for his visit. But I guess I was wrong. Well, hurry up. Go get the wine. Samuele will wait till there's wine on the table."

"No, no, Ernesto. What I came for is not that important, and we don't have to have wine on the table for that. Sit down, please," he said to the woman. "My sister is getting married this week-end. I was going to ask Franca to be the witness with me. I wanted to ask in front of all of you."

"Lucia, getting married? To whom?" Ernesto asked, startled.

"Silvestro. His first wife died, as you may know, and he's asked Lucia to be his wife."

"That is good news... Hurry up, woman, this also calls for celebration. Go get the wine. Franca, set up the glasses."

Franca went over to the closet while her mother disappeared through the back door. In a few moments she came back with two bottles of white wine. Ernesto took one from her, and, after wiping the dust off with a cloth, proceeded to open it, being sure not to unduly shake the bottle. It was his own *spumante* and he knew how to serve it.

"I made it with my own hands--my own process, from grapes on the sunny side of the ravine. I dare you, Samuele, I dare you to find another like this anywhere. I dare you!" he repeated with pride. He wound the corkscrew into the cork; then, with a decisive and steady pull, being sure to keep the bottle at a precise angle to allow the air to escape above the liquid, he opened the bottle to a big pop, without spilling one single drop.

"You will see," he said in admiration of the light golden color, "that it is unique." He poured some into his glass, lifted the glass and drank it. "Exquisite! Simply exquisite!" He then placed the bottle over each glass, allowing the sparkling and foamy liquid to pour noisily into each of the five glasses. On seeing they all had their glass in hand, he proposed the toast. "To Lucia! That she be healthy and bear boys!"

"Oh! father!" protested Franca.

"To peace," said Samuele.

"To us," interjected Franca, causing both her brother and mother to look at her.

The five drank up the spumante except for the mother, who was not a drinker, as she always claimed. Nevertheless, she took a sip and kept the glass in her hand. On seeing Toni finishing his glass, she turned hers over to him. Embarrassed by the stares and the glare of his father, Toni refused to accept it.

"Drink it yourself," he said to his mother, who was not expecting that answer.

In the past, his mother always gave Toni, who accepted without fail, whatever she thought had the quality worthy of her son.

Seeing his son repudiate his mother's habitual offering, Ernesto immediately picked up the bottle and refilled his son's glass. Then, waiting for Samuele to finish his, Ernesto refilled it again.

"This calls for a greater toast," Ernesto said. Without revealing the words of the toast, he picked up his glass and gulped it down as though he were drinking beer.

"What's the toast?" asked Samuele, amused.

"It was a personal one. Go ahead, drink up and then tell me if this wine isn't the best you ever had," he continued with his bragging while he opened another bottle.

Samuele emptied the glass and so did Toni and Franca, who turned her eyes toward her mother, who finally drank her full glass of *spumante*.

"I am assuming it is all right for Franca to be a witness," Samuele said, wanting reassurance.

"Don't even ask. Here, have some more wine. And, by the way, you haven't said whether you like it or not. That isn't important. What's important is the fact that you're drinking it... That's it, drink up," he said with a wide smile on his face. He also refilled his own glass and immediately put it away with Samuele quickly following suit.

It was already dark outside when Samuele noticed how late it was, and asked permission to leave. He also asked if he could talk with Franca alone.

Soon after, Samuele and Franca walked out into the open. The evening was serene, the moon shining directly from across the distant mountain skyline, a fresh easterly breeze sweeping over the open fields and coming all the way from the Adriatic Sea through the Appennine mountain passes and across the valleys.

The two walked, almost completely unconscious of the fact that they were taken up by the magic spell of the evening. When they came by the well, out of sight of the house, Samuele put his arm around her waist. A few seconds later, he extended his hand over to her breast. Franca began to breathe heavily.

"I love you, Franca," he said in a soft tone.

Franca turned to him, her eyes shining bright.

"I'd like to count the stars in your eyes," Samuele said.

"Why?" Franca asked, not having the faintest idea why Samuele had said. Still, she waited to hear his answer.

"If I were to count the stars in your eyes, you'd be here forever with me. There are more stars in your eyes than there are in heaven."

"I'd be happy if you kissed me half as much as the stars in heaven or where ever else they may be."

Franca turned to him, and Samuele, still looking deeply into her eyes, wrapped his arms around her waist, pulled her close to him, and began to kiss her mouth. Franca drew tighter against him until both locked completely in each other's arms, kissing in joyous passion, whispering their love for one another at short intervals. It was Franca, however, who repeated the words of love more often than Samuele, who said them with more conviction and deeper feeling.

"Franca, Franca," he repeated, breaking slightly away from the embrace. His hand over her breast, he felt like screaming, almost crying out the name of God. Franca bent slightly forward, and Samuele opened the remaining buttons of her blouse, exposing Franca's full white breasts. While she caressed his neck and head, Samuele placed his face in between her breast, kissing first one then the other nipple. Her eyes closed, Franca lifted her face to the sky, her mouth open as she pulled Samuele deeper into her breasts.

"I've been waiting such a long time for you. I thought you'd never come. I love you--I love you, Samuele..."

Samuele kissed her open mouth with passion. For the next few moments, the two breathed on one another's breath.

"Franca," he whispered in her ear, "Franca, Franca, Franca," he repeated, trying to appease his overwhelming passion. With his face pressed against her breast, he repeated her name several more times.

"Yes, yes," she answered as she caressed his head and face. "I love you so much. I want to be completely yours, all yours, and forever. Samuele, I love you so much"

With his eyes closed, locking within the pleasure of those passionate moments, and to assuage the frustration over his unwillingness to sexually consummate his love, Samuele again assured Franca of his love.

"You made my life possible. I dreamed of moments like these, and I did not want to die before experiencing these moments with you... Please forgive me. I don't know why I am telling you these things. I love you, Franca; I love you... Forgive me for loving you this way. I cannot let anything happen to you, nothing. I shouldn't continue to love you. Oh, how I wish you had rejected me! Now I can't help but be drawn to you. And I am wrong, I know. I am wrong," he repeated with a conviction that alarmed Franca.

He had gotten off on a tangent and was making no sense. While he talked, his passion diminished into rationalization, to the horror of Franca, who listened while she continued to hold his head pressed against her breast.

"I am wrong," he continued. "I am very wrong. Nothing can come of this. Nothing," he repeated in a pathetic tone.

"Stop, stop it; you're scaring me. What's the matter, Samuele? Here, look at me. Tell me, darling, what is the matter? Tell me, tell me. I thought you enjoyed making love to me. I want to make love to you no matter what happens to me. I don't want you to think of me. I love you. You're the one that counts. Please tell me what is bothering you. Please tell me."

"You are young and vigorous. You have a complete life ahead of you."

"What do you mean?" she asked in a tone hinting despair.

"I'm not being fair to you. I am taking advantage of you."

"What do you mean!"

With his head pressed deeply against her breast, and his eyes so tightly closed as to form tense wrinkles vibrating on his forehead, Samuele asked her once again to forgive him, reminding her that whatever happened, she should remember how much he truly loved her.

"I love you more than life itself. More, more," he stated.

"Then tell me what is tormenting you. Love me, make love to me. I want to be yours. I am yours. Take me. Kiss me again. Kiss me."

Samuele kissed her with resurging passion. With one hand clinging to his neck, Franca slipped her other hand down to his trousers, these being the moments she had also hoped to enjoy, and with Samuele only.

As she slipped her hand inside his pants, letting passion take its course, on hearing her mother's voice call from above, Franca quickly pulled up her hand while Samuele, breaking the embrace, picked up her blouse.

After answering to her mother's intrusion, Franca did not make another attempt at trying to learn what was troubling her lover. The moment was too precious and the kisses enthralled her whole being.

"Kiss me, kiss me!" she repeated with palpitation when Samuele moved his head to her side. Pulling back slightly, she began to cover her breast. After having looked deeply into her starry eyes, Samuele moved his hand gently over her breast and kissed it once again.

"Life," he murmured thoughtfully, "life is so amazing--so much beauty, so many secrets, so many unexplainable things; here--both of us--a good example! Life is worth living and death is our enemy. It's not enough that God assures it to us; we shorten it ourselves at every moment and for the most stupid reasons, and we do it on full stomachs. Franca, Franca, oh, Franca! The blood runs cold and only to make the heart beat. Franca, we kill without hunger."

"What do you mean? What are you talking about?"

"Please forgive me. It's just one of my moods."

"No, no, no! There's more to it. Tell me, I beg you. Tell me, tell me!"

Samuele looked up as Franca's voice grew louder, reaching the house.

"No," he answered softly, putting his hand gently over her mouth. "No," he continued, "there is nothing, nothing. I promise you to love you as you want me to love you. I promise. Please, do not worry. There is absolutely nothing wrong. I just haven't completely forgotten my war experiences, that's all. Sometimes, they haunt me, that's all... See what you did when you raised your voice. Someone's opening the door. Quickly, button up your blouse. Here, let's walk to the center of the pathway."

"Franca, Fr-a-n-ca!" her mother called from above.

"What do you want?" Franca replied.

"What are you doing? Come on back up."

"I'm coming, can't you see," Franca answered rudely as she walked toward the house with Samuele at her side, holding each other's hands right up to the door, where, for fear of being seen, separated without speaking one more word. Finally, when Franca motioned she had to go inside, she turned to face Samuele.

"Goodby," she said as she looked deep into his eyes for a prolonged moment.

Feeling her searching eyes, Samuele answered good night in a low voice. Then, in a lower tone, he told her he loved her more than the earth itself.

"I do too. I love you as much," she answered in a voice which was almost a whisper, her emotions not allowing her to say much more.

"I'll be back to get you," Samuele said after moment of hesitation.

"Yes," she answered almost inaudibly.

She turned and walked fast to the house. On seeing her disappear through the door, Samuele turned and began to walk back home.

On the solitary and dark road, Samuele walked slowly, limping unconsciously as he went along. Occasionally, he glanced into the sky to observe the bright stars. Each time he looked up, though, he always paused to look at the moon, thinking to himself how many times he had expressed the desire to end his life on earth and for his soul to migrate to the moon.

"It won't be long now," he said aloud, his eyes fixed on the orange disk. "It won't be long now," he repeated, and then went on walking back home.

Behind him, with her arms on the window sill, Franca looked out at the road over which her lover was walking, pondering the heavens, but thinking about Samuele, wondering what had happened to him and worrying over their troubled love-making. Not knowing that Samuele had just paused to look at the moon, Franca, too, glanced at it with this difference: she looked at it while Samuele confessed to it.

When the two were finally in their beds, staring face up at the ceiling, the moon continued on its silent journey.

Before finally closing his eyes, Samuele, though slightly, began to cough.

CHAPTER 27

By the following Saturday, Samuele got all the records. Maria, too, made the preparations for the informal wedding banquet, with Lucia helping, though she concerned herself mainly with the wedding dress for herself and the clothes for her son.

About an hour before going to church, Silvestro arrived, dressed in the dark suit he had worn at his first wedding, and with him all of his daughters, wanting them to see the ceremony so there would be no question in their minds who their new mother was going to be.

With his eyes partially closed, Silvestro asked Lucia if he was properly dressed. With a smile, Lucia replied in the positive. Silvestro's eyes opened wide, and he smiled happily. Then, after recommending their best behavior, he ordered the children to go play in the yard, telling them to keep neat as well.

"Not the baby," said Lucia. "I've got to dress him up. Here, you go to the yard with them," Lucia asked the little girl, who quickly got in front of the group and ran to the yard, where Samuele was looking after the animals.

While Silvestro held his baby on his knees, and Lucia was going around making her last arrangements, Franca knocked at the door. Silvestro went to answer.

"Silvestro!" exclaimed Franca, "what are you doing here? The bridegroom is not supposed to see the bride before the ceremony."

"That's old stuff for us. It doesn't apply to us," he answered with a slight smile. He opened the door to let her in. "It applies to you, though," Silvestro continued. "And be sure Samuele doesn't see you before your ceremony. It could bring you bad luck."

"I don't know even know if there's going to be one at all."

"What do you mean?"

"I was only kidding."

"Where's the rest of your family?"

Franca explained she had come alone, that the rest of her family would be coming later, after the church ceremony. She looked around, noticing how everything had been spruced up. Then she asked where the rest were.

"Lucia is upstairs, and Samuele, Maria and the children are in the yard. I'm here minding this one. He doesn't want to keep still."

"Give him to me. I'll go to the yard."

"Only if you bring him right back. Lucia has to dress him."

Franca took little Samuele into her arms and walked out to the yard. The first to see her was Maria, who approached the young woman with a smile.

"I'm glad you came. I see you were already in the house. This little one is going to have his own mother and father in a little while. It should make you very happy, does it?"

"Yes, Franca, it does. I have thanked God for all He has done for us. I hope all goes well with you and my son. He told me he loves you."

"Yes," she admitted almost without emotion.

Franca's "yes" left Maria puzzled. Maria, however, did not ask Franca just what that yes meant. Besides, Samuele was coming from around the barn with the bull and the children noisily following behind and looking up at the little girl riding high. On seeing her on the bull, little Samuele began to yell, motioning that he wanted to join the group. Franca immediately walked toward Samuele with the boy in her arms. Little Samuele raised his arms, wanting to get on the huge animal, and his uncle took him from Franca and put him up behind the girl.

Then, turning to Franca, Samuele began to speak.

"You look very beautiful," he said as he stared at her, causing Franca to lower her head slightly.

"I'm glad you think so. I am sure no one else does."

"Thank you for coming. I have the rings and I want you to see them. Let me bring them around first. Here, come with me. I also want you to see how well trained this animal is. Isn't he magnificent?"

"He is big, and beautiful."

"And intelligent too... O.K., kids, here we go."

As the bull went out, the children gave a shout, running from one side to the other, making a noisy rumpus. When one of them almost ran into Franca, she squeezed closer to Samuele, who gave her his hand.

"Would you like to have a ride?" he asked Franca jokingly. Franca refused with a smile.

"What time is the ceremony?"

"At eleven. We have plenty of time."

At the end of the ride, Franca asked Samuele why he had behaved the way he had the other night. "I almost doubted you loved me," she said.

"No matter what happens, remember one thing: I have always loved you and I always will."

But Samuele felt he was making a mistake in telling her that he loved her that much, concluding that making love with her might also be a mistake. Yet, he truly loved her and could not stay away from her especially now that he was living with the warmth of her love. Even the kissing had achieved a new meaning for him.

And Franca, who had longed to be loved, admitted to herself--when she was alone and rational, that the love in which she and Samuele were indulging was perhaps the best she could ever have expected, knowing, however, that if Samuele should change his mind and consummate their love as if married, she would be ready to satisfy his wish and fulfill her own desire for physical love.

"I am in love with you more now than ever," she answered, those thoughts persistently in her mind.

But the frown on her forehead indicated to Samuele that she was troubled.

"I must not do anything that might eventually harm you," he explained.

"You said that before. What are you afraid of?"

"Afraid! No, Franca, I'm not afraid of anything. I never made a decision or did anything from fear."

"What is it then?" she insisted.

The ride had come to an end, and the children had become more obstreperous.

"Nothing, Franca, nothing. I want to love you. Give me time to clear my mind... Hold on, kids, here comes the first."

Samuele lifted off his nephew, who was already being called little Sam, then the Marcello's little girl. As he was about to take the bull into the stall, Silvestro's children began to pester him for a ride.

"If you all behave, this afternoon I will give each of you a ride. Now, go into the house and get ready. We'll be going to church in a little while. Go on, now, and behave."

The children turned around and walked silently toward the house. Maria intercepted them and accompanied them in to help with the last details. She held her grandson by the hand.

"Your mother is very happy and proud," Franca commented.

"I know. She was never that happy, and even now, she's still holding back. But she's the happiest she's ever been. You never know how things turn out at times. Well, will you give me a hand with this animal?"

"Sure."

Samuele walked ahead, leading the bull to the stall with Franca following right behind. When the smell from inside the stall reached her nose, Franca stopped, telling Samuele that she was not going in.

"Why not?" he asked.

"I have a wedding to go to. Besides, I put on some real perfume. I'll wait out here."

Inside, Samuele laughed. He quickly tied the animal to manger and quickly walked to the door. Noticing part of her skirt overlapping the outside of the door, Samuele sneaked his arm out. Grabbing her by the wrist, he pulled her into the doorway. Franca fell into his arms, kissing him passionately.

"For this, I'll step into your stable anytime," she declared with a smile.

"Let's go now; it's getting late," he said as he kissed her gently.

Placing her hand over her face, Franca walked out of the stall with him.

"You're the most beautiful I have ever seen you," Samuele said.

Franca glanced at him for a moment, her eyes sparkling. Then, she looked away into the horizon.

About five minutes before the ceremony, the group left for the church, except for Maria, who stayed behind to take care of the house and to begin setting up the table for the wedding dinner.

Before she left, Lucia listened to a last piece of advice from her mother: to enter the church through the back door and to exit through the main door heads up. Lucia protested but nevertheless conceded.

When the group found itself walking to church by the back road, Samuele was the first to question why Lucia had taken that route.

"Mother's wish," she replied without a trace of resentment.

Lucia walked next to her husband-to-be hand in hand with the chatting children behind, except for little Sam, who walked between his uncle and Franca, who, on lifting him by his hands into the air, screamed with happiness.

When they got to the church, Don Alfonso was waiting by the back door. He greeted Lucia and Silvestro and congratulated them, telling the couple how lucky they were, and bidding them to go in.

In a few seconds, the group was seated in the front rows while behind them gathered numerous friends and relatives trying to get seats near the compact group of the usual old women monopolizing the better parts of the benches.

Lucia listened to the Mass, her hand on her forehead almost throughout while Silvestro sat straight and never moved. The children examined the colored paintings on the walls, their eyes always seeming to pause on the bleeding statue of Christ on the cross. Samuele and Franca, on the other hand, listened to the Mass, occasionally exchanging loving glances, while behind them, the old women whispered.

At Communion time, Lucia, Silvestro, and Franca went to the altar, followed by practically every woman in attendance.

Don Alfonso gave the Communion first to Lucia, then to Silvestro. When he saw Franca, he paused, then gently placed the host in her mouth. Without moving forward, Don Alfonso looked out at the group, fixing his eyes on Samuele. When the old woman next in line to receive Communion noticed the priest staring back, she turned her head slyly to see what was going on. Don Alfonso caught her action and immediately went to her before she could turn completely around. Her eyes closed, she received her Communion. After crossing herself with a severely devotional movement, she walked silently back, hands over her breast and chewing on the host.

With the termination of the Mass, Lucia, Silvestro, Franca, and Samuele joined the priest, where the two altar boys had already set up the stools for the marriage ceremony.

Lucia was first to kneel, then Silvestro, while Franca and Samuele stood behind. In her dark dress and with her new permanent wave, Lucia looked distinguished and beautiful. Silvestro looked at her like a boy caught in his first infatuation.

Don Alfonso, as he performed the ritual as expeditiously as possible, kept on looking at Samuele, who, to avoid further glances, stared at the marble floor. Finally, Samuele had to look up when Don Alfonso asked for the rings.

Samuele took the rings out and handed them to the priest; then, taking Franca by the arm, they walked to one side. Having blessed the rings, Don Alfonso proceeded with the rest of the holy rite. Finally, when the priest pronounced the famous words making Lucia and Silvestro husband and wife, Lucia began to cry. With tears in her eyes, she threw her arms around her husband and kissed him. Then, turning to her brother, she did the same thing, to the controlled consternation of the old women who had never seen kissing inside their church. On seeing Lucia kiss her husband, the women moved only their eyes. When she kissed her brother, they could moved both their eyes and heads.

Don Alfonso, on the other hand, after having patiently waited for Lucia and the group to move away, with apparent preoccupation turned to Samuele.

"You didn't take Holy Communion."

"No."

"I was hoping you would. It's not enough to say you have faith in God. You also have to show it."

"The ways to God are many. I told you, out of respect for you, that I have maintained my faith in God. I also told you that I owe my life to our faith. Don't pick me up on everything I do or do not do. Besides, this is no place to discuss this matter," Samuele rebutted in a serious tone. "And, by the way," Samuele continued, with an obvious but important afterthought, "we don't exist for the church; vice versa, it exists for us. Likewise, God exists for us," Samuele stated not knowing whether he was talking heresy or according to church doctrine. In pronouncing the word God, however, Samuele was making an effort to control his pronunciation, having come to terms with his subconscious' reactive propensity.

Don Alfonso drew back with sudden perplexity. "I don't think I truly understand what you are saying."

As the two talked, the group moved outside the church while Franca waited inside under the statue of the Archangel.

"What I am trying to say is that religion ought to concentrate on the individual, to make him better, to make him a better citizen, to make him aware of his civil status, of his rights, and not to make of him a conquest, a soldier for God's army. God does not need this type of believer. He wants a responsible and responsive human being. Make us healthy citizens, Don Alfonso and God will love you and the church that much more."

"We concentrate on fulfilling the glory of God. By so doing, we try to better our people."

"No, no, you don't. But I don't want to have an argument now."

"Has Tina been influencing you?"

"Tina! Yes, Tina. I haven't thought about her since we both saw her last. No, Tina is no different. All she wants is to add names to her list. She understood--rather, her leaders have understood--that their power lies in large bodies of followers. They're not out to care for them, to heal them, or even guide them, though they always say that is exactly that which they do. Look, how many hospitals are there around here? How many schools are there that are not specifically aimed at recruiting young boys and girls for the seminary and convent? These things are not there for the people, but for the people to serve the church."

Don Alfonso became disturbed by Samuele's tendentiousness.

"All I am trying to say is that the people who come to your Mass are old women for the most part. You're not reaching the young ones is what I am trying to say. You've got to change something... Listen, Don Alfonso, I did not want to offend you in any way; at the same time, I cannot hide my feelings from you. Anyhow, Franca is waiting there. Do you see her? We have to go home for dinner, and we have reserved a place for you; my mother is expecting you. You will be coming?"

Don Alfonso hesitated, not about the invitation but by Samuele's stand.

"Well," Samuele insisted gently.

"Yes, yes, I'll be there. We'll go on with our discussion another time."

"There isn't much more I can add to what I just said. I don't have answers. Let me go; I'll see you later."

Samuele left the priest at the altar and walked toward Franca, who was slightly angry for having had to wait.

"Mother told me to invite him over. So, I had to."

"It didn't have to take you so long," she complained passively. But, almost immediately, she more than managed a smile. "Anyhow, is he coming?"

Samuele nodded as he put his arm around her waist. Outside, a larger than expected group of people had gathered in front of the church to congratulate the newly--

weds. Then, on seeing Samuele and Franca, they began to cheer. Samuele smiled at them warmly. While Franca looked into his face with pride, many of his friends approached him to shake hands.

With all their children behind them, Lucia and Silvestro walked down the road with Samuele and Franca following behind. From each side of the street, people greeted and congratulated Lucia.

On reaching Mr. Banno's house, Samuele noticed that Mr. Banno was seated alone in his yard, his head down and unresponsive to the street activities. After telling the group to go on, he and Franca walked up to him.

"Hello, Mr. Banno."

"Hello, Samuele," he answered, raising his head. "I am happy for you and your sister... Hello, Franca."

"I am sorry for what happened. I am truly sorry. I wish there was something I could do."

"Thank you for your consideration. We don't deserve much, however. I am glad to see all is turning out well. We needed someone like you around here. And I am glad I sold you the land. Of course, you know I had my own reasons. Nothing turned out as I had hoped. I deserved it, though."

While the two men talked, Rosa appeared from inside, and walked over. After glancing at Franca, Rosa began to talk to Samuele.

"I want to apologize. I'm sorry for the trouble I caused you," she said in a low and submerged voice, with her father pathetically looking into her face.

"Things could have turned out worse. We know where things stand. Let's start anew. We're alive," Samuele said. confidently.

Then, looking at Mr. Banno, Samuele repeated the same thing to attract his attention. Mr. Banno, however, continued to stare into Rosa' face.

"Yes, we are alive," Mr. Banno repeated meaninglessly.

"Thank you for talking with my father, Samuele; I truly appreciate it, after all we did to you."

"If you don't mind, I'd like to come over some evening and drink some of your *aglianico*, Mr. Banno."

"Any time, Samuele, any time."

"We have to go now," said Samuele. "My mother is waiting. Goodby."

With his arm around Franca' waist, they walked away under Mr. Banno's eyes focusing on Samuele's slight limp. Rosa, on the other hand, stood with her head bent, staring at the lucky couple.

Maria had set the table. Ernesto, who had arrived alone, was already munching and drinking. On seeing Samuele, Ernesto commented on the quality of his own wine.

"It doesn't look like my wine," answered Samuele. After having tasted some, he quickly saw that the wine was not his.

"Strange," he commented, "it is very good, but it's not mine. I have tasted it before, though."

"So have I, a lot, as a matter of fact. Here, give me some more," Ernesto asked jovially.

Soon Maria came from inside with a trail of children behind. When they reached the table, she assigned given seats to each, leaving empty chairs between them. Then Silvestro and Lucia came out. When all the food was on the table, the adults sat down. After asking everyone to be quiet, Maria said grace, after which, Don Alfonso appeared at the gate.

"Just in time," shouted Ernesto. "We haven't started yet and Maria just said grace."

Don Alfonso walked over and sat on the chair next to Samuele. After he crossed himself, Don Alfonso said another but very brief grace amid the noise of the impatient children, and immediately began to eat the steaming *pasta asciutta* (maccheroni with tomato sauce).

"This macaroni is delicious," commented Don Alfonso.

"I'll have some more," spoke up Ernesto, first to finish his dish.

"There's plenty more to eat, Father," assured Franca, who knew how much her father was capable of eating, and how often he overdid it.

"Don't worry, I have plenty of room in here," he answered, his hands rubbing his rather expansive stomach.

"I know, that's what I'm worried about," countered Franca.

"Here, pour me some more wine, will you, Maria. Give more to Don Alfonso."

"The wine is very good, too," commented Don Alfonso.

"You'd never know whose wine it is," said Maria.

Then she explained that Mr. Banno had brought it over when the rest were at church. They were all surprised, especially Samuele, who felt sad.

"Who's getting the meat?" asked Ernesto after he had consumed his second plate of pasta.

"Father!"

"Well, after the macaroni comes the meat, isn't that right, Don Alfonso? And with the meat comes the wine. Franca, go on, pour the wine for everyone, including the children."

"I guess you're going to have a real banquet when Franca gets married," Don Alfonso remarked.

"They haven't said anything about it yet. When it happens, Don Alfonso, you'll be the very first to be invited."

Samuele and Franca looked at each other. The rest listened to an exuberant Ernesto monopolizing the table chat at the expense of Lucia and Silvestro, who hardly said a word. They laughed, however, whenever anyone said something even close to being funny.

Soon, the main course was placed on the table. Maria had prepared several types: rolled *braciola* cooked in tomato sauce, broiled chicken, and rabbit in marsala wine. The side dishes included home fried potatoes with peppers preserved in vinegar, green lettuce with *radicchio*, and fresh-cut beans. At one end of the table were various fresh fruits, including dark blue figs, pomegranate, red oranges and tangerines, muscatel grapes, and a sundry of dried fruit as almonds, hazel nuts, walnuts and figs.

Slowly, the group consumed the dinner, though the children finished ahead of the adults. Ernesto, the happiest of all and the one who sat most tenaciously by the table, occasionally looked at the big elm tree, taking a deep breath as though he were sighing, but continuing to eat without interruption. The only other time Ernesto looked away from the table was when the children ran around the table screaming at the top of their lungs.

Finally, when the meal ended, Maria took out the wedding cake and Lucia brought out the *spumante*. Taking over from Lucia, Franca filled the glasses with the sparkling wine while Maria began to cut the cake. The children immediately scurried around the table back into their seats, and soon, all was quiet.

Don Alfonso got up. After requesting the rest to rise, he took it onto himself to propose a toast to the newlyweds.

"No one knows in what form God displays his love for us. We want to thank You, O Lord, for all You have bestowed on us, not only in this fine food, but for having made this day possible--a day in which these two young people, after years of tribulation, hardships, and of sin, have finally been joined together. We want to Praise You for your grace, O God, and to ask You to continue giving them the love You so benevolently bestow on your creatures. May both of you live in the light and happiness of our Almighty God."

Quietly, the adults clinked their glasses and drank to Lucia and Silvestro, who in turn thanked Don Alfonso and the rest of their friends for having been so kind and for having made their day a joyous one. Silvestro added that he did not deserve all this, and that he was extremely grateful.

"May you live happily together and enjoy this precious life," Samuele added. Raising his glass, he bowed his head to his sister and brother-in-law. Then looking at Franca, he drank joyfully.

"Thank you," answered Lucia, almost overwhelmed.

Lucia wanted to say more, but couldn't, and Silvestro felt likewise. Besides, the attention had shifted to the children, who went on eating their cake, a rarity for them. In no time, they finished their portion. Not prone to sweets, Ernesto sneaked his piece of cake to the oldest girl in exchange for the glass of spumante.

Silvestro, who ate his cake slowly, helped his son, sitting on his lap. Occasionally, the father allowed the boy to sip the spumante. Silvestro's eyes were wide open by now and taking part in the conversation. Before he spoke, however, he always looked at Lucia first as though seeking her approval.

"Have you seen Samuele's bull?" Silvestro asked of Don Alfonso, whose mouth was full of cake.

The priest first replied with a nod; then, after dunning his cake and sipped his spumante, he answered an embarrassed Silvestro.

"Yes, yes, I have seen the animal. Samuele has the finest specimen I have ever seen. The people are going to get a treat the day of the feast. We're going to have the most beautiful celebration this year, and the Obelisk is the brightest ever. Yes, yes, there's a real treat for the people this year, and they deserve it. We've gone through a lot. We need this celebration."

While the priest talked, the rest listened. But only Samuele understood the undertone of the words, and was pleased to note Don Alfonso's special message.

Don Alfonso had understood the social needs and knew the methods to use to reach the people; he also knew there was a time and place for everything. The idea that the church should have existed for the people and not vice versa still bothered the priest, however. He hadn't thought about it in those terms.

Now, because of Samuele, Don Alfonso began to wonder and to better consider another priest from Sicily, Don Sturzo, whose activities were being covered in the press, especially his return from exile in the United States. Italy had just finished a hard and humiliating decade with the Fascists in power. Now that the war was over and the Fascists defeated, Don Alfonso felt confident.

Don Alfonso momentary relapse came to a sudden end when little Samuele suddenly began to shout to his uncle wanting to ride the bull. Shaking his head from the loud voice, Don Alfonso looked at the little boy sitting on his father's lap.

"All right!" answered Samuele.

The rest of the children jubilantly began to jump in the air, all shouting discordantly as they ran toward the stall. Silvestro, on the other hand, with his son in his arms, walked over to the stable. Going into it, Silvestro noticed there was enough space at one end for additional animals.

"Why don't I bring them down? I have a few little ones that will never fatten up at my place. Besides, I want to give them to you."

"Bring them down; bring them all down. We'll build a wing to the side. As a matter of fact, I think you ought to think of moving down here altogether. There isn't much you can do up there. You'll never get anywhere there. Here, you can help me, and, in not too distant a future, I see you taking charge here. You know, I'm not planning on staying around here forever."

"What are you going to do?"

"I don't know. Anyway, we have something going here. Talk it over with Lucia and see what she says. I am sure my mother won't mind. There's plenty of room here and the schools are better around here. With all the kids you have, you ought to think about those things as well. I'll help you with everything I have."

Silvestro listened, unable to believe his ears. Dumfounded, he told Samuele that he would talk it over with Lucia and that he would not object if she were in agreement.

Walking over to the bull, Silvestro wondered about fortune. It was true: it existed. But, what did he do to deserve all this, and was it just reward? As he walked past the cows, he noticed them all turning their heads and looking up.

Samuele untied the huge animal, and walked it out of the stable. On appearing at the door, the children screamed. Silvestro walked over. With a heave, he placed his son on the bull, which turned its neck to look at the little rider. Samuele, in turn, lifted the little girl up behind the boy. Then, giving the rein to Silvestro, Samuele walked behind with the other children. After a short ride, Samuele lifted up Silvestro's youngest daughter, telling the three to hold on to each other. Seeing the animal reacted favorably both to the noise and to the added child, Samuele added a fourth, to the amazement of everyone present. With Silvestro leading the animal, the group walked over toward the table.

Ernesto, who was finishing the wine in the remaining bottle, declared that, in his life time, he had never seen such a phenomenon, with Don Alfonso making similar comments. The priest, in fact, did not hesitate to bless both the animal and the children.

While the priest went through his ritual, Silvestro smiled proudly while Lucia glowed. Maria, who sat by herself at one corner of the table, looked on with tempered joy.

"You're all coming down," said Samuele to their disappointing groans. "Franca is going for a ride," he quickly added.

Though the unexpected announcement made Franca laugh aloud, the children cheered with joy. Franca, however, really thought that Samuele was kidding.

"Hurry up," Samuele insisted with a smile.

When Franca failed to move, Samuele walked over and took her by the arm. The children, who had been taken down by Silvestro, waited in ecstacy. When Samuele lifted Franca onto the animal, the children laughed and cheered to Franca's temporary embarrassment.

"All set?" Samuele asked.

"No, let me down," she answered.

Taking the rope from Silvestro, Samuele led the bull away under everyone's watchful eyes.

"Be careful," Samuele said to the animal; "there's precious cargo aboard."

Ernesto, who had followed the incident with interest, asked Maria if he could take a nap somewhere. After Maria pointed to a place under the elm, Ernesto smiled with gratitude.

"But now," Ernesto said, "if you're planning on bringing out more food or wine, be sure to wake me. Now," he continued, pointing his finger at her, "don't forget," he emphasized as he made his way to the tree.

"As a matter of fact, Maria," interjected Don Alfonso, "I had better be going too. I need my siesta, but I'll be back later this evening."

"Come back whenever you wish, Father."

"Goodby, Mr. Don Alfonso," called Ernesto, causing Lucia to burst out laughing. Don Alfonso, who hadn't expected the extra title, also smiled, not without remarking, however, that he had never seen anyone eat and drink as much as Ernesto, who was quickly lost to the outside world.

"That's why he's so red in the face," Don Alfonso continued.

After Don Alfonso had gone, Lucia asked her husband if he wanted to take a rest. Used to an afternoon nap in the field, Silvestro answered that he did. Lucia asked her mother for them to go rest upstairs. Maria, naturally, did not object.

"I'll be right back," Lucia said to her mother.

"Don't hurry. I will clear the table."

"Are you sure?" Lucia asked, a smile on her face that caused Silvestro to feel embarrassed.

The two went away, leaving Maria by herself. While she was clearing the table, Samuele returned with Franca and the children, Franca still riding the bull.

"Everyone's off to sleep. Why don't you go too?" Maria suggested to her son. "Franca can stay here with me to help with the dishes, if she doesn't mind."

Franca laughed with her mouth wide open. Maria also smiled.

"Yes, go ahead, Samuele, go take a nap. I'll stay here with your mother. I want to talk with her anyway. If we need help, I'll send one of the children to get you."

"All right, I will. Let me put this beast away first."

With all the adults gone, Franca and Maria worked to get the table cleared, while the children played quietly in the courtyard.

About two hours later, Maria heard her name called from the street. It was a friend bringing a gift for Lucia. Maria asked the old man to enter.

Skinny to the bone, in a worn jacket twice his size, and trousers mended in several places, the old man made his way cautiously circumspect to the table where Franca stood staring on his trembling hands. Not seeing Lucia, he quickly asked Maria Lucia's whereabouts.

"She and Silvestro are taking a nap," Maria answered matter-of-factly.

"Already!" he exclaimed, a grin on his face, causing Franca to smile, and, soon after, Maria to follow suit.

"Kids, go call Samuele. He's in back of the stall. Tell him we have a visitor."

The children ran off all together in a chase, the little ones straggling behind.

"That's all right, Maria. I have to go anyhow. My wife is getting on in years, you know. I have to be by her side all the time," he said as he placed the newspaper-wrapped gift on the table and proceeding to pull a chair from under the table to sit down.

"May I offer you some wine?" Franca asked with hesitation, having heard him say one thing and doing another. Nevertheless, she found the strange old man spirited and charming.

After giving Franca a thorough eye inspection, and obviously approving of her figure, the old man looked at pitchers of red and white wine.

"At this age, you know, I'm not supposed to drink much. As a matter of fact, Maria, I hardly drink these days. But I don't think a little bit of white wine will hurt me, do you? Here," he said, having picked up the glass with the largest bottom and pointing it to Franca, "just pour the bottom--to know what it tastes like... just to taste it."

Taking the man literally, Franca picked up the pitcher of white wine, and began to slowly pour it into the glass, making sure the stream was small and taking extra precaution not to spill any, as the old man's hands continued to shake. Franca filled the bottom, then lessened the stream to a stop. But the man did not take away the glass. Franca looked up to receive the sign to stop. Instead, he continued to hold the glass out while Franca limited the flow to a trickle. Maria, wise to his tricks, smiled. Franca, seeing him still holding the glass, continued to pour until the glass was full to the brim.

"Pour no more," he said. Then, bringing his trembling hand to his mouth, and without spilling a drop, he paused for a moment, his eyes fixed at the bedroom across the yard.

"*Salute*! (Health)" he said, his eyes focused on the bedroom. "To your daughter and her new husband. May they have boys. They already have one anyway, ha, ha, ha," he continued with a chuckle that even made Maria smile.

He brought the glass to his lips, spilling but one drop, drank the wine down to the bottom of the glass, then held out the empty glass at a startled Franca.

"Franca, just another bottom..."

At that moment, Samuele made his appearance with the children following behind. Soon after, Silvestro and Lucia appeared--Lucia full of smiles.

"You all slept well, I gather," the toothless, thin-lipped old man said to them, smiling more with his eyes than with his mouth.

In a few minutes Ernesto made his way to the table, rubbing his eyes. On approaching the table, Ernesto recognized the old man for the geyser he was.

"I don't think I have had the pleasure of drinking with you, sir. Won't you join me in a toast to the newly-weds?"

While Ernesto was filling his glass, the old man had already finished his.

Unexpectedly, Mr. Sorrentini appeared at the gate, with a gift for Lucia: a set of glasses with bottle.

"This looks like pure crystal," Lucia remarked, thanking Mr. Sorrentini.

"Fill one up," interrupted the old man. "I'll tell you if it's pure crystal."

"I'll have to wash them first... Silvestro, pour him more wine."

"Right here," answered the old man, once again bringing his trembling hand forward. While Silvestro poured the wine, the old man turned to Mr. Sorrentini. "Don't you play the accordion?" he asked. And without giving the man a chance to answer, the old man continued: "Go home and get it. Lucia got married, and we need music to liven up this party."

Mr. Sorrentini stood there with his mouth half open. Looking around to see what the others thought of the idea, he easily understood there was need for music. Without saying a word, he turned around and began to walk toward the gate.

"And don't forget your two buddies. We want an orchestra," the old man yelled.

Don Alfonso returned a while later. He too was bringing a gift for Lucia and Silvestro.

"Let me guess," the old man intervened, having become the undisputed center of attraction; "it's a missal! Surprise! surprise... Lucia, if you don't want it, I'll take it home to my wife."

"Why?" asked the priest.

"She's always saying the rosary. Maybe with the book she could pray to herself, quietly, you know."

"I thought she didn't know how to read," Maria interrupted.

"She doesn't; that's why she ought to have the book. Beside, she can't see anyhow. So, Lucia, you had better keep it. Silvestro will put if to good use."

Everyone laughed, including Don Alfonso. Then suddenly everyone stopped laughing on seeing Enrico and Tina appear at the gate. Don Alfonso's smile froze on his lips.

"May we come in?" asked Enrico.

"By all means," replied the old man, looking at the voluptuous Tina. "Bring her too. Don Alfonso wants to know her secret."

"What's that?" asked Ernesto.

"He wants to know how she attracts so many young men."

Once again, they all laughed, and Don Alfonso joined in the laughter.

Tina, who had heard the remarks, also laughed.

"We've brought you a gift," Tina told Lucia as she handed over the packet.

"What else is new? Everyone's bringing gifts. What's in it, booze?" asked the old man, who had everyone in stitches.

"No, I am sorry," replied Tina, her undersized sweater accentuating her curves.

After giving her his typical review, the old man focused on Tina's short skirt.

"The reason for the short skirt is that you ran out of material. Enrico needn't worry, there's plenty under it... "Oh, I almost forgot: you bring other spirits," commented the old man on the verge of offending Don Alfonso and Maria.

"Give him more wine," said Enrico, attempting to diffuse the attention away from Tina.

"If you don't mind, Enrico, I'd rather get it from Tina."

After kissing Lucia on the cheek, Tina accommodated the exhilarated old man. Holding his glass up at the level of Tina's face, with his hand trembling more than ever, and while Tina began to slowly pour the wine, he slowly lowered the level of his glass, forcing Tina to bent. When her breast was abundantly in full view, as a man of a certain age, he asked her to pour the wine slowly and gently.

"God bless you," he commented, "you fill well," he concluded, looking straight at Tina's sweater. He then raised the glass to his mouth and immediately did away with its content.

Mr. Sorrentini returned with his friends, each carrying an instrument. Without much fanfare, the men quickly took their places under the elm tree and began to play, thus attracting the neighbors and the near-neighbors. Before long, about twenty-five young and old gift-bearing friends, walked into the yard, with the young ones quickly beginning to dance to *saltarelli* and *tarantelle.*

Samuele, who saw the wine supply disappear, used it as an excuse to ask Franca to help him get more from the wine cellar. Finally alone, Samuele took her into his arms and kissed her passionately. Franca kissed him back with as much ardor. When Samuele tried to break away to fetch the wine, Franca pulled him back and kissed him again.

"I'm so very happy for your sister Lucia."

"She's lucky, and Silvestro even more fortunate. But it's better this way."

"And us? Is it better this way?" she asked, her face becoming sad.

"There is nothing wrong with what we are doing."

"I want to get married because I want to be loved."

"I love you."

"Yes, yes, I know. This afternoon, thinking of your sister Lucia and Silvestro almost made me sick to my stomach with envy. I wanted to be there with you."

"We have plenty of time for that," he said as he put his hand over his mouth, the humidity making him cough.

"You said that before, and it worries me now more than ever. The other night, after you left me, I couldn't sleep. Horrible thoughts went through my mind. And when I finally fell asleep, I had the worst nightmares. Why, Samuele, is this happening to me? Is it because I am too much in love with you, or is it the fear that we will not be able to consummate our love? If we love each other so much, why the hesitancy?"

"I am sorry, Franca. I hoped to bring you joy and all I seem to be doing is cause you suffering."

"No, no, please, don't feel that way. It's just that I am a woman, and you're the only one who makes me feel this way. It's so frustrating to be so much in love and not make love. It's getting harder and harder, and I can't stand it this way."

"Wait till the day of the feast. I want to be sure I know what I am doing. As soon as I am sure, I will tell you, and probably before the feast... Come now, help me with these bottles," he urged, his eyes full of compassion.

Franca put her arms around his neck and kissed him. Outside, meanwhile, more people had gathered. When the two appeared with the wine, everyone cheered except for the old man who looked at them sternly.

"What else did you do down cellar beside getting that wonderful stuff, eh?"

Samuele smiled; Franca, on the other hand, turned red.

"Ha, ha, see that! She's blushing. Everybody look: she's blushing" the old man let out with a cunning laugh.

Everyone turned to look at Franca. Seeing herself suddenly on the spot, and feeling the need to redeem herself, she immediately retorted that she and Samuele had certainly done no more or less in those few minutes than he and his wife would do in similar circumstances, with the difference that they did not have to do it in the wine cellar. To that, everyone cheered, and even Ernesto applauded his daughter for her resourcefulness and ability to stand on her own two feet.

"We're long past that, my dear Franca. Now, we leave it to the Holy Spirit."

"Is that why she prays every night?" asked Ernesto, causing everyone to burst into an uproar, except for Don Alfonso.

"We ought to have fun, and I agree. Please stay within respectable limits."

Maria apologized to the priest. And for a while, hardly anyone said a word. Even the musicians stopped playing.

"Tina!" called out the old man, "if I were but ten years younger, I'd be spinning you all around this yard like no other man. Dull Enrico, here, doesn't even know how to dance. You should have seen us do the tarantella."

"I'm ready to show them. How about you?"

"Strike up the band," he ordered.

"And what type, Sicilian or Neapolitan?" asked Mr. Sorrentini.

"The new version."

"And what is that?"

"The *trembling* tarantella, if you will."

With that, the old man led Tina to the center of the yard amidst the cheers of the children and the laughter of the grown-ups. At the sound of the music, he grabbed Tina by her hands and began to dance. After a few short rounds, more tired from the amount of wine he had imbibed than from old age, he finally decided to stop.

"Let's go, big man, take over," he commanded.

Enrico stepped onto the floor and started to dance. Before long, the children joined in, then a few couples, and finally everyone except Don Alfonso, Maria, and the old man.

"See what I started?" the old man said to Maria.

"They're all having fun."

"Sure, Maria, and they need it. Here, pour me more wine."

"Don't you think you've had enough?" asked Don Alfonso.

"You don't think there's wine where I'm going, do you?" he asked, raising his head heavenward.

"I wasn't thinking of that. I just thought too much will make you sick."

"I agree," added Maria.

"Agree to pour another glass, Maria... that's it... all the way up. Oh, stop. Thank you." Having gulped half, he turned to the priest. "This is the last glass. I know when I've had enough," he said, and quickly finished the remaining half.

Without greeting anyone, as they were all dancing, he slowly picked himself up and slowly walk to the gate, his legs seeming to bow under his body, his hands trembling more than before. At the gate, he turned around, waved at Maria and Don Alfonso, and disappeared just as he had appeared--out of nowhere.

When the tarantella was over, everyone rushed to the table to look for a seat, while Ernesto looked for another glass of wine. Not seeing the old man, both Ernesto and Samuele asked his whereabouts and were disappointed to learn he had gone.

"His days are numbered," commented Ernesto sadly.

"Funny, he was the first to come, and the least expected. He came in quietly and left in the same way. If weren't for him, none of this would have happened," Samuele said to Franca.

"He enjoyed his stay, however."

Samuele fixed his eyes on Franca's, having understood what she meant.

"You're right, Franca. He had a great time for himself and was also the life to the party. At one time or another, we all give and receive.

"You're doing the same thing with a difference: you're not willing to let go."

"Franca, Franca," he repeated affectionately, "let's find a place to sit down; my legs are tired. Do you see what you have to put up with."

"There's a place."

The two walked over, attracting the attention of many of the guests. When Samuele and Franca sat down on the grassy ground the guests laughed.

They hadn't been seated but fifteen minutes when the last unexpected guest appeared at the gate. It was the Cavaliere, dressed in his usual white suit. Samuele saw him and walked over to meet him.

"I heard about the wedding and thought to join you, if you don't mind."

"We're honored. Please come in and join us."

"I came for a specific reason."

"Yes?"

"I would like to see how the bull reacts to the music and noise."

"Do you want me to bring him out?"

"Certainly, if you don't mind."

After having announced the Cavaliere's presence to the guests, who showed their due respect by bowing to him, Samuele asked the band to start playing and the people to dance. He also told them that the Cavaliere wanted to see the bull's reaction.

With a glass of wine in hand, the Cavaliere waited by the table. Ernesto, who was seated at one end, spoke to the distinguished guest.

"Samuele has the finest animal of our region."

"Yes, know; I've seen it."

"He also has some of the finest wine."

"Yes, I'm noticing. I notice," the Cavaliere said, raising his glass. "May I have some more? I want to drink to the health of the bull."

"The bull! That's a new one on us. Not a bad idea, though. We've been drinking to Lucia and Silvestro all afternoon. You're right, we should start with something else. To the bull!" Ernesto always ready to join in.

With smiles on their faces, the two men drank. But while the Cavaliere placed his glass on the table, Ernesto refilled his. Raising his hand and looking in the direction of the Cavaliere, he toasted once more.

"To the bull!" Ernesto repeated raising the glass to his mouth. The Cavaliere, however, joined him in only in laughter.

A cheer on the part of the children attracted the Cavaliere's attention when Samuele appeared at the door leading the huge bull. With the music in full blast, and the people dancing and making noise, Samuele moved toward the center of the commotion. At one point, the bull stopped, his eyes slightly wild and circumspect. The band stopped playing, and the people retreated.

"No!" called Samuele, "go on playing."

The band resumed again slowly. Samuele put his hand on the bull's neck and began to talk to the animal at the same time. Then, slowly the bull reacted to Samuele's commands. When the band played full speed, and the people went on dancing, Samuele walk to the center without any difficulty.

The Cavaliere was impressed by the control Samuele had over the animal. He was more astounded when, in the middle of the dance, with people jumping and moving in every direction, Samuele ordered the bull to back-step. Then, loading the animal with four children, his nephew, Marcello's little girl, and Silvestro's two other children, Samuele went through the regular routine while the musicians played and the people cheered--just as they would during the actual pull of the Obelisk.

"Remember, Samuele confided, as though the animal were understanding, "there's precious cargo aboard."

Samuele felt a deep excitement as he directed the animal amidst the noise and the music, his eyes, however, always concentrated on the bull's huge head.

"Whoa!" Samuele finally said, and the animal came to a complete stop. One by one, he brought the children down, as the band played and the people clapped and cheered.

Excited, the Cavaliere filled his glass with wine and turned to Ernesto, who was still intrigued by the animal's feat.

"Eh!" shouted the Cavaliere, causing Ernesto to turn. "To the bull!" the Cavaliere shouted before beginning to drink his wine.

Ernesto quickly got his glass. While the Cavaliere was drinking, the rosy-cheeked jubilant Ernesto raised his glass.

"To the bull!"

With the sun setting, the wedding celebration also came to an end. One by one, the uninvited guests took leave of Maria's family, each one affectionately shaking Samuele's hand. Standing by his side, Franca also shared in the accolades.

The saddest part of the evening came when little Samuele had to leave his girl friend who, with tears in her eyes, kissed her little friend goodby. Samuele quickly uplifted her spirits by promising her that little Samuele would be back soon and for good.

CHAPTER 28

With the addition of Silvestro's calves, Samuele's stable became the largest in town. Buyers from such cities as Naples were already stopping by to do business with Samuele. The rapid expansion was due to Samuele's busy schedule on the road, his continuous buying and selling, and his ability to choose the better specimen for himself.

He also took complete control of Mr. Banno's land which he fenced to allow the cattle to wander and feed in the open field--something of a rarity in the region where everyone kept the cattle inside for fear of thieves. When farmers from other areas began to note Samuele's achievements, they began to experiment with their versions, those same farmers, however, preferring to offer to sell to Samuele rather than on the market. Suddenly, Samuele found himself becoming a clearing house for sellers and buyers.

On one of his trips to a nearby village, he came across the owner of a piece of land that lay practically abandoned near his own land. With little negotiation as the offer was an honest one, Samuele found himself buying the land. With this acquisition, he now had plenty of land to satisfy his business needs. What he was lacking and unable to buy, however, was his health.

Knowing he had a limited amount of time left, he also felt the need to plan for his future, doing so without arousing suspicion as to his motives. As a result, Samuele kept on asking Silvestro to spend more time with him. And because the business was growing, Samuele took Silvestro to the various markets, making sure to introduce him to his business colleagues.

In the evening, Samuele began to go to bed earlier than usual. There, by himself, he would recall his war days, in particular his time in the concentration camps. Occasionally, he took out the wallet and stared at it for long periods of time.

Unbeknown to him, Maria often stopped outside the room, knowing something was wrong and afraid to ask. She even put her ear to the door but never heard anything from inside except for an occasional cough. Once, however, she thought she heard him cry.

With a few weeks remaining till the day of the feast, Samuele decided to go over the grounds and stop by the home of the Cavaliere to see the progress for the installation of the Straw Obelisk.

On his way over, Samuele met Enrico and Tina with whom he had wanted to talk, since the two had appeared together at Lucia's party, wondering what had happened to Enrico and Tina.

On seeing Samuele, Enrico was first to speak.

"Samuele, where are you going? Come on over, we want to talk with you."

"Hello Enrico and Tina, how are you?"

"Oh, hi, Samuele. I wanted to talk with you at Lucia's party, but you were so busy. I'm glad to see you. Do you have a moment? Have you heard about Enrico's future plans?"

"No," Samuele answered, not interested in getting in any long-winded conversation. Tina understood Samuele's mood right away.

"You can spare a couple of minutes, I'm sure. We wanted to ask you for an opinion and I believe you could advise Enrico. Oh, by the way, Toni is also planning to immigrate. No one knows about this, except for you and me," she said, giving an importance whose value only she understood.

"Toni! Where is he planning on going?"

"We're going to Australia."

"Good, good... great place! There's a lot of virgin land down there. Besides, I'm told that many immigrants are doing well. Who knows, people like Toni and Enrico might even spread the word about our Obelisk and arrange for it to be drawn in Australia or where ever else our people may be... By the way, I also understand there are many people without religion in those parts of the world. You're planning on following them, right?"

"Ah, no," she replied, fully understanding Samuele's sarcasm.

"Oh, I can't go; my work is here. You know, Samuele, it's easier to talk with people that profess nothing than to talk with those who think they profess something. One is conditioned; the other is not. One is a slave; the other can be freed from ignorance."

"Very good Tina, and you succeeded with Enrico and Toni."

"Enrico's gotten so much better. Oh, there's a lot more work to be done. It wasn't so easy at first, believe me."

Turning to Enrico, Samuele asked what had made him decide to change religion. With a snickering smile on his face, Enrico told Samuele that Tina's new religion just seemed to have made more sense.

"I understand," Samuele said. Then, half-smiling, half-laughing, he added, "You're all right, Enrico, you always get what you want."

Tina's face reddened.

"Did I say something to embarrass you, Tina?" Samuele asked in a mocking tone.

"Oh, go ahead, Enrico, tell your friend here some of the things you saw with your own eyes. Tell him, so he won't have any more doubts. Oh, yes, he might even want to listen afterwards."

"I should have doubts" said Samuele, "about something specific?"

Refusing to answer, Tina looked at Samuele angrily, but urged Enrico to speak on her behalf.

"We happened to go by this place, one afternoon. This man was crossing the street. He didn't look before he started to cross. A car was coming along and hit him. A lot of people gathered around, but no one helped. Later on at the hospital, the man needed blood. No one volunteered except a friend of Tina. That saved the man's life."

"This is the basis of your conversion?"

"Yes," interrupted Tina, an expression of satisfaction on her face.

"What's this supposed to prove, Enrico?"

"That one religion exploits the people; another helps them."

"Do you know the difference between a religious and a civic act. Do you know the meaning of personal responsibility?"

"Why?" Tina asked in a tone close to anger.

"I've seen avowed atheists help enemy victims."

"Come now, Samuele, how can you believe in a religion that pre-supposes that we are born in sin? How can you accept such pessimism?"

"You're partially right," answered Samuele, which caused Enrico to liven up on hearing his friend agreeing, if only partially, with something Tina had said. "You're technically right about original sin, which may explain the act of Baptism--to wash the sins away..."

"...And they don't use soap," commented Enrico in an effort to be funny.

Samuele didn't even wink; he simply went on. "As far as pessimism is concerned, any religion that offers love and happiness can hardly be called pessimistic."

"Those are only words," Tina asserted.

"It is a belief."

"Do you believe in it?"

"We're not talking about my beliefs; you're discussing yours and I'm not interested. I have things to do. Goodby, Tina." Then, putting his hand on Enrico's shoulder, Samuele continued. "You're doing well. A real hero, our new Caesar. You and Toni fit well together," Samuele said, and, with those words, Samuele left the two in complete silence.

He hadn't walked but twenty yards, when Tina called to him. "We'll go on with our discussion when you have more time."

Samuele turned out of respect, but did not answer, angry at himself for having engaged them in that conversation.

The street was already being readied for the up-coming feast. Everywhere workmen were busy with the preparations. Lights decorating the street were already partially installed, and one arcade practically completed.

At the town hall, Samuele walked through the ample corridor used as the depository for the many panels of lacework embroidered in shining straw. There were also many wooden frames, and ahead, the Cavaliere's well-lit and spacious workshop full of embroidered frames everywhere. At the far corner, the Cavaliere was giving his finishing touches to a medallion of the Grieving Madonna for mounting on the main panel of the Obelisk.

On seeing Samuele, the white-robed Cavaliere quickly walked toward his guest. After shaking hands, he offered to show Samuele around the shop. In the tour, he explained how he had gone about doing the work and how each panel was going to fit into the over-all frame being readied at the site. All the items in the shop were being gathered to be brought to the sight for assembly of the obelisk-type tower whose size had grown taller with the years.

He also explained that he had to re-condition and rebuild much of what he had done before the war, damaged by mice or simply rotted, this being one of the reasons why he was not able to build the Obelisk to a new height. He promised, however, that if things went well, he would redesign the frame to make the Obelisk taller.

"Then we'll be needing to have the bulls like the one you have," he told a Samuele engrossed in the description of each piece and amazed at the amount of effort the Cavaliere was making to create the intricate and very beautiful lace of straw.

"I'm astonished," admitted Samuele. "When I was young, I did not see it as intricate and as beautiful with so many parts. How long have you been working on it?"

"Samuele, this is not a year's work. It is the work of a lifetime. I'm never finished, never!"

"Why do you do it? What makes you want to build and rebuild a thing like this. You're not getting rich."

"Rich!" the Cavaliere laughed aloud. "Rich!" he repeated ironically. "If you want me to be the wealthiest man alive, make sure your bull does his part and does it well. When the Obelisk reaches its destination and everything and everyone is safe and sound, then I consider myself the richest man in this world together with those of us that make it possible. You understand, I am sure."

Smiling, Samuel answered in the positive. While he looked at the Cavaliere, however, Samuele turned his face aside, shielding a slight cough with his hand.

"Yes, Samuele, there's a lot of patient work in our Obelisk. And, you know something, a lifetime's work can go down the drain by the wrong pull of one rope, or by a timid or wild animal, or by an ill-tempered animal bearer? One action, just one single action by someone, anyone, can ruin more than two centuries of tradition and destroy decades of my own creations. This is one reason why I visited you so often."

"How about the others, you must have picked them."

"Yes. Ten are veterans and only you and one other are the novices. Confidentially speaking, though, you have the strongest and best behaved animal of them all. I don't mean to be repetitious, but yours is the finest animal I have ever seen. You'll be attracting a lot of attention. Can you handle it?"

While the two men were talking, Don Pietro, the town's doctor and a personal friend of the Cavaliere, walked through the door. Jovially, as was his habit, he greeted the Cavaliere and Samuele.

"Is the statue of the Madonna in place?" Don Pietro asked.

In the conversation that followed, Don Pietro became alarmed by Samuele's cough even though it was slight.

"You know, Samuele, I was always interested in you ever since you came back."

"Oh!"

"If what I heard is true, your return is a miracle. You may not know, but I have been talking with Marcello. He's told me a lot about you. It's amazing you both made it."

"There were times when we didn't think we would. But here we are."

"Samuele, would you mind my giving you an examination--more for medical history than anything else. Would you mind very much? I would also like to look at your foot. As a doctor, you can understand my curiosity."

"I don't have the time, not at this moment. Some other time later I'll be happy to oblige."

"You must have gone through a lot," interrupted the Cavaliere, who began to wonder why his medical friend had suddenly gone off on that tangent. There must have been a reason, otherwise the Cavaliere knew that Don Pietro wouldn't do a thing like that.

"I am back, and alive. I had my share of suffering. Thousands, however, suffered without reward of life. Knowing those people died in the way they did saddens me each time I think back to them, to that whole stupid war. You people here have no idea what happened to us in Russia nor what took place in Russia and in Germany. And now I read that Togliatti is back."

"We didn't know much, it is true. Remember, we hardly had radios and only once in a while we got the paper. With Mussolini we got propaganda; during the war we got nothing. As for now, who knows what we're getting. But Togliatti is back and heading the Communist Party," Don Pietro responded, brushing his large black mustache with his hand. "But, Samuele, please! Let me take a peek at your foot. I'm intrigued, and I'll be brief."

"Right now, here?"

"Yes. Just take off your shoe and sock, that's all."

Samuele obliged. Placing his foot on a footstool, he untied the shoe, then took off his sock.

"There it is," he said.

"Interesting," exclaimed the doctor as he looked at the bluish, toeless foot. Practically half of the front had frozen off. "Very interesting," continued Don Pietro, bending down to examine it. The Cavaliere looked on with amazement.

While the doctor inspected the foot, Samuele's slight cough became more persistent. Covering his mouth with his hand, Samuele tried to see their reaction. Not noticing any, he felt relieved, especially when Don Pietro paid no apparent attention.

"It's a wonder you are alive," commented the doctor as he stood up. "You may put your shoe back on... What kept the rest of you from freezing to death?"

"I didn't completely freeze, as you can see."

"That's amazing," Don Pietro said, knowing when to stop.

"Considering how many died, I guess it is amazing."

"Well," said the Cavaliere, "there are just a few more things I'd like to show you. Come on, Don Pietro, come, I haven't shown you these pieces either. I think you will like them."

The two followed the Cavaliere, Samuele now limping more than before. Don Pietro noticed it but said nothing, acting as though he was not noticing Samuele's more pronounced limp.

Finally, when the Cavaliere was through with his tour, Samuele asked to be excused. Both the doctor and the Cavaliere shook Samuele's hand affectionately, and Samuele was out of the shop.

"What was that all about?" asked the Cavaliere.

"He's a sick man. I think he is very sick. I don't like what I see in his eyes and face. His days are numbered."

"What!"

"What is wrong!" the Cavaliere exclaimed, his tone one of great alarm.

"I'm not sure."

"How's this going to affect him at the pull? You know the strain--five hours is a long time! And, will he get along with Minico?"

"He has plenty of strength left for that. Don't worry about that. As for the helmsman, I believe they'll get along."

"Sure?"

The doctor nodded. "Amazing how he pulled through."

"How did he make it, anyhow?"

"Marcello told me they shielded themselves with those who were dying and by using their clothing."

"God!"

"*God* is right. There's more and I cannot tell you except for this: Palmiro Togliatti, who is being received as hero in some circles around here, worked for the Soviet Union; he helped the Russians decide whom to execute and whomimmig to indoctrinate, the result being that those who were executed were better off than those left alive. How do you like that for an eye-witness report?

"Let's change the subject. Is the statue of the Madonna in place? You never did answer."

"You never gave me a chance. You were too interested in Samuele right from the beginning. That poor bastard, and the rest of those poor devils: we'll probably never know what happened to them. At least Samuele is alive and I'm glad Marcello is telling you the story, not that anyone is interested. *Thousands died without reward of life*. You heard him, didn't you?"

"If only those whose avocation is war had a profession like mine--to keep people alive instead of killing them, or a hobby like yours--to keep building our Obelisk and keep people awed and happy, Samuele and the rest of us could live our lives more or less according to our inclinations. Look at him! He has the courage to think he can live as he wishes when we fixed, for him, the number of days on this earth. We set his lifespan, my dear friend, and I am sure he knows it. He also knows that hundreds of thousands of unaccounted Italian soldiers were lost in Russia and little is said about it."

The Cavaliere did not answer. He simply nodded his head. Then, moving to a frame with the face and head of the Madonna embroidered on it, the Cavaliere asked his friend to help him lift it onto the wooden bench.

CHAPTER 29

Franca did not have many opportunities to go to visit Samuele, but every time she could find the least excuse, she would find herself on the way toward her lover's house. With but a couple of weeks remaining for the feast, Franca was anxious to be with Samuele to see how he was doing during these hectic days of preparation.

On this particular day, she also intended to fix a date, if possible, for their wedding.

Samuele was in the yard when she appeared at the gate. He had the bull under harness, the type he was actually going to use to pull the Obelisk. Samuele was by himself as Maria and the little girl had gone to visit Lucia.

"Ciao!" Samuele said on seeing her, his voice revealing an obvious affection.

"Ciao!" she answered flirtatiously as she opened the gate and walked toward him.

She wore a light bell-shaped dress that swayed with her walk. Her hair was pulled back so that her whole face was completely visible.

"I came to tell you something."

"Something important?"

"I used it as an excuse to come see you and get away from that place."

"Kiss me first."

Samuele put his arms around her and kissed her. Then, pulling back, he stared into her face, her smile filling him with lyrical happiness.

"What are you staring at?" Franca asked.

"At you, at your beautiful face." He caressed her cheek then kissed her gently for a prolonged time.

But the bull, which was standing quietly behind them, observing the two lovers, unexpectedly moved forward and pushed Samuele forward as he was kissing. Separated by the huge bull, Franca laughed heartily.

"He's jealous," complained Franca.

"He wants to go on with the training... Oh, by the way, what was it you came here for?"

"My brother Toni is emigrating."

"For Australia?"

"How did you know?"

"He's going with Enrico."

"Yes!"

"Good riddance. This country isn't losing much and the other gaining less. But, one can never tell. Both might become very successful, especially if willing to work. I heard about people like your brother in America, how well they've done. I think they'll be fine."

"After what he did to you?"

"It's history now... Here, help me with this animal, will you?"

"I guess it doesn't matter anyway."

"What are you talking about?"

"I despise him, but I feel a little sorry for him, and I would like him to be present at our wedding."

"Our wedding?"

"Well?"

Samuele had not thought about that at all. When she pushed him for an answer, the smile on his face disappeared.

Franca became concerned. "You do not want to marry me?" she asked in a sweet but rather apathetic voice.

"I do, I want to marry you. I always wanted to marry you, and you know it."

"Lately, you've acting as though you don't want to."

"No, Franca, no. I have been busy, what with the training here, tending to business, getting things organized. I've been very busy. But, don't think I have not been thinking about us," he said, seeing the need to bring back the look of candor on her face. "I have chosen a probable date and was going to tell you after the feast."

"Please tell me, tell me now!"

"The eighth of December, the day of the Immaculate Conception."

"Samuele, Samuele!" she exclaimed with excitement, as she threw her arms around Samuele, kissing him hard and reacting like a child having received who knows what unobtainable gift.

Samuele held her by her waist and lifted her high up into the air. "Are you happy?" he asked.

"Happy! I'm in heaven," she cried.

"Hang on, you're going for a ride," he suggested, lifting her up onto the bull's back. "Now that my nephew is gone, you have to take his place."

As Samuele brought her around the stable, she smiled with joy.

CHAPTER 30

The sixteenth of September was a typical harvest day. While most farmers were engaged in the process of making wine, Samuele had to be present at a nine o'clock meeting with the Cavaliere, Minico and the other members of the team.

At exactly nine, the twelve men with their huge animals were welcomed by the Cavaliere at the road junction by the bottom of the hill, one of the most difficult places through which to manoeuvre. For this reason, the Cavaliere decided to meet at that corner to emphasize the seriousness of their task, and to impress upon the men the great responsibility they had undertaken. It was not a child's game; rather, it involved dangers, both for themselves and for the multitude of rambunctious spectators, many of whom were already gathering around.

The first thing the Cavaliere did was to introduce them to each other. In turn, they then scrutinized with admiration each other's animal. Minico, whose job was to stand just below the Cavaliere, balancing on the tiller post as an acrobat on a high wire, had the responsibility to coordinate the movement of the six teams, his orders stemming from the Cavaliere.

Except for Samuele, who was in his early twenties, the others were for the most part in their late thirties and older as evidenced by the deep creases on their faces and the rough skin of their hands. Minico was the ranking senior member, both for his age and for his experience. He was second only to the Cavaliere.

As for their looks, four had green eyes, two jet black, and the others had brown eyes. They were broad of shoulders, chest and hips, and all of them under six feet in height. All had natural strength coupled to a tough expression on their faces. The unkind land which they had been working to derive their subsistence had molded them to reflect the harsh terrain. In spite of the evident strain on their faces, each reflected an enormous amount of light in their eyes, partly due to their being the proud owners of those prize animals, and partly because they had been chosen for this important mission. They smiled at each other when they were introduced and even chuckled over their animals.

"Gentlemen," the Cavaliere called out to them, "let's get down to business. There are several things we have to accomplish this morning. I need to have your attention throughout so there will be no questions afterwards. You have to become familiar with the course. You have to know by heart the dangerous areas--here, for instance, where we are standing, is most dangerous because the buildings restrict our movement.

"As you know, the Obelisk is being assembled. I want to do a dry run from there to here with the animals teamed up under yoke. In that way, we will learn about the course: braking when going downhill, pulling when going uphill, changing the ropes around large trees, limiting the ropes to the front and back when on the street, and learning my commands.

"Remember the mission: to get the Obelisk from there to here, in about five hours, and do it without damage to property or injuries to our animals, to us, or to the spectators.

"Last, but not least, I have to choose the first animal, and we will do that now as this position is an important one. Whomever I choose will be receiving commands directly from me, and he will extend those commands to the rest of you. You will appreciate this method the day of the pull. The noise will be so great that my voice will not reach much further than the first team. Coordination, therefore, is important, especially if we have to change direction, which will happen many times, guaranteed. The choice is mine to make, and I would like to announce it now, if there are no objections," he said, and waited to reveal his choice of Samuele.

The twelve men looked at one another without comments. When no one objected, Biagio, the most talkative and spirited of the group, said he would not mind being chosen for the number-one position, but that if he wasn't chosen, he would accept any other. The way he spoke, his manner of opening his mouth to show his gold tooth in contrast to those blackened by nicotine--made the others laugh aloud, and he, laughing at himself.

"It doesn't matter to me who is chosen," said Samuele. "Choosing now seems premature, though. We ought to wait until after we've completed the dry run."

"It makes sense," admitted the Cavaliere, with the rest quickly in agreement and all nodding at each other and then at Samuele.

"All right, now. Let's get started."

With the Cavaliere and Minico in the lead position, the group began its journey to the sight of the Obelisk. Automatically, the twelve men and their animals coupled off with Samuele, who found himself to be in the second position alongside Biagio, who also seemed pleased in that position. As they walked, people greeted them, while children gathered in groups and walked beside the team--the same children who, about two weeks earlier, had already gone to the site riding the single-axle, two-wheel cart. In their chatter, the children almost always exclaimed over the tremendous size of the animals with their extended horns--their accolades bringing no end of joy to their owners.

"Beautiful ox you have there," Biagio said to Samuele. "You should have kept him whole; he'd be worth a million to you. Everyone would be coming to your stable."

"It's a bull," answered Samuele, matter-of-factly.

"A bull!" exclaimed Biagio, looking at the animal with fiercely proud eyes. Then, looking back, he yelled to the rest, "It's a bull! You know where to bring your cows."

The men burst out laughing. Even the Cavaliere laughed.

"How much?" said the one behind Biagio. "I have a couple ready for mating."

Samuele smiled and told them that the bull was not old enough for that.

"A big bruiser like that not old enough?" commented another. How old is it?"

"Nicola told me to wait at least a year," Samuele answered with a chuckle.

Each man in turn contributed his own sexual comment, causing the Cavaliere to smile once again, somewhat maliciously.

Meanwhile, more children gathered. Even adults were standing by the roadside. Some of the animals reacted to the noise by swinging their horns from one side to the other, and staring in their direction. Just below the incline, the Cavaliere stopped the group.

"Look," he said, his hand forward.

The men looked up and saw the summit of the Obelisk with the Madonna in place reflecting rays from the sun.

"How do we get there?" asked Samuele.

"There is no road from here to there... This is another important point. The stretch, from here to there is crucial. We will be inching our way down this steep incline. I don't want to upset you, but in more than two centuries, the

Obelisk fell only once, and then we had the Second World War. We're planning to keep it in balance from beginning to end.

"Look there. See the ground? The wheels will sink into the soil if we're not careful, and those trees and vines will be in our way. Gentlemen, analyze every inch of the ground. Remember, we may have to stop where the incline is the steepest."

Slowly, the men left the macadam street, walked over the soft shoulder and into the open field, leaving an evident trail behind them. The further up the hill they went, the more the huge Obelisk came into view. Samuele came to a quick stop. With the sun shining from behind, the partially completed structure appeared like a tremendous dark tower with the rays of the sun piercing through the empty slots, like stigmata. High above floated several cumulus clouds, adding an aura of mysticism. On seeing them, Samuele felt awed by their mysterious beauty. Silently, he examined the structure and marveled at its complexity.

Aware of Samuele's sensibility, the Cavaliere told the story of how the tradition began. Though speaking to the whole group, the Cavaliere directed his comments mainly at Samuele, to whom the Obelisk was a symbol of beauty. To the others, the Obelisk was a tall and big structure, having commented along those lines from the time it appeared before their eyes.

As they neared the Obelisk, the men walked with their heads turned upward, all staring toward its summit, and not looking where they were going. Finally, when the Cavaliere halted them, they lowered their heads.

"Take a five-minute break," the Cavaliere told them. "Then, get the animals ready for yoking."

Under the supervision of Minico, the men, each with his beast behind, dispersed in the area, while Samuele stayed close to the base of the Obelisk, admiring the various medallions and sculptures. He examined the thick wheels and the steel axle, then the long tiller post to harness the first team. He also examined the yoke fastened across the post. Behind him, the bull seemed to be observing the very same things.

The Cavaliere approached Samuele. "That's where I will be," he said pointing to the platform above the first story. "And right here," the Cavaliere said, placing his hand on the tiller post directly beneath the platform above, "is where Minico will be standing giving the more specific orders on when to go forward and when to stop. His position and responsibilities are crucial."

"It's not very safe: neither on the platform nor here on the post."

"Neither is the position of the first team. In truth, your position is not only the most dangerous, it is also the most demanding, physically and emotionally. Imagine, Samuele, when the Obelisk tips to the front, its weight falls on the tiller post; we have had instances wherein the animals were almost crushed to death. Likewise, when the Obelisk tips to the rear, the weight forces the tiller post upward; and we have had instances wherein the animals were almost strangled to death. You see, therefore, the first team carries the real burden. Samuele, you do see the importance in choosing the right combination of men and animals..."

Samuele listened to every one of the Cavaliere's words. However, the words *you do see*, with the emphasis on *do* revealed a different state of emotion on the part of the Cavaliere, and Samuele was not prone to deciphering it.

"Did my suggestion interfere with your plans? Samuele asked in a subdued voice.

"Temporizing doesn't usually give good results."

"I'm sorry," replied Samuele.

The problem was that the Cavaliere had come to an additional realization: he was choosing between Samuele and his bull--the best qualified both for the animal's appropriate size and strength, which were superior to those of the other animals, and Samuele, who emotionally and physically was at his wits end. The Cavaliere feared that their rigorous journey might mean the last nail into Samuele's coffin. Yet, there was the Obelisk with its Madonna whose safety was entrusted to him, and there was Samuele with only one chance for his day in the sun!

Having agonized over the decision, and feeling a deeper comradeship with this young man who had withstood the Siberian hell, the Cavaliere's decision had assumed a graver meaning.

"Are you prone to premonitions?" the Cavaliere asked.

"No, Cavaliere, absolutely not."

"Do you like the Obelisk?"

"The most imposing thing I have ever seen. I am truly excited. I can't imagine how you do it. It is a marvel."

Samuele's sincere admiration pleased the Cavaliere. "Does it make you happy to look at it?"

"It makes me extremely happy to know that human beings are capable of accomplishing these feats. It makes life exciting; it helps us to bear anguish; it makes us even forget, if only temporarily, the atrocities we bring on our fellow human beings. It's too bad the feast lasts only the day."

"It lasts three days, but nothing goes on forever... Five minutes are up. I'll meet you by the other cart. The men are already gathering."

Among them were several brakemen, who had come by themselves.

Almost immediately after exchanging salutations, the Cavaliere, having privately consulted with Minico, told them he was ready to announce his decision for the first team.

"I have chosen Samuele for the number-one position with Biagio as his team mate..."

After a hearty cheer accompanied by the usual chatter, each of the men congratulated Samuele and Biagio. Then, without further ceremony, the men placed their animals under yoke.

After the harnessing, they stood by their sides. The Cavaliere and Minico took their position at the front of the two-wheeled cart, while the brakemen manned the ropes. A small crowd had gathered and anxiously waited for the forward command. Finally, the Cavaliere gave his first command to Minico, and Minico, swinging his stick forward, passed the command to the six teams.

"Forward, march!" he shouted at the top of his lungs, and the animals began to pull, amid the cheers and excitement of the small crowd.

About one-and-a-half hours later, the group came to a stop in a reserved space just below the church.

"And this, as you all know, is where the Obelisk will be anchored.

"Gentlemen, well done. I have chosen well. We have the best combination of men and animals we have ever had. I am sure we will make all of our compatriots proud.

"There is no question in my mind that we will have the most spectacular pull ever. No question in my mind."

The men, with great big smiles on their faces, hugged their animals as they listened.

"Now, are there any questions? This is the time to clear up anxieties, doubts, or whatever else you may have."

"I am concerned about the narrow street below here. I don't know how the ropes will be manned. There are houses on both sides."

"When we get there, we shall have to stop. While the Obelisk is standing still, the men holding the lateral ropes will have to split up: some will pull along the sidewalks; others--very few, naturally--will have to pull from the top of the roofs and from balconies. The ropes will be handed from one group to another, from balcony to balcony, from window to window, and from roof to roof. There is no doubt this is a critical place. You ought to also remember, Samuele, that the forward and rear ropes will be extended. Most of the balancing will be done by these two teams."

"Do you know approximately how many people will man the ropes?" Samuele asked.

"We never know from year to year, but it is in the many thousands--you can imagine how difficult it is to control so many people. This year, we expect more people than ever in that we're celebrating the end of the War. And speaking of the War, I want to take this opportunity to welcome back our Samuele, wishing him God's speed."

"Many thanks for your thoughts, Cavaliere. What was the year you had the largest crowd, and how did you handle it?"

"In 1936, King Umberto assisted in the pull. Obviously, his presence attracted national attention, and crowds came from all over. We had no bad incident of any kind. By the way, the King presented us with the gold medal."

"A couple more questions, if you don't mind," Samuele said. "One, I understand there's a special rope to the Madonna. Who got that? Two, are there particular things we should be on the lookout for, for prevention sake?"

"The highest bidder was Mastro Berardino, the wine-maker from Taurasi. As for prevention, we should be sure to have all ropes manned so as there are no loose ends. Remember, the ropes are intertwined with solid twenty-inch wooden sticks. It is absolutely necessary that they be off the ground at all times."

The men listened with their mouths open. It seemed to them they were on the verge of accomplishing an impossible task. The Cavaliere, however, wanted them to feel that the whole manoeuvre, if properly executed, should only generate excitement and thrills.

"I don't want you to over-react, and not to worry too much about the manoeuvre here. After all, this is not the first time we've done it. If we are as careful here as we have to be throughout, we'll have a successful pull. In any case, just remember the Madonna is at the very top and she will always be at our side, as she always has been. Now, are there any other questions or comments?"

"The men who will be on the ropes, do you have them picked out?" asked Biagio.

"No! We have never chosen teams. The men may come from any place. Everyone has a chance at pulling the ropes. Remember, for many it is an honor."

"Will they hear your commands?"

"We will have guides on all sides of the Obelisk and as far up as the fourth story. There will also be people to relay the commands. Besides, they will move with the animals. Samuele, and you, Biagio, yours is the key position, as I said before. If we start too abruptly, the Obelisk will bend and sway to the back; if we stop abruptly, the Obelisk will bend and sway to the front. Naturally, if we have to come to a sudden stop, then stop. But we have to avoid these jerky starts and stops as much as possible. Anything else?"

None of the men spoke. However, they stared at the Cavaliere, waiting to be dismissed. When he saw there were no more questions, he began to speak again.

"One last thing: here are the ribbons for you to tie on your prize animals. Good luck."

After having received the streamers, the men first shook hands with the Cavaliere and Minico, and then each went his way.

CHAPTER 31

Friday evening, after Samuele and his mother had taken care of the stock, and Maria and the little girl left the stable, Samuele remained behind. While the huge bull ate hay from the manger, Samuele looked on silently. Occasionally, the animal returned a glance. Samuele caressed its neck; then he passed his hand under its throat, over its shoulders, over its hind legs and up to its back. When he came to stand in front of the bull's head, Samuele ran his hand up and down its flat face. He stared at the animal's head for a long time, thinking and, at the same time questioning himself and the animal about the meaning behind the up-coming event.

"What does it all mean?" he said aloud, the animal lifting its head to Samuele. "Yes, what does it all mean? Why? Tomorrow you and I will have to follow a course that might be dangerous to us and to the thousands of bystanders. Yet, we do it. Why? You don't know, do you? Or, you do know, and refuse to tell me. You won't tell me because you cannot speak. But you understand me. You always understood me. Always!"

The bull kept on eating, while his master kept on speaking, his soliloquy relaxing the animal as a mother reading to a suckling child.

"It seems all living creatures have to endure at least one of this type of task in their lifetime. Tomorrow will be my last--and you?

"How many more will you have to undergo before the knife pierces your throat?

"I can't tell you how many horrible tasks my friends and I sustained; few of us beat them off. But now, my time has come. I feel the knife at my throat.

"I remember when my strength was like yours. I thought I still had some when Toni proved to me otherwise. Besides, once it goes, it doesn't come back. Nothing really comes back, nothing...nothing at all. Only a short while ago I began to realize how precious life is. I felt the magic that first evening with Franca. I thought then that what lay ahead would be better and greater, and it proved true--it is true! You cannot imagine how much I desire her love--I desire it more than ever, and yet I have to abstain from it. I have to forego it. Can you imagine, here is the thing I want most, it is here, and I cannot partake of it. The desire torments me, because I know that if Franca should have a child, and I will be gone, you know what will happen to her. Oh, sure, she will live. I don't want her to live like that. I have seen so much unhappiness over similar situations; there can be much anguish.

"The things we are capable of doing to one another! You do not understand; yet, you are capable of suffering, if only physically, and you do suffer. If only I could know your feelings tomorrow. But I won't. Nor will you know mine no matter how many times we will exchange glances. I might yell at you, you might bellow at me, and neither of us will understand each other's true feeling, except to execute the commands given me and those I give you. In the end, that's what life is all about, isn't it? And maybe it is better this way. It must be, otherwise we would have been created differently.

"Tomorrow, your strength will help pull the Obelisk---man's creation, and you're taking part in the fulfillment of one of man's undertakings. Your strength will help make the day a success.

"Tomorrow, people will be reminded of man's dual capability: they will see a thing of wonderment such as our Obelisk, and hear extermination systems of war that took place a few years earlier. It is true your species is raised and slaughtered by us, making sure that nothing goes to waste--your work and finally your carcass. Nature commands us to satisfy our hunger, and your sacrifice gives us health. There is a reason, therefore. There is a reason!

"There is a reason," Samuele repeated, lowering his voice as he continued to reflect on his past; the melancholy in his eyes was not evincing a desire to return to those experiences. On the contrary, he wanted to raise more such bulls and to pull more obelisks.

"But, let's face it. You're an exception. And the Cavaliere, who said you are a rare specimen, is also an exception. And yours truly, in all humility--yes, I am an exception.

"Unfortunately, there are far too few of us in this world, far too few."

The bull picked up a mouthful. As he chewed it, he looked into his master's eyes while Samuele, in turn, watched the animal's expression.

"I see neither happiness nor anguish in your eyes; I do not know how you feel, even now that you are eating. Yet you obey me. There must be more to you than your docile expression. I know there must be."

Samuele caressed the animal. He scratched behind its white big ears which the bull collapsed on feeling tickled. Samuele then put his hand over his mouth to restrain his cough.

Outside, the sun was about to disappear behind the mountains to the south of Naples. Franca, wishing to be with her lover, persuaded her father to walk over to Samuele's house, saying that he ought to be helping Samuele during the pull.

They found Maria preparing supper. The little girl was seated at one side playing with a makeshift doll Lucia had made. Franca told Maria that her father wanted to offer his help during the pull. When Maria told them that Samuele was in the stable, Ernesto immediately left for the stable thus giving Franca the opportunity to speak with Maria.

Franca wanted to ask Maria several questions that she had not dared to ask in the past.

"How is the little girl getting along?" Franca asked, knowing this to be the best way of beginning and directing the conversation.

"She's doing well, Franca. She misses her mother terribly. Samuele, though, more than makes up for both her father and mother. Samuele is her father, and it is just as well that she never knew Marcello."

"I am glad to hear she is getting along. Samuele is very kind to children. I hope he will be as kind and as good to our own children."

"I am sure he will, Franca," Maria answered, as though she knew the wedding was pending. "He will love your children. I can tell by the way he cares for this little one here. You know, my grandson adores Samuele."

"Did he tell you about our wedding date?"

"No, Franca, he did not."

"I'm surprised."

"Did you set a date?"

"Yes, he told me the eighth of December, the day of the Immaculate Conception. I was sure he had told you. Apparently, he doesn't say much about me."

"Franca, he has been busy. He's done a lot in a very short time. When he comes home, he either works in the stable, or is here playing with her. After he eats, he goes upstairs, and I don't hear from him any more."

"How does he look to you?"

"What do you mean, Franca?"

"I was just wondering. One evening he had a coughing spell."

"I heard the coughing. I'm trying to find a way to suggest his going for a visit. He started this coughing after the fight with your brother."

Without arousing suspicion in Maria--at least Franca thought so for the time being, she attempted to change the subject.

"I see supper is almost ready. Do you want me to go call him?"

"Usually she goes; if you wish you may go with her. I'll finish with the table."

"Don't set anything for us. We've already eaten," Franca said as she left, hand in hand with the little girl. Maria stood still and watched the two pass through the door, while crossing her hands over her breasts.

"Really, now..." Ernesto was telling Samuele when Franca met them returning from the stable. "I'll be on your right side all along. Nothing is going to go wrong. In any event, I want to enjoy the spectacle up close with you..."

"Hello, Franca."

"Hi, Samuele." Franca went to his side, while the little girl moved up front to be picked up. As they walked, Franca extended her hand to Samuele, who held it tight, his thumb caressing her soft skin. He turned to look at her, wanting to tell her the difference between the first time he tried to hold her hand and she refused because they were rough, and now he was caressing her soft skin.

"Franca tells me you have set the important day," Ernesto commented, while walking leisurely toward the kitchen.

"Yes, the eighth of December, the day of the Immaculate Conception."

"A great choice," answered Ernesto, trying not to place any special meaning to the word *immaculate*. Franca, however, knew better. Virginity was still considered a requirement.

"Yes, I agree. The date is appropriate."

Although Franca well understood the conversation, she was also concerned about her Samuele, fearing the worst, and willing, should fate intervene, to go against customs, a fear that Ernesto had of his daughter.

With these troubling thoughts, the three entered the kitchen. Maria stared at her son's face. Samuele felt that something had happened, but did not know how to ask. Instead, he went to the corner of the kitchen to play with the child, whom he hugged and kissed, and she enjoyed every moment of it.

"She acts as though she were your real daughter," remarked Ernesto.

"There isn't much choice," Samuele answered.

"Not too many would do what you're doing."

"That's right, not too many."

Franca then spoke up, telling her father that Samuele had not yet had supper, suggesting, therefore, that they go do their shopping and stop by on their way back.

After the father and daughter had left, Maria asked her son why he had not told her of his wedding plans.

"No reason, Mother, no reason at all. As a matter of fact, I think I forgot all about it."

"You did!"

"I know, Mother, it sounds awful, but I did. When I told Franca that, I just wanted to make her happy, that's all."

"What are your plans? Can you tell me."

"My plans are to get Silvestro and Lucia situated here with us. I want Silvestro to learn about every aspect of my work because I might like to do something else and I want him take over."

"Take over! And you?"

"I don't know. I don't want to do this all my life. I want to try something else. I don't know yet. I haven't thought about it much...Mother, can we eat now? I think the child is hungry."

Maria placed the food on the table, filled his glass with wine, and then filled her glass and the child's with half water, half wine. While Samuele ate with the child on his lap, Maria kept looking at him, while Samuele avoided her glances. He played or talked with the child, asking mainly if she missed her little friend.

"Yes," she answered in a thin and timid voice.

"Well, he's coming back, with all the other kids. How do you like that?"

"Hurray, hurray!"

Samuele smiled. Then, putting his hand over his mouth, he coughed. Maria looked at him. Samuele raised his eyes to hers. When he saw her staring at him, he turned to look at the child and lowered his head altogether.

"Are you ready for tomorrow?"

"Yes, I think I am."

"And the animal?"

"He's in better shape than I."

"Why, is there something wrong?"

"With me! Why do you ask?"

"You said you're not in the same shape. Besides, you're coughing, and I am worried about you."

"No one is as strong as he. As for the cough, it comes and goes. I've had it before and it went away."

"Do you want some more wine?"

"Yes, thank you."

Maria poured the wine and looked at her son. Samuele felt her stare but did not dare look up.

After supper, Samuele told his mother he was going to bed, explaining that he needed all the rest he could get for the pull the following day.

Maria thought it strange that her son should want to go to bed so early, especially when he knew that Franca was returning. But, she was not going to say anything to change his mind.

"Will you go to church with me in the morning?"

"Certainly, Mother, I'll take you to church tomorrow, and again Sunday to hear Mass. Tomorrow, I have some business to attend to."

Samuele set the child on the chair and walked upstairs. A sudden fear overcame Maria. She stared at the upstairs door, then walked silently over by the door, attempting to listen but hearing nothing. She went downstairs, cleared the table and put the tablecloth away. She then returned to stand in front of the same door. Once again, she heard nothing. Downstairs again, she began to wash the dishes, and, once every so often, she returned to the door. Finally, she held her ear to the door. And, again, her attempt was in vain. She was standing by the door when she heard a knock at the front door. It was Ernesto and Franca.

"Samuele's gone to bed. He said he wanted to rest for tomorrow. I don't know what's wrong. He's acting strange."

"Naturally he's acting strange. Anyone in his position would act strange. He's got butterflies in his stomach, that's all," replied Ernesto with an unconvincing smile on his face.

"Butterflies!" exclaimed Maria, even more worried.

"No, Maria, you don't understand. Samuele is nervous, that's all. The same thing's happening, right now, to the rest of the team. I can assure you that the Cavaliere is probably shut up in his own room."

"If that's the case, why do they do these things?"

"For us, Maria, for us... Come on, Franca. We had better be going."

After the two left, Maria took a deep breath, feeling somewhat relieved over the possibility that Ernesto might be right. She walked over to the little girl.

"It's bedtime, my child," Maria said, taking the little girl into her arms.

CHAPTER 32

Next day, the sun rose from the east with a brilliance that seemed unsurpassed. The people everywhere were making last-minute preparations for the festa. The square and its streets were already filled with people going to church and with booths displaying numerous items of merchandise. In some, salesmen had already begun selling their wares. On one side of the square, the huge covered platform on which the symphony orchestra was going to perform had been completed. On the other side was a second platform not as refined in its finish as the other. On it, the band from Gioia dei Colli was going to perform its specialties: marches and overtures by Rossini. Around the platform, musicians had already gathered. Their contract required them to play throughout the morning. In the evening, they were to alternate with the symphony orchestra, and also provide background music for some of the stage skits to be performed by professional actors from Naples.

Samuele, Maria, and the little girl arrived at the square about fifteen minutes before Mass began. When they entered the church, whose altar was laden with flowers, Maria and the child sat down. Samuele, instead, made a tour of the church, stopping in front of the altar, and then going out the door on the other side. As the Mass was going to be long, he decided to visit the animal fair being held in an empty field adjacent to the square.

Slowly, Samuele walked over to the fair. Many people, already recognizing him, greeted him and wished him a successful afternoon pull.

After looking over the animals, he bought five calves and arranged for their delivery. Then, he went back to the square. As he walked across to the church, he ran into Tina, dressed in a light cotton skirt and sleeveless blouse. All the men were looking at her, and some commented on her appearance, but she paid no attention to them.

Tina, who was secretly carrying a torch for Samuele, immediately called out to him.

"Hello, Samuele! Hey, what brings you here?" she asked with a smile, her white teeth shining within her large sensuous lips.

"My mother is in church."

"And you're here with the men while the women are inside?"

"If you were there, you wouldn't be outside with us. Look, they're staring at you."

"Ah, do you think they have reason to?"

"Sure," he answered, pointing at her breasts.

To one side, an older man belonging to a clique of salesmen remarked aloud that Samuele was also pointing in the right direction.

"I don't know what you have been thinking about, but, oh, I'm interested in explaining my religion to you. I wish you'd give me a chance, that's all I ask."

"And Enrico?"

"Oh, Enrico! Yes, what about him?"

"How has he reacted to your religion?"

"Oh, well, he is not too intelligent. He is not a bad kid, though."

"Kid?"

"Well, he is a little young, and, oh, he hasn't been around..."

"...Women?"

"Oh, no, that's not what I mean. He hasn't been around like you, I mean."

"I've been around, and I've come across people like you."

"Oh, but I don't know how to take your remark."

"Take it any way you want. Look, I've got to go."

"Don't go away; Mass is not over yet. Oh, you see, I come here every Sunday at this time. The sermon is about to start-oh, yes, it will come over the loudspeakers. It will fill the whole square. You have to wait anyway. You may as well hear all about Jesus Christ with me. I promise not to say a word about it throughout the sermon. Nothing. You can see, eh. I am not asking much."

"I had intended to stay here."

"Oh, good. I thought you might be afraid to spend time with me. By the way, that is one of the hardest things for me to overcome. Ah, you see, they would all come to talk with me--including women--but they don't dare for fear of being conspicuous."

"If they were to talk with you, they would strengthen their belief in their own religion which, I think, is pretty good."

"Oh, I don't believe so. I hope you forgive me. You know, I am--I have to be frank about certain things."

"It doesn't matter to me... Let's go there to the bar. I'll treat you to a vermouth. That way, we can sit and listen..."

"...And also see what's going on, can't we, eh?"

Happy at the outcome of her conversation, Tina swaggered across the square beside a limping and taciturn Samuele, and maintained a serious expression on her face.

Seated at a table, they could see and hear all that was going on in the square. Immediately across from them, the musicians were tuning up their instruments, the horn and drum players making the loudest sounds.

Soon a voice came over the loudspeaker system, and it was of Don Alfonso: "My dear brothers, today we celebrate the feast of our patron saint. In this morning's sermon, I want to speak about the life of our Grieving Madonna, the Mother of our Lord Jesus Christ, our Savior. Our Madonna learned the meaning of forgiveness from our Lord, Jesus Christ. Let us learn from the teachings of Jesus, our Savior, as our Madonna learned from Him.

"Our lives have to follow the examples of our Lord Jesus if we are to gain paradise. One of the very first things we have to learn is to forgive. Not to forgive is to claim we are perfect. Jesus Christ, the son of God, though perfect in every respect, forgave; he forgave his enemies as well as his own people..."

The voice of Don Alfonso, saying the special Saturday Mass, filled the square, but everywhere people went on with their affairs. Samuele and Tina listened silently. Then, suddenly, while the priest was in the middle of a long sentence, the band struck up a very noisy and fast march that completely drowned out the voice from the loudspeaker, the rhythm so catchy that the men walking across the square unconsciously marched to the beat of the music.

Samuele and Tina looked at each other, but kept their silence. Then they looked at the band and enjoyed the music. When the band finished the colorful march, the priest's voice filled the square once more.

"...in our Lord Jesus, our Savior. This is a day to remember. It has been such a long time since we have been able to pray in public to Jesus and to our Madonna for peace in the world.

"In the past few years, we saw so many tragedies, so much destruction. Why, I ask you, why? Because we did not learn from the example of our Lord, Jesus Christ. And, we did not learn from our holiest Madonna, who has been grieving for the death of her son, and now not only grieves for us, but also for the millions of victims from this last war.

"When will men..."

The band struck up another tune: Wagner's Overture from *Die Walküre*. The entire square and the hilly roads leading into it were filled with the music with the people nearer to the band giving up talking altogether, the music being so loud and so stirring. Others, especially those in the adjacent areas, talked during the lyrical passages, but stopped talking when the horns, reinforced by the drums, played so as to drown out every verbal activity.

Once again, Samuele and Tina looked at each other; then, without saying a word, turned their faces toward the square. After about five minutes, the band stopped.

"...our Lord. God sacrificed his Son, Jesus Christ, for us, to deliver us, to offer us salvation. Our holy Madonna is a symbol of sacrifice, the One who intercedes for us, the Mother who works on our behalf, the Mother who understands our sins. She is the Mother who is also aggrieved by our sins. Let us not add to Her grief through our sins. When we sin, let us go to Her for help. She will be there with open and consoling arms.

"Let us follow the examples of our Lord Jesus Chr..."

A loud and heavy drum roll filled the air. This time, the musicians had moved from the stand and gathered in a marching formation in front of their director leading them in Rossini's *La gazza ladra* overture. After the drummers' in-place crescendo was reached, which literally drowned out every part of the town, the director pointed to the wind section, and the loud band began its march through the square and down the side streets, with a horde of children noisily marching behind. No matter where the band went, one couldn't hear anything but the loud and rhythmic drumbeat accentuated by blasts of the French horns.

After about fifteen minutes, the band reappeared in the square with the children following behind. Approaching their platform, the band executed a slow about-face; then, after squaring off in perfect formation, the band leader, pointing to the drum section, and with his arms frantically waving in the air, brought the drummers to an ear-shattering crescendo. After sustaining it for about one minute, wherein all eyes were on him, he flung his arms once around, and in a split second, bringing them down, he brought the music to a sudden stop, to the wild cheers of everyone.

"...Holy Ghost, Amen."

"Oh, I told you I wouldn't say a word. Did I keep my promise?" Tina asked in a deliberate child-like manner.

"Yes, you kept your promise... How could you not. No one else spoke either. Do you want another vermouth?"

"Ah, no, Samuele. I don't want another vermouth. I want something else."

"What?" Samuele asked curtly.

"You!" she exclaimed in a subdued but sultry voice, and without her habitual *ohs* and *ahs*.

Samuele had understood from the beginning that Tina was coming on to him; though she was not his type sexually and spiritually. Nevertheless, he was curious about her religious motives.

The problem with religions, including his own, was that there have been so many upheavals in the name of God--upheavals that left trails of blood of millions and millions of people. Many who were prematurely made to see their maker, and, always, in the name of that God.

He vividly remembered the several one-sided conversations (Samuele knew little about religions) he had with this would-be, comrade-in-arms atheist in one of the Siberian camps. Samuele distinctly remembered--and this made a big impression on him--his co-prisoner saying that while men cannot do without religion, the same men use it to gain or to consolidate personal or group power, noting that at the basis of every schism, religious revolution or reformation, the genesis is to be found in the struggle between those in power and those seeking that power.

It doesn't matter whether they are called schisms, revolutions or reformations, or any other name, the basis is generally the same, and the results corroborated by the premature death of millions of innocent followers ultimately sacrificed in the name of God or its equivalent.

"You want me to become a follower of your religion?" Samuele asked, the image of his doomed comrade in sight.

"Ah, there's more than religion in my heart," Tina said, coquettishly.

"As in Enrico's heart?"

"Must you always bring him up, eh!"

"I would like to know where you stand, what's the meaning behind it all. Do you, yourself, understand what you are doing? I have the impression you do not. Are you seeking power for yourself or for others, or don't you know?" Samuele asked in a recalcitrant tone.

"Oh, my religion is all-encompassing."

"And others are not?"

"They're probably, oh, what shall I say, more moralistic?"

"Morals, what's that got to do with anything?" he asked, his tone verging on anger.

"Your morals? Oh, you'd forget your morals because my religion is not about morals. In the end, you'll feel nothing immoral, nothing."

"Your religion teaches that?"

"Well, my religion deals with what's natural; it does not avoid nature."

"You keep your morals, your nature and your philosophy; I'll keep my religion."

"Eh, Samuele, don't be angry. Why do I have the impression that you're afraid to be alone with me, ah?"

"I never planned to be alone with you."

"Oh, that's a shame. I'd assure you I would not do anything compromising."

"If there's compromising, it will be with someone else."

"Franca, for instance, eh?"

"Yes, especially Franca, if the question of compromising were an issue... But look, the people are beginning to come out of the church..."

"...Oh, you mean the women."

"Women, I guess," Samuele answered, as he stood up.

"Wait," she pleaded.

Two older men were walking their way. They were talking to each other and had not seen Samuele and Tina. When they got close, Tina stopped them.

"Good morning, gentlemen."

"Good morning," answered the older of the two.

"Did you like the sermon, eh?"

The man looked at his friend as he turned the palms of his hands outward, not knowing what she was talking about and turned to his friend for a possible explanation.

"Oh, well, did you like the priest's sermon?" insisted Tina.

"We didn't hear anything."

"Weren't you here, eh?"

"Ya, we were here, but who the devil cares about the sermon. It's the same thing over and over again. You hear one, you've heard them all. Besides, we've got work to do."

"Thank you."

"What else do you want to know?"

"Oh, nothing else, thank you. You were both very kind."

"We were?" The men shrugged their shoulders and went on their way.

"I also have to go. Goodby," Samuele said, and walked away, leaving Tina by herself, devastated, but smiling to those passing by.

As for Samuele, he did not get the answer to or the proof of his comrade-in-arms' observations. "Perhaps, another Teresa," he said to himself on the way to meet his mother and his little girl coming out from the church.

CHAPTER 33

Dressed in their best clothes, people from everywhere flocked into town and around the perimeter of the Obelisk.

An hour before the journey was to begin, thousands gathered around the monumental tower of straw. Children scurried about, yelling and jumping all over the place; older boys indiscriminately climbed the ropes, some even climbing and walking on the tiller post. Young girls and women, however, dressed in colorful costumes, either stood in admiration of the boys' unbridled activities or in defiance of their buffoonery and hooliganism.

Throughout the crowd, salesmen shouted magniloquent about their unique products. One, selling sunglasses especially designed to view the Obelisk, was surrounded by would-be buyers. When a old man asked to try the glasses before buying them, the salesman, lowering his sunglasses down to his nose, assured him that the glasses fit all sizes and that no where in the world were better glasses sold for less.

"I'll take a pair," the old man said.

"Take two pairs; pay half the price for the second."

"Me too!" yelled a voice from the side.

"Two pairs for me!" echoed another.

In no time, the man sold all but ten pairs with people continuing standing and pushing in front of the stand.

"Sorry, I'm running out and cannot sell under cost. One for the price of one on the next five, take it or leave it. No more seconds!"

The salesman immediately sold the five.

"Five remain. Double the price and the glasses are yours."

After having sold his complete stock, the salesman told the crowd he would finally join them to view the Obelisk, as he did not have to worry about selling his wares.

"Does anyone want to buy the pair I have on?" he suddenly asked, triple the price, and it is yours."

"I do!" yelled the first man in line.

No sooner had the salesman gone through the motion of sitting back to enjoy the spectacle, another salesman from the opposite direction appeared selling the same glasses at a slightly higher price. When the people heard his voice advertising the glasses, they quickly rushed to him. The first salesman, meanwhile, his hand polishing his big mustache, extended his secret wink of the eye to his colleague about to sell out his stock of cheap sun glasses.

From below, the six teams of men and animals began to appear in intervals on the crowded scene, with practically everyone converging on them, wanting to look at the ribboned huge animals and trainers. Silently, with their chests expanded, the men cautiously made their way through the crowd.

Samuele, with his bull, appeared on the scene together with his entourage which included Franca. Once again, the crowd began to shout and to move down to meet him. On being surrounded, the bull began swinging its long horns from side to side, and stepping with his hind legs sideways as a warning to the people to stay away. Samuele quickly turned to the bull and began to stroke its neck. When the crowd finally opened a frontal pathway, Samuele made his way forward.

Some people, however, noticing the animal's reaction, lost some of their initial enthusiasm. Nevertheless, the crowd moved forward with Samuele, who quickly realized an element of present danger: the control of so many unwieldy people. He had not expected such a movement and thought that if they acted that way now, they certainly would get out of hand during the pull. With this in mind, he reached the platform, where he was welcomed by the other members of the team.

A tremendous cheer coupled with hand clapping suddenly arose from the crowd. Again, they moved down the path where the Cavaliere and his friends were approaching in a horse-drawn carriage. He waved his hands as a token of thanks.

Not far behind were the remaining members of the team, having the same difficulty moving through the dense crowd of about twenty-thousand.

"Harness them," ordered the Cavaliere.

Under the general cheers of the crowd, the men, under Minico's supervision, went about their chores. After Samuele and Biagio had yoked and then harnessed their animals to the long and sturdy tiller post, the rest, after bringing their animals side by side in place, extended the heavy rope from below the cart, along the post, and securely tied onto each of the six yokes. After completing their final safety inspection of the equipment, they reported their readiness to the Cavaliere, who was standing with Don Pietro and Don Alfonso at the base of the Obelisk.

"The crowd worries me, Cavaliere. They're going to get in everyone's way," Samuele said, with a Biagio nodding his agreement.

"Naturally," answered the Cavaliere, looking directly into Samuele's eyes. "Naturally the people pose the biggest danger of all. It has always been so. Leave that worry to me, to Don Alfonso, to Don Pietro, and to Minico. They'll help us. Besides, these other gentlemen here are in charge of the ropes, and they know what to do. This is not our first time. The brakemen are also in place.

"If there are no questions, we will all go to our posts.

"Brakemen, are you checked out and ready?"

The brakemen and their assistants stepped forward to report they were completely ready.

"Rope leaders, are you all ready to assume your posts?" The more than fifty answered with a loud "Yes."

"Samuele, how about you and your animals? Are you ready?"

Each of the six men answered in turn that they were as ready as ever.

"Don Alfonso, Don Pietro, any observations?"

"They all look in fairly good health to me. The animals above all are bigger and stronger than ever before."

"I will speak to them," Samuele answered, "and I am sure we will take good care of our Madonna."

"If that is the case, go to your posts."

Amid a tremendous uproar from the crowd, the men walked to their posts. The Cavaliere, Don Alfonso, the mayor, Minico and the rest of the guides climbed from within the Obelisk to their respective platforms around the Obelisk.

When the Cavaliere took his command position, the crowd cheered once again. With the appearance of Don Alfonso, the cheers subsided, his appearance meaning that the pull was about to begin. Don Alfonso raised his arms to the crowd. When silence came, the Cavaliere spoke.

"My dear friends..." he began, an overwhelming cheer interrupting him, "dear friends, the war is over..." he stated, the crowed interrupting him again with thunderous shouts of *viva la pace, viva la pace* (long live peace). "...Yes, the war is over, and now we can continue with our great tradition. What we are about to do, on this glorious afternoon, is unique in the world. Nowhere else will you find an obelisk with the magnificent Madonna at its top being pulled by a team of animals and men such as we have in our region. This is truly an unusual day, my dear friends, a day that all of you make possible in one way or other. It is a day that has to go on, every year, as in the past, as it has to be, from now on... No more war!" he exclaimed to another thunderous response. "...Every year, yes, every year from now on, we have to have our festa; our Madonna has to ride high," he stated to a *si, si* (yes, yes) response from the people. "When She doesn't, we will all suffer. The people of the world will suffer, and we all must choose between a Madonna riding our Obelisk and tanks riding herd on our humanity. In the past three or so years, our Madonna did not ride. As a result, the world saw a most horrible and ferocious war, the war that took so much from us, especially so many dear ones from our homes. You and I had nothing to do with it; it was started elsewhere and we had to share in the disastrous consequences. Remember, though, we do not have wars to have tragedies.

"Tragedies when least expected, even this very afternoon, unless we are diligent and resourceful. Yes, that is right, unless we--all of us, every woman, every child regardless of age, every man--unless we are all careful, unless we follow instructions, tragedy can surely strike us on this beautiful and glorious afternoon.

"Please, pay attention to our commands. Pull or release according to my commands. For those on the wheels and the many on the brake-ropes, be sure to respond to my commands.

"Our first responsibility is to stay out of the way of the ropes. The men on all sides have to balance the Obelisk; no one else can. So, stay away from them unless you're manning the ropes.

"Our second responsibility is to be silent during the crucial manoeuvre. You may cheer all you want after each manoeuvre. Take the lead from the band.

"Throughout the journey, do not explode any fireworks. The sudden noise may startle the animals. There will be great fireworks tonight, and a couple in a few minutes.

"Stay clear of the Obelisk. This year, it is the tallest ever. Should it fall, God help us, we don't want anything to happen to anyone.

"As you know, we are travelling over private property. Traditionally, the proprietors allowed us to use their grounds. That does not mean we should destroy plants or damage property. Be considerate, and let us be grateful in our use of private property.

"That is all I have to say," he said. Pausing to let the cheers quiet down, the Cavaliere began again.

"We will now receive the prayer from Don Alfonso..." The crowed responded with another thunderous cheer, causing the animals to step sideways. Samuele shouted to the men to keep calm, while he held a grip around his bull's neck.

With the Cavaliere on one side, Don Alfonso began.

"In the name of the Father, the Son, and the Holy Ghost, Amen," the people repeated the prayer with him, many of them on their knees. "Our Father, who art in Heaven... Amen.

"Brothers and sisters, you all heard the wise words of our Cavaliere. Without him, we would not have this bright and big Obelisk; without him, we would not be paying homage to our Madonna in this unique and exciting way. God wants us to share in this joyous day. Let us be sure that all goes well--do only what you are to do. We have a long afternoon, and a long night. I noticed the many stands with their merchandise. I also noticed the grilles. I am sure there will be plenty to eat. I know there is plenty of entertainment--two orchestras! Let's be sure that nothing spoils all the entertainment planned for us. Above all, let us insure the safety of our Madonna. Her reaching safe harbor means a safe harbor for us.

"Our Father, which art in Heaven... Amen."

After crossing themselves, the crowd burst out in another thunderous cheer. After blessing, Don Alfonso disappeared within the Obelisk and was replaced by the Cavaliere's assistant.

"Everyone to his assigned place!" shouted the Cavaliere. Then turning his sight downward to his left, he gave the sign for the fireworks.

Suddenly, a couple of heavy blasts shattered the tranquil sky, causing many un-expecting people to panic--memories of bomb drops and machine gunning still in their psyche. The animals reacted likewise with Samuele quickly responding to his bull's uneasiness, as did the other men.

The Cavaliere and Minico looked at Samuele. On receiving his nod, the Cavaliere gave his order:

"For-war-d-dd!"

The animals moved, and the crowd yelled with excitement. Up front, Samuele controlled the pace. The Obelisk bent in all directions, swaying according to the terrain and to the people pulling the fifty or so ropes. The tall structure bowed and bend in any direction, according to where the greatest pull was applied. The task was to keep the Obelisk in a perpendicular position, and for animals and men to move in coordinated and synchronous formations.

The team of men and animals pulled appropriately, with the first team absorbing the major part of the burden. The lead animals brought their heads close to the ground during starts. During abrupt stops, they could be thrust upward and hanging from the lifting tiller post.

The huge wheels sank into the soft earth; with the ropes tight on all sides, the rope-bearers walked slowly with the Obelisk.

Everywhere there were cheers and sighs, orders given, precautions taken. Ernesto and Silvestro walked close by, their eyes wavering from the top of the tall Obelisk to Samuele, who walked backward so as not to miss the

Cavaliere's orders. Constantly talking to his bull, Samuele also turned to the other men to be sure the weight was evenly distributed, especially during the many starts and stops--about every fifteen minutes. During the first phase, two large chestnut trees were already uprooted by the taut ropes.

During the break, the Cavaliere ordered everything rechecked. Just before he was ready to begin again, he warned about the ground rise with its steep incline ahead.

"We will stop before the rise. Then we will have to inch our way over and then down... Forward, move!"

Once again, the animals brought their heads to the ground as they pulled the mighty Obelisk forward. They were already perspiring. The air rushed from and through their nostrils covered by white mucus profusely dripping to the ground. Slowly, but steadily, they pulled under the leadership of Samuele, who had shown himself an expert at receiving orders and in retransmitting them to the rest of his team.

Samuele continued to walk backward, his eyes and head turning in every direction, to the tip of the Obelisk, to the face of the Cavaliere, to Minico, to Biagio, to the other men in front, and to Silvestro and Ernesto, whose encouragement engendered greater confidence in Samuele.

As he went forward, Samuele already sensed when to slow down and when to move faster. But, he never moved faster than a slow walk. In the past it took about four hours to complete the journey; this year they planned to complete it in five hours to allow more breaks and more rest for the animals.

Just before the incline, the Cavaliere gave his order to stop. When the animals came to a complete stop and the ropes secured, the brakemen engaged the brakes. The Cavaliere then announced a ten-minutes break to which the crowd burst out into cheers.

During the break, people crossed the terrain, many going from one rope to another, while others who had stood idly by now decided to join other rope handlers.

At the end of each of the many ropes, as many as four other ropes were added to allow more people to take part in the pull. And, as in the past, the end of each rope was manned by girls and mainly by boisterous boys whose ripped shirts and, in many cases, torn pants, showed their preference to be dragged on the ground.

During these breaks, groups of youths ran from one rope to another, throwing water bags at each other, and wrestling themselves to the ground in heaps, in their exuberance, always succeeding in hurting themselves. No wonder so many sported bruises and cuts on their backs and legs.

Samuele, meanwhile, wiped down his animal with a towel provided by Ernesto.

"Good idea, Samuele. Always care for those who work for you. You are right, Samuele. How about you, how are you doing?" the Cavaliere asked of the others, bending down, and pleased to receive positive nods.

"My brother-in-law, Silvestro, went to get something for them as well," Samuele reported, "and he should be right back."

After he finished, Samuele passed the towel to Biagio. Silvestro soon returned with two heavy cloths. While the two sponged down the animals, the Cavaliere held a brief conference with the men from above his platform.

"You saw the demand for great strength from your animals, and you saw their mouths bent to the ground. That's nothing compared to what's ahead. Most of you know what's ahead from past experience. Going up the slight incline, your animals will be pulling on their knees, especially the first team; going down on the other side, your animals will be pulling mainly with their hind legs. Yours, Samuele and Biagio, as a matter of fact, will be doing just that on both sides. Don't worry, however, resiliency is with us.

"An additional group of men will be helping you this time on each side of the cart. Unless you have any questions, I'm ready to start."

There being no questions, the Cavaliere ordered the two side ropes to the front. With the ropes extended, he spoke to the additional teams.

"It was never intended that the animals alone would pull the Obelisk by themselves, especially over these inclines. Likewise, the brakes alone will not be enough when going downhill. The duties of those in the back is to help with the braking when needed. Your duty, on the other hand, is to pull. I will call to you when I need pulling power, and I will call to the back when I need braking power. Be sure to immediately respond to my orders. Any question?"

While the Cavaliere was having his conference, one of the older children decided to tie the common heavy wooden log at the end of the rope so that he could more effectively pull with his friend. After having tightly made the knot, he left it on the ground, and would return to it when the pull began. Meanwhile, they joined other boys running from one rope to another, with some climbing up the ropes, challenging others on who could climb the highest.

On receiving the signal that the Obelisk was about to go forward, the same boy, who had tied the log to the rope, finding himself pulling on another rope, decided to stay with the new rope. Meanwhile, no one picked up the extended rope to which the boy had tied the log.

Having received the all-ready report, the Cavaliere gave the order to continue, and the crowd cheered tumultuously.

Slowly, the animals went forward, helped by the twelve teams of men. As all eyes and energy were concentrated in the forward position, and although the rear rope was being manned, no one picked up the slack on the remaining end, and no one saw the log entangled in the roots of an old olive tree.

Suddenly, the back rope became taut, taking with it into the air dozens of pullers, and causing the Obelisk's base to be pulled forward while the entangled rope pulled the top of the Obelisk to the rear, to the consternation of everyone.

The added weight on the rear brought the tiller post suddenly into air with the first animals' hind legs barely touching the ground while the front legs dangled in the air. Minico did all he could do to keep from falling to the ground. When the Obelisk swung backward, it made the center pole rise, lifting the first team of animals into the air.

"Hold! Hold! Back! Back!" the Cavaliere cried out desperately to all sides amidst general panic and consternation.

Samuele, seeing his bull hanging to the point of strangling, climbed on to the front of the pole and began to disengage the bow that was cutting into his bull's neck.

"No, Samuele, no!" yelled Minico. Samuele looked up.

The forward rope handlers, seeing the Obelisk falling to the rear, pulled extra hard, forcing it to swing forward, bringing the animals down to the ground and onto their knees, with the tiller post heavily on their necks.

Ernesto, who had noticed the taut rear rope, rushed to its end, with Silvestro behind. On seeing the cause, Ernesto rushed back to the Cavaliere.

"Back up, back up, the rope is caught."

The Cavaliere continued the order.

"Back, back, back!" Minico yelled desperately to the rest, his hand frantically waving his stick.

Meanwhile, Ernesto and Silvestro were already heaving with their shoulders on the huge wooden spokes of the wheels, pushing toward the rear, and yelling to the other men to push with all their strength.

"Animals back, the rest hold fast," ordered the Cavaliere desperately, the crowd crying in fear, women screaming everywhere.

With sweat running down his entire face, Samuele moved to the side of his bull. With both hands against the animal's chest, he pushed with all his strength, with the rest of the team in unison following suit. As they inched the cart backward, the Obelisk began to regain its equilibrium.

Ernesto rushed to the rope once again, and was relieved to find that someone had already disentangled it.

With the Obelisk centered, and the animals in their normal position, the Cavaliere ordered a twenty-minute break. The people sighed with relief.

Climbing down from his platform, the Cavaliere ran to the rear through the thick crowd gathered around the olive tree to find Ernesto with the log in his hands.

"That's what did it," Ernesto said to the anxious Cavaliere. "The boys tied it inadvertently. It entangled in these roots."

The Cavaliere gazed at the log. Lacking the courage to speak, he turned. With his head bowed, he walked to the front of the cart.

Samuele had his arms around his animal's huge neck, his face pressed against it, while Silvestro was wiping down its huge back. Biagio and the rest also wiped down their animals.

"Samuele!" the Cavaliere called out. "Samuele!"

Samuele raised his head, his arms still tight around the animal's neck.

"He almost died," Samuele said as he stared into the Cavaliere's eyes.

"Worse than that, many people might have been killed. You helped save the day. The training you gave your animal paid off. No one was expecting to have to back up. Ernesto, by the way, was the first to detect the cause."

Samuele turned his glance away from the Cavaliere and looked directly into the bull's eyes, contemplating the animal's indifference to the call of imminent death. Still breathing heavily, the animal turned its head up to his master, while the Cavaliere, placed his hand on Samuele's shoulder.

"Death is the last thing you want, isn't it?"

Samuele, his eyes still fixed on those of his animal, and with one hand covering his mouth, nodded to the Cavaliere. After a brief moment, he spoke.

"I'd rather die myself."

"No, Samuele, no one is going to die, not while I am in charge... Samuele, are you able to continue?"

"Yes, I assure you."

"Biagio, the rest! Are you able to continue?"

"Yes," answered Biagio with an air of self-confidence.

"Good, good. Go on with your care. As soon as I am ready, I will let you know."

With the music playing in the background, the Cavaliere was about to leave when Ernesto appeared, his shirt out of his trousers, and looking more than disheveled.

"I want to thank you personally for what you have done."

"I did no more than what others would or should have done."

"Yes, of course. You're a great man, Ernesto. I expect you at the banquet this evening. If anyone challenges you, tell them you have my special invitation."

"Thank you, Cavaliere. I do not know where I will be."

"Continue to stay by the side of Samuele for the duration of the journey, will you?"

"Yes," said Ernesto.

After the Cavaliere had made his rounds, he appeared on the platform again to a round of applause from every direction. Those sprawled on the ground rose to their feet in giving him a standing ovation.

"That was a close call," he told the crowd that listened without as much as a whisper among them. "That was the closest since it fell the last time.

"It shall never fall again!" he yelled to the people who answered with a resounding and exhilarating cheer.

"A good part of the journey is ahead of us. Let's keep our eyes open and let us be attentive to detail.

"Ready, everyone?

"Ready, Minico?

"Ready, Samuele?

On receiving the nod, the Cavaliere gave the forward command. The animals, digging deep into the ground, pulled their precious cargo forward with little effort, until the upward slope ahead.

When they came to the upward slope, the Cavaliere ordered even and steady heavy pull, not wanting to risk the wheels sinking into the ground.

The animals pulled with all their might, their noses almost touching the ground, and their masters encouraging them to continue with all their strength. Samuele, keeping his right hand on his bull's side, pushed and talked at the same time.

"Steady, steady," he kept saying, his eyes fixed on the Cavaliere, who called out to the six teams to keep pulling.

Sweat profusely dripping down their faces, the six men kept up the steady pace, walking backward to insure they were pulling as directed by their Cavaliere, their groans and grimaces easily reaching his ears and eyes.

"We're almost to the top," the Cavaliere shouted. "I'll tell you to slow down at the crest."

Waving his hand, Samuele maintained the steady speed, with Biagio and the rest ready to slow to a halt.

Ordering the brakemen to be ready, as the wheels went over the crest, the Cavaliere yelled to the brakemen. But, in spite of their best efforts, they could not quite hold the Obelisk from moving faster forward.

"No stumbling! Steady, steady!" yelled the Cavaliere.

Samuele, heeding the advice, moved forward at the faster clip. During the dangerous descent, the men pushed against the animals' chest, their loud *wuo*'s and *wua*'s intended to avoid a run-away Obelisk.

In the rear, the brakemen applied all the pressure they could to the wheels, while men, women and children hung low to the ground manning the brake-ropes. Luckily, the huge wheels cut into the ground thus helping hold back the speed. Meanwhile, the men holding the rear ropes, planted their heels into the ground, while the boys slid on the ground as the Obelisk went forward. Those on the side ropes slowly and cautiously moved forward, helping to hold the structure in equilibrium. The crowd also moved forward, cheering and yelling.

With the sun behind the mountains, its distant rays bounced off the golden embroidery of the Obelisk standing against a blue western sky, the light shattering into a thousand shades of reflective colors.

Franca, Maria, Lucia and the children followed the Obelisk within a reasonable distance, but always in sight of Samuele. Franca, of course, kept her eyes exclusively on Samuele, her mind conjuring up her plan of seduction, while Maria, who also kept her eyes exclusively on her son, maintained her beads active with her constant secret prayers. Lucia, meanwhile, kept the agitated children in check.

The pull resumed, the animals pulled with evenly distributed strength.

"At this rate, we'll get there in no time," commented Biagio, happy over the fast pace.

"I agree," answered Samuele, who now walked forward, only occasionally turning back to check with Minico and the Cavaliere. Their heads horizontal, the animals pulled the precious cargo speedily forward, with Samuele keeping pace, though his limping was more noticeable.

Don Pietro, who had been keeping close watch on Samuele, but always from a distance, noticed Samuele's condition deteriorate. Having observed every move of his, Don Pietro, while the crowd moved forward with the oncoming Obelisk, sought out Franca. During a moment when the excitement of the pull had reached a high peak, and seeing Franca standing to one side, Don Pietro approached her.

"You are Samuele's fiancé, aren't you?"

"Yes," she answered, surprised that the doctor should be asking her that question.

"Are you in love with him?"

"Why?" she answered, an obvious frown on her face.

"Well, are you?"

"Yes, I love him. But why are you asking me this?" she asked, the doctor's persistency worrying her.

"Take care of him; he's a good man. I have seen few like him. He deserves a lot of love."

Franca clasped her hands over her breasts, and almost covering her mouth with one hand, finding it hard to believe that the doctor should have asked her about her feelings.

"Love! He's asked me to marry him before Christmas."

"He did?" Don Pietro asked, slightly incredulous.

"Yes, doctor, he has asked me, and I said yes. But why are you asking me all this?"

"I wanted to express my concern to you."

"As a doctor or as a friend?"

"Both! No, probably more as a doctor. From what I see, he went through a lot. He's seen few happy days and I doubt he will see too many truly happy days, although he is still vigorous and he seems sincerely happy, especially because he knows that you really love him, heart and soul."

"What are you trying to tell me?" she asked in a low voice, an expression of sadness pervading her face. "What are you trying to tell me?" she asked again, her eyes fixed on his.

Don Pietro did not answer. He stared taciturnly into her sad face.

"He hasn't got much longer to live, is that what you are trying to tell me?" she asked.

Don Pietro nodded. Then, placing his hand on her shoulder, he began to speak again.

"Give him all the love you can while he can love you back. He deserves to be truly loved, and nothing less than that."

On the opposite side, Enrico, Tina, and Toni quietly followed the Obelisk by moving with the crowd. Unbeknown to Enrico, Tina kept her eyes almost always on Samuele, while commenting that the whole thing was void of true or meaningful religious values.

"Whatever it is, it is fantastic and all the people, pulling together, seem to be enjoying it," Enrico answered almost wryly, Tina detecting a tone she had not observed.

"Oh, you're enjoying the spectacle!" she said, half asking, half exclaiming,

"Yes, I am."

"You too, Toni, ah?"

"Sure! It's really something, carrying that thing on that two-wheeled cart, and balancing it!"

"Oh, but it's not religion. It's void of all religious sentiment."

"Who cares?" answered Toni, who had watched his father in action.

"Wait a second now," objected Enrico. "If it isn't religion that started the whole thing, what did and what is it then?"

Remembering the conversation she had earlier with Samuele, Tina, seeing she was getting nowhere, secretly concluded that they had been captured by the mass hysteria of the spectacle, as had everyone else, with the exception of Samuele whom she kept in her constant sight.

"I tell you what, Toni, why don't we three go get Rosa and spend the evening together. It's going to take at least another couple of hours before reaching its destination."

"Good idea!" Toni answered with a sparkle in his eye.

"No, I don't want to go now. I want to see the Obelisk through. We can go afterward," answered Enrico, his head held high, looking at the summit of the golden structure.

The locked wheels left two deep ruts in the ground as the Obelisk moved down the slope, the animals moving forward effortlessly.

With everyone following a sustained pace, the men holding the center left rope could not swing it over a young poplar. As the rope touched the upper half of the tree, it pulled it right out of the ground, roots and all. On the other side, meanwhile, the leader of the upper rope team called out to the Cavaliere to stop. Ahead, there was a large tree and they had to go around it. While the Obelisk stood still, they ran around the tree. When the force of hands re-gathered, the leader signaled the Cavaliere to continue.

When the six teams brought the Obelisk safely to the flat portion of land, the Cavaliere gave a ten-minute break. Descending from his platform, he called Minico and other the leaders for the last conference.

While he waited for them to gather, he congratulated Minico, Samuele, Biagio and the rest of the team.

Up ahead, there was a drainage ditch running through the fields. It was not steep, but presented particular difficulties.

"Once we start crossing it, we cannot stop, because the soil is very soft. We have chosen what we feel is the best place for the crossing. The men have already scraped off the edges, so our going in and out should be easier. The crucial point is the release time for the braking teams and the immediate take-over with full strength by the animals assisted by the ground forward rope handlers. If we hesitate but one second we'll sink into the ditch.

"Gentlemen, if we get stuck in the ditch, another set of animals will not suffice to pull us out. So let's be alert during the crossing. Don Alfonso, we will need your prayers."

"I have been praying all along and I will continue to do so."

The men reported back to their posts. In the remaining minutes, the crowd moved in and around, people asking all sorts of questions of each other and making thousands of comments. Franca, Maria, Lucia, and the children joined their three men. Running to Samuele, the children immediately asked to be put on the bull's back, and Samuele quickly obliged.

Ernesto told the women that the Cavaliere invited him to the banquet. As he was not cut out for that type of formal affair, he asked Franca to go in his place. Franca's face lit up at the news.

"Only if you don't mind," she said to Samuele.

"I assumed you were coming."

"Dressed like this, Samuele!" Franca said, as if to chide him.

As they were talking, the man selling the special sun glasses, the one who had run out of stock at least two times, approached the group with a box full. Recognizing him as the one who had sold Mr. Banno the glasses, Samuele was amused.

"No thanks, we don't need glasses. Besides, it'll be dark in a couple of hours. Please leave us alone."

"But these glasses were specifically designed to view the Obelisk at sunset!"

"Go try this crap elsewhere," intervened Ernesto with a menacing voice.

"Not to worry sir," the salesman shot back. He then turned to Samuele.

"I was admiring the way you handle the animals," the salesman said, as he glanced at little Samuele sitting on the bull.

Noticing the rest of the children, the shrewd salesman picked up a pair of glasses and gave it to the boy, who extended his hand to get them while the others looked on with envious eyes.

"Thank the man," urged Lucia, proud that the salesman had picked her son to receive the glasses.

Little Samuele, instead of thanking the smiling and anxious salesman, kept on looking at the glasses. When no one else spoke, the salesman began to walk away, keeping his eyes on the group with the hope that one would break down and call him back to sell to the rest of the children.

"Wait a second," called out Maria. The man raced back.

"That's all right," interrupted Samuele.

"Go on your way... Mother, can't you see he did that on purpose. He thought he could sell glasses to all of us. Don't worry about the children. The glasses aren't any good, anyhow. The little one will break them in no time."

No sooner said, they heard a click coming from the boy. In trying to open the sun glasses, the plastic handle snapped. Holding the two pieces in his hand, little Samuele turned to the group with sad eyes. Samuele looked at him and burst out laughing. The rest quickly followed suit on seeing the boy about to burst into tears.

Cavaliere gave his command to move forward. When they arrived at the edge of the ditch, the Cavaliere ordered another stop. After summoning the brakemen for last-minute instructions, he ordered the journey to begin again.

The problem was that if the brakemen locked the brakes thereby blocking the wheels, the wheels would sink deeply into the ground and to an unwanted stop. They had to apply just enough additional force to keep the wheels turning, thereby making the take-over for the forward teams to effectively take over.

The challenge was in coordinating two opposing pulling forces: the rear force of the brakemen, and the forward force of animals and men. The secret to success rested in a split-second manoeuvre wherein the rear force was to be released just as the wheels came to the center of the ditch, and for the front force to take over at exactly that instant.

As the wheels were about to go over the edge, Samuele and Biagio waited for Minico to give the order. As they moved, Minico kept looking at the center of the ditch. The instant the wheels reached center, Minico yelled for the brakemen to release and for the forward forces to pull.

At that instant, the animals pulled full force, their frothy mouths scraping along the ground, while the men on the ground ropes heaved their weight forward in one synchronous action. Without sinking, the wheels turned upward over the steep incline and onto to flat land. That having been executed successfully, there remained one more important hurdle before reaching the macadam road ahead.

At about three-quarters of the journey, at the junction to the town, the route changed drastically from farmland to the macadam or stony street lined with one to four storied houses and many light posts.

From here on, the transportation would require a power based on a combination of special techniques and handling rather than a power based on the strength of men and of animals.

On seeing the huge tower moving in the field, some of the musicians abandoned their instruments and ran irresistibly toward the Obelisk. After finding places on the ropes, they helped with the pulling. At about twenty meters from the edge of the field, the Cavaliere gave his order to halt. The front ground ropes were disengaged, as they were no longer needed. The brakemen and the leaders of the rear ground ropes walked to their last conference.

"Most of the men of the front ropes are moving to help with the rear ropes. As you can see, what we have ahead is the steepest though shortest descent. The problem is that the distance is too short between the edge of the field and the edge of the road. It means that this time the animals will be practically walking on their hind legs, with the first team, as usual, having to bear the burden. If they should stumble, you can imagine what can happen as we will be moving full speed. So, Samuele and Biagio, don't stumble," the Cavaliere said, a smile on his face, which caused them all to smile.

"Brakemen, on my command, block the wheels so that they will not sink. The men on the rear ropes will have to hold, letting the Obelisk slide down to the lower level. Samuele and Biagio, have your animals hold. Then they must pull to relieve the weight of the third team. Minico, here, knows all about the distribution of weight, and he will guide you. All right, let's go."

At the edge of the drop, the brakemen locked the wheels, which immediately sank about three feet into the ground while the rope men held fast. Midway, two animals momentarily collapsed under the added weight.

"Samuele, pull!" yelled the Cavaliere.

With the front team engaged, the rear animals slid on their hind legs. But as the middle team engaged fully, the rear animals bounced back, and all held accordingly. When Minico gave the command to turn, the Obelisk was on the macadam road, facing in the direction of the distant church. The people cheered wildly.

With the Obelisk secure, the musicians ran back to their instruments. The band leader brought up his baton, and in a couple of seconds, the band began to play a loud march to the tremendous cheers of the exuberant crowd.

From there onto the final destination, the pull would assume a more complicated aspect due to the houses and light posts lining the unevenly paved street, and the Obelisk would have to kept in equilibrium mainly with front and rear ropes. The lateral ropes would be few and to be handed over to specific individuals stationed on roofs and balconies.

The crowd, too, would have a different make-up, in that they would move either to the front--forced, therefore, to walk backwards--or to the rear, with fewer people scattering on the smaller side streets. The only other consideration, during this last phase, would be the semi-darkness, giving the Obelisk's intricate straw lacework different shades of colors reflected by the whiteness of the houses and the electric lights from the street and from the homes.

During this phase, the rate of the forward move would be more or less controlled by Minico, with his flying stick.

The Cavaliere, satisfied with the new rope configurations, ordered the Obelisk forward. This time, the six teams of men and animals pulled steadily and effortlessly, their tendency to go faster than was recommended. Yet, because of the lateral ropes, they had to make several brief stops, giving people chances to talk with one another or engage in negotiations with the various salesmen.

During the breaks, Samuele always wiped down his animal, helped by Silvestro and Ernesto. The families of the other members of the team also joined full force, and rejoicing with wide smiles over what already was a successful and spectacular pull.

And people of all ages moved in, curious about the state of the animals, and wanting above all to see the expressions on the men's faces.

Franca, seeing her lover's face completely wet, went up to him and in front of everyone wiped Samuele's brow. At first, Samuele felt embarrassed, and Franca hesitated. His smile, though, gave her confidence. She passed her handkerchief over his face, holding her little finger gently against his skin. Samuele looked at her in appreciation of the secret caress and Franca smiled.

"I got no one to do that to me," comically commented Biagio, who was wiping his animal.

"Who'd want to do that to you. Can't you see how old you are," answered the third man, causing everyone to laugh, including Ernesto, who had watched the whole scene with certain pride.

Above them, heads appeared on the roofs of the houses with the crowd quickly shifting its attention to them.

Franca asked Samuele if he minded her going home with him after the pull. Samuele answered that he did not mind in the least. On seeing the attention diverted, Franca began to talk to Samuele in a serious tone.

"Will we have a chance to be alone?"

"No, I don't think so," Samuele answered in an even tone of voice.

"I want to spend some part of this day alone with you. We have to, unless you don't want to."

"You know I do!"

"You don't seem too enthusiastic over the idea, though."

"Franca, I have to tell you in words?"

"I want to feel you want me, you desire me, you want to love me."

"All of those things, everything, and more; I feel all these things for you."

"We'll find a way to be together?"

"Yes, we will."

Franca's expression changed. She felt like wrapping her arms around him in front of all those people, and she would if Samuele had been the kind to allow her to do so. With her eyes fixed on his, with a resigned and sure expression on her face, she began to speak again.

"I love you with all my heart and soul. If I should ever lose you for any reason, I don't know what I'd do. I love you," she said, moving her lips slightly forward in the form of a kiss. Understood her intentions, and with his eyes fixed on hers, he nodded in agreement.

With that positive gesture, Franca had to think of a way of arranging it, and to do it in a way so that no one would think there had been anything between them. Silvestro, however, presented the real problem, and, at the same time the only possibility of achieving her goal.

"Did you get the skirt as a wedding gift? I hadn't seen it before today," Franca asked Lucia.

"Silvestro got it for me a week ago. By the way, are you going to the banquet with that dress?"

Not having thought it through, Franca became startled.

"That's right!" she exclaimed; "what should I do?"

"I don't know," replied Lucia. "Don't you have a better one?"

"Yes!" Franca exclaimed suddenly. "Yes," she repeated, having thought of the way to achieve her goal. "You know, while Silvestro and Samuele feed the animal, I can go home and change dress."

"That'll take too long. If they have to wait for you, we may just as well spend the evening alone."

"Silvestro can come back as soon as he finishes."

"That's true," Lucia agreed.

Shortly before the pull was to begin, people already moved to the front or to the rear of the Obelisk. With Samuele standing alongside his bull, Franca moved to him.

"How do you like my dress?"

Samuele squinted, not expecting that kind of question. "Fine, fine, but why are you asking me that now?"

"Do you think I should come with it to the banquet?"

"I don't know. But why would I think about that now? There are other things on my mind."

"How long will it take you and Silvestro to feed the animals?"

"About five minutes, not much more than that. Why?"

"Well," replied Franca with a smile on her face, "I have to go home to change."

"How long will that take?"

"About twenty minutes, if not more."

"All that time!"

"When you finish, you can send Silvestro back. You can either wait for me there, or you can come by my house."

"We'll see."

"Never mind, stay home, wash, take a nap and wait for me."

The Cavaliere stood on the platform. After looking at Minico, he turned to Samuele and to the rest of the team. Satisfied that all was under control, he gave the order to go forward, to the crowd's cheers which reverberated in the street.

As the animals pulled, the people kept their eyes to the ground to see the reaction of the animals on hitting the stone section of the road.

A few yards ahead, the pavement changed to flat rocks. The Cavaliere talked to Minico, signaled to Samuele, who was walking backward so as to be in visual contact with him. Samuele slowed the animals down, warning each of the owners to keep one hand on the side of his animal when the pavement changed.

Just before reaching the stone pavement, he and Biagio placed their hands on their animals. When the animals hesitated and began to stir, Samuele quickly began to talk, with Biagio and the rest of the crew following suit. The animals, however negotiated the transition without much difficulty.

Slowly, the men and animals moved cautiously over the treacherous pavement without serious incidents, with the Cavaliere making frequent brief stops to allow the side ropes to be handed from house to house, while the people watched anxiously. As the crowd was compact on both sides, and because of the houses, the heat on this part of the course caused the men to sweat profusely and the animals to drool in abundance. With the suspense subsided, and the crowd's noise subdued, the sounds clearly heard were the heaves and groans of the twelve men pulling with their animals up the slightly steep and slippery road.

"Steady!" ordered the Cavaliere. "We're only yards away."

The last few moments were punctuated with tremendous heaves of the men, who pulled with all their might. As the men pulled and groaned, they looked to the Cavaliere and to Minico for the signal to halt.

When finally they reached their destination, the Cavaliere felt relieved for having completed his mission successfully. After manoeuvreing the Obelisk with the face of Madonna looking directly toward the church's campanile, and after the ropes were secured to the surrounding balconies and walls, the Cavaliere called on Don Alfonso to the platform for the final benediction.

In a matter of seconds, Don Alfonso appeared on the platform.

"In the name of the Father, the Son, the Holy Ghost, Amen. We wish to thank you, oh Lord for this, the greatest of our days. All of you, together with our six teams of men and animals have literally accomplished a miracle.

"We thank you, Lord, for having given us the strength, the energy, and the intelligence in accomplishing this arduous task, and we beseech you to give us the wisdom in resolving our human differences as we solved the difficulties we encountered today.

"May God bless you all, and may our Madonna intercede on our behalf for better and richer harvests.

"One last word: keep your wheat stocks, and your contributions coming to our Cavaliere. He needs to refurbish several panels.

"May the Lord be with you, and may our prayers bond us as brothers and sisters where ever we are!"

With that, he blessed the people and, after crossing himself, stepped down behind the platform. With their heads bowed, the people crossed themselves in silence. Then, in a spontaneous burst of joy, they let out with the greatest cheer of them all, a single sound that resounded throughout the town and in every small street.

After allowing the crowd to quiet down, the Cavaliere began his concluding remarks.

"My friends, I wish to thank Minico, and Samuele with his fellow handlers. But I wish to express my greatest admiration for the animals. They were superb."

In hearing those words, the crowd once again let out a great cheer in honor of the Cavaliere.

"And now," he said in a loud voice, "my last command: Release the animals!"

It is hard to imagine, not being there, the exhilaration and the exuberance that the people felt for having participated in the grandiose feat, and to sense their deep-felt gratitude for the Cavaliere and for his team of men and animals.

After the supports had been checked, the Cavaliere allowed the owners to unyoke their animals.

Samuele was first to free his. With his arms around its neck, and while Silvestro and Ernesto were already rubbing the animal dry, Samuele waited for Franca coming forward with her handkerchief, and running with her arms open wide.

"You were wonderful," she said. "I love you," she whispered.

"And I love you," he answered in a firm and loud voice.

After a brief time wherein the twelve men, joined by relatives and friends, exchanged compliments, with the animals being decorated with additional ribbons and with pictures of the Madonna, with Franca to his side, Samuele turned to his brother-in-law to reassure himself about the evening plans.

"Silvestro," Samuele said, "you will come home with me. I need help with the bull, to be sure he's well."

"I'm coming, too, remember?" interrupted Franca

Samuele had not expected Franca to be so full of fervor and enthusiasm.

"Absolutely," answered Samuele. "How about your father, will he mind?"

Ernesto did not mind, knowing that if his daughter and Samuele wanted to do anything, they would and could, just as Toni had.

Lucia perceived that Franca was up to something, but was not sure about the details.

"Franca, be careful. You don't want to end up as I did," Lucia said in a friendly and circumspect tone.

"I don't understand."

"I think you do. Samuele is such a wonderful man, and I think you will be a great wife. Don't risk spoiling it."

"How do you know how I feel?"

"I've been through it. You have the same manner, the same expression. You even talk in the same way."

"There's a big difference in the two situations."

"I'm not talking about the situations. I'm talking about us, the two of us, us women."

"Why did you make love to Silvestro?"

"I liked him all right, and I was attracted to him. Seeing so many people killed, though, I thought I'd least enjoy a sexual relationship while we were still alive." Lucia rationalized, and she knew it.

"In other words, the thought of dying made you do it--in other words, you wanted to love and be loved for fear of dying and not have consummated that love," Franca queried, directing the conversation.

"We did it, we enjoyed it, I paid the price of scorn, my son did not have his father, my mother rebuked me in every turn, and we're the luckiest people in the world, thanks to Samuele. I could have ended like poor Rachele," and so can you! And you know, Franca, I only want the best for you and for my brother," Lucia spoke in earnest. "I worried more about my mother whom I didn't want to hurt. Of course, I ended up hurting her."

"Lucia, do you know how much I love your brother."

"I know, it's written all over your face."

"Can I tell you what I feel deep inside?"

"Yes."

"Provided you won't say anything to anyone?"

"Yes."

"I don't think..." Franca began, but quickly interrupted when Enrico and Tina approached them to say hello.

Lucia brushed them off fast, wanting to continue with the conversation. Unfortunately, Maria approached them, followed by Ernesto and Silvestro. Samuele, finally free from admirers, joined his group as the two women exchanged glances.

The band played one tune after another while the people moved around through the area. Many fell prey to the wandering salesmen, who dispatched post-war products manufactured in the general area.

At one side of the street, four women were broiling steaks; at the opposite side, cherries and grapes were being sold while children gathered around the ice-cream carts and candy salesmen. Older men, on the other hand, attempted to buy *original* American cigarettes while women bargained for *imported* silk stockings guaranteed to wear three years.

"If you keep them in the drawer!" remarked a wry old woman, causing many bystanders to burst into laughter. Nevertheless, many bought the flimsy stockings.

"There!" Samuele exclaimed to the children, "here's something for you," he said as he pointed to the hat salesman displaying a bunch of colorful straw hats. "Hey! come on over. The kids want a hat."

The salesman rushed over and began to place hats on the children's heads, asking if they fit. The children, however, showed little enthusiasm for the idea and hardly answered the man.

"I guess the kids don't like them. They're too cheap-looking," Samuele said to the disappointed salesman.

"They're three for the price of one?"

"I guess not."

"Look, these here are better quality. Try them on."

"Same price?"

"I'll let you have them for the same price."

"One extra for her?" Samuele asked pointing at Franca. The salesman agreed. And because these hats had streamers attached, the children were happy. After each child was fitted, Samuele pulled out the money to pay the man, who refused, wanting to fit the rest of the group. Ernesto interrupted.

"I could use one. The sun gets in my eyes when I look at the Obelisk. We'll take four more for the price of one."

"It's a deal. By the way, I sell two for the price of one. But because you worked so hard today, I'm glad to let you have the hats for less. Thank you and good luck," he said. Then waving a hat with one hand, he went on to other people, leaving Samuele and the children laughing and smiling.

Unexpectedly, Toni approached the group. After he had nodded politely to Maria, he walked directly toward his father to ask if he minded his going to get Rosa.

"You're asking me? You're old enough. Do what you want."

Without saying another word, Toni turned and went on his way, Ernesto murmuring aloud over the potential of his son becoming a man. Gazing at a pensive Ernesto, Samuele went over and placed his hand on Ernesto's big shoulder, the gesture revealing several things to Ernesto, who smiled.

"This is also my great day," Ernesto said.

Maria, noticing the happy expression on Ernesto's face, approached him.

"I wanted to ask you about your wife. She's not here."

"Strange fact she agreed to come. Coincidentally, she learned her father was seriously ill. So, she went over there."

While the two talked, Samuele fixed Franca's hat. As he pressed it to one side, Franca told him how much she loved him.

"...and I hope to show you tonight," she added in a serious tone, causing Samuele to draw back.

He looked into her eyes filled with an unusual serious expression the likes he had not seen in her before. Even Silvestro noticed.

"What's going on between you two?"

"Nothing, Silvestro, we were just playing," answered Samuele jokingly. To be sure that Silvestro believed him, Samuele picked up Franca and placed her on the bull, Franca shouting, causing everyone to smile except for Lucia. When Franca pleaded to be taken down, Samuele obliged. But Lucia kept on looking at Franca with a serious expression on her face.

"Look!" exclaimed Franca, pointing to a bunch of children dancing to the music of the band.

"That's nothing yet. Tonight, there's going to be a real show. Dancers are coming from Naples," Samuele answered. Then, turning to Silvestro, Samuele asked if he was ready.

With Silvestro leading the bull forward, Samuele and Franca followed behind, hand in hand.

"Don't be long!" Lucia said to Silvestro, who, bending over, kissed both Lucia and little Samuele. "Come right back. I'll need help with the children."

"Don't worry. We'll make it fast. But I don't know about Franca. She wants to go to her house to change her dress."

"You can be sure it'll take her a full hour, if not that" commented Ernesto.

CHAPTER 34

By the time Samuele broke away from his colleague, Franca had completed her plan.

Once out of the crowd of whom so many stopped to congratulate Samuele for his feat, Samuele, Silvestro, and Franca stepped up their pace, all three anxious to get the animal home, to complete their chores, and return to the festivities. Of the three, the most anxious was Franca, who, proudly walking hand in hand with Samuele, was mentally putting her final touches to her secret plan. And Samuele holding her hand served only to accentuate her desire of hurrying home. She kept a steady fast pace, often complaining that Silvestro was not walking fast enough.

"Hang on," Silvestro protested. "The pull is over. We're only going home!"

On arriving at the stable, Silvestro rolled up his sleeves, ready to go to work. While Samuele held the animal's reins, Franca began to speak aloud as, being sure she was talking to both men.

"If I go home right now, I should be back in about half-hour to forty minutes. You will wait for me, won't you, Samuele?"

"Half-hour to forty minutes!" repeated Silvestro, his eyes closing slightly at the thought of having to disagree with Franca.

"Is that too long?" she asked innocently.

"It'll take Samuele and me but a few minutes to do our work."

"You're dressed for the evening, but Samuele and I are not. We can't be going to the banquet in these clothes.

"You go back; Samuele and I will come as soon as we've washed and changed. Remember, I have all the way home and back!"

"It's all right with me," answered Silvestro, shrugging his shoulders.

"Don't stay too long," urged Samuele, not daring to smile.

"It'll take me more than forty-five minutes, I am sure," Franca said. "Well, I must go. Don't forget, Silvestro, to go right back. Lucia needs your help."

"She did it without my help all day!"

"That was today. Now it's early evening, and little Samuele will want to be with his father... Anyhow, do as you wish... Samuele, I'm going. Don't leave without me!"

Leisurely, Franca walked out of their sight. Once on the other side of the road, she began to run, and, instead of following the usual route to her house, she cut across the open fields like a fox pursuing a jack rabbit under a warm early evening sun. In about five minutes, she was in front of her house, being received by her dog. She opened the door, ran upstairs, put her dress in a bundle, and in a few seconds, was running over the same ground with the bundle on her shoulder. In less than five minutes, she was back at Samuele's house.

Instead of going in, she hid across the street, looking and waiting for Silvestro to finish his work and to return to Lucia. After a few interminable minutes, Silvestro brought out a pitcher of water with a wash bowl. He combed his hair, and finally left with his jacket in hand.

Having waited until Silvestro was out of sight, Franca walked to the yard, still breathing hard. When Samuele saw her, he was startled. Nevertheless, on opening his arms to her, she flew into them without hesitation. He lifted her into the air and turned her around a couple of times. On stopping, they kissed.

"What took you so long?" commented Samuele, a wide grin on his face.

"I would have been here sooner if I didn't have to wait for Silvestro to go. Besides, did it ever take you less than eight minutes to my house, both ways?"

"Even when I walk fast it takes me no less than fifteen minutes each way."

"So, we have at least thirty minutes to ourselves and just for ourselves. I've been waiting for ages!"

Arm in arm, the two lovers walked toward the house, the sun still shining on their back; its rays, spreading across the valley, bounced off house and into their faces.

"Look how beautiful," he said when he went to close the window of his room. The sun shone directly into his face.

Franca did not answer. On turning to get her response, he saw Franca in the nude, her clothes on the floor. He gazed upon her for the briefest moment, the sun's rays falling on Franca's body.

"Please turn once around, would you?" he asked, in disbelief of what he was seeing.

"Why, Samuele?" she asked in a subdued voice, one hand over her breasts, the other covering her pubic hair.

"Go ahead, I'll tell you after."

Showily and deliberately, Franca made a complete turn as if a statue on a revolving pedestal, except that she was naturally beautiful, her body full and vibrant.

"Just as I thought. There's a marble statue of a young Greek girl at the museum in Naples. She's gorgeous and about your size--perfect proportions, except for her back..."

"...You don't like my back?"

"The Greeks didn't usually finish the backs of their statues..."

"...And?"

"...And you are totally beautiful!" he said as he walked to sit on his bed.

Franca stepped over to him. His face pressed against her belly, she put her hands around his head, pressing him tightly against her. Samuele responded by placing his arms around her waist. Bringing his face up between her breasts, he began to kiss her.

"Samuele, I love you," she said in earnest, and answered in like manner. "Please, Samuele, get up."

Bringing himself on his feet, he kissed her deeply.

"Wait," she said, as she began to unbutton his shirt. "Please take off your clothes."

Samuele moved aside and began to undress while Franca, having removed the bed cover, slipped between the sheets. With her head on the pillow and her body resting on the bed, she waited for him. He looked at her, and she was beautiful, her face serene, her eyes deep, her mouth closed. His clothes off, he stepped to the edge of the bed to kiss her. She opened her mouth to his, and pulled him on top of her, bringing the sheet over them.

"Samuele, I love you," she said as she moved his body onto hers and wrapping her legs around his. "Please, Samuele, be gentle."

"Yes, my love," he answered. "I've been wanting to be with you in this way, to enjoy each other's love. But, we cannot go all the way. We must wait for that."

"No, Samuele," she said in a soft voice, resolved to consummate their love, "No, my love. I want you to make love to me because I want to make love to you. Just be gentle. It is my first time, and I have never felt as I do now. My being with you in this way is a far greater experience than I imagined, and I don't want you to worry about anything, no matter what happens."

With that, Samuele became pensive and slightly withdrawn. Feeling the change, Franca moved her mouth to his, kissing him passionately.

"For me, please do it for me," she beseeched, her hand moving between their bodies.

With her hand, she guided him until she felt him comfortably inside, Samuele responding more to her movement than to his passion. With her hands around his neck, she brought his mouth on hers. With their lips locked, Samuele extended his hand to clutch the edge of the mattress. Holding the back of her head within his elbow, he held her tight against his mouth and began to thrust himself gently and more secure into her. On reaching deeply within, Franca gave out a sudden moan. Samuele withdrew.

"It's all right," she said with a smile; "it's all right," she repeated as she brought her hand down. "Wait a second...there...yes, just like this for a few seconds."

With his clutching the edge of the mattress, Samuele controlled his action, and with his upper strength, dominated her body. Franca enjoyed being held firm into his body, feeling more confident than ever about Samuele's response to her. Under his firm and constant clasp, Franca remained happy and responsive to his gentle rhythm.

When Samuele tightened his grip, she felt him deepest inside her. As he was about to reach his orgasm, she tightened her legs around him, and with her hands around his neck, she drew him to her with all her strength, holding him until climax, and continued to hold him tight until long after Samuele released his grip on her.

"Stay, stay like this!" she repeated.

Clutching the edge of the mattress and repositioning the back of her head into his arm, Samuele pressed her open mouth into his. Breaking the kiss, Franca urged him to stay inside her.

Through the opening by the window, the sun's rays which reflected on the wall had slowly faded until there was hardly a trace of light.

Samuele opened his eyes. While Franca's head was on his arm, and her face pressed against his chest, he raised the bed sheet and pushed it back, causing Franca to look up.

"I love you," she whispered without moving. "I want to stay here forever."

Samuele stroked her gently on her face. As he was about to touch her lips, Franca kissed the palm of his hand. He shifted to one side. As he held her breast, he glanced toward the window. Seeing the sun's rays had disappeared, he released his hold on her breast.

"The sun's gone. There are no more rays!"

"There are always rays, Samuele; there is always sunshine. Now I know the meaning of those rays and of that sunshine. They will be mine for as long as I live. Samuele, our love has made it possible, and I will be forever grateful and faithful to you."

"It's gone, see! There are no more rays. Hurry, we have to go."

Samuele got up and went to his dresser. Still in bed, Franca looked at his white body standing against the dimming background light. Half dressed, he turned toward her. There were tears in her eyes.

"Franca!" he murmured in a low and soft voice.

With the bed sheet up to her neck, Franca--with one hand over her womb, and the other on the pillow supporting her head, and with her eyes fixed onto his--remained reflectively.

"What is wrong, my love?" he asked.

"My love?" she repeated sobbing. "The light has gone, and it will come tomorrow; but, it has gone from me."

"Yes, my darling, I know. I understand, and I am happy for what we had." On his knees, he kissed her gently. "Well, then?" he asked as he wiped her tears. "There is always a tomorrow, always. I believe in it. Today may have been our tomorrow. We must live for these days because when they are fulfilled, life becomes complete. Almost complete... Come, get up; it is getting late, and we've stayed as long as could. I don't want them waiting for us."

Samuele took her hand and pulled her up. As Franca put her arms around his neck, Samuele placed his arms around her waist, drawing her against him.

"Franca, Franca! Let's hurry."

"I don't care if they find out you're my lover."

"Lover!"

"Yes, my lover, my only love. Samuele, you don't know how much I love you, how much I have longed for this very day. You've fulfilled my dreams and given meaning to my life. And now, I don't know if I will be able to bear it. I don't know..."

"What are you talking about? You're not making sense. We both wanted this, and I am not sorry. Nor am I your lover. I'm only one who completely loves you," Samuele said assuredly.

"Just as I have always wanted. 0h, God..."

"God! God..."

"*God*! Why are you repeating that word?"

Samuele squeezed her against him. His eyes closed, he groaned as he moved his head back and forth against her face. Franca opened her eyes and kissed him on his chest.

"I understand... I think I understand. It's all right; you don't have to repeat or tell me anything. Nothing, nothing, my love... You're right, we had better go. We had better hurry or they'll be suspicious."

Franca, with her arm over her breasts, moved to the chair. After putting on her undergarments, she went to the mirror next to Samuele, who was putting on his shirt. She turned to help him with the buttons, then combed her hair. Though her eyes were dry, they shone brilliantly.

And their future?

It had just begun.

CHAPTER 35

"Here they are!" exclaimed Lucia on seeing Samuele and Franca breaking away from a group of people that had stopped to congratulate him.

On seeing her son so soon, Maria felt relieved, and glanced at Ernesto, who looked back without saying a word. Silvestro, holding his son in his arms and surrounded by his other children, squinted at seeing the two so early, thinking he should have waited.

Samuele and Franca, in complete view of their families, made no attempt to avoid the people approaching them; they even chatted with them.

"You made it fast," Lucia commented, staring into Franca's face, and noticing a change in Franca's expression. Franca, however, was not smiling, nor acting as sprightly as before. Lucia understood what had taken place, but said nothing. Though she understood Franca's need, nevertheless Lucia remained sad.

"We would have been here sooner if we hadn't stopped for so many people congratulating your brother-hero."

"You look very pretty, Franca. You also look more like a woman with that pretty dress," Maria commented.

"Thank you," she answered with a touch of humility in her tone.

"We had better go to the banquet," interrupted Samuele. "The Cavaliere said arrive at just about this time. Afterward, we'll join you in front of one of the orchestras, depending on which one is playing."

"Go along," replied Ernesto, who had stood in the background staring at his daughter. Suddenly, he realized his daughter was a woman, and a beautiful one at that.

Samuele picked up the little girl and kissed her on her forehead.

"No one's paid much attention to you, eh! Well, tomorrow, I'll give you a big ride. How about a pretty smile, now?"

The little girl quickly accommodated him with a big smile. Then, unexpectedly, she put her arms up to be picked up, and put her arms around Samuele's neck.

"Lucia, will you hold see my baby, here?"

Lucia took the little one into her arms and stood next to her husband, holding their little Samuele. The other children gathered around them looking at Samuele and Franca disappearing into the thick crowd.

At the huge hall in the municipal building, most of the guests had already arrived, and were standing in groups, talking about the successful pull sipping sweet vermouth from tall thin glasses.

The first to welcome Samuele and Franca was Don Pietro.

"Samuele, Franca, come in. We were just talking about you. How do you feel?"

"Exhilarated."

"And you, Franca?"

"Couldn't be any happier," she answered, implying, however, that a similar day would never repeat itself.

"You look beautiful, Franca... Congratulations, Samuele. You're a very lucky man!"

"Lucky in which way?" Samuele asked, a grin on his face.

"For having such a beautiful woman by your side."

"I'm glad you clarified it; I didn't want it any other way."

Samuele and Franca looked at each other. Then, following the doctor, they walked to the large group at whose center stood the Cavaliere in a shiny new white suit, surrounded by the men, who made the feat a success, and their well-dressed wives.

Franca, with a dress that barely reached the top of her knees, was in direct contrast with the older, more conservatively dressed women in age, in beauty and in femininity. Franca no longer hesitated in extending her hand to the men, who invariably kissed it, or to the other women, including Biagio's wife, whose hand was as rough as her hands had been.

"Biagio told me about Samuele, that he is a great man. They all did a wonderful job."

"Yes, they did, and Samuele is very fond of Biagio."

The Cavaliere came up to Samuele and Franca. After shaking hands with Samuele, the Cavaliere took Franca's hand and kissed her soft skin. Franca smiled at him.

"Help yourselves to an *aperitivo*; supper will begin soon."

Samuele walked to the corner of the room where the drinks were being served. Unbeknown to him, Don Pietro, who was chatting with Minico, looked at him from the corner of his eye. Samuele limped slightly, almost unnoticeably, except for Franca, and for the worried-looking doctor, who did his best to hide his concern. He turned to Franca, however.

"Love him with all your heart," he said, his hidden despair reminiscent of fictional characters from a by-gone era.

Franca did not answer. She lifted her eyes to his and remained silent. As there was no need for the doctor to prescribe medicine, she, nevertheless, understood his good intentions. But the suggested cure brought chills to her spine. She turned away from Don Pietro to reach for the glass that Samuele was offering her.

"Wait, don't drink yet," asked the doctor, hurrying away. Back with a glass of his own, and in the company of Minico, Don Pietro continued with a new-found smile.

"I'd like to drink with you. No, I want to drink to the two of you. Well, cin-cin!"

"And likewise from me, cin-cin," said Minico bringing his glass up.

"Health and happiness," added Samuele, with Franca repeating Samuele's words.

At the large horseshoe-shaped table, the Cavaliere sat at the center, Don Alfonso, Don Pietro on each side, whereas Minico sat in the center between Samuele and Biagio, the remaining ten men with their respective wives (or fiancés) sat on the other side of Minico. When everyone was seated, the doctor struck the glass with his knife, and the guests immediately stopped talking.

"We had a most glorious day, and a very exhausting one. I am sure we are all hungry, However, we cannot begin until Don Alfonso gives us his blessing. Therefore, Don Alfonso!"

"In the name of the Father..."

Except for Samuele, everyone made the sign of the cross, including Franca, who turned to look at Samuele. Don Alfonso noticed it too, but went on.

"Yes, we had an exhausting day: thrills, and close calls. The important thing is that you brought our Madonna safely back to our church, and you deserve our congratulations and God's blessings.

"Let us give our thanks to God for continued peace in our community and in every community throughout the world.

"In the name of the Father, the Son, and the Holy Ghost, Amen."

Silence immediately turned to chatter, accentuated by widespread sounds of wine glasses being struck to other glasses, while the antipasto was being served.

Soon, the waiters brought out *manicotti* and *tortelloni.* For the main course, they served *vitello a la milanese*, home fries, a variety of cooked vegetables, including beans, and salad. As for wine, the celebrants were served the best *aglianico* of the region. With the last course, composed of a variety of local cheeses, the waiters served *moscato bianco.* For desert, they served *mille foglie* with *spumante* and, finally, *espresso.*

With the *spumante* still being served, the Cavaliere stood to propose a toast. Having invited the guests to rise, he brought his glass forward.

"Ladies and gentlemen, I wish thank you for your participation in today's grueling pull, and I hope the food and the wine of this evening is a worthy reward," he began, drawing a comprehensive and laud applause. "You know what the Obelisk means to me personally, and to all of us. Today's successful pull marks the beginning of a new era, a rebirth for our area and for each one of us.

"Let us drink to this re-birth with its promises of progress, prosperity, and happiness."

Buoyed by the Cavaliere's optimism, the guests drank gleefully. When he resumed and thanked them all from the bottom of his heart, the guests burst out with applause. Samuele and Franca turned toward each other and kept up the clapping.

"Friends, I am not entirely deserving of this tremendous applause. I could not have done anything without your participation, and what pleased me the most is that we worked as a team.

"In these occasions, common sense dictates that we be brief in our remarks, and to refrain from listing names especially at gatherings such as ours with so many deserving individuals. Please allow this one exception.

"Might I mention the name of Samuele, knowing what he went through during the war, he has come back with a spirit worthy of emulation: forge ahead, create, forgive and give!

"Ladies and gentlemen, let us be thankful for his return. May God give him life, and the happiness he so richly deserves."

Don Pietro stood up and began to clap. Immediately after, everyone, including the Cavaliere--but not Don Alfonso--joined in the applause. Samuele stood up and bowed to all. Then, giving a quick glance at Franca, who had tears in her eyes, he put his arm around her and sat down.

"Look," said Don Alfonso to the Cavaliere, "Franca is crying."

"Yes, I noticed. And she has every right to cry. We human beings are evil, and God is not doing much to make better."

"Cavaliere! what are you saying?"

"Nothing, Don Alfonso, nothing. Look, Samuele wants to say something."

"I am overwhelmed and I thank you from the bottom of my heart," he said and quickly sat down amidst another round of applause.

He extended his hand to Franca and felt her trembling.

"Franca, a good part of the evening is still ahead of us. Let's not give up. Come, eat the rest of cake. It is delicious."

CHAPTER 36

By the time Franca and Samuele joined their families, the festivities were in full swing. The band was playing the *Neapolitan Tarantella*, and about eight young men and women dressed in costume were dancing on the stage. The fast beat of the music lifted the people who followed the music by beating their feet on the ground or by swinging their arms. All around the stage, children played and danced.

Samuele and Franca sat down on chairs provided by Ernesto. With his arm over his mother's shoulders, Samuele listened to the wonderful music and watched the dancers in their movements. He was so exhilarated that he wanted to pick up his nephew and dance in the middle of the square.

When the number ended, the band leader, who also acted as the master of ceremonies, announced the next song, *Core Ingrato*, to be sung by Di Stefano, "a tenor to be discovered.

"He will be accompanied by a special section of mandolin players."

The lanky maestro then turned around to prepare his band. The tenor walked to the microphone amid an enthusiastic ovation. The maestro turned to the violin section, then to the tenor.

Di Stefano began to sing with a full and vibrant voice, keeping the people spellbound. Even the children listened without making any distracting noises. Only Samuele dared speak.

"I used to ask myself," he whispered into Franca's ear, "I used to ask myself, when would I be returning to the land of mandolins. Listen to it, listen to it all. I never dreamed it'd be like this?"

Franca squeezed his hand. She raised her face close to his for one second, but did not comment. She understood what he was trying to say.

The singer went on, completely wrapped in the lyrics. When he came to the end, he sang with so much power that the people began to cheer before he could finish. Nevertheless, his voice soared over the clapping and the cheering. Immediately after ending, he hurried to the rear, leaving behind him a screaming crowd.

"Yes, ladies and gentlemen, that was our Di Stefano, our young and talented singer," the band leader announced. "Would you like to have him back?" The crowd began to scream once again. When the noise subsided, the band leader went on. "Ladies and gentlemen, Mr. Di Stefano will be back with us during the second half. Now you must listen to the other orchestra. But don't forget to come back."

Clapping and cheering, the people got up and walked to the other stage. There they found the symphony orchestra already assembled and the musicians tuning up their instruments. A sign announced Rossini's *Semiramide Overture*, a work most people had not heard before.

While the musicians went on tuning their instruments and the people scurried around for the best seats, the many vendors 'sang' about their products. Meanwhile, the ice cream salesmen were virtually surrounded by young and aggressive children. And there, the same salesman was selling sunglasses for the up-coming fireworks.

"Don't let the bright lights ruin your eyes. Observe the orchestra with my glasses, you'll hear the music better."

Even Samuele got a chuckle out of it.

The maestro appeared on the podium in full dress and bearing a white baton. Tall and slim, he signaled his musicians to get ready. Then, pointing to the drummers in the rear of the orchestra, he gave the signal, and the music began.

The accent was on the string section, accented by the wind instrument. Once again, the people were enthralled as they listened to the very end without taking their eyes off the musicians.

During Tchaikovsky's *Capriccio Italiano*, the people, recognizing the popular refrains, began to sing along with the orchestra: "Dad's against it, and so is mother; how can we make love?"

"That's not our problem," Samuele whispered into Franca's ear.

"How I wish it were that," she answered in a serious tone.

Silently, the two lovers listened. But, as the evening progressed, and the air became cool, Samuele began to cough, but not loud as to be distracting.

"You still cough once in a while?" Franca said, turning her statement into a question.

"Yes," answered Samuele.

"It hasn't gone away?"

"No."

"Why don't you let Don Pietro visit you?"

"I've been through many hospitals."

"You never told me that."

"There was no need to," he replied without too much concern. "Listen, isn't this part beautiful?"

"It is. It's very beautiful."

From beneath the square came the aroma of broiled steaks. Silvestro, who had not eaten very much, asked Lucia to go with him for a snack. Maria agreed to mind the children. Quietly, the two made their way through the crowd.

"I guess they don't like this music," Samuele remarked to Franca.

"I don't know. Maybe they're going to get something to eat."

"Are you hungry?"

"No, a little thirsty, though."

"Would you like to go for a walk. We can get something on the way."

Once out of the crowd, the two walked hand in hand. Franca held on tight, very tightly but hardly said a word as they walked along the rocky sidewalk, occasionally stopping to look at window displays.

When they looked at each other, however, they stared deep into each other's eyes, each understanding what the other felt and knew, and neither daring even to mention a single word about the future, or about their marriage. Worse, Franca knew that she and Samuele would never marry.

Franca walked silently. She squeezed his hand and Samuele reacted by caressing the top of her head. She felt like crying, but did not dare, at least not for the remainder of the evening.

Unconsciously, the two found themselves under the base of the towering Obelisk. Samuele felt a strange surprise.

"Look at it!" he said as he stopped. "It looks mysterious. The base is lit up by the lights of the arcades while the top is in semi-darkness. Look!" he exclaimed with excitement. "The moon is passing over the tip. The moon!"

Franca glanced at the Obelisk, pushing her head back. On seeing the full orange moon, she felt a chill run down her spine, the second time she had felt those tremors that day. Now, as she glanced at the silent voyager, she felt a strong desire to ask him what it meant to him, but decided she had better not. She did not want him to have recollection of the past, especially the most recent past involving her brother Toni.

"The straw toward the tip is shimmering," Samuele said.

"You're right, and it's so beautiful," she answered with her face lifted to the star-filled sky.

"Man is capable of doing many things," Samuele commented, "such as bringing joy to other men."

"Man!" she enunciated the word with evident scorn.

Samuele waited for her to say more. When he saw she was not going to continue, he asked her what she meant.

"Nothing, just nothing. You're absolutely right. The Obelisk is beautiful," she said, her tone harsh at the beginning and soft toward the end of the sentence.

Then pressing her face hard against his chest, she continued emotionally. "It's probably too beautiful."

"Let's go to the other side. There is less light there."

The two walked to the scarcely lit corner, linked by a high wall on one side, and by another wall leading to the church. Passing by the central door of the church, Franca made the sign of the cross with Samuele gazing at her in silence. At the corner, they stood with their backs against the wall, looking at the dark side of the straw Obelisk. The light shining from the opposite direction created a sort of halo around the statue of the Madonna.

"Just as with the moon's halo," he pointed out to Franca.

Franca did not answer, but looked for a few brief moments. Then, suddenly, she stood in front of him, her arms stretched to him. Samuele took her into his arms and they kissed passionately.

"Franca, darling," he said in a tremulous voice. "Stay close to me; let me hold you," he asked pleadingly, his eyes half-open as he pressed his face to hers.

Franca locked her arms around him and squeezed him with all her strength. As they stood together in deep silence, a strain of music reached them from the square.

Above their heads, the hands of the clock moved forward. Suddenly, they were awakened from their trance by eleven blows of the clock bell.

From the door of the church, two old women dressed in black walked out silently, their heads bowed. Franca looked at them with her eyes wide open. Suddenly she felt a strong urge to go into the church.

"I want to go in."

"What for?"

"I want to pray. I forgot... I haven't prayed in a long time. I feel like praying."

"I'll go in with you."

Franca had not expected Samuele to accompany her and was surprised by his offer.

"You don't have to if you don't want to."

"I do want to. You make it sound as though I never go to church."

"To pray?"

"Yes, to pray. I say more prayers than my mother, and certainly more than Don Alfonso."

"I never doubted that you pray."

Inside the church they walked slowly toward the dimly lit altar, the little bronze crucifix laying on its huge marble slab. The niche above the altar was empty, but a large picture of the Grieving Madonna hung to one side.

Franca kneeled by the wooden banister in front of the Madonna, and made the sign of the cross. Then, sinking her head between her hands, she began to pray. Samuele knelt beside her, looking at her head between her hands, then at the small crucifix. He stared at it until Franca raised her head. She looked his way for an instant, then she looked at the small carved Christ, continuing to pray. Finally she made the sign of the cross and got up. Samuele also got up and walked out.

"I feel better," she confessed.

"I'm glad. Are you ready for your drink now?"

"I'm not thirsty."

"I thought you said you..."

"I know."

"Why don't we go back?" he asked, putting his hand over his mouth to hide the cough.

Franca looked up to him, then nodded her approval.

As they passed under the Obelisk, they admired it once more, with their eyes following its glittering surface to its summit. On reaching the square, they were listening to Puccini, *Madame Butterfly*.

Maria was alone with the children. Ernesto went after something, and Lucia and Silvestro had not yet returned. She rejoiced to see her son, and so did the children, with the exception of little Samuele sleeping on her lap.

"The music is about to end. I hope the others come back soon. The children are tired, and so am I. We should be heading home," Maria said, trying not to complain.

"Yes, Mother," agreed Samuele, putting his hand over her shoulder, as he had done earlier in the evening, the gesture bringing no end of joy to her.

Having received a grateful smile from his mother, Samuele sat down next to her, and Franca did likewise. Soon the music finished. The people stood up to clap, but not for very long. They were anxious to move to the other platform to secure the end seats having a view for the fireworks. A few minutes later Ernesto returned. Then came Lucia and Silvestro. As they picked up to go toward the other platform, they could already hear the voice of DiStefano singing the lyrics from the *Capriccio*.

The *maestro* then announced that as a last number the band was performing a special number by the mandolin section, *La vita è bella e tu lo sai* (Life is beautiful and you know it.) Everyone was enchanted by the typical Neapolitan melody whose spirit was certainly in consonance with that of the spectators.

"You see how much more there is to life?" Samuele whispered into Franca's ear.

"I concluded there cannot be more than we've lived this day."

"There is, I assure you," he said in complete earnestness. "I never dreamed this possible, and here I am!"

"If there is a next day."

"No one lives forever. But, having lived today, does it matter that much if tomorrow doesn't come?"

"It matters to me," she said abruptly.

"Of course it does, and it should. It also matter to me, Franca. But tell me, are you happy for what happened today?"

"Yes, I am happy though it is already a dream. Talking to you now with that music--I don't know. The whole thing is like a fairy-tale. Everything seems so beautiful, and why am I so sad? Why am I so happy?"."

"It is not a fairy-tale, except that ours came true. Look, everything is real: the little one sleeping in Lucia's arms, and the little girl here with her head on my mother's lap. Here they are, sleeping; they lived their day and now they're in another world. You can see that. They can't hear the mandolins and they can't see the things going on around them. But these things are happening, and you and I are enjoying them. And the children, unbeknown to all these things, are preparing for another tomorrow..."

Which was Franca's problem, because she had just begun to experience life and she had found it greater than she dreamed, and one day's experience was not enough. She wanted more, though down deep she knew there weren't many more days ahead and knew she could neither do anything about that nor show despair over her situation.

Franca and Samuele moved to another part of the square which overlooked extensive and open farmlands below. Above, the sky contained thousands of stars shining brightly against an infinite dark-bluish color.

Three teams from different cities competed for the prize awarded by the Cavaliere to the most original and best fireworks display.

With the first explosion, some of the older people were taken by surprise and ran for cover. Soon, however, the second burst appeared in the sky. This time, the sky was lit with scintillating colors floating downward and then dying.

For twenty minutes, single shots burst into the starry sky. While the people watched with gleaming eyes, the older children watched with awe and as always waited for the next volley.

Samuele and Franca stood in the background holding hands. Whereas Franca looked on perfunctorily, Samuele looked at the man-made display of bursting light like a child. During those moments, he forgot the real fireworks he had been subjected to and joined the crowd in praising the spectacle.

When the single volleys ended, the three teams began with their multiple bursts. In every direction, continuous explosions created fantastic forms of myriads of colors. Samuele watched with his mouth open, trembling with excitement. For the moment, he saw more stars in front of him than there were in the sky.

Franca, on the other hand, looked more at Samuele's face, analyzing his child-like expression of apparent excitement, and could not understand how he, in his conditions, could be so interested in the event. When he coughed, he automatically put his hand over his mouth.

She kept looking at him for a while longer, then she lowered her head. She looked up again when she felt the pressure of Samuele's hand on hers. A tremendous multiple burst had caused him to react, and automatically he squeezed her hand. He felt too much joy and could not entirely hold it within himself.

When the three teams finished their individual competitions, they joined in for a big finale. The sky suddenly grew bright, its bursts illuminating the top of the Straw Obelisk. Multi-colored stars floated through the air as more rounds went up. Then suddenly, the noise subsided and the sky became dark.

For a few moments, no one made a sound. Finally, when their eyes got readjusted and they saw the moon and the stars once again, the people went into thunderous applause.

Samuele glanced at the moon. Then in a serious tone he pressed his face against Franca's.

"The moon!--I reached it tonight!"

THE END

EPILOGUE

The Straw Obelisk is a metaphor for peace. Because it is also the product of man, the army tank is a metaphor for war.

The plot of *The Straw Obelisk* is the struggle between good and evil. When men's efforts are expended on behalf of good, the result is an obelisk of straw as enduring as one of granite; when men's efforts are expended on behalf of evil, the result is a tank as obsolete as rust itself.

Because the characters in *The Straw Obelisk* were grafted on real individuals--hence, a work of fiction, they have assumed an identity entirely different from those individuals.

The historical individuals entered my psyche during the war years, roughly from 1942 when I was about six years old, to 1947 when, as an eleven-year-old boy immigrating to America, I became completely and definitively separated from them. During those growing-up days, however, I observed--as a boy--how they interacted among themselves and how the war impacted on their lives.

Once those individuals entered my psyche, their alter egos (if that be the driving force) insisted on being developed. Because of that insistence, I began to give intelligence or content to my words in creating their persona; they rebelled, however, insisting on re-developing themselves as characters with their own souls, their own persona, and their own pathos, and, to my amazement, they succeeded in attaining that goal, at my expense.

The issue of separation was related to my situation only in that, as a young boy, in immigrating, I had to learn a new language, acquire new friends, and even learn how to live with a father, a brother and sisters who were absent from my life during those formative young days. In my new environment, however, I grew and developed my own soul, my own persona and my own pathos. On the other hand, the characters in *The Straw Obelisk* remained static while the individuals who made possible *The Straw Obelisk* evolved or changed separately and on their own.

Suddenly and painfully, I was dealing with the issue of a three-way separation:

a) the separation of a divided family--half in America, half in Italy--and my not knowing my father, brother, and sisters during those formative years,

b) the separation from my friends and relatives, who went on living without any connection with me, and, worst of all,

c)the separation between my fictional characters, loathe to change, and their historical antecedents, who, as individuals, evolved their own souls, their own persona, and their own pathos.

Except for the characters who are happy with what they are, and my early friends and relatives who went on with their lives however they did it, the three-way separation affected me, and only me in that I have had to live with a void. Whereas my characters, together with their historical antecedents, have continuity and may have already completed their life cycles, I have had to struggle with my own separation from my family, with the separation that my characters had with their antecedents, and with the separation I had with my early friends and relatives.

To fill that void, I made trips back to my village to learn what I may have missed or may be missing; the answers I found there were more than satisfactory. I saw individuals; I saw the Straw Obelisk; and, as for you, the readers, having read the story, and seeing the pictures hereafter, you yourselves will have become witnesses to the truth of *The Straw Obelisk.*

Two notable authors attempted to fill their voids. Alex Haley may or may not have gone to Africa and may or may not have located the historical antecedents of his characters in *Roots*. The question may be: To what extent are his characters fiction or non-fiction? Considering a separation of about 200 years, and the land mass of a continent, his task was formidable indeed.

With Marcel Proust, on the other hand (with his initial *A la recherche du temps perdu* and his conclusive *Le temps retrouvé*), we are made to consider the perplexing ramifications of time, as though time has human dimensions. Proust made me realize that as human beings, we can do the following:

a) We can lose something and, eventually, find it or not find it,

b) We may have an experience, lose it from memory and, eventually, recall it in various degrees, or

c) We can invent or create experiences which we can then recall in various degrees of clarity at a later date.

We cannot, however, find that which we did not lose, nor recover an experience we did not have. Time exists beyond us. It cannot be lost; it cannot be found; and, it is not recoverable.

Which is exactly what my characters tried to tell me, that it is futile to be in search of the so-called lost time, which is an impossibility. By creating my characters (or re-developing themselves as they claim), I fulfilled my void, and thus came to terms with the pain and sorrow of my own separation.

On going back to my original manuscript after about twenty-three years, I attempted to revise the characters; however, from Franca to Samuele, from Banno to the postal clerk, each and everyone refused to be changed. The

Cavaliere, in fact, demanded of us to re-read the following paragraph, to better digest its content, saying, in addition, that human beings are often surrounded by opposing forces that, unless managed, can create havoc with our lives:

> *The challenge was in coordinating two opposing pulling forces: the rear force of the brakemen, and the forward force of animals and men. The secret to success rested in a split-second manoeuvre wherein the rear force was to be released just as the wheels came to the center of the ditch, and for the front force to take over at exactly that instant.*

On a recent visit to my town, many individuals were still there. Although we recognized who we were, we did not know what we were. And our attempts to verify any of our attributes, or details of facts, proved elusive. On both sides, we were frustrated at every point.

In searching for the historic Franca, for example, I was told that another young lady had a still-born baby out of wedlock, and that she died soon after because of her unfulfilled love. As for Samuele, I learned nothing more than what I actually remember: he was my second cousin, having returned from Russia, singing, in his baritone voice, sad songs in the Russian language to the line of poplars or to the canaries nesting there, and he, limping, died from consumption.

As for poor Rachele, may she rest in peace, she committed a peccadillo; yet, she was killed, which means that when it comes to things of the heart, the heart remains more obtuse than ignorance itself.

In searching Maria's house, which has since been rebuilt on the same abandoned Roman subterranean aqueducts, I came across Samuele's spiritual *last will and testament*. It contained an itemized list of his worldly goods he left for his beloved. To my great surprise, he also bequeathed me his wallet, with a note recommending I keep it close to my heart. Reading it made me cry. And I still cry each time I read it. No wonder the wallet has become a metaphor for tears.

As for the Obelisk, when I wrote about it, I had not seen its majestic structure. During those war years, it was neither assembled nor drawn. From 1946 to today, luckily, the feast of the Straw Obelisk (Carro di paglia) was celebrated every year. I had a chance to see it in 1946 except that I was sick in bed for that whole week. In May of 1947, some five months before the feast, I left Italy to join the rest of my family living in Boston, and did not go back until many years after I wrote *The Straw Obelisk.* I was astonished to note that the Obelisk was as I had depicted it, and that the pulling by the six teams of men and animals essentially as described. What entered my psyche, on seeing it for the first time, after so many decades, was my realization that for me the Straw Obelisk now stands as a true metaphor for peace.

PHOTOS
of faces and places in the surrounding areas of the Straw Obelisk

1-4

5-8

9-12

13-16

17-20

21-24

25-28

PHOTOS
of the Straw Obelisk
as is drawn today with
the participation of
thousands of people
under the direction
of Mr. Giotto Faugno

29-32

33-36

37-40

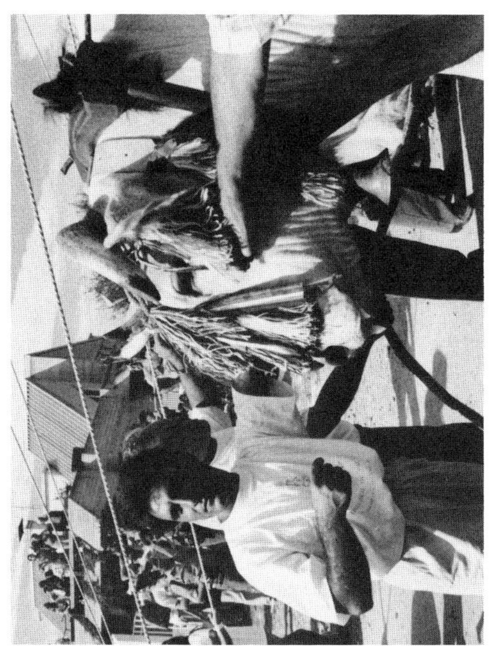
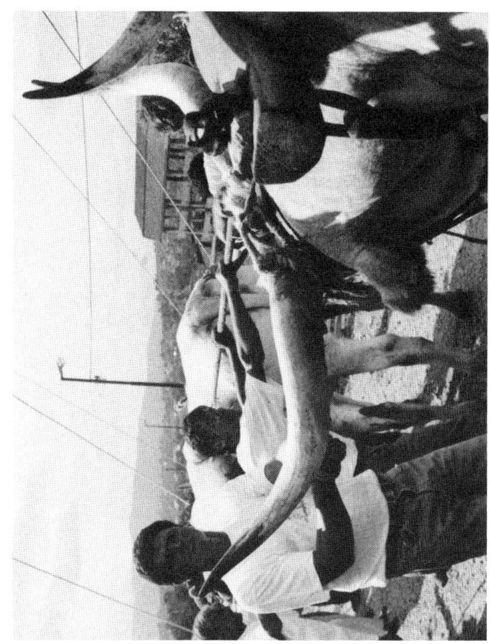
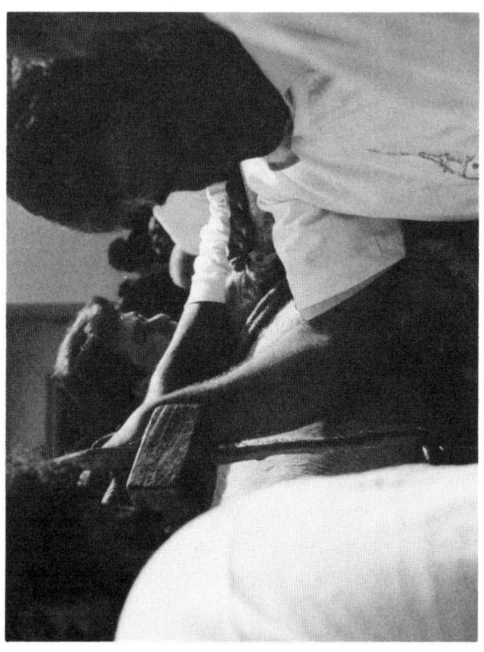

41-44

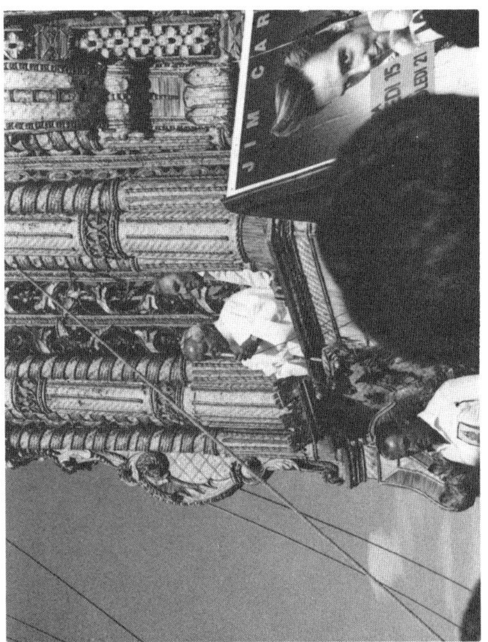

45-48

49-52

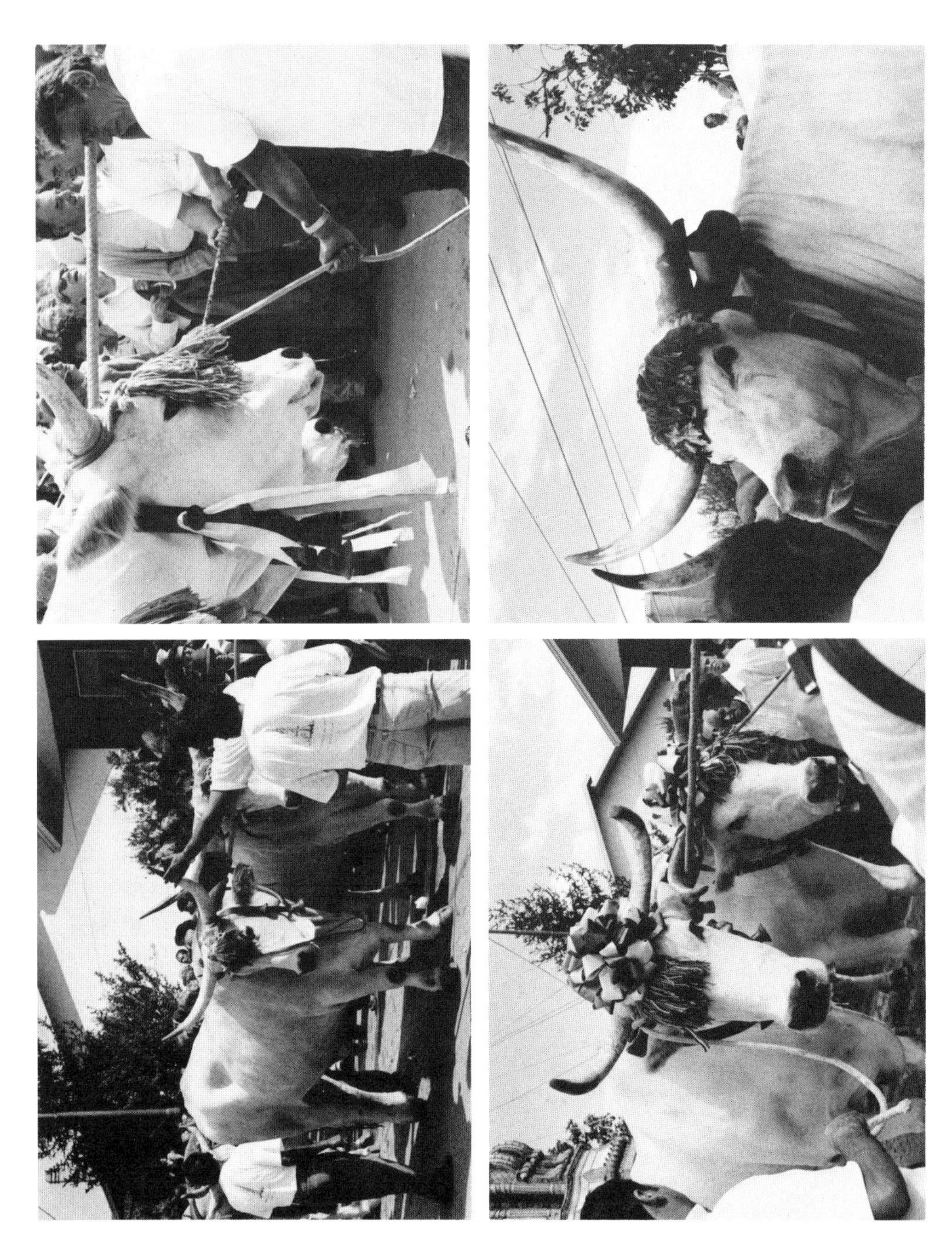

53-56

7-60

61-64

5-68

BOOKS OF ITALIAN AMERICAN INTEREST

AMERICA'S ITALIAN FOUNDING FATHERS by Adolph Caso includes works by Beccaria and Mazzei. Cloth, ill., ISBN 0-8283-1640-4, $25.95.

DANCE OF THE TWELVE APOSTLES by P.J. Carisella reveals Italy's biggest sabotage of a German plan to destroy Rome. Cloth, ill., ISBN 0-8283-1935-9, $19.95.

DANTE IN THE 20TH CENTURY by Jorge Luis Borges et al includes articles by several American and European scholars on Dante. Cloth, ill., ISBN 0-9378-3216-2, $25.95.

FROGMEN--FIRST BATTLES by William Schofield and P. J. Carisella tell an authenticated story of the birth and deployment of underwater guerrilla warfare by the Italians of the World War II. Cloth, ill., ISBN 0-8283-1998-7, $19.95.

INFERNO by Dante Alighieri, by Nicholas Kilmer, illustrated by Benjamin Martinez, is rendered into modern English with a separate illustration for each canto. Cloth, ISBN 0-9378-3228-6, $19.50.

IMPERIAL GINA--The Very Un-Authorized Biography of Gina Lollobrigida by Luis Canales tells the story of this great Italian woman and actress. Cloth, ill., ISBN 0-8283-1932-4, $19.95.

ISSUES IN FOREIGN LANGUAGE AND BILINGUAL EDUCATION by Adolph Caso recounts the plight of limited English-speaking students and their struggle to introduce the Italian language into our public schools. Paper, ISBN 0-8283-1721-6, $11.95.

ITALIAN CONVERSATION by Adele Gorjanc offers easy to follow lessons. Paper, ISBN 0-8283-1670-8, $11.95.

LIVES OF ITALIAN AMERICANS--They Too Made This Country Great by Adolph Caso has 50 biographies of those who contributed in the formation of the U.S. Cloth, ill., ISBN 0-8283-1699-6, $15.95.

MASS MEDIA VS. THE ITALIAN AMERICANS by Adolph Caso explores, critically, the image of the Italian Americans in the media. Paper, ill., ISBN 0-8283-1831-X, $11.95.

ODE TO AMERICA'S INDEPENDENCE by Vittorio Alfieri is the first such composition written on the emerging nation, in Italian and English by Adolph Caso. Paper, ISBN 0-8283-1667-8, $11.95.

ON CRIMES AND PUNISHMENTS by Cesare Beccaria influenced Jefferson, Adams, Washington and many more. To a great degree, America owes its present form of government on this book. Introduction by Adolph Caso, paper, ISBN 0-8283-1800-X, $5.95.

ROGUE ANGEL--A Novel of Fra Filippo Lippi by Carol Damioli traces the tumultuous life of this Renaissance man who was both a great artist and womanizer. Cloth, ill., ISBN 0-9378-3233-2, $21.95.

STRAW OBELISK The) by Adolph Caso: effects of World War II on a southern Italian village. Cloth, Ill. 0-8283-2005-5, $24.95.

TALES OF MADNESS by Luigi Pirandello, translated with an introduction by Giovanni Bussino, includes of the best of Pirandello's short stories dealing with the theme of human madness. Cloth , ISBN 0-9378-3226-X, $17.95.

TALES OF SUICIDE by Luigi Pirandello, translated with an introduction by Giovanni Bussino, includes some of the best of Pirandello's short stories dealing with suicide. Paper, ISBN 0-9378-3231-6, $14.95.

TO AMERICA AND AROUND THE WORLD--The Logs of Columbus and Magellan by Christopher Columbus and Antonio Pigafetta contains the first reports on the first voyage to America and the first voyage around the world, edited and with an introduction by Adolph Caso. Cloth, ill., ISBN 0-8283-1992-8, $25.95.

WATER AND LIFE by Adolph Caso contains poems in the original English and Italian. Paper, ISBN 0-8283-1682-1, $11.95.

YOUNG ROCKY--A True Story of Attilio (Rocky) Castellani by Kinney-Caso tells the life story of one of America's great boxers of the fifties. Paper, ill., ISBN 0-8283-1802-2, $11.95.

WE, THE PEOPLE--Formative Documents of America's Democracy by Adolph Caso contains document and lengthy commentary on the formation of America's Democracy. Cloth, Ill. ISBN 0-8283-2006-3, $22.95.

At your local stores,
or directly from the publisher:
Visa-Master Card orders only: **1-800-359-7031**
(Postage and Handling: $3 each).